KALEIDOSCOPE

A NOVEL

HUGO N. GERSTL

PANGÆA
PUBLISHING GROUP

KALEIDOSCOPE

ISBN 978-1-950134-56-4
Pangæa Publishing Group
www.PangaeaPublishing.com

Cover image:
Kaleidoscope © GAB.COM

Fleuron image © Freepik.com
Linear mandala © Freepik.com

Cover design and typesetting by
DesignPeaks@gmail.com

For information contact:

PANGÆA PUBLISHING GROUP
25579 Carmel Knolls Drive, Carmel, CA 93923 – USA
Telephone: 831-649-0669 – Email: info@pangaeapublishing.com

To

GISELLA AND RICARDO,
VANESSA VALLARTA, ERIC DAUCHY, AND LESLIE FINNEGAN

AND, AS ALWAYS, FOR MY BELOVED
LORRAINE

Hugo N. Gerstl Collection

See below some of Pangæa Publishing Group's bestsellers by the same author:

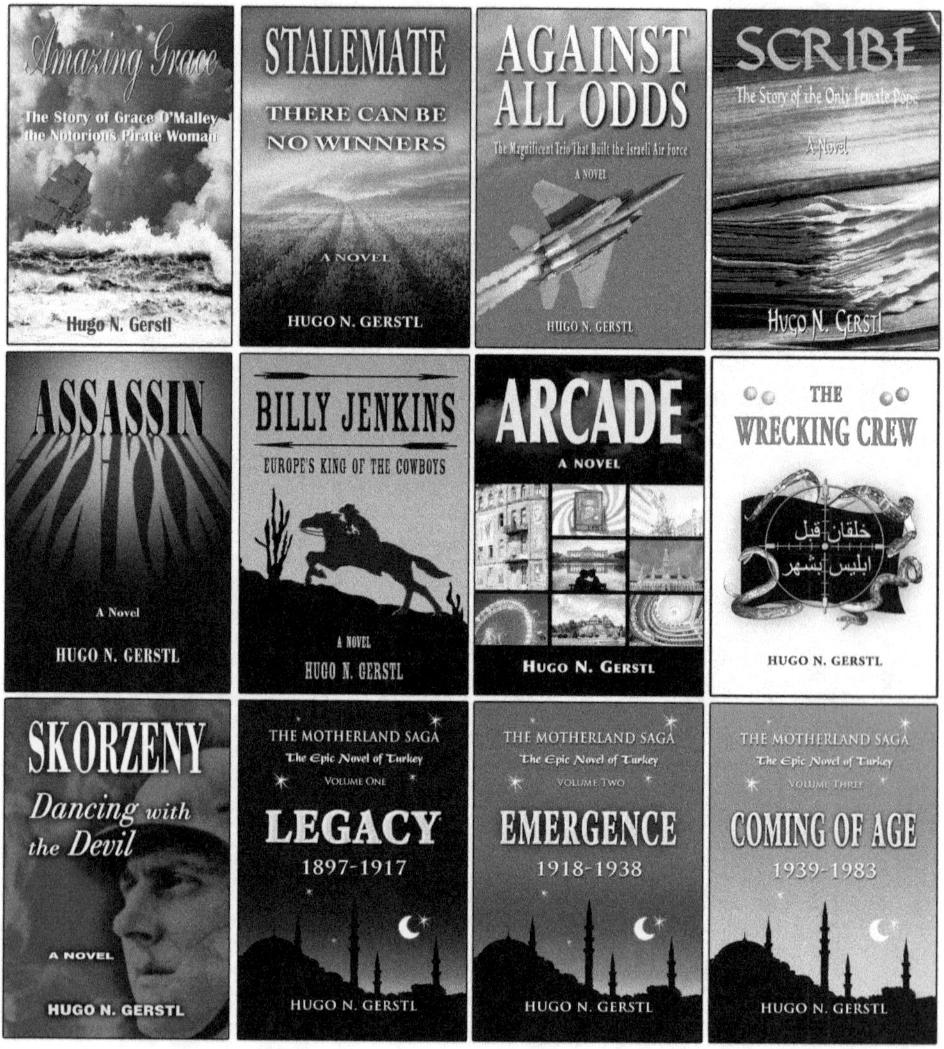

Do not miss them on your shelf!

For Hugo N. Gerstl's complete novels list and descriptions, go to www.HugoGerstl.com

PANGÆA

Pangæa Publishing Group
25579 Carmel Knolls Drive
Carmel, CA 93923
Email: info@pangaeapublishing.com

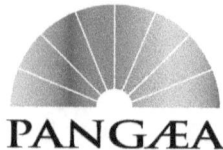

LEST WE FORGET ...

THIS BOOK CELEBRATES THE SMALLEST OF EXTRAORDINARY ACHIEVEMENTS

BY SINGLE HUMAN BEINGS

WHOSE INDIVIDUAL EFFORTS WERE NO GREATER THAN A GRAIN
OF SAND ON THE BEACH

BUT WHOSE COLLECTIVE EFFORTS MADE UP THE ENTIRE BEACH

AND CHANGED HISTORY

BOOK ONE

LARA

1938 - 1939

1

EARLY 1938 – NEW YORK CITY

During her first fourteen years, aside from being the only daughter of Milton Rosensohn — yes *the* Milton Rosensohn of Revson's Department Store — Laurie Rosensohn was no one's idea of a "catch." She was all too painfully aware of that sad fact. She had always been the "nice" girl, the "good" girl, the obedient daughter. By the time she reached her twelfth year, Laurie was ten pounds overweight, her skin had prematurely broken out in "zits," she was painfully shy, and, worst of all, she had no way of hiding what she perceived to be a large "Jewish" nose. Not that anyone ever *said* anything to her face, or even behind her back, at least nothing she ever heard, but Laurie somehow just *knew* …

Her classmates in eighth grade had a habit of passing around "slam books," spiral-bound 6" x 9" notebooks which could be flipped from one page to another. On the first page, there were two sets of numbers. The first had names of the students who filled in answers. Some kids filled in their real names; most filled in imaginary names. That list might look like:

1. Charlie Chaplin

2. Jackie Marks

3. King George of England

The second set of numbers contained numbered questions about classmates, such as:

1. What do you think about …?

2. What would you like to do if you went out on a date with …?

3. What is the sexiest thing about …?

On the next several pages, each page had the name of a different student with the same two sets of numbers. The first set really didn't matter much, because most eighth graders wrote in fictitious names, but Laurie could not help looking at the second group of entries for each student. The entry for Billy Tennant, for example, displayed:

1. WOW! What a dreamboat!

2. Make out and French kiss the whole night

3. Everything, including things I can't mention.

Of course, when Laurie raced through the pages to find what people thought about her, her hopes were invariably dashed.

1. O.K.

2. Read a book or stay home.

3. ?

Slam-books may have been just for fun, but for some, like Laurie Rosensohn, they were painful reminders of her shortcomings.

By the time she entered her second year of high school, while most of her girlfriends were asked out on dates, the phone calls Laurie received were few and far between, and none of them were invitations. But by that time, Laurie had discovered an inner resolve. God did not create junk or losers, and even if He did, she felt she was neither. For one thing, she excelled in French, German, and modern history. She read prodigiously — everything she could get her hands on. Thankfully, she had outgrown her pimples, and while she was still a little bit *zaftig* — the *Yiddish* word meaning having a full, rounded plump figure, she was by no means obese. But her dark hair was determinedly kinky, and that nose …

Laurie's one really close friend, Hannah Sapin, was smart, loyal, popular, and a bit on the wild side. Laurie often found herself fantasizing when she listened to Hannah's tales, not bothering to separate imagined truth from wishful thinking. As always, sooner or later, talk between them turned to perceived "adventures" with the opposite sex. "Why last night …" Hannah would begin, her eyes lit by the smoke from a distant fire, "Abe and I …"

"If I only had your life," Laurie would counter. "All these guys seem to be out for one thing, but I can't even *give* it away."

"Don't worry, my dear," Hannah would say. "Your time will come. You're smart, savvy, and …"

"Oh, right," Laurie rejoined. "You're going to Vassar next year. It's off to City College for me. And what with my nose the size it is, a guy can't get within two feet of me even if he wanted to kiss me …"

"There's more to life than that, Laurie."

"Such as …?"

By the end of her first year at City College, Laurie's grade point average, while respectable, was not good enough to enable her to transfer to Columbia, but she was by no means dismayed. She knew her "B" average was not the result of laziness or any brain deficiency, but was based on the fact that she was taking a full 15 units *and* working twenty hours a week, often more, for the Union of Socialist Workers. At last, she was going to make her most precious dream come true. Even more important, she had accomplished the means to make it happen, without the knowledge or assistance of her parents, who would have written the check which, for them, would have been no more onerous than buying lunch at the automat on Times Square.

Laurie felt elated as she entered the offices of Aaron Hirschberg, MD, ENT, Otolaryngologist, clutching the $300 she'd saved from her employment. For the past six months, she'd been reading articles in *Collier's* and the *Saturday*

Evening Post about rhinoplasty and how more than nine out of every ten young women who'd undergone that operation were thrilled with the results.

When Doctor Hirschberg entered the small, tastefully-furnished office, to which Laurie had been led by the receptionist, she felt a sense of security and confidence. The doctor was only a couple of inches taller than she, an older man, perhaps fifty, with kindly eyes, and a warm, welcoming manner. He treated her with not the slightest hint of condescension.

"Thank you for coming today," he began. "I understand you've earned every penny of my fees on your own, as well as carrying a full load at CCNY. That tells me a great deal about your character."

"Thank you," she said, not knowing what else to say.

"Frankly, I'm surprised that you wanted this operation ..."

"Surprised? Doctor, you don't know how long I've been hoping ... thinking about ..."

"You're concerned about your appearance?"

"I am. It's been years and I've always felt like the ugly duckling."

"Really?" the doctor said, slipping a peppermint Lifesaver into his mouth. "Would you care for one of these?"

"Thank you, no," she responded.

"Well, Laurie — if I may call you that?"

"Of course."

"I don't find you the least bit unattractive, and I say this professionally."

"But, doctor, are you telling me you don't notice my ...?"

"I don't consider your nose to be an impediment. If you're talking about what you think is a 'Jewish' nose, the same might be said about a huge number of people throughout the world, just about anyone with a Semitic background."

"It sounds like you're trying to talk me out of something I've wanted since I was a child."

"No, my dear, nothing could be farther from the truth. The fact of the matter is that you are a beautiful young woman, maybe not in your own mind, and maybe you see something other people don't see when you look in the mirror. If I perform plastic surgery on you, you'll look a little bit different, maybe prettier in your own eyes, and I'll make a little money from the operation. But I ask that you give this some serious thought. Not everything beautiful has to be 'pretty.'"

"I've given it a lifetime's worth of thought, Doctor Hirschberg," Laurie said, a bit more emotionally charged than she'd wanted to sound.

"I trust you haven't discussed this with your parents …?"

"Why should what they think make any difference?"

"I don't say it should. You're very much an adult and I won't insult you by treating you like a child. All I'm asking is that you think about what I've said. A couple of weeks one way or the other won't make a bit of difference."

"Laurie, what foolishness is this?"

"It's not foolishness, Daddy. Three weeks ago, I had saved $300 and even went to a surgeon to discuss having a nose job. Since that time, I've given this a lot of thought. Professor Pasinetti and I have discussed this for the past three months. People in Spain are dying, simply because they believe everyone should be free to express their opinion and be left alone to live out their lives in peace. Wouldn't you agree with that idea?"

"Of course, I do. You know we support the same cause. We can't let that madman Hitler overrun Europe, but …"

"Dad, you and mom write big checks, but that's not enough," she'd replied. "The brigades are putting their lives on the line. I need to show my support in more ways than throwing money at the problem."

"Laurie, you can do so much to help from right here. Jacob has just been made a junior partner at Cravath, Swaine & Moore," he said, mentioning his daughter's presumptive fiancé. "I'm sure he could find you an important position where you could do more than any fifty men to assist … Have you talked to him about it?"

"I mentioned it, and …"

"Yes?"

"It seems Mr. Mueller and I are no longer affianced."

"What? But …?"

"We agreed to disagree. Besides," she continued "if you must know, the sparks never really flew between us. I know you and mom were all for it, and I hate to break it to you this way …"

Milton Rosensohn extracted a Philip Morris cigarette from a pack he kept in his jacket pocket, drew on it sharply to calm himself, then asked, "Does your mother know about this … this proposed 'adventure' of yours?"

"No, Dad."

"You know it will break her heart. And she's not the healthiest woman in the world."

"I'll be as gentle as I can, Daddy."

"What did he say?" Hannah Sapin asked the next day.

"What do they all say?" Laurie replied. "Stay here and stay safe. There's no need to risk your life."

"Give enough money to the cause and the problems will go away. When you have money, the 'green poultice' is their cure-all for everything," Hannah said sarcastically.

"Uh-huh. They can't stop me, though."

"Good for you. Could I ask you a favor, though?"

"Of course."

"I just got offered a job at the *New Republic*. It would really give my career a boost if you could write me while you're in Spain. First person direct-from-the-front and all that."

"Absolutely. But how can I be sure it'll get to you? I've heard international mail delivery is pretty spotty from Madrid."

"Drop letters off at the American Embassy. Work your charms on a junior attaché there. I'm sure he'd help an American woman in distress. After all, that's his job."

Twenty minutes after she'd waved goodbye to her parents from the deck of the S.S. *Normandie* enroute to Le Havre, Laurie Rosensohn tore up her driver's license, her student identification card, and her Revson's Department Store discount card, and watched as myriad tiny pieces floated from her fingers into the calm Atlantic Ocean. The one thing she kept was her New York Public Library card.

Still a virgin when she'd boarded the huge ocean liner, two days later she'd happily given up that status to a boy who, like her, had joined the International Brigades. Cut loose from the strictures of her cosseted life of entitlement and privilege, she engaged in previously forbidden fruits which had been denied her: cocktails, cigarettes, and, yes, even a puff or two of marijuana. She felt it was time to explore *another* part of life as well, one she had only heard about, and …

Of course, a new life meant a new identity, and when she'd met the handsome young man at dinner one night, he'd introduced himself as Joel Raskin. "I've been watching you since the first night. If you'll forgive my being so forward, might I ask your name? I couldn't look you up on the registry."

"That's easy to cure," she replied. "I'm ... Lara ... Lara Gard ..."

They were together the rest of the voyage.

Later, she learned Joel had lasted barely three months before he'd returned to Chicago after having heroically manned the bastions as a desk clerk in Barcelona, two hundred miles from the nearest front.

2

When Lara first arrived in Madrid, it was still in Republican hands, although it had been under siege since November 1936 and, as she was told by her neighbors when she was assigned to her two tiny rooms on *Calle 12 de Marzo,* things seemed to be getting worse by the day. Toledo, less than an hour away, was under Rebel control, and the Nationalists ensured that the Spanish capital, the biggest war prize, lived uncomfortably from day to day, even from hour to hour.

Five days after her arrival, she wrote the first of many letters to her best friend.

"Dear Hannah,

"While my dream had been to destroy the enemy as a frontline soldier, I've been put to work at the office of the chief of procurement. Standing in line is a constant feature of daily life. My companions refuse to abandon their spot, even as the bombs fall around them, in the hope of taking home a bone for stew or a sweet potato. Lentils — 'resistance pills' — are the staple that's meant survival for countless families. Housewives come up with solutions that include making omelets with orange peel, or sausage out of breadcrumbs. Breaded fried onion rings make do for fish. Some children have never seen a banana or chocolate. The main topic of conversation

in many households is, 'What would you eat right now if you could have anything you wanted? ... '"

In Cataluña, where the rivers Fluvià and Toronell join, lay the village of Castellfollit de la Roca, a series of two or three-story mud-brick or dark basalt cubes stacked one against the other, looking like a town that had once had a normal shape. Then, by some incredible force, it had stretched out over a mile-long basalt formation. Houses perched precariously close to the edge of a 165-foot drop-off and wound along the cliff overlooking the countryside and the rivers that flowed beneath the town.

A land of brown hills punctuated by lush stands of pine and olive trees below a constantly hot blue sky, Castellfollit sat more than a thousand miles northeast of Madrid, seventy-five miles north of Barcelona. To the traveler's eye, it stood high above the road, remote, silent, and brooding. *Go on to the next village*, it seemed to say. *To Olot or Besalú. You will like them better.*

Many of the town's houses and streets, which harked back to its medieval beginnings, were built of the dark volcanic rock that served as a pedestal for the town. Castellfollit's six-foot-wide main street bisected the entire plateau, narrowly pressing between houses which strained to remain on the cliff face.

Castellfollit de la Roca, and all the surrounding countryside — the lemon groves, the olive trees, the fields where sheep grazed on stubble, and, most importantly, the only basalt mine still being exploited in Spain — belonged to Don Juan Carlos of the noble family Caceres, which had dominated the area since time out of mind. The Don and his elegant wife, Doña Rosalia, now in their mid-fifties, had been benevolent stewards of their bounty for more than three decades. They believed that upon their ultimate demise — God willing may it not come for several years — their eldest son, Don José, thirty-eight, would assume his parents' mantle, and life in Castellfollit would continue as it had for the past several hundred years. The elder Caceres' only concern was that Don José was as yet unmarried and had not sired any known heirs to carry on their name.

The Caceres' middle son Theo had dutifully entered the priesthood in the age-old tradition of nobles' second sons, and, in thanks, the senior Cacereses had made the appropriate contribution to *Iglesia Madrè*.

Their youngest son, twenty-one year-old Don Ramón, posed a different problem. A year-and-a-half ago, Ramón had joined the *Partido Socialista Unificado de Cataluña,* a marriage of socialists and communists, who'd aligned themselves with the Republican Loyalists in what was already being called *La Guerra Civil Española.* Worse yet, Ramón announced he was joining the Army of the Republic within the next month and would be relocating to the capital.

At hearing this news, Doña Rosalia burst into inconsolable tears. In the vain hope that Ramón would come to his senses, for indeed he was her favorite, she sequestered herself in her private quarters for three weeks. Alas, her suffering proved fruitless, since by the time she emerged, Ramón had left his native village.

Taller than most, dark-skinned, with sensual lips and a gently curved nose, his brown eyes soft and deep, and a thick mane of coal-black hair, he was not unaware of the effect he had on the young — and not so young — women of Girona province, most unmarried, but some matrons as well. He knew in his heart that his future lay beyond the inhabitants of his tiny village, and that it was time to seek his fortune, if not in Barcelona, then in the huge city of Madrid.

At the end of April 1938, Ramón Caceres set out on his 1100-mile journey west.

3

On July 14, 1938, Lara awakened to the excited chattering of several inhabitants of 57 *Calle 12 de Marzo*. The first voice she heard was that of *La Señora*, the imperious widow Maria Evangelista Sebrun, who had appointed herself *decana* — doyenne — of the apartment building, and thus was first to hear and learn about all the news in the neighborhood.

"A new fellow from the east has come to town," *La Señora* began amid the excited 'oohs' and 'ahhs' of the twenty female inhabitants, most of whom had been without a man for months. "Very young, but very much a man, you can tell," she continued.

"Not to worry," a thirtyish woman wearing a tight skirt and a thin, low-cut blouse that displayed her ample curves, responded. "In this school, he'll learn everything he needs to know in a hurry."

"And maybe give us a few lessons as well," a young matron chimed in, salaciously massaging a cucumber she'd purchased in the street market earlier that morning.

Although Lara, whose high-school Spanish had increased dramatically during her brief time in Spain, had been accepted by her neighbors, *l'Americana* remained hesitant to engage in their prurient conversation, silent but not unfriendly, as the apartment building ladies continued the morning's juiciest subject of gossip.

"Do you know where he'll be staying?" another one of the group asked.

"He's perfectly welcome to stay with me," the brunette in the tight outfit said. "José's been away for six months and there's plenty of room in my empty bed," she mock-sighed.

"The neighborhood warden told me he's been assigned to the four-block area surrounding our apartment building," *La Señora* said, taking a more serious tone. "The *Falangistas* and their allies are stepping up their attacks. They say the new man spent a month with the commandos learning how to organize civilian units to defend their own neighborhoods."

Amid the disappointed wails that arose, Señora Sebrun continued, "As much as we like to joke about this, it's become a matter of personal safety, even life or death. Don't think the Nationalists aren't bragging about their manhood and what they intend to do if … when … Making love is one thing … Getting raped or worse is something else … Just remember La Pasionaria's words, '*It is better to die on your feet than to live on your knees!*'"

The courtyard grew silent for several moments before the questions began. *La Señora*'s responses were brief and to the point. "He'll spend two hours each day and two hours each night with a group of six apartment dwellers at a time. We'll learn how to sew and hang black curtains to cover the windows at night, how to fire small sidearms, and, in some cases, anti-aircraft weapons and submachine guns. How to manufacture homemade explosives. How to react if and when dealing with the most horrible and grisly personal matters. And, of course, there's our ancient fallback: pouring boiling oil onto the street when the enemy marches by at night."

Señora Sebrun concluded, "He is twenty-one, his name is Ramón Caceres, and he comes from a small village in Cataluña. That's all I can tell you because that's all I know."

"You may not believe you're on the front lines, but here, there are no front lines. Madrid has been under siege for two years. It is not a city *at* war, it is a city *in* war, and in war you sleep with your boots on," Ramón said.

It was the third week of class — two hours each Tuesday from five to seven in the evening, and two hours each Saturday night from ten to midnight. Lara's group consisted of five women and Lukas, a Dutch freelance journalist with a tic in his right eye, a short, dour man who cleared his throat several times a day, smoked tiny, smelly cigars, and had stopped filing stories months ago. Actually, he'd stopped doing much of anything. He had expressed to Lara a few days ago that he wanted to leave the city. Somehow, he could not, yet he seemed to loathe everything about it. Mostly the unbearable tension of the place, the doom which hung over it every waking hour.

"But, Señor Caceres, some things seem quite unnecessary. Wearing boots when you're sleeping ...?"

"You are a soldier, Señorita Gard. Soldiers learn to sleep no matter what," he said gently. "If you find it too uncomfortable, Señorita, I understand. All I ask is that you do your best. I will learn from you and I'll just do more myself. If it comes down to that and we're together at the time, I'll do your job as well as my own."

She started to say something, but the words died in her throat. *How can he be saying this? I mean nothing to him. I'm simply another of his students in the art of survival. Yet he's saying he'd die for me — or anyone else under his care — and I believe he means it.*

Anywhere but here, she might have thought him an insufferable boor, a self-important ass, and hated him wholeheartedly. But this wasn't anywhere, it was here, and here, where everything was upside down and inside out, somebody had to be Ramón Caceres, somebody had to set the example.

"Thank you," she said, turning to face Caceres. "I am sorry if it seems like I don't take what you say seriously enough."

"Not at all, Señorita Gard," he said, smiling at her. "If I expect more from you it's because you've already proved how capable you are and how much you've already helped the cause."

She felt a sudden warm tingle creeping up her neck. Half an hour later, at the conclusion of the lesson, Lara stayed behind after the others had departed.

"Yes, Miss Gard?" he asked. "Is there something I've missed?"

"No, Señor Caceres. I was just wondering if you've eaten anything yet?"

He glanced at his wristwatch. Quarter after seven. "Not since this morning. Tuesday's my busiest day."

"If you'd like, I made some gazpacho and bought a loaf of French bread this afternoon. I'd be happy to share them with you."

"You're sure it wouldn't be an imposition?"

"It would be my pleasure. I'd appreciate the chance to talk to someone other than myself and the occasional 'war widow' from a nearby apartment. Would you mind if I asked you to call me Lara, since we'll be out of class?"

"Only if you address me as Ramón," he replied.

She reached out and shook his hand as though they were business associates.

During dinner, while he ate voraciously, Lara turned on the black Bakelite Emerson radio that sat on the nearest table. She'd bartered for it some weeks ago, and it was her prized possession. Most nights, she listened to the scratchy, static-filled broadcast from the B.B.C. Sometimes, if the conditions were just right, she could hear the much weaker signals from farther east, Berlin, Warsaw, even, on the rarest of occasions, Moscow. As she was tuning the right-hand knob and watching the needle move around its half circle, a powerful signal came over the airwaves, dominating every other station. An unctuous male voice smacked his lips noisily.

"Ahhh," the voice sighed. "What an evening to enjoy a crisp bottle of LaBodega *fino* sherry while my inamorata and I await our delicious repast of *paella*. Plenty of shrimp, chicken, and sausage, which stiffens the … ah … resolve of our virile Nationalist soldiers — you ladies know what I mean — when this dreadful war comes to its predictable end and the true heroes rule *toda España.* In fact, we have plenty of everything in our midst, while the loyalists starve and dine on stale bread and half-rotten potatoes. This is Radio Sevilla, the voice of Andalusia and I am so happy to spend part of each evening with you …"

"Bastard!" erupted from Caceres. "Sure, rub our noses in *mierda*, asshole!"

"Quiepo de Llano. Falangista General de Llano. Their Fascist puppet spokesman. Unfortunately, his audience is much greater than ours," Lara said.

"You can hear him all over Spain and the sonofabitch never hesitates to let everyone knows his Nationalists are drinking the finest wines, while we struggle to get stagnant water out of our rusty pipes. And what his 'heroes' are going to do when they get hold of every Republican woman within sight."

She glanced at Caceres, but remained silent.

"I'm sorry for my outburst," he said. "It's just that we are fighting for a real cause. The other side seems to have all the high cards, the Moorish brigades, the Condor Legion …"

"There's nothing to forgive," she said. "Nobody knows from one day to the next if we'll even survive. The Germans bomb us only when they know they'll escape unscathed. They're too much in love with their Messerschmitts to smash them up on our hillsides. The Italian pilots are different."

"Oh?" he asked. He cut two thick slices from the loaf and handed one to her.

"I saw what was left of one of them three weeks ago, when his fighter crash-landed in a wheat field outside the city. I was told by the sergeant of the firing squad that some of our militiamen had captured him and when they carried him back to the city, tied hand and foot to a pole, he cursed his captors all the way back to Madrid. When they stood him against the wall of the police station, he refused the blindfold and sneered at the four marksmen detailed to shoot him. But when he fell, he just looked like a bundle of rags. They brought a horse to drag the body away, one of the horses that used to do the same job for the bull on Sunday afternoons."

"You actually witnessed this?"

"Not really. I happened to walk by just as the horse was hitched to what was left of him. The sergeant made a clenched fist and said, 'Don't pass, Señorita. It's best not to look.' What he meant, of course, was *'Observe this dirty work. These are our slogans come to life.'* In a way, I felt he was praising me for *not* turning away."

Lara stood up, went to a nearby counter, and returned with a platter bearing a pitcher half-filled with wine and two ceramic cups. "Water may be stagnant and hard to come by, but thank God you can still buy a liter of *rioja* in the market place for a few céntimos," she said, placing the pitcher on the table between them.

Caceres smiled, poured some wine for each of them, and held his cup up to the light, pretending to assay it as though it were a premium French Bordeaux, "Ahh!" he sighed, imitating General deLlano. "The nectar of the gods ... and the goddess," he said, bowing in Lara's direction. "I propose a toast. To the loveliest woman in this room ... and the most courageous. May I ask what brought you to this hell, Lara? Somehow you don't seem like the 'armed tourist' that Winston Churchill calls the foreigners who come to Madrid."

"I wish I could give you a direct answer, Ramón. I grew up on Park Avenue in Manhattan, New York, a rich, spoiled *kugel* — that's a noodle-and-raisin pudding we Jews bake and eat on holidays. But it's come to mean a dumpling, a girl who's been given every privilege money can buy and who expects life will always be that way."

"You are *Judía?*"

"Yes. Like so many *Communistas* before Señor Stalin started the *Yezhovschina,* his big purge two years ago. I was sent to all the best schools, got engaged to marry the right boy, did all the things I was supposed to do. If life had continued the way it had started, I would have been crushed to death by a parlorful of huge-breasted aunts wearing diamonds the size of your fist, an overstuffed apartment with a twittering canary, and the requisite miniature *kugels* and *Mervyns* — the male equivalent of a *kugel.*"

"But …?"

"I escaped. A real *shande*, a great shame to my parents. I haven't heard from an aunt or a cousin, and only one classmate since I joined the International Brigades. Had I known what I was getting into —. No, that's not really true, Ramón. In its own twisted, perverted way, I fulfilled my dream. We're all going to die sooner rather than later. And for all I know, a year from now I won't even be a memory. Maybe not even a black-and-white photograph that some overpriced 'society' colorist in Manhattan painted in 'natural' colors sitting on my mother's night table."

Caceres sipped his wine thoughtfully.

"I was right when I toasted you as the most courageous woman in this room," he said softly.

"More likely the most stubborn or stupidest," she replied. "And you, Ramón?"

"In my village, I was what you would call a 'Mervyn third class.'"

"Meaning?"

"Had I been the firstborn son, I would have succeeded my parents in owning our village, the king of all I surveyed, the emperor of three thousand hectares."

"Seventy-five hundred acres — about half the size of Manhattan. You said 'had I been the firstborn son.' But you're not the firstborn son?"

"Not at all. The second son historically became a priest."

"Which you're not."

"Correct, Lara. I'm number three, which means I'll eventually own whatever I earn. If I'm lucky, a small farm on the outskirts of an even smaller village. So … Madrid and the Second Republic, which could cease to exist within a year."

"But you're committed to it?"

"I'm committed to the idea of a better life for everyone."

By the time they'd finished their dinner, darkness had spread over the city. With electricity an undependable utility, Lara lit two large candles and they continued their conversation, albeit in an entirely different direction.

Suddenly, apropos nothing at all, Lara asked Ramón in a direct, no-nonsense manner, "Are we to become lovers?"

In ordinary times, Caceres would, have been shocked. Instead, he answered matter-of-factly, "Every human being is entitled to *some* happiness. There's no reason we shouldn't find happiness for whatever time we have. Do you find me attractive?"

"Do you find *me* attractive?"

"Since the first day I met you. Why else would I have been so cautious in dealing with you? I've always been taught to hide my feelings."

"That's not the way I perceived 'hot-blooded Spanish *dons*,'" she said, breaking the tension which precedes the first tentative moves toward the greatest pleasure a man and a woman can achieve with one another. She reached over and stroked his face. Very gently.

Words were a burden, and they did not speak again until much, much later that night.

And it was even better the second time.

4

"*Dear Hannah,*

"*For the time we had left, our relationship deepened into a loving friendship. When Ramón assumed greater responsibility in the hierarchy of the deteriorating Republican forces and resources, he'd been sent farther afield to participate in the Battle of the Ebro, and we spent less and less time with one another as that battle wound down to its conclusion.*

"*Now, the Battle of the Ebro is finally over. It broke the back of the Republican forces. The ultimate Nationalist victory now looks inevitable.*

"*The Republican Army of the Ebro consisted of 80,000 troops, the Nationalists fielded 90,000. The difference was Franco's troops were supported by 500 first-class planes supplied by the German Condor Legion and the Italian Aviazione Legionaria squadrons, while the Republicans were able to field only 35 fighters and 40 second-class aircraft. The aircraft supplied to the Rebels were invariably flown by top-of-the-line Luftwaffe and Italian pilots. ...*"

He was on his way to the Ebro battlefield when he came upon the wreck. He immediately joined the crew at its grisly labor. They worked until dawn

— hard, dirty work — by the weak beams of flashlights, amid drifting smoke that rose like steam from the river and blew gently across the road where they labored. To avoid the periodic flooding of the Ebro, the builders of the railroad had erected a packed earth ridge for the tracks, not very high, but it had added to the speed of the train and had sent the engine and the first three cars onto the road in a tangle of splintered wood and bent iron.

At the start of the bombing run, the train's engineer, acting from instinct, stopped the train, knowing that had he given the engine full steam, the enemy, which relished bombing a moving target and most likely derailing the train, would attack immediately. But the conventional wisdom of railroad engineers had failed him. These bomber pilots had seen the train slowing to a crawl, then stopping, and they were not fooled.

Most of all, Ramón thought, as he heaved on the end of a railroad tie pressed into service as a lever, *someone, not knowing the range of German bombers had decided that trains could run during daylight. And here was the result of such stupidity.*

As they took the wreck apart, pulling away boards, prying loose wheel carriages and axles, they came upon the bodies, most of them dead. Now and then, they found one still alive and carried him down to the road, to be taken back to Tarragona by private car or taxicab, which had been called in from neighboring towns. But for the most part, the bodies were twisted into impossibly grotesque positions by the force of the wreck.

"What happened?" Caceres asked a miraculously uninjured sergeant.

"We fought against a Nationalists column west of Madrid, and it was a nightmare. Our forces were very brave, but the Rebel field guns chewed us up from a distance, and machine gun fire mowed us down."

"Weren't there reinforcements, Sergeant?"

"If you want to call them that, Señor. Some miners arrived from Asturias to fight by our side, but they had no guns. When we took the field against organized military forces, we learned the simplest tactical truth: we lost: lives, armaments, everything. We believed the righteousness of our cause would somehow protect us. And we were wrong."

Shortly after this conversation, the chief of police from some nearby town made his way to the scene in pants, boots, and pajama tops, and took charge of the rescue efforts.

Two boxcars of live steers had traveled with the train, heading toward the markets of Tarragona. Many animals had been injured in the wreck. Some had managed to make their way into the fields, where they bellowed without stop in pain and terror. The policeman tried to ignore it, but he could not. Finally, to the relief of everyone, he rounded up a detail of the survivors, handed them pistols, and sent them off, limping and shuffling, wandering through the mist and smoke, to find the animals and put them out of their misery.

Toward dawn, a westbound train passed slowly on the remaining track. Loyalist reinforcements headed for the Madrid front, all of them wearing red scarves. They stuck their heads out the windows and gave clenched-fist salutes to the workers on the road, calling out patriotic Republican slogans. In one car, they were singing. Caceres had seen this before, a train of new volunteers passing a train of dead and wounded. He did his best, with shouts and smiles and salutes, to help them not to see what was on the road.

At daybreak, Ramón Caceres was relieved by a company of infantry and he collapsed against the side of a car, sitting in the weeds by the side of the road. His hands, black with axle grease, soot, and dried blood, with a slice across the palm, had bled themselves dry. He sat quietly in a kind of stupor, watching the mist burn off as the early morning sun found the river. The pale green water flowed lazily by. He wanted to put his aching hands in it for as long as he could stand the cold, but he was too exhausted to move.

Dear Hannah,

On August 19, Colonel Yagüe Blanco, the "Butcher of Badajoz," took command of the Nationalist forces. Supported by six divisions and the German Condor Legion, Blanco's forces broke the Republican lines.

From that point forward, the end of the battle was never in doubt. On November 16, the last Republican troops recrossed the Ebro. The Battle of the Ebro was over. ... "

"Civil war is like a fight between lovers," Ramón said to Lara. They were eating paella, which she'd managed to put together from the ever-diminishing stocks available in the Madrid market. "Each side knows precisely how to infuriate the other. And now, this city is starting to die."

"Don't you think it's time for us to leave, darling? I've done my duty, taking the 3:30 'til sunup shift on the roof every other night since you were sent to the Ebro."

"Where would we go?" Caceres asked. "I've heard there's a refugee camp just inside France, Gurs. Seventeen thousand crushed into space built to house three thousand. I'm being sent to Valencia for two weeks, Lara. Will you be alright?"

"God knows," she replied. "What choice do I have?"

12:20. She did not have to be up on the roof until 3:30. She became conscious of the clock ticking. Lately, she'd managed to sleep, propelled by the exhaustion of simply surviving in the beleaguered city and by their frenetic lovemaking when Ramón was beside her.

12:23. At this rate, she'd be an old woman by sunrise. She turned on her left side and hugged her chest. It was not the same as when Ramón held her close. Not the same at all.

12:24. Damn! She tried to turn on the light, but the electricity was off. Went to the sink in the far corner of her room and tried to splash water on her face, but the water was off. Peered at the clock.

12:26. Went to the toilet, which didn't flush. She'd have to wait for the time she could pour a potful of water into it. Once a day. Maybe. If she was lucky.

12:28. Tried to find a half-comfortable position on the lumpy mattress. Used up another two minutes.

At a little after 1:00, with no sleep on the horizon, Lara pulled on her white woolen socks, making sure there were no lumps, laced up her boots, checked the safety on her Bergmann Bayard M1912 pistol, then stuck it inside the waistband of her corduroy pants. She had stood in line a full day at the armory to get that pistol. She pulled a heavy tan sweater she had purchased at the *mercado de ladrones*, the thieves' market, over her work shirt, then tied a red neckerchief around her throat. It was as much of a uniform as anybody had.

The rain had stopped, although lightning still flashed over the Guadarrama. Lara moved through the dark streets of the city, hemmed in by three-story buildings. A dog barked some distance away. She could tell it had been barking for a long time — its voice was almost gone. *It doesn't know what else to do, so it barks.*

From the apartments high above her came the sense of restless sleep. Too many terrible things had happened in these narrow streets centuries ago — and perhaps three or four nights ago as well.

Calle de Plata. Where medieval silversmiths had kept their workshops.

Now, so many Communists. Am I one, too? No, I don't think so. I want democracy. Are all the Jews Communists? Hitler says so. Jews hate injustice, that's what it is. I would like to shoot Hitler. If I did that, they'd march me in glory up Flatbush Avenue. Even Mr. Stein of Stein's Glassware would approve, and he's a Republican.

Avenida Saldana.

There was a big market here on Wednesdays. An old lady with a moustache gave her something free every time — parsley, beans, figs … Now the street was deserted. She glanced at the wristwatch her *bubbe*, her grandmother, had given her for her seventeenth birthday.

1:45. Less than two hours before her watch started. Perhaps now she could snatch an hour of sleep. Not enough, but better than nothing.

On Monday, February 27, 1939, Lara returned from a full day of mailing out fundraising letters for various defense committees, surprised and delighted to find that Ramón had returned from the South. Even more astonished to find a large bouquet of wildflowers in the pitcher normally reserved for the bulk *rioja* she purchased once a week. And a hot dish of beef stew, *real* beef stew, waiting in a pot on the stove.

He was even more desirable than she remembered. True, his face carried the strain of increasingly difficult times, but he was her man, and that's what really mattered. During their dinner, Ramón uncorked a bottle of expensive wine, poured draughts of it into wine glasses, and toasted her.

"Ramón, would you mind telling me what is this all about?"

"Of course. The world is crashing down around us, but it doesn't matter anymore. On March 12, my enlistment is up and it will be the last *La Causa* sees of me."

"Have you told your parents about *us*?"

"Uh … not yet. Because of … circumstances … but I'm certain once they meet you, they'll accept you — us — with open arms." Ramón verbally shifted gears. "You're an American. The chances of you getting out of Spain are much better than mine. You should register with your Embassy as soon as possible."

"As who? I came here without a passport. My only identification is through the Brigades under a different name, by way of my New York Public Library card."

Later that night, they celebrated their coming freedom in the most wondrous way lovers can. They drifted off to satisfied, dreamless sleep, wrapped in each other's arms. Although they'd kept the radio on at very low volume, they didn't even awake when the B.B.C. interrupted its evening broadcast of contemporary music with a brief announcement.

"Ladies and gentlemen, His Majesty's Government, speaking through Prime Minister Chamberlain, and Monsieur Daladier, the French Prime Minister, have jointly announced that effective tomorrow morning at 9:00 a.m. they will officially recognize the Nationalist regime of Generalissimo Francisco Franco as the sole legitimate government of Spain. Please stay tuned for further bulletins as we receive them."

Two weeks later – March 9, 1939 – Madrid

Lara sat on the roof of the crumbling three-story apartment building, the Labora Fontbernat submachine gun lodged between her legs, its makeshift bipod of questionable use at best. *My nightly watch — hah! — what a laugh that is. I'll be lucky to last a week. Ten p.m. to two tomorrow morning. Then, if I'm still alive, back to my flat. No electricity. No water. The nightly smell of unwashed bodies. The smell of fear. Fear of death … or worse.*

They'll be coming any moment now. What the hell am I still doing here in this shithole city in the valley of the shadow of death? Twenty-five next week if I even make it. Happy fucking birthday! No. Birthday or not, there'll be no fucking.

They had come at 9:45 the night before last. Two of them. Dressed in dark work clothes, their red scarves stuffed into their shirts so she could hardly see them in the near dark of her apartment.

"Señorita Gard," the taller one, Ramón's age, had said. She noticed he was close to tears. "Señorita Gard …" he started again. "We … we …" He coughed uncomfortably.

The other man, older, reached into his coat pocket, withdrew an identification tag on a metal chain and an indecipherable pasteboard card and wordlessly held them out toward Lara.

She felt the cold numbness and tears had already flooded her eyes before the younger man mumbled, "He was a good man, Señorita. A brave man. He died so that others might live. His work detail came upon a mine … Before the others could stop him …"

The dam broke ten minutes after they left. Her screams could be heard throughout the crumbling tenement building. For all she knew, they could be heard throughout the whole dying city of Madrid. It didn't matter. They went on and on and on until she had vomited her insides out and her throat was so raw from the fire of her grief that when La Señora finally found her and managed to pour the strongest, vilest wine she could find down her throat, Lara simply collapsed, shivering uncontrollably, and fell into her cot.

She may have slept an hour that night. She never knew if she slept at all. The cold was beyond endurance. She alternately mumbled and screamed Ramón's name with the last sounds she could make. In the morning, La Señora came back with a bucket of warm water, with which she bathed Lara's face, and a cup of hot, strong coffee. Somehow or another, the younger woman slept through the day and into the evening.

Ramón had been twenty-two, so wedded to the cause, so passionate when they came together. She had never been asked to identify the body, nor could she, were she asked. He'd probably already been buried in some hard-packed field somewhere in some nameless hills outside the town.

And yet, the second night after she'd received the news of Ramón's death, she was on the roof of her apartment house. There was hardly anyone left. And someone had to stand guard. So Lara stood guard in her misery, in what could be, God willing, the last night of her life.

Looking into the tiny pocket mirror earlier that day, while there'd still been daylight, she'd seen a face that looked ten years older than it had only a month ago. Skin chapped and roughened from the incessant sun, her long chestnut hair chopped to a short bob, an ungainly nose with a bump — *a Jew nose* one of those Nazi bastards had remarked less than a month ago when the noose was tightening and those 'volunteers' of the Condor legion had strolled openly along Madrid's *Gran Via*, like conquering gods.

It was only a matter of days … maybe even only a matter of hours. With no passport in hand and the regime collapsing, her only thoughts turned to survival.

2:30 a.m. Her replacement, a young matron, spoke in low tones. One never touched whoever was on guard duty. The one being replaced, exhausted, barely holding herself together, might accidentally discharge the weapon.

"Señorita Gard, your shift is over. Please try to get some sleep. I was widowed myself three months ago. The pain never goes away. We can only hope that someday …"

Lara nodded solemnly. "Thank you, Sofia," she said, daring to wrap her arms around the other woman. "As hard as it is for me to say anything now, I really mean that."

She handed the submachine gun to her friend. It took her only moments to reach her tiny apartment. Strange. The door was unlocked. Had she forgotten to lock it? She really couldn't remember. Not that it mattered, of course. It was just that …

She felt rather than saw a presence in the pitch-dark room.

"Hello? Hello?" she ventured. "Señora? Señora Sebrun?"

Suddenly, she felt a hand snake around her waist while another grasped her mouth.

"Silence," a voice — a male voice — rasped.

She started to struggle, then stopped. The smell was so familiar. *It can't be you, Ramón. You're dead.* She tore free of the hands, turned to face him.

"Ramón?" What emerged from her throat was the querulous voice of a small child.

"*Si. Ja. Yes. Oui.* And I love you *so* much, my darling. *So very, very much …*"

5

"How did — ?"

"There was no work detail. The two men who came to see you? Friends. Friends I could trust. But we must leave, right now, tonight. I've decided to terminate my military service early."

"But —?"

"I'll explain in the car. It's in the alley behind this building. Grab whatever you have. There's food in the car, gasoline enough to get us where we're going — maybe. By tomorrow at this time, Madrid will be in Franco's hands and the war will be over. No one can predict what the Generalissimo will do by way of retribution. That's why we must leave *right now.*"

Moments later, they struggled into the tiniest car Lara had ever seen.

"A Fiat Topolino," he replied to her questioning look. "Three years old. My parents sent me the money when I told them what I planned to do. The car's Italian, small enough that it won't attract too much attention, and we don't have to stick to the main roads.

They had been in the car less than three minutes when they heard the sounds of a crowd singing in the streets and tanks rolling down the same streets in the opposite direction.

"We're getting out just in time," he said.

"We could go west to Portugal," Ramón continued. "Two hundred fifty miles. Seven hours. through miles of Nationalist-held countryside. We could travel south through Republican territory. Take passage on a boat to Tangier, Morocco. Risky. Northeast to Port-Bou? Even riskier."

Republican Spain's only major overland route to southwest France would subject them to the heaviest surveillance imaginable, but even that would be preferable to the smugglers' route through the Pyrenees. In the end, they decided to head north to Bilbao, almost exactly the same distance as the Portuguese frontier. It would take the rest of the night and an entire day, but it was the fastest way out of Spain.

Forty-five minutes later, Lara and Ramón were still trying to get out of Madrid. Burning buildings, fire trucks skidding on streets, wet from a slow, persistent rain that had started at dusk. The Gran Via, Madrid's main boulevard, was blocked by Nationalist tanks. Smaller streets were blocked by refugee campsites — tarpaulins rigged upright with broomsticks to keep out the rain.

At dawn, they were forced to stop at an intersection as private cars being used as ambulances sped past. Finally, they found themselves on the road to Burgos. But they began to see men in Falangist uniforms standing beside the highway, so they moved onto the narrow secondary lanes that went through the villages.

Less than an hour later, the car started sputtering. Moments later, it stopped altogether. Although the black night had turned to a lighter gray, there was little to differentiate the land.

"Any idea where we might be?" Lara asked.

"None," he replied. "North of Madrid, south of Burgos and nothing I can see except wheatfields in every direction. Not a building, not a living thing. I haven't seen a road sign or another vehicle since we left Madrid." He exited the car, opened the hood, and was immediately hit with a blast of hot air, the ticking of a cooling engine, and the smell of burnt oil.

"Do you have any idea of what's wrong? Or how to fix it?" Lara asked.

"No, I don't," he muttered. Embarrassed by his display of temper, he hurriedly said, "I'm sorry, *Querida.* It's just that I feel so useless and —"

"Look ahead of us, Ramón!" Lara nearly shouted. "*Si Dios quiere, todo estará bien!*"

"What the —?"

Sure enough, a middle-aged man with a wen on his nose, wearing a straw hat that looked like it was filled with — and smelled like — goat shit, approached them, peddling one of the oldest bikes they'd ever seen. The bicycle's basket contained a loaf of bread and the man was humming a wordless tune.

"*Ayuda, Señor*! Help, Sir!" they called out in unison.

The fellow pointed to his ears, shook his head, and smiled at them.

"*Por favor, Señor!*" Ramon shouted as loud as he could.

Lara spun her hands, one around the other, to indicate a spinning engine, then stopped and moved her right index finger across her throat.

"Ah!" the man smiled agreeably. "Autoa! Bai?"

"Bai!" Lara agreed. "Basque," she murmured to Ramón.

The man dismounted from his bicycle and walked over to the Fiat. Almost as an afterthought, he reached into the engine and signaled Ramón to start the car. It started.

The man refused to take money and waved to them as they moved off. They began to speak of what they would do when they got to France, maybe even all the way to Paris.

Two hours later, the sun midway between the horizon and the zenith, Ramón said, "When we come to a spot off the road —?"

"Me, too," she responded.

They'd stepped out of the car, went to different sides of the road, and had barely relieved themselves when a German spotter plane appeared and swooped low to have a look at them. When it disappeared over the horizon, they ran back to the Topolino. Some cover, no matter how small, was preferable to being caught in the open. The plane returned, buzzed the car, then left.

At dusk, they worked their way around the outskirts of Burgos, found a shack with an ancient, hand-operated gas pump, and bought fuel from a suspicious peasant woman who overcharged them mercilessly. They pooled their remaining pesos to pay her. The woman went into the shack to retrieve some coins for change. They saw her watching them through the window. Lara pointed out to Ramón that there were no telephone lines going into the shack. "All she really wants to do is steal our change," she said. They drove away without it.

The road began to climb through forests and the tiny car sputtered and started to stall. Ramón pushed the gas pedal to the floor. The car faltered, then roared ahead. *Watered gasoline,* he thought. Later, after the sun had gone down, they came to the Rio Nervión, eight miles from the Atlantic. When they got to the seaside port, they saw a line of fishing boats.

Ramón got out of the car and wandered down a street of dockside bars and sailors' haunts, making sure the car was locked and parked under a streetlamp, and that Lara was completely hidden from view under a heavy woolen overcoat which, in turn, was covered by a duffel bag. She was so exhausted she couldn't move, and she smelled so ripe from nervous sweat, no bath for two days, and the fetid odor coming from inside the car. that she concluded no man, particularly a drunken sailor, would think to have his way with her.

Not long afterward, a hand banged hard on the window. Lara came to her senses prepared to fight or flee, when Ramón introduced a barrel-chested, middle-aged fellow, sporting a bushy moustache and wearing a suit and tie. "I'm your captain," he said, smiling at the startled young woman, "I don't normally dress like this, but my brother got married this morning and I served as his best man."

Over a shared bottle of *rioja*, they came to agreement. Ramón and Lara offered the Topolino and two submachine guns in exchange for passage to France. "Good," the man said.

They reached France the following day, wading ashore at the fishing village of Saint-Jean-de-Luz. Shoes in hand, they walked up a narrow brown-pebbled beach to a low seawall.

Lara, breathing a vast sigh of relief, bent down and kissed the wall. *"Vive la France* and thank God!" she exclaimed. "Look at that!" she continued, pointing at a man wearing a uniform with a gray cape over it. "A *flic*, a policeman who looks just like a picture I saw in a *National Geographic* magazine back home! I can't wait to try my high school French! Come on, Ramón!" she said, grasping her lover's hand and pulling him toward the officer.

As they approached the policeman, Lara noticed his eyes widening appreciatively as he glanced at her skirt and colorful, low-cut peasant blouse. *"Bonjour Monsieur le sergent,"* she said, bowing deferentially. "We are so happy to be in France!"

"Your French is quite elegant," he replied, smiling genially. "You are …?"

"Américaine. My fiancé is Spanish. Republican."

"Ah," the officer said. "Hélas, there are so many in his position. Have you eaten?"

"Not since yesterday afternoon, Sergeant."

"You flatter me Mademoiselle. I am merely an officer." He extracted a small red apple from his pants pocket, cut it with knife, and offered half to each of them. As they greedily bit into the fruit, he asked, "I trust you have the appropriate papers?"

"Why do you think we had to leave Spain like this?" Ramón said.

"Hélas, again," the policeman said courteously. "In that case, I fear I must arrest you."

6

March 12, 1939 — St. Jean-de-Luz, France

They had been extremely fortunate. The *flic* who'd arrested them in Saint-Jean-de-Luz was sleepy and the sun, high in the sky, made for an unseasonably hot day. He'd been on duty at the south end of the town, only six miles away from the Spanish frontier, since five o'clock that morning. If Lara and Ramón had been dropped off by an illegal boat, it was nowhere to be seen. The Commissariat, the police prefecture, was located at the northern end of town, farther away than the frontier. His shift would be over in fifteen minutes. Little Henri was visiting grandmère that afternoon. He could imagine Amélie waiting for him at home, alone. He could picture her in a provocative bathing suit. Perhaps even less … They'd been married three years and it had been ten days since …

He glanced over at the two young people, who seemed not at all disturbed as they munched on a second apple he'd shared with them.

Refugees, he thought. *If I arrest them, they are fined a few francs and sent back across the frontier, their escape is ruined, and they face almost certain death. Perhaps that's the way it is in Spain, where they're so busy killing each other they could care less about the truly important things. Thank God, things are different in France.*

"Donostia?" he asked, using the Basque name for San Sebastian, twenty miles down the coast.

"No, your excellency, Madrid," Lara replied in French.

"Three hundred miles away! How in the world did you get here?"

"We bought a Topolino in Madrid, then traded it for a coastal trawler ride over the French border."

"*Mon Dieu!* Are things that bad?"

"Worse, excellency," Lara continued. "We've been without food, water, or electricity for days. Guards on every road into and out of the capital. It's particularly hard for a *Juive* now that every European border is closing to us?"

"Your man? He is *Juif* also?"

"No, sir. *Católico*," Ramón replied. "But a Loyalist. What do you intend to do with us, officer?"

"Will you be staying in St. Jean?"

"If at all possible, we'd like to make it to Paris."

"Can you ride a bicycle, *mes amies*?"

"Five hundred miles? I hardly think so," Lara said.

"Sixteen miles to Bayonne. Have you any money?" the policeman asked.

Lara reached into a pocket in the fold of her skirt and withdrew two wrinkled twenty-dollar bills and a ten-dollar bill, which she showed to the officer. "United States money?" he asked.

"Yes."

He did some quick calculations in his head. "If I fine each of you forty francs for your 'infraction' and charge you an additional twenty francs for the cost of my brother-in-law driving you the sixteen miles to Bayonne, that will leave you nineteen hundred francs, which should be enough for bus fare to Paris, and allow you to live for three months in the capital, provided you're very frugal …"

An hour later, after he'd gone to the local bank to exchange dollars for francs, taken one hundred francs out, and remitted the remainder to Lara and Ramón, the *flic* pocketed half of the 'fine,' five francs from the portion he gave his brother-in-law, and his twenty-franc commission from the well-dressed, dignified banker. He felt this was a far more judicious solution than simply taking these young people to precinct headquarters, feeling that justice had truly been done. And that young love had been served in the process.

Four Months Later – July 1939 – Paris

A hot, sultry day in the French capital. Not a hint of a breeze. The sour stench issuing from numerous public urinals on virtually every corner was overwhelming, since much of what was deposited there spilled over onto the adjacent sidewalks. Numerous smells competed with the urine: the sweet, enticing aroma from cinnamon-laced *babkas,* the hot, yeasty tang of freshly-baked bread; the earthy, pungent redolence of frying potatoes or onions; the hearty savor of roasting beef brisket. The musty whiff emanating from tiny bookstores with too many books and not enough space for the limited amount of air, and the very human odors of coffee, Gauloise cigarettes, and perfume covering the sweat issuing from unwashed bodies.

Welcome to the *pletzl,* the heart of Jewish Paris in the middle of the *Marais,* spread over the 3rd and 4th arrondissements: overcrowded to bursting, poor to the point of penury, smellier than the *Les Halles* market or the slaughterhouses of *La Villette,* the throbbing heart of the world's greatest city.

Inside their small, third-floor walkup apartment at the corner of Rue Sainte-Antoine and Rue du Prévot, the tension in their living room-cum-dining alcove was palpable. They had argued again, the third time this week, over anything and nothing: Ramón's scuffed, unpolished shoes, Lara's bra, panties and stockings which hung from the glass door of the tiny shower stall and dripped all over the linoleum floor, making it slippery to the point of danger when Ramón had to use the toilet in the middle of the night. The rent which they could not afford to pay until a few days beyond the due date each month. The conversations between them about his homesickness for the lonely spaciousness and solitude of his days in the hills and fields below Castellfollit de la Roca, where one could walk for hours without seeing another soul; about how much she missed the crush of humanity on Broadway or Seventh Avenue or the East Village; the conversation that snapped and crackled with wit and challenge; a hot corned beef sandwich at the Second Avenue Deli, complete with coleslaw *and* potato salad *and* Doctor Brown's Cel-Ray tonic.

On Saturday morning, July 15, Lara and Ramón spoke seriously with one another as they sat in the small dining alcove looking toward the Saint Paul metro station.

"Part of the problem is we see less of one another in peacetime Paris than we experienced in war-torn Madrid," he began.

"Ramón, we came here with little more than the shirts on our backs and no *permis de séjour* or work permits. Which means we're at everyone's mercy. We have a choice: either we work long hours for some rapacious swindler for almost no pay or we starve."

"We have each other ..."

A lot of good that does us. I wake up at 4:30 in the morning five days a week so I can make sure everything is set up and laid out at the bakery before the six o'clock crowd staggers in after a night on the town — a little too much wine, a bar fight, the neighborhood whores sweaty and exhausted. By quarter-of-eight, the snotty kids on their way to school, businessmen buying pastries for the office, secretaries, and shop clerks take their places. That continues 'til half-past-nine when I'm finally able to sit on a hard wooden stool near the cash register for ten minutes.

Monsieur LeVie, the patron, who's always jolly to the customers, is a dour bastard. I have to dodge his attempts to pinch any soft spot he can find and I'm on my feet until the shop closes at five. After that, I spend another hour — for which I don't get paid — emptying garbage, mopping linoleum floors, and scrubbing the slatted wooden baseboards behind the counter. By the time I get home, you're either walking out the door or already gone, and I'm flat-out exhausted. And you work from six in the evening 'til after midnight as a busboy at Stolly's where you make less than the lowest-paid streetwalker's pimp. By the time you get home I've only got two hours' worth of sleep before my day starts. That's hardly what I call 'having each other.'

"Lara, should we go back to Spain and try to survive there?"

"I don't know. What would happen if I got pregnant?"

"Are you telling me —?"

"Thank God, no. That would raise an even bigger set of problems. Where you grew up, your parents wouldn't know how to handle that we even slept with one another before we were married, let alone how we'd raise a child other than in the Catholic church ..."

She poured a cup of chicory coffee into his mug and one into her own.

"Let's keep this conversation civil, Ramón. You think either of us has the energy to hop into bed and screw our brains out with all that's been going on? Not to mention that my mummy and daddy would not be particularly pleased if their little *kugel* brought home a little *sheygetz* or *shiksa*," she said, using the Yiddish pejorative for a non-Jew. "As it is, we've still never told either of our parents about our relationship."

"So, what do you suggest?" Ramón asked, a hint of bitterness in his voice.

Both of them had raised their walls of defense and neither was willing to concede that each had raised that ultimate question in their own mind during the past few weeks. It was Lara who finally backed away from answering. "We should take time to think this through."

"But —?"

"Something we might have considered before we fell in love so quickly."

During the next month, things did not get better. Lara and Ramón were scrupulously polite toward one another, almost as if each were searching for a way to coexist and go on with life without reigniting painful feelings. Neither attempted to blame the other for what they realized was happening. Each Saturday morning, Lara found solace in getting up early, walking to the *Agoudas Hakehilos* Synagogue, ten minutes from their apartment, and mingling with her coreligionists. Much of the Spanish population in Paris spent time in the Sacré-Cœur Basilica in Montmartre, the highest point in the city, on Sunday, and Ramón, eager to hear his native tongue and to learn news from back home, started attending services there on a regular basis. Neither accompanied the other to their respective places of worship.

On August 23, 1939, Joachim von Ribbentrop and Vyacheslav Molotov, the German and Soviet foreign ministers, signed a non-aggression pact in Moscow. Late in the evening of August 31, 1939, a small group of German operatives dressed in stolen Polish uniforms seized the Gleiwitz radio station near the border of Germany and Poland and broadcast a short anti-German message in Polish. The "false flag" operation was organized by the Gestapo to make the broadcast look like the work of Polish anti-German saboteurs.

Five hours later, 1½ million German soldiers, 2,000 aircraft, and more than 2,500 tanks crossed the Polish border. Great Britain immediately gave the Nazis an ultimatum: pull out of Poland or else. Hitler ignored the ultimatum. Two days later, on September 3, 1939, the United Kingdom and France declared war on Nazi Germany.

On September 8, 1939, in a tiny village in Cataluña, Don José Caceres, the first son and presumptive heir to Castellfollit de la Roca and all the surrounding countryside, dropped dead of a heart attack less than a month after his fortieth birthday.

When the Spanish Civil War had ended, six months before, half a million Republican Loyalists escaped to France. Although many ended up in the internment camps in southern France — Gurs, St. Cyprien, and Les Milles — a few thousand had migrated to the capital. News from home spread most quickly to the churches. Two days after Don José's death Ramón learned of his brother's demise.

September **10, 1939**

Milton Rosensohn had heard from his daughter less than half a dozen times since she'd embarked for Madrid a year-and-a-half before, but he was neither a fool, nor was he without resources. He was aware that Laurie had been living somewhere in Paris for the past six months. When he contacted Hannah Sapin, Laurie's best friend, she told him his daughter had been using the name Lara Gard for the past year, and while the two girls hadn't kept in touch except for a dozen letters during Lara's time in Spain. Hannah, who was still working as an investigative reporter for the *New Republic*, had her own resources. Together, they posted letters to Laurie Rosensohn and Lara Gard, *Poste Restante* at the American Express office in Paris, and placed advertisements on the front pages of *Paris-soir* and the *New York Herald Tribune – Paris Edition*, which read, "Lara Gard - Please contact your father or Hannah S. at American Express Paris."

Lara, who'd decided to earn extra money on the days Ramón attended church, happened to be working the early shift at the bakery when a customer left a copy of *Paris-soir* on the counter. As she was clearing his dishes and the newspaper away, she happened to glance down at the paper and saw the ad. It was September 10.

More than her curiosity was piqued.

They spent the next two days, alternately clinging to one another, trying to rekindle the passion that had brought them together, screaming blame at one another, and mishandling the ultimate knowledge that they were spending their last moments together: not childlike, but childishly selfish.

Finally, Ramón told her, "With Theo married to Mother Church, I have no choice."

"I could go with you," Lara replied dutifully, while inside she was thinking *please say no.* "There's not much future here for me with you gone."

"This is Paris. You're a beautiful woman, and …"

"Not appropriate to be the Doña of the 'Mervyn first-class' of Castelllfollit de la Roca," she responded bitterly. Moments later, she burst into tears and grasped him to her tightly, her emotional roller coaster totally out of control. "I'm so sorry I said that, Ramón. But I still love you so much, so very much," she sobbed.

As she looked up into his face, she saw him choking up. "And now, *querida mia*? What happens now, my dearest one?"

She tried to regain control and finally said so softly he almost didn't hear it, "There'll always be a part of me that will love you. I guess that just a part of growing up. Let's try to remember we came in in love, and we went out that way as well…"

7

SEPTEMBER 29, 1939 – TIMES SQUARE, NEW YORK CITY

Two weeks after she'd disembarked from the *Normandie* at New York harbor's Pier 88 and the day after a beaming Milton and Sophie Rosensohn reintroduced their daughter, "Lara — you know, like the Russian countess Larissa" to an assortment of relatives her parents' age — *like I told Ramón, 'huge-breasted aunts wearing diamonds the size of your fist in an overstuffed apartment with a twittering canary'*— she'd finally been able to reach Hannah on the phone. They arranged to meet at the Automat in Times Square. Since it was only eleven, they were virtually alone once they'd entered the huge emporium of cheap eats just ahead of the midday crush.

After plunking their nickels into the slot, turning the requisite plastic knobs, lifting the glass doors, and helping themselves to their French-drip coffee and chicken pot pies, they found a table toward the back of the room where they could chat to their hearts' content. Hannah's first question was not unexpected.

"What was he like?"

"Dreamy, at least at first," Lara replied. "A hot-blooded Latin, just like in the movies. And, of course, since it was wartime ..."

"Did you use a … you know …?"

"In a Catholic country? They weren't even available."

"You wrote he was a younger man …"

"Twenty-one."

"Oh, wow! So why would you possibly give it all up and come home to this?"

"His big brother suddenly died, the family needed the son and heir to come home to run the village they owned, and the idea of a Jewish American woman from New York City didn't quite live up to their expectations."

"And?" Hannah asked, arching her eyebrows.

"No more war, big city, no money, I worked all day, he worked all night."

"So, daddy's urgent summons to come back home wasn't the only reason you decided to return? I somehow surmised from your last letter that the bloom was off the rose."

"You are so-o-o perceptive Miss Ace-reporter for the *New Republic*."

"Let's get another cup of coffee and some *real* pie for dessert," Hannah said.

After they returned, Hannah lit a cigarette, offered one to Lara, who declined, and continued. "What, exactly, do you plan to do back in the Big Apple?"

"I hadn't really given it much thought. Being a spoiled *kugel* is not my idea of fun."

"I'd hardly think so. How was your big reunion with the *mishpocheh*, all your relatives?"

"Do I really need to tell you? Just shoot me if I ever become one of them."

"How can you say that?" the *New Republic* reporter asked. "After all, you get the chance to live in the most exciting city in the world."

In response, Lara pressed her lips tightly together, stuck her tongue in between, and blew a noisy Bronx cheer.

"I figured as much. How soon would you want to be back in Paris?"

"How does ten seconds sound? You'd know how different life is in Europe if you ever go there."

"Oh?" Hannah asked. "And just what makes you think I haven't been there?"

"What do you mean by that?"

"I think it's time we take a little walk," Hannah said, glancing at her wristwatch. "It's 12:30 and it's so crowded and noisy here, I can't even hear myself think."

"You're kidding me! You've been to Europe half a dozen times and you didn't once think to visit your best friend?"

"And exactly how was I supposed to do that? Walk into the middle of a war zone, find some local, and ask, 'Oh, hello there, are you a Nationalist or a Republican? My friend Lara Gard is with the International Brigades. Do you know where I might find her? No, she never gave me her address. Doesn't *everyone* in Spain know Lara Gard? Oh, sorry to bother you. Have a nice day.'"

"But I mailed you quite a few times …"

"Uh-huh. Return address *Poste Restante*, American Express."

"Point made, Hannah. I apologize," Lara said. "But after I moved to Paris?"

"Same answer."

"I hope you're not furious with me."

"Of course, I'm not. To answer your next question, zero time in Spain, once in Lisbon, three times in Paris, the same number in London, and once in Geneva."

"The *New Republic* sent you to all those places?"

"Well … not exactly. The *New Republic* gave me unpaid leave time so that my other employer could show me what was going on."

"Your *other* employer?"

"Well, not *officially*. That employer doesn't even exist."

"Should you be talking to me about this?" Lara asked, turning her head to the left and to the right to see if anyone else was listening.

"If it doesn't exist, who would even know what it's about?" Abruptly, Hannah shifted verbal gears. "How much do you know about the latest war?"

"Hitler's obliterated Poland and nobody's bothered to stop him. England and France have declared war on the Reich, but not a damned thing has happened. Words. And words are cheap. Like all the help the Republicans received during my time in Spain."

"You're getting all your information from the newspapers and the shortwave?"

"Where else could I get it?"

"You've heard of SIM? The *Servicio de Información Militar?*"

"No."

"And you fought for the Republic?"

"Absolutely, but I never once heard of them."

"The Spanish Republic's spy service from August 1937 to the end of the civil war last March. I'm sure you've heard of the American secret service?"

"No, I haven't."

"That's because we don't have one."

"How can that be?" Lara asked.

"Because we've never really been attacked from outside the country. We've always gone 'over there.' But all the European nations, no matter how small, have had them for centuries."

"So, we haven't learned from them?" she asked Hannah.

"Not if you listen to our Secretary of War. Mister Stimson has often said, 'Gentlemen do not read each other's mail.'"

"And you don't agree with him?"

"Absolutely not. Lara, I'm a Jew. You'd have to be deaf, dumb, blind, and stupid not to know what Hitler's government has in mind for Europe's Jews. Read the *New York Times* … Listen to Walter Winchell …"

"Does this conversation have anything to do with your new job?"

"Not only does it have *everything* to do with my it, but it may concern you as well."

"Why do I feel I'm being recruited into another army?"

"Because, my dear, that's exactly what I'm trying to do." Hannah replied sweetly. "Of course, this may not happen tomorrow or even in a matter of months."

"I'm listening."

"The boss man just happens to be in Manhattan this week. He's meeting with people to try and interest them in his new project, the one that doesn't exist. I mentioned your name and your background to him and he said he'd like to talk to you. No job offer, just a chat."

After a short taxi ride to Rockefeller Center, they were whisked by elevator from the ground floor to Room 3603. The sign on the door said, "Private Meeting." There were no other identifying marks.

As they sat patiently in the adjacent waiting room, one of the tallest women Lara had ever seen opened the door. Lara estimated she was in her late twenties. She had an unusually high-pitched voice for someone so large. "Good afternoon," she greeted Hannah and Lara. "You must be Lara Gard. I'm sure my boss is looking forward to meeting you. Oh, I'm sorry, I seem to have neglected my manners. I'm Julia McWilliams, the boss's assistant this afternoon. I'm …"

She was interrupted by a ruddy-faced, gruff, white-haired Irishman in his mid-fifties wearing a military uniform with the eagle insignia of a colonel on each shoulder. His dignified face broke into an ingratiating smile. "Good afternoon, Miss Gard. I think you ought to know that I met your father a couple of years ago…"

The colonel remembered the incident clearly. "I needed a civilian suit to wear at some fund-raising event and when I got to the hotel that morning, I found my wife Ruth had neglected to pack it. The hotel recommended your father's department store and the folks at the Waldorf Astoria got me in to see Milton Rosensohn within the hour. By 1:30 that afternoon, I had the most elegant suit in the entire hotel. Of course, you used a different name back then, but he took me into his private office and showed me your picture. He was so proud of you …

"But I fear I might be boring you. Won't you and Hannah join me in my inner office? Don't be put off by the eagles on my shoulder boards or the name Donovan on my nametag. If we're going to be friends, you might as well call me 'Wild Bill,' just like everyone else does."

"A spy service?"

"You might call it that, Lara. Everyone on the beltway, starting with that horse's ass who's running the FBI, is trying to block it. Like I'm poaching on his territory or something. Seems I've only got one friend, but when you have that friend, you don't need many others."

"F.D.R." This from Hannah.

"Oh, I've got a few others."

At that moment, the woman they'd met in the anteroom entered bearing a silver tray, four cups and saucers, a pot of tea, and a plateful of Italian biscotti.

"Thank you, Julia," Donovan said. After she departed, he said, "Great gal, that one. Twenty-seven, not married, no boyfriends, seems to think she'd overpower any man. I've got the perfect match for her…"

"Sounds like an Irish *shadchan*, doesn't he?" Hannah quipped, using the Yiddish word for a matchmaker.

Not the least bit uncomfortable, Lara retorted, "And you're not trying to get me interested in becoming a spy?"

"Ladies," Colonel Donovan continued, "I prefer to call it an intelligence-gathering agency. That is, if it ever gets off the ground. So far, President Roosevelt has made me what he calls a 'Coordinator of Information.' No one knows what that means and that's just as well."

Lara, who was already working on her second almond biscotti, sipped at her tea to clear her throat, got into the spirit of the game immediately. "I trust that means you're in charge of putting together something that has no meaning, no rules, no history, and, let's be frank, no money."

"Bingo."

"Is anyone else helping you to organize this … thing?"

"A Canadian, William Stephenson."

"A spy?"

"A higher-up in MI-6, the British outfit. The President asked me to use him for help in getting started. We've already got a bunch of volunteers who're paying their own way and we're going to start training them at a secret camp in Canada in a year or two."

"I don't suppose I've heard of anyone in your little cabal," Lara said, obviously enjoying the informal repartee.

Equally amused, Donovan retorted, "Maybe one or two. John Ford's on top of the list …"

"*Stagecoach!*" Lara exclaimed.

"Then we've got that kid who wrote *The Devil and Daniel Webster* …"

"Steven Vincent Benét," Julia interrupted as she came into the room unannounced. "I hate to interrupt your name-dropping, boss, but the Curies' daughter is waiting in the reception area. Shall I bring her in?"

"Sure, why not?" Donovan said, to the gasps of Hannah and Lara.

Ève Denise Curie remained in the room less than half an hour before excusing herself. When the three of them were alone once again, Lara said, "Hannah told me you wanted to have a brief chat — and that I might somehow fit into your plans?"

"Ah, yes, a sweet, shy, retiring type who wants to remain a *kugel*. And don't look at me like I shouldn't know the lingo because I'm a *sheygetz*. You better believe some of my best friends are Jewish — and not in the way the Democrats throw it around. I'm a dyed-in-the-wool Catholic Republican who lobbied and voted *against* Roosevelt *twice*. I just happen to think that the Jews are getting a truly shitty deal from Hitler and his thugs."

"I'm listening," Lara said. She realized that this conversation had turned dead serious.

"I know about your efforts in Spain and I know you've never turned your back on the Jewish philosophy, 'If a million people say you're wrong and you believe in your heart that you're right, you be the one who speaks up for what you believe in.' Lara Rosensohn Gard, there's going to be some very ugly times for your people in the years ahead. I want to offer you a job where you'll be in the front lines saving as many Jews as you can. Does that interest you?"

8

March 13, 1940 – Somewhere in Southeastern Canada

As Lara disembarked from the bus along with thirty-five other passengers, she shivered in the frigid thirty-eight degree temperature and looked across the snow-dusted field toward two prefabricated Nissen huts. Approaching the buildings, the new inductee read the words on a small, plain wooden sign: Sixth Departmental Training Center.

Moments later, six huge twin-engine aircraft roared by at low altitude, their wake leaving one the loudest sounds Lara had ever heard. Although she involuntarily clamped both hands over her ears, she could not escape the violent tremors that shook the ground under her feet. Even before the noise from these behemoths abated, Lara's eyes were drawn to eight smaller planes, which suddenly turned and seemed to soar straight up, without appearing to lose any speed. Within seconds, when they were almost out of sight, the aircraft entered into a steep dive and turned southeast toward the direction from which they'd originally come.

"Avro Manchester bombers and Hawker Hurricane fighters," Lara heard from an anonymous voice addressing the crowd. "Our boys will give it to the Jerries good and proper."

Shortly afterward, the flat scrubland surrounding them was silent, except for the movement of twenty-six males and nine young women, including Lara Gard and Hannah Sapin, being herded toward the two huts.

Within minutes, Lara found herself in the women's barracks, two rows of ten bunk beds with small cabinets at the head and on each side of the beds. Beyond the sleeping area, the hut contained latrines, showers, and washrooms sufficient for twenty-five inhabitants.

A squarely built woman in her mid-thirties, her brunette hair cut quite short, wearing a Royal Air Force uniform, stood at the entrance to the women's barracks. She called out sharply, "Find a bunk! Put whatever you brought with you on the bunk. Take the numbered tag off your bunk and carry it with you. The same number is on your headboard, so you won't get confused when you come back. Don't worry, no one will steal anything you brought. Line up at the other side of the hut. Someone there will send you to the quartermaster for clothing and supplies. It's now oh-nine-forty. When you get your stuff, bring it back and hang it in the closet next to your bunk. Carry your numbered tag with you at all times. Meet back here at eleven-forty. That'll give you fifteen minutes before mess."

Half an hour later, each woman returned to her "bedroom" with two pair of khaki shirts and slacks, a pair of gray shorts, a baseball cap, a sweatshirt, a tee-shirt, three pairs of cotton panties and bras, two pairs of thick socks, and a pair of sturdy black shoes. At 11:30, ten minutes before they'd been told to return, both the men and the women presented themselves to a tall, broad-shouldered man who'd greeted them when they first got off the bus.

"I'm not familiar with military talk," Lara murmured to Hannah. "But I think 'mess' means food."

The 'mess hall' turned out to be a buffet featuring some of the best food she'd ever eaten. There was as much as she wanted and more. A raised stage stood at the center of the room. When most of the men and women had eaten their fill, a distinguished-looking man walked up to the stage. Lara thought she recognized him.

"Pardon me, but isn't that —?" she asked the man who'd escorted them into the dining room."

"Yeah. He's the guy from *Lost Horizon*, you know, what's his name …?"

"Ronald Colman?"

"Yeah, him."

The recruits kept eating and talking spiritedly, hardly paying attention to the man on the stage. As invariably happens, in a large room full of noisy, active people, it is the one person who stands silently, saying nothing, who eventually captures the attention of everyone in the room. So it happened here. The noise and bustle slowly died down, like air leaking out of a balloon. It wasn't long before all eyes centered on the man who was softly tapping the microphone.

When everyone was silent, the strikingly handsome actor, often compared to "The King of Hollywood," Clark Gable, opened his mouth to speak. At least five of the women in the audience, Lara and Hannah among them, sighed audibly.

"My God," Lara told her best friend, "now *there's* a man you could trust with your life."

"Ladies and gentlemen," Colman began, "I cannot thank you enough — my homeland across the pond and the United States of America, the greatest country in the world — can never thank you enough — for what you have volunteered to do. As courageous as each of you are, it is almost certain that history will never recognize you. You will be fighting against some of the deadliest, most evil people who ever lived. If you live or die only a very few people will even know what you've done. But yours are necessary lives, and we don't intend to waste even a single one. For the next three weeks, you'll be learning survival skills. When you're done, you'll be men and women of steel, right out of the Superman DC comics."

This last remark drew a few chuckles from some of the men in the audience.

Colman continued, "The war you'll be fighting will not be conventional. You won't be on the front lines. Your job will be to learn things the other side doesn't want us to know. You'll be spies, plain and simple. If you're caught, we can't even acknowledge you exist, and you'll most likely be hanged or shot without a trial."

Uncomfortable coughing from many in the audience.

"During the time you're here, we'll try to teach you the skills that will enable you to come home, or at least even the odds that you might survive with your head still attached to your shoulders."

Holy God, Lara thought to herself as she lay on her bunk that night, *just what did I sign up for?* That thought passed quickly, replaced by another. *I don't know, but a woman of steel, or as the Bible says, a woman of valor, sounds pretty damned good to me. Assuming I survive.*

Next morning, reveille sounded at 4:30 a.m. Two huge drill instructors (God knows what army *they* came from!) waited at the front door of the hut as the half-asleep recruits relieved themselves, pulled on their pants, sweatshirts, and running shoes, and groggily stumbled out the front door.

"Okay, little kitties, time to start shapin' up!" a tall, fierce-looking man with buzz-cut blond hair and a red face shouted. "We let you folks sleep an hour more than you needed. In that hour you've put on two pounds of ugly fat. So, we'll do some warmup exercises before we start our little trot!"

Thirty minutes later, a slimmer man in his mid-thirties took over from the blond giant. "Ladies and gents, it's time for a relaxing little jaunt before we have a bite to eat, if that's all right with you. Let's get moving!"

What followed turned out to be a three-mile run through the ugly scrub, up sand dunes, down steep rock-strewn pathways, around sharp bends. By a mile-and-a-half, Lara was sweating profusely, despite the frigid temperature, and her throat felt parched and sore because of her heavy panting.

"C'mon, Gard, get your lazy little *tuches* in gear!" shouted Hannah Sapin, who'd been running ahead, but who'd taken the time to circle back to goad Lara on. "You aren't fifty yet, and you're chuggin' along like my *bubbe*!"

Lara swore good-naturedly, stopped, took a few deep breaths, and started running again. Fortunately, the last part of the run back to the camp was mostly downhill on hard-packed earth. The running coach was neither sweating nor breathing hard when he got back to the field, but she also realized, not without pride, that she and Hannah were in the front third of all the runners.

"Okay, people," a third trainer said. "For a bunch of sixty-year-olds, you didn't do too badly. Chow's ready in the mess hall, then it's morning class."

Breakfast was every bit as hearty and delicious as lunch and dinner had been the day before. Afterward, the trainees were directed to an assembly room. A pleasant, recorded female voice came over the Public Address system as they entered the large room. "Take any empty seat you find. You'll be able to see and hear well from anywhere in the room. You need not take notes. There will not be any tests after this session. Class lasts two hours. If you have to go to the latrine, I suggest you do so now. Class starts in fifteen minutes."

The lights dimmed and the audience's eyes turned to the movie screen, from which "America's Everyman," Jimmy Stewart, addressed every person in the room.

"The motion picture you are about to see tells the story about what, for years, was one of the most advanced and progressive countries in the world, like America, a safe haven for Christians and Jews, native-born and immigrants, that echoed Emma Lazarus' words on the Statute of Liberty."

Stewart's image was replaced on the screen by that of a woman everyone in the audience immediately recognized. "But that all changed on January 30, 1933, when Adolf Hitler was named Chancellor of Germany and the Nazis came to power," Katharine Hepburn continued.

"Many of you will find what you're about to see shocking and disgusting. Some of you may need to excuse yourself to go to the restroom and vomit. That is acceptable. The purpose of these and similar lessons will be to show you exactly what you'll be up against and why it's so important that you build up resistance to the sickening sights you will see. While you may be used to some degree of violence and even murder in your own backyard, you will never have experienced atrocities on this scale. Let us move on." The lights went all the way down.

What followed were scenes familiar to most, if not all, of the audience, but were nevertheless disquieting. Six-foot-six-inch tall President Paul von Hindenburg, well into his declining years at 84, handing the chancellorship over to Adolf Hitler, a man three-quarters of a foot shorter. The mammoth parades in Nuremberg in 1935, the unfurling of 21,000 flags. Cut to a shot of Hitler signing the Nuremberg laws, which removed citizenship rights of German Jews.

1936: steel, coal, aircraft, and tank factories churning out weapon after weapon after weapon, and the rearmed military forces trotting out new tanks, armored cars and aircraft. A view of cars speeding both ways on the first *autobahn*.

Jews on their knees, scrubbing streets in the middle of Vienna, SS bullies urinating on their heads and then standing over the humiliated and demoralized *Juden* while these 'subhumans' licked up the urine. Six-year-old children writing with chalk on their families' shops: *My parents are filthy Jewish Christ-killers. Please do not shop in this store.*

For the next hour, unspeakable atrocities unfolded as scene followed grisly scene. *Kristallnacht,* concentration camps, the ill-fated, voyage of the S.S. St. Louis, the Wehrmacht marching into Vienna amid thousands of cheering Viennese. Neville Chamberlain announcing "Peace In Our Time," followed by a furious Winston Churchill excoriating the Prime Minister, "You were given the choice between war and dishonor. You chose dishonor, and you will have war!"

A map of Europe appeared on the screen showing a black stain expanding over areas controlled by the Third Reich: Austria, Czechoslovakia, and Poland. Black arrows pointing at Denmark, Norway, Belgium, the Netherlands, Luxembourg, and France.

The Luftwaffe and the Wehrmacht obliterated Poland. In the final image, the town of Guernica, Spain was shown on a happy, peaceful market day. Two minutes into the film, hundreds of German and Italian fighters and bombers rained a two-hundred-yard-wide path of destruction, obliterating the defenseless town and killing over half its inhabitants. The screen darkened for a moment. Then the following words appeared:

"CHANGE DOES NOT COME WHEN ONE SEES THE LIGHT.
CHANGE COMES WHEN ONE NO LONGER WANTS
TO LIVE IN THE DARKNESS."

The house lights went on. Slowly.

9

By the end of the second week, Lara had not only accommodated to the training schedule, but found she actually enjoyed it. Up at 4:30, exercises, the run, which had now lengthened to four miles, a mammoth breakfast, followed by morning class. Her days at university had been a series of social events aimed at pairing her with a presentable, appropriate husband. Jewish, of course. Even better if he was a doctor or a lawyer with a major Wall Street firm.

Boring. She thought back to a time less than two years ago.

How could I ever go back to a life like that after Spain? And Ramón? I wonder what he's doing now? Those were horrible times, but God was it wonderful when …. Maybe …?

Although her daily visit to the bathroom scale showed neither a gain nor loss of weight, it seemed to Lara that her waist and hips somehow seemed more taut. *If Ramón could see me now … if his hands could be all over me …*

Although she was nowhere near the top of her class, Lara made it a point of pride to do *more* than what was required. It all started to come home when Hannah commented, "Lara, you've changed in the last two weeks. For awhile, I thought you weren't going to make it."

"You don't know how right you are, Hannah. Last Thursday evening, I got called into the commandant's office. I thought I'd been doing so well, but I was almost in tears when I left. He was blunt. *I'll say he was,* she thought. *'You're not a spoiled little brat anymore. I'll give you one more week, and if you don't get your act together, you're out of here next Monday. What is it you don't understand about 'When these people come after you, you won't be able to survive on your charm?' That means you've got to be on top of things every moment, and from what I've seen you're not concentrating, you're not where you need to be.'*

"And?" her friend prodded.

"Friday was 'cry day,' and cry-night. My first thought was he was picking on me because I was Jewish or because I was a woman and I was ready to take a bus, a taxi, or something back home and forget about this whole thing. He seemed so unfair. But then I thought, *he was hired because he's supposed to look out for every volunteer Colonel Donovan picked. Could he be looking out for me? Letting me know he wanted me to survive?*"

"That could be, my friend," Hannah rejoined. "I must say I never found him to be unfair and I'm just as much a Jew and a woman as you are."

When she arrived at her regularly scheduled martial arts class at three o'clock on Wednesday afternoon of the fourth week, the usual instructors were not there. Instead, a pugnacious-looking little man stepped forward and stood silently. *He's one of the ugliest human beings I've ever seen,* she thought. *More like an angry little frog than a person.*

As if reading her mind, the short fellow said, self-deprecatingly, "The first day of this course you got to see and hear Ronald Colman. Welcome to the second half of survival school. Today you get the dregs." When he smiled, it didn't make him look better. Only more sinister.

"The good guys," he continued, "don't always get to look like pretty boys. My kind eats those handsome pansies for dinner, and we spit out the bones afterward. You better not mess around with Rico Bandello, y'hear?"

Half a dozen members of the class, recognizing the speaker from his most famous movie role as the ultimate gangster, called out, "*Little Caesar!*"

"You got that right," the little man said. "My real name is Emanuel Goldenberg, which wouldn't mean a thing to you, but if I introduced myself as …"

I thought I recognized him, Lara thought. *That's Edward G. Robinson.*

The applause was sincere and much more than polite. As Robinson stepped forward, he spoke in more 'normal' tones. "Folks, those of you who've seen gangster movies may think you've seen the real thing. But the *real* Mafia dons are truly the sharks in the ocean. They learn to survive and they've got to live with that instinct every day. They damn well better know how because if they don't …" The next words went unsaid.

"In their own way, which is not what 'society' thinks of as the 'right' way, they are patriots. I'm a Roumanian Jew, and I'd rather have those 'gangsters' at my side than a whole chorus of angels singing Hosannas."

At that moment, two middle-aged men came forward. The first was a slender fellow with a pencil mustache. The other, an obese man, looked like he could kill you by *sitting* on you. Each of them looked like someone none of the trainees would care to meet in a dark alley. Both sported a bulge in the breast pocket of his tight-fitting jacket which did not appear to be a wallet.

"Ladies and gentlemen," Robinson continued, "up 'til now you've learned about how to avoid the bad guys discovering who you are and why you're there. You've been exposed to the way regular Army forces fight. It's clean, it's a good way to defend yourself and put off an attacker. It's most definitely *not* the way you're going to operate when you get to your ultimate destination and you're facing the unexpected." He turned to the man on his right and the larger man on his left.

"You're about to start learning what's *different* about the way *you're* going to war. We're not going to teach the enemy how to be nicer, we're going to teach them that you don't fuck with *our* agents. If they mess with you, they're going to get a lesson in *pain management*."

Moments later, he introduced the smaller of the two men, Artie 'Dandy' DiGirolamo, and the huge man, Max 'Fats' Bruno.

DiGirolamo invited the class to sit on chairs spread around the room. He wheeled out a plastic skeleton like one would see in a doctor's office. "The first thing we're gonna learn is what parts of the human body are the most sensitive to pain. I'm sure each of you guys know the seat of all pain, which is place where you get the most pleasure, the family jewels. You've heard the saying, 'When you've got 'em by the short hairs, their hearts and minds will follow?' That's not just based on real pain, it's based on *perceived* pain, you know what I mean?"

"Yes sir," Lara, who, two weeks earlier, might have hesitated to say anything, was surprised to find herself responding. "What he needs to make him think he's bigger, stronger, and more *virile* than other men."

"Correct, Miss …?"

"Gard, sir. Lara Gard."

"Good thinking, Miss Gard. I don't mean to embarrass you, you being a lady and all, but …"

"Mister DiGirolamo, I was in Spain during the Civil War. And let me tell you, sir, if we're serious about survival here, it does none of us any good to beat around the bush or pretend that women are inherently different — somehow less courageous than you big, brave men. I've changed bedpans, wiped the asses of dying men, and helped birthing mamas deliver baby boys who'll probably grow up thinking little girls are there to screw and make babies...

"And to answer what I'm sure will be your next question," she continued sweetly, "despite a man talking about 'having a hard-on,' the balls and the sack holding them are the softest part on a man's body, meaning he wants to protect them before any other part."

"Well said, Miss Gard," DiGirolamo said. "By the way, a woman's most sensitive parts are in the same area. You'll be coming across almost as many female enemies as males. They used to refer to it as a 'honey trap' back in the day. Would any of you feel the slightest hesitation to whack a woman's pussy with the stock of your rifle? I see some of you look pretty squeamish. Better get used to it, people. If it comes down to her snatch or your gonads you're gonna have to make that decision in a split second."

One of the men got up shakily and stumbled out of the room.

DiGirolamo continued. "Better he gets sick now. You're all going to be faced with that decision sooner or later and you better get used to it. Let's take a short break."

Less than five minutes later, the trainees sat nervously on the edge of their seats, their eyes and ears riveted on the little man with the mustache.

"Let's look at some other major pain points." DiGirolamo explored in detail where you could hurt a man most: the inside of the elbows, the kneecaps, the ankles, the fingers, the wrists, the nose, eyes, ears, cheekbones, the bottom of the feet ... "The Turks taught us that last one," he said. "Tie a man down so he's lying on his back and his feet are bare. Take a hard object, any type. Hit him on the bottom of his feet over and over again. It doesn't even have to be that hard. Within an hour or two, the guy won't have a mark on his body but his own mother wouldn't recognize him. He'll be so crazy with pain and terror he wouldn't know his own mother. Nice touch. The Turkish cops still use it. Very effective."

"Mister DiGirolamo, what's the most original way you ever killed a man?" This from the back of the room.

"Come on up, sir, and I'll demonstrate."

When the man was standing near him, DiGirolamo drew back his right arm, extended his right hand with fingers straight and tight together, took calculating aim, and drove his hand very slowly, like a spear, into the man's solar plexus, stopping just short of his stomach. Imagining what it would feel like if 'Dandy' had moved in anything but slow motion, the fellow who'd asked the question instinctively clutched at the pit of his stomach.

DiGirolamo reared his rigid right hand back, then drove it, again very slowly and stopping short of the mark, into the volunteer's Adam's apple. Finally, DiGirolamo, using his stiffened hand like the flat blade of a knife, swung it sideways at the underside of the model's nose, stopping just before he hit paydirt. The smaller man was not even breathing hard, nor had he worked up any kind of sweat.

"Sir, you would now be dead," he said. "It's all in using a stiff hand. You can kill a man by jamming it up under his breastbone and tearing his guts, or you can smash his Adam's apple so he strangles. Or you can hit him hard under the nose. That breaks the bone at the bridge of his nose and drives the splinters up into his brain." DiGirolamo picked up a glass of water from a nearby lectern. Turning to his fellow lecturer, he said, "Okay, Fats, your turn."

The larger man addressed the students. "Boys and girls, I'm sixty-eight years old. As you can see, I'm too fat to run and I'm too fat to fight without a little help from my friends."

He extracted a small handgun from his breast pocket, held it up, then shoved it back into the pocket. Next, he took a small curved knife from his jacket side pocket.

"These weapons are small and handy. Hardly powerful enough to kill anyone, but you can stop an attacker long enough so you can safely get away, provided your assailant doesn't have similar equipment. If someone gets close enough to you, the knife will inflict pain in the sensitive places my colleague described."

"On the other hand," Bruno continued, "assuming you don't want him to get that close, a quick shot to the chest should be enough to do it. By the way, how many of you carry a key ring with car keys, house keys, door keys, rabbits' feet … all kinds of keys with you every day?"

Almost every hand shot up.

"That, my friends, can protect you better than most weapons." He signaled DiGirolamo to come to within two feet of where he stood. "Dandy, can you hold out your key ring and I'll show these people what I mean."

When the smaller man did so, Bruno wrapped his hand around one of the keys so that the blunt end pushed against his palm, then made DiGirolamo's hand into a fist. He approached his colleague threateningly, then said, "Use your key as if it were a knife."

DiGirolamo thrust his fist forward.

"No one will be expecting that," he said, "but the pointed end of the key can do the job of a stiff blade."

For the next hour, the two thugs — for that's exactly what they were and they made no pretense of being otherwise — entertained and instructed their audience with the less savory side, of the business in which they had been involved for many, many years.

While the trainees had earlier disciplined themselves to the coolness with which they approached their martial arts instruction, they now found themselves opening their minds to a completely different regimen, the art of inflicting pain in the most effective manner.

For the next thirty days after they left the physical aspects of the training camp, the 'students' immersed themselves daily in 8-hour-long intensive language and customs lessons of the places to which they would be sent. Already proficient in Spanish and reasonably well-versed in French, Lara learned colloquialisms, the culture of the countries which would host her, and a detailed introduction to the manners and manner*isms*, including the heavy-handed sense of humor and the particular accents, of the occupying Teutonic gods from Hamburg, Essen, Leipzig or other regions between the Rhine and the Oder Rivers.

And when, at the end of that time, she passed all of her final examinations in everything she'd been taught, Lara was posted to Barcelona with responsibilities that extended to France and OSS headquarters in Switzerland, at the end of May 1940.

BOOK TWO

STEFAN

1939-1940

10

September 8, 1939

The man who called himself Stefan Varga stood on the tiny wharf at Sandomierz, Poland, his head in his hands, quietly weeping. Two days before, he had witnessed the annihilation of General Kaciszewski's Polish Defense Forces at the Battle of Łódź opening an unobstructed path to victory for the Wehrmacht. Earlier this morning, after he'd retreated south and east to this redoubt, he'd received the telegram.

"Regret inform you your wife and son killed when building bombed STOP. Return HQ Warszawa soonest STOP. Rowecki."

Momentarily, he heard a piteous whine. Opening his eyes, Varga saw a half-starved terrier mix of some kind. The dog looked beseechingly at him. Each of them looked defeated, not expecting any more from life, except perhaps another well-aimed kick.

"From the looks of us, I'd say we're both down on our luck," he said to the canine.

The dog cocked his head inquiringly. Varga reached into the pocket of his shabby military uniform and withdrew half a loaf of black bread and a few chunks of salami. "Not much, I'm afraid, but we can split it between us," he said, tearing the bread in two pieces. He placed half of the bread and some sausage on the ground in front of the animal.

When the mongrel hesitated, Varga said, "Go ahead. You look hungrier than me."

The dog sniffed at the feast momentarily, wolfed it down in three bites, turned, and trotted away.

Well, at least I made somebody a little happier.

Shortly thereafter, accompanied by the scrape of wood against wood and the strident blast of an airhorn, an ancient one-stack river tug, which had seen much better days, indeed much better *decades,* docked at the pier: *Nadwiślańska Księżniczka,* the *Vistula Princess.*

A short, rotund man with an imperious handlebar moustache and the manner of someone who'd been on the water most of his life, addressed the man waiting on the wharf. "Captain Varga?"

"That's me."

"Major Nowak said you're looking to get to Warszawa."

"I am."

"Seems I'm almost the only one going in that direction nowadays. I heard … that is …" he looked down. "I was so sorry to hear …"

"It happens," Varga said stonily.

"This damned war," the skipper continued.

"Aren't they all?"

Captain Varga stood at the intersection of Marszałkowska and Aleje Jerozolimskie — Jerusalem Street — gazing silently at the pitiful pile of stucco and bricks that had, only a few nights before, been a three-story building of stately beauty, a place of happiness and peace, his home. Now, there was nothing left for him to bury but memories. Varga was so numbed by what he observed that this was simply one more gift from hell.

That night, alone in a small, nondescript hotel room in a poor workers' quarter of town, not knowing or caring who heard, lying sleepless on a narrow cot covered with the thinnest of blankets, the tears came, following by his agonized moans as he faced a future devoid of Helena. Her warm breath against his neck as they slept in a wordless embrace. The early mornings when they drifted in and out of sleep, only to feel the shock of cold air as the covers were pulled off and an all-too-familiar little voice, called out impatiently, "Mama ... Papa ... I've got to make pee-pee ... and I'm hungry!"

Gone.

As was the likelihood of peace. Or happiness. Ever again.

For the next three days, Varga tried to make some semblance of sense about what had happened, not only to his beautiful young family, but to the graceful, elegant city on the Vistula. The water works, gone. The telephone exchange, gone. The electricity grid, 80% demolished. Three-quarters of the neighborhood pounded into rubble.

Section IIb of Military Intelligence, Varga's unit, had suspected something was coming. But certainly not of this magnitude and certainly not in civilized Europe — not again, a scant twenty-one years later. With the invading army less than ten miles from the center of Warsaw, the Polish High Command had hastily reassembled in small pockets of resistance throughout the city. At one of those outposts, Captain Varga, a logistics professor in civilian life, assumed command.

Poland was at war — no, it was increasingly clear that Poland was *losing* the war — but you couldn't just stop fighting. Stefan Varga simply could not abandon his adopted homeland. He was a soldier. He knew he didn't have long to live, and, with the loss of his family, he didn't really care. But honor demanded that certain things had to be attended to, and then matters could run their course. At the very least, he wished he could have said goodbye to his wife.

On September 15, the remains of Military Intelligence gathered at what was left of its headquarters to carry out its final order: "With the exception of classified documents identified by department directors, all files will be destroyed by 1800 hours."

Captain Varga watched, emotionless, as this work was done. Watched, apparently, without feeling. Perhaps he didn't care, or perhaps he cared too much. Whatever the truth, no one could read the message, if any there was, in his veiled eyes.

"Good evening, Captain Varga. Thank you for meeting with me." The speaker, a tall, exceedingly handsome man, with a full head of tightly-curled, coal-black hair, sat across from Varga in a small, comfortable hotel room in Pruszków, ten miles southwest of Warsaw

"Bronislaw Urbanski spoke highly of you, Colonel Rowecki," Varga began.

"I realize the rank seems pretentious, first because I'm only five years older than you, and second, because the Polish army does not recognize me as anything more than a lieutenant. My 'troops,' such as they are, simply call me *Grot.*"

"A *nom de guerre?*"

"I suppose you might say that, although the 'war,' such as it is, seems pretty one-sided. Have one of these?" he said, holding out a box of small cigars."

"Thank you," Varga said, as Rowecki lit it for him with a silver-wheeled lighter. "You asked for this meeting, Colonel?"

"I did. As of tonight, there are fifty-one German divisions — a million-and-a-half soldiers and thousands of tanks — in Poland. Our air force was blown up on the ground the first morning. England and France have declared war on the Reich, but that's all they've done. America doesn't give a damn, so, as usual, we find ourselves alone. We have — or *had* — half a million troops. So far as we know, we've suffered a hundred thousand casualties and another hundred thousand taken prisoners. Things are probably worse than that. But this is not the first time, and this is Poland. For *us* at least, not everything is necessarily lost."

"I agree, Colonel."

"But the regular army does not." Rowecki paused, lit a cigar of his own, and said, "We want to offer you a job."

"'We,' Colonel Rowecki?"

"The ZWZ, the *Związek Walki Zbrojnej.*"

"The Union of Armed Struggle?"

"An underground resistance, Captain Varga."

"I see."

"You have a choice. You can go to one of the regular combat divisions — suicidal as it sounds, the higher-ups in the regular army have decided to make a stand in two of the eastern provinces. The *nation* is defeated but the *idea* of the nation mustn't be. If that's what you want to do, to die on the battlefield, I won't stop you."

"Or?"

"Or you can come to work for us. It's not an easy decision, but time's the one thing we do not have. The city's almost entirely cut off. By tomorrow, there'll be no getting out. Shall we go for a little walk, Stefan — may I call you that?"

"Of course."

They walked in silence for a while. A flight of Heinkel HE-111 bombers passed overhead. Both officers looked up, then waited. The bombs fell on the southern part of the city. The sound of steady, distant thunder. Silence returned as the sound of engines faded.

"Well?" Rowecki said.

"The ZWZ, Colonel."

"You know what the Germans will do if they get hold of us?"

"I'm sure it won't be pleasant."

"I'm pleased with your decision. There'll be a meeting in my office in the ZWZ's temporary headquarters, twenty miles east of downtown Warsaw at 0930 tomorrow morning. Any questions?"

"None, Colonel."

"Oh, and one more thing …"

"Yes, sir?"

Rowecki reached into his jacket pocket and produced two shoulderboards. "As of this moment, Stefan Varga, you are officially commissioned a Major in the *Związek Walki Zbrojnej.*"

"Thank you, sir," Varga replied.

"We're glad to have you with us." They shook hands. The colonel saluted. The major returned the honor.

11

THURSDAY, NOVEMBER 2, 1939, WILNO, LITHUANIA

8:30 a.m. Stefan Varga, wearing blue overalls, a heavy wool sweater, and a dark, well-worn leather jacket, stood outside a shabby workers' canteen in the city where he'd been born. Although it was still autumn, frost flowers had already appeared on Wilno's sidewalks. Despite his protective clothing, Varga found himself shivering and rubbing his hands inside his pants pockets, trying to keep warm. He'd been told by Colonel Rowecki that his contact would meet him on the Moscow Road, a block east of the Café Vienna where he now stood.

"Just beyond the Napoleon sign," Rowecki had said. "He'll find you." Moving several yards up the street, Varga came to the venerable signpost, one of the city's most famous landmarks. Looking east, he read, "On June 24, 1812, Napoleon passed this way with 422,000 men." Circling the stanchion and looking west, toward Warsaw, he mused sardonically on one of history's great ironies. "On December 14, 1812, Napoleon passed this way with 4,000 men."

"Major Varga?" Stefan turned found himself staring at a short, slightly pudgy man of sixty, with rheumy, watery eyes behind thick, steel-framed glasses and a beard which at one time might have been trimmed in a neat VanDyke manner, but was now simply a thin, wispy mass of smudgy gray.

"Professor Kholodenko?"

The older man sighed. "*Used* to be. Jewish professors of theoretical science, haven't done so well in the Ukrainian S.S.R. lately."

"So, you've joined the great migration to the Soviet Workers' Paradise?"

"For the moment," the older man replied. "Given what's happened in the West, it seemed like the safest alternative until three months ago. Now, who knows?"

"Ah, yes, the infamous Molotov-Ribbentrop Pact. How long do you think it'll last, Professor Kholodenko?"

"One never can tell," the professor said. "To quote an old Catalan saying, 'With sufficient saliva and patience, the elephant screws the mouse.'"

"That may be so," Varga replied. "But which one is which in the strange misalliance?"

"That remains to be seen. I trust you know why Rowecki sent you here?"

"Not really," Varga said. *Most likely a do-nothing mercy job to help me think of something other than Helena's and Jovan's deaths, twenty-four hours a day.* Out loud, he continued, "Something about transporting papers to Roumania."

"Ah, yes, papers," Kholodenko murmured noncommittally. "They're stored at the Saint George Catholic Church on Sirvydo Street. We should go there together so you can choose which ones you'd like to take."

"Which ones *I'd* like to take?"

"Colonel Rowecki said he felt you were one of the few officers whose discretion he trusted to save the most important of these documents. Do you do speak Yiddish?"

"Of course," Varga responded.

"Good. That will make our task easier."

They walked three blocks north to *Gedimino prospektas,* Wilno's main thoroughfare, where they hailed one of several Polski-Fiat Junak taxicabs.

When the taxi dropped them off at the entrance to the church, Professor Kholodenko spoke briefly with an elderly priest, *Monsinjoras* Matis, who, by his wrinkled hands and crepey skin appeared to be well into his seventies. The two approached Varga.

"Ahh," Father Matis intoned. "You are the officer sent by Colonel Rowecki? He said you were to be entrusted with a small portion of the *Žydų* papers — originals — that we are storing here in case we are invaded at some time in future."

"I must apologize *Jūsų Šventenybė*, Your Holiness," he continued. "To be truthful, I have no idea what or why —?"

"*Mano sūnus,* the monsignor replied gravely, "It is not always given to us to know the answers to those heavy questions. We are aware of the Germans' intentions as regards your people. If something untoward were to happen … well … it would be shameful to destroy all memory of the parent religion."

The priest beckoned them to follow him upstairs to a large hall, which reminded Varga of his days in the university library.

"Father, there must be thousands of documents in this room. I taught logistics which supposedly made me an expert on how to move things from one place to another, but I would have to commandeer seven or eight freight cars to move the contents of this room anywhere. And my resources, even in peacetime, would be nowhere near what I would need."

The priest laid his gnarled right hand on Varga's wrist. Stefan found the gentleness of his voice and the soft, smooth feel of the ancient skin comforting. "My Son, your Colonel Rowecki knows all this. He asked that I condense the core of everything you see here, the very heart of the most meaningful portions, into a single briefcase you could carry with you."

"But that's —?"

"Impossible, you say, Major Varga? Recall, if you will, the story of Hillel, one of Judaism's most humble and celebrated sages. Your Talmud recites the tale of a gentile skeptic, who stated publicly he would accept Judaism and convert only if a rabbi would teach him the entire Torah while he stood on one foot. First, he went to Shammai, one of Hillel's colleagues, who was so insulted by this ridiculous request that he threw the apostate out of the house. The gentile did not give up and went to Hillel and made the same challenge. Hillel responded, "What is hateful to you, do not do to your neighbor. That is the whole Torah; the rest is simply commentary — go and study it!"

Varga thought back to his time in the Talmud-Torah, the smoke-filled one-room schoolhouse. *I remember on my first day, when I was six years old, my parents brought me there and asked me to touch the cover of the book I was supposed to study, then lick my fingers immediately afterward. I did, and found my fingers were sticky and tasted as sweet as honey. Several years later, I learned this was a trick every teacher pulled on first-day students. Before the child came to* cheder — *the schoolroom* — *the teacher wiped a bit of honey on the book cover. He would then explain that the taste of learning would remain sweet in the student's memory for the rest of his life.*

"Hillel also said, 'If I am not for myself, who will be for me? But if I am only for myself, what am 'I'? And if not now, when?" Varga remarked.

Professor Kholodenko smiled. "So now you understand the duty Colonel Rowecki has assigned to you, Major Varga. You have been designated to carry the story of our people to distant lands at a time when, for all we know, a goodly portion, if not all, of our brethren might well be destroyed, and to entrust that tale to those who may be the surviving remnant."

"Go with God's blessing," Father Matis said, handing Varga a leather satchel.

After he left the church and said his farewells to Professor Kholodenko, Varga walked for miles through zigzagged streets where stones in ancient buildings leaned or sagged. Past crowds of Orthodox Jews in caftans and curling earlocks, gossiping in front of tiny storefront synagogues. Past Wilno's housewives in print dresses, carrying home garlic sausages and black bread from the street markets. Past dogs and children playing soccer on cobblestone streets, and old men who leaned their elbows on the windowsills and shouted to other old men across the street from their tenements. It was every quarter of every city in East-Central Europe.

Reaching his hotel, he trudged upstairs and carefully placed the heavy, but manageable, satchel onto the end table next to his bed. Twilight had embraced the city. From the growling in his stomach, he realized he'd not eaten a thing since breakfast.

Stepping out of his hotel, which occupied a grimy sidestreet in the underbelly of Wilno, he was hit with an icy blast from the north. He bundled his jacket tighter, appreciating the warmth of the black lamb's wool karakul on his head. Standing on the cold pavement, he loosened his wrists and shoulders and rolled his head round his collar to relax his neck from the day he'd just finished. When he reached *Gedimino prospektas*, he turned his mind outward and let the city's conflicting smells, sights, and sounds envelop him. The stink of Russian petrol, tobacco, cheap scent, and icy water running in the gutters. The sporadic charges of city buses, the belching brown lorries thundering through the potholes in pursuit. The eerie emptiness in between. The latest conquerors in the back seats of Russian limousines with their blackened windows, the unmarked buildings, splitting before their time. Were they office blocks, barracks, or schools?

The dough-faced boys smoking in the doorways, waiting. The chauffeurs and taxi drivers reading newspapers in their parked cars, waiting. The unspeaking group of solemn men in greatcoats and hats, staring at a closed door, waiting.

Continuing along the wide street, Varga paused at windows spotted with an accumulation of dust and frost, examining what they offered. Painted wooden dolls. For whom? Dusty tins of fruit or perhaps fish. Battered packets hanging from red string, contents a complete mystery. Jars of pickled herring. As he approached a parking garage, a drunken peasant woman pushed a bunch of dying tulips wrapped in newspaper toward him. Rummaging through his pockets, he found a crumpled *lita* note and pressed it into her withered, wrinkled hand.

Ducking into a small basement restaurant farther along, he found the place more than two-thirds filled, with customers quaffing more beer and mead than eating food. The waitress, a large-boned middle-aged woman nodded at him and gave her best excuse for a grin, displaying a mouth filled with steel fillings and teeth brown from years of harsh cigarettes.

"You new here?" she asked.

"Born in Wilno but haven't lived here for awhile."

"What'll it be?"

"*Apynys Kosmosas*," he replied, indicating a winter beer brewed in Kaunas, Lithuania's second city.

"Good choice. You eating?"

"Uh-huh. First, *Šaltibarščiai,* beet borscht. How's the *Bulviniai Blynai*?"

"Best potato pancakes in Wilno. You like 'em with sour cream or apple sauce?"

"Both, please."

"You a Žydas?" she asked, not unkindly.

He affirmed that he was Jewish and an officer in the Polish military.

"Lots of 'em coming this way. *Boches*, too. And the Russkies pushing back from the other side. Gonna be some interesting times. I don't know if you'd want to be around here."

She left his table and returned minutes later bearing the coal-dark brew and chilled pink soup. Varga looked around the large, noisy room. Soviet enlisted men in khaki uniforms with red shoulderboards, roughhousing and joking with their comrades, their looks trained on an assortment of whores of every age and size. Lawyers and notaries in charcoal gray suits and somber ties, sitting in varous corners of the room, holding hands with much younger, attractive women, obviously not their wives.. Varga felt a momentary tug of emotion.

Helena had died less than two months ago. He'd not even thought of another woman since … But he was a man, not yet forty. He knew what he needed as well as he knew that he was not unattractive. Still …

12

The following morning, Varga awoke at nine, took the ancient lift, which protested dramatically as it descended ever-so-slowly to the breakfast room. He helped himself to a pot of hot tea, four hard rolls, and a plate of kippered herring smothered in fried onions. He spread butter and loganberry jam onto the rolls, and smacked his lips, anticipating the delight of the salty-tasting fish before greedily wolfing his meal down.

Returning to his hotel room, he examined the satchel. The leather was dense, pebbled, the hide of some unknown animal, covered with a thick, fine dust. He wet his index finger and drew a line through it, revealing a color that had once been dark chocolate, but was now faded by time. The seams were hand-sewn, sturdy work which appeared to have already lasted fifty years and would most likely last another fifty. A portmanteau, like a doctor's bag. Two sides opened evenly, and held together by a brass lock.

He put one finger on the ingenious lock, a perfectly circular opening which did not suggest the shape of its key. Inserting an odd-shaped key which Father Matis had provided him. Varga heard an emphatic, satisfying *snick* as the lock opened. Whatever was in the satchel was covered by a blue-and-gold satin sheet.

As he lifted the cover, he fingered an array of brittle, faded papers and a few small books. He carefully extracted two slender handwritten notebooks of poetry by someone named Chaim Grade, of whom he had never heard and another book written in faded blue ink, a thin novel called *Satan in Goray*, by another unfamiliar name, Isaac Bashevis Singer.

His excitement grew as he dug deeper into the pile: two letters written by Sholem Aleichem. *My God, over 100,000 people attended his funeral in New York thirty years ago. Tevye der Milchiger,* a series of short stories, had been a worldwide phenomenon. Next, a postcard written by Marc Chagall. As he plowed through the rest of the papers, he found commentaries on the Torah and the Talmud by the eighteenth century scholar, Elijah ben Solomon Zalman, the Vilna Gaon, the most influential interpreter of Jewish thought since the Middle Ages.

Varga spent the next two hours poring through what amounted to a first-person enyclopedia covering the hardscrabble everyday lives of the Jews of Eastern Europe when the region in which he grew up was the center of the Jewish world. *These must be saved.*

An astronomical guide with a set of dials to calculate when religious holidays should fall, given variations in the lengths of Jewish lunar months. A weathered agreement from 1857 between a yeshiva in Vilna and a union of water carriers. Finally, Varga's hands trembled as he lifted the last document out of the briefcase: a 1933 'autobiography' by a malnourished fifth grader, Bebe Epshtayn, describing how her parents forced her to eat by telling her beguiling stories. "When I would open my mouth, they would pour in food," she wrote. Attached by a paperclip, Varga gazed for several minutes at a yellowed photograph of a serious-looking dark-haired girl of ten. *Who knows what ever became of her? Who knows what will ever become of these writings, of the world I knew as a child, unless I do my part to save them?*

As he turned into a large courtyard, Varga found much of the morning sunlight blocked out by several large, decaying two-story buildings. No more than ten feet separated each tenement from its neighbors. A narrow, muddy lane provided the only walkway between the structures. For the most part, that path was congested by clotheslines strung from first-floor casement windows of one edifice to the next. Each line bore bedclothes, towels, clothing, and underwear, which hung dripping from six feet high to less than a foot above the wet ground.

He wandered deeper into the rabbit warren of crumbling structures until he came to the address Professor Kholodenko had given him. The bottom half of the building's exterior consisted of small, half-destroyed gray bricks, a quarter of which were missing. Above these, a few irregularly shaped light pink stones. Still higher, flat, dark-red, facing stones, which climbed up the front to the white wood-framed windows on the second floor.

Once inside, Varga sought out the building's directory of tenants. No Kholodenko, but quite a few units had no names beside them. He heard a door open on the second floor and looked up to see the professor summoning him. "Up here, Major!"

Once he entered his host's apartment, Varga was surprised to find that Kholodenko's flat was large and, though not modern, luxurious: Oriental carpets covered nearly every square foot of the floor; expensive, high-quality furniture, the pieces obviously hand-selected and chosen with a connoisseur's eye; original paintings, no prints. Johann Strauss *sohn's Kaiser-waltzer* issued from an HMV phonograph, adding an uplifting cheeriness to the surroundings.

Professor Kholodenko beckoned his guest to an alcove, from which Varga gazed out at a panoramic view of the neighborhood. The older man brought small cups of Turkish coffee and honey-sweet baklava to the table after Varga had seated himself.

"The briefcase?" Kholodenko asked without preface.

"Secure in the hotel's 'left luggage,' as you suggested."

"Good. The proprietor's Jewish, so I don't think you need worry."

"If you'll forgive me, Professor, I still don't know why Colonel Rowecki sent me to Wilno. He said my contact — I'm assuming that's you — would provide me with the details."

"Correct," Kholodenko replied. "It has something to do with the contents of the briefcase."

"I'm not surprised," Varga said, sipping the thick, syrupy liquid from the demitasse cup. "What escapes me is the purpose of my mission. What would this have to do with a *Polish* underground operation? And why?"

Kholodenko held out the plate of sweetmeats. Varga took two of them and placed them on a napkin in front of him.

"Saving Jews serves Poland's interests."

"Since we're both Jewish and men of the world, Professor, we need not mince words. We've been harassed and chased out of Europe just about everywhere we've tried to settle for hundreds of years. Russia and Poland may have tolerated the *Yehudi* who were forced upon them, but there's never been love lost between them. Until recently, thank God, the Germans treated us kindly." He took a square piece of honeyed pastry between his thumb and index finger, biting into it. "And the Turks, of course," he said, savoring the nutty sweetness of the baklava.

Professor Kholodenko said nothing for several moments, nursing his own cup of coffee. When he spoke, his words were delivered in a slow, thoughtful cadence. "Nearly half this city is made up of our *landsmen*. Of thirty-five million Poles at the time of the invasion, one of every ten were Jews. You know, of course, Hitler has plans for all of Europe's Jews."

"If Jews are so unpopular in Poland, why would our government be interested in protecting them?"

"The enemy of my enemy is my friend. Europe has almost ten million Jews. The United States has half that number. The German *bund*, Father Coughlin, Westbrook Pegler, and their brand of isolationists, are doing everything they can to keep America out of the coming war, or, at the very least, neutral. American Jews are not only vocal but extremely influential in politics, the movies, and the print media. The New York *Times* ...."

"Pulitzer, the Sulzbergers ..."

"Correct. You've seen how much help we've received from France. Only England and the United States stand between an independent Poland and one that's carved up by the Russian Bear and the German Eagle. So far, the United States sits on its hands doing nothing while Britain could fall in the next year."

"But if Poland could somehow show our American friends how serious we are about protecting Jews —?" Varga mused.

"Exactly. Poland is a nation of farmers living in the last century: rolling hills, no natural barriers to immunize it from attack from the outside. History has taught us over and over again that Poland's only hope of survival is to live by its wits, rather than by force of arms."

Kholodenko continued, "What Colonel Rowecki has in mind won't save a single Jew. And these papers, which might have value to someone, somewhere, are symbolic rather than critical. What your senior has in mind is a test of your intelligence, endurance, and ingenuity. If you succeed, I'm sure he has bigger things in mind."

"Pardon me, Professor, but you're still talking in riddles," Varga said, his tone impatient.

"Very well, Major, I'll be blunt. The colonel sent you to Wilno for a reason. If you'll join me in my den, I'll show you rather than tell you ..."

When Varga seated himself, Kholodenko stood to his guest's right and pointed to a jagged yellow line on the map which descended from the Baltic Sea at the northwest corner of Lithuania to the eastern border of German-aligned Slovakia at its juncture with Poland and Hungary. "This line divides Poland into German and Soviet spheres of influence. Wilno, or Vilna as the *goyim* call it, is quite close to that line. Your job is to get yourself, the briefcase, and its contents safely into Roumania, which, for the time being, is still a safe haven for the Polish government.

In order to do so," he continued, "you'll have to navigate through dangerous territory, including the Pinsk Marshes and the Ukrainian S.S.R., which nominally belongs to the Soviet Union but it's anyone's guess where their sympathies lie."

"Seems a fairly simple, direct route," Varga said, tracing south on the map with his index finger. "Wilno to Bialystok, to Lublin, thence south to Lvov and the Roumanian border."

"On paper, yes," Kholodenko agreed sardonically. "But Bialystok is barely in the Russian sector, Lublin is presently Wehrmacht territory, Lvov disputed between Poland and Ukraine, Hungary neutral but more-or-less aligned with the Reich. A lovely route maybe. 'Safe?' I hardly think so."

"You don't trust that the vow of friendship between Hitler and Stalin will be eternal?"

"Do you?"

"Perhaps for a year, maybe less," Varga replied. "Maybe long enough to let the ink dry on the concordat. They've already started punching holes in the 'spheres of influence' when they think no one's looking."

"Five years ago, I'd have said 'Whatever you do, stay on the Soviet side of the frontier. Our people have it better there than it's been anywhere else in five hundred years,' After all, Jews played such a huge role in the Bolshevik Revolution … But then Vissarionovich and his Georgians, — even Jewish cannibals, got hungry. Nice people," he finished sarcastically.

"What do you recommend, Professor Kholodenko?"

"Stay as far east of the dividing line as you can. Improvise, Major Varga. That'll be your key to survival. Good luck."

13

Varga awoke early, lying on top of his raincoat, the smell of the hay beneath him sweet, freshly cut. He looked up at the barn roof, the early light barely glowing between the cracks where the boards had separated. Stretching to alleviate the momentary stiffness he felt, he stood, walked over to the broad, open window — what the farmers used, standing on their wagons, to pitch forkfuls of hay into the loft. It was just after sunrise. A shaft of sunlight illuminated a cut field, strands of ground mist rising through it. A narrow road of packed, sandy soil passed less than a hundred yards from his lodging of the night before.

He saw three men walking down the road, wearing black shoes, black leggings, long black coats, and broad-brimmed black hats. *Hasidim* on their way to *shul*. Their faces were white as chalk. One of them turned and looked at him, displaying neither curiosity nor challenge. They made no sound as they walked. Then they were gone.

Poland.

He had entered the country the previous day. A taxi, two trains, and a ride in a wagon on a cold day followed. A dog who growled deep in his throat, yet wagged his tail. A peddler on the road. Varga knew he would not arrive anywhere in particular any time soon. He was where he was, where travelers slept in barns. An old woman, a kerchief around her ancient face, had said he was welcome. The sun had set, the moon had risen, and he'd slept in total peace in an unknown place.

He leaned against the sagging wood adjacent to the window and watched the day break. A band of storm clouds moved east. Here and there, light broke through the clouds, a birch forest appeared on the horizon, and a rye field turned to green as he watched. He remembered the wet smell of morning earth, crows calling as they flew along the curve of a field. He had once lived in this part of the world, a long time ago. Sometimes he had ventured beyond the winding streets, beyond the outskirts of town, and he'd seen such mornings when he was a little boy, when he'd awakened long before anyone else, in order not to miss any of the miracles.

"Hey up there, *pan*, are you still asleep?"

Leaning out the window, he peered down to find the old woman looking at him from the yard. She wore a sweater and jacket on top, a broad skirt below, her left hand on her hip, her right hand leaning on a stick to support her small, sturdy body. Her dogs, a big brown one and a smaller black-and-white one, stood by her side and stared up at him.

"Come along to the house," she called. "There's coffee waiting."

She hobbled away. The dogs romped around her, sniffed the bushes, lifted a leg, and pressed the earth with their extended forepaws to have a morning stretch.

Seeing no one in the vicinity, he stood by the open loft window and relieved himself. The dogs trotted around the area below him, occasionally looking up. Sighing from one of life's minor pleasures, Varga descended to the bottom of an earthen stairway.

When he reached the ground, he saw that the old woman had left two large wooden buckets by the well. He knew she wanted him to bring the water in. First, he took off the white linen shirt he'd purchased in Wilno just before he'd departed that city two days ago. Then he worked the squeaky pump handle and splashed himself with surges of icy water from the spout. Shivering in the early morning air, he rubbed himself dry with the shirt, then put it back on and combed his hair with his fingers.

Next, he filled the buckets and staggered into the kitchen, determined not to slop water onto the floor. The farmhouse, an old drystone building, had a low ceiling, a tile stove with a large crucifix on an adjacent wall, and glass windows. The coffee smelled strong and invigorating in the kitchen's close air.

The woman brought coffee to him in a china cup that must have been close to her own age. "Thank you, *Małababcia*, little mother," he said, taking a sip. "The coffee is very good."

"I always have it every morning except when the wars come. Then you can't get it for love or money. Not around here, you can't."

"Where am I?"

"Where are you? Why you're about halfway between Bialystok and the Białowieża Forest — that's where." She shook her head at such a question, made her way to the stove, and using her skirt as a potholder, withdrew a pan of bread from the oven. She placed the pan by the side of his coffee, then went off to the pantry, returning moments later with a bowl of white cheese covered with a damp cloth. She put a knife and a plate in front of him, then stood by the stove while he ate.

He knew if he asked her to sit with him, such a request would offend her sense of propriety. She would eat when he was done. He sawed off the heel of the bread and covered the steaming slab with white cheese. "This is delicious," he said.

"You must be on your way south," she said.

"I'm on my way to Lublin."

"Lublin!"

"Then to Lvov."

"Blessed Mother, Lvov. You're a long, long way from there. They say the *Niemców* are in Lublin. You'd be safer to stay in the east. Pinsk or Rovno. Lvov is a Ukrainian place, you know," she told him.

"Yes, I know."

"They say it's in Poland, but I don't think so. You'll want to watch your money over there,"

"Have you been there, *Małababcia*?"

"Me?" She laughed at the idea. "People from around here don't go there."

When he was done with breakfast, he put a few złoty under the rim of his plate. Back in the barn loft, he spread his map out on the hay, but wherever he was, he could not find the name of the place. When he came out of the barn, the old lady and her dogs were taking a cow out to pasture. He thanked her again, she wished him a safe journey, made the sign of the cross to protect him on his way, and he headed down the narrow, sandy road in the direction he'd seen the *Hasidim* walking earlier.

Half an hour later, he reached the closest thing to a village. It wasn't much. A few log houses scattered on both sides of a dirt street, a man with a shaved head and a cavalry mustache, his thumbs hooked in suspenders as he lounged in the doorway of what Varga took to be the village store. He saw a tiny Jewish ghetto on the other side of the village: women in wigs, a *Hasid*, yarmulke pinned to his hair, chopping wood in the little yard outside his house. Pale children with *payess*, uncut curly sidelocks, springing out from around their ears. He walked on for five minutes and the village was no more.

Alone again on the broad Polish steppe, Varga walked through seemingly endless fields that ran to the forest on the horizon. The sun grew hotter, the satchel heavier, and he started to sweat. The fields on either side of the narrow road were alive with the buzz and whirring of insects. The black, moist earth had a certain smell to it, rotting and growing, sweet and rank at the same time. From this perspective, his journey from one city to the next, and then to the next after that, seemed frantic and absurd.

TEN DAYS LATER – NOVEMBER 17, 1939 – SOUTHEASTERN, POLAND

Varga found a small, remote Polish army post, just on the border of the German and Soviet zones, which, miraculously, had not been overrun by the Wehrmacht and which, equally implausibly, had been overlooked by the Russian forces. He presented his official identification card to the post commandant, Lieutenant Rakowicz.

"Welcome to the only military establishment in Poland that's somehow been spared from the war — so far. How is it in the capital?"

"It's ceased to exist for all I know, Lieutenant."

"That bad?"

"Worse, I'm afraid."

"Who was your last commander?"

"Colonel Rowecki," Varga said.

At that, Rakowicz's face lit up. "Rowecki was my boss when I was in the 55th Infantry Regiment in Leszno. You couldn't ask for a better man. When did you last see him?"

"About a week ago." Varga proceeded to explain his assignment to the lieutenant. "Confidentially, Colonel Rowecki enlisted me in the ZWZ and promoted me to major ten days ago. He appointed me courier to get the contents of this briefcase to the military command-in-exile presently in a top-secret location over the Roumanian frontier."

"I see, Captain ... uh, I mean Major. In that case, permit me to give you any assistance I possibly can. I don't know how much influence I still have. Lublin's shaky at best and everyone who can is trying to get as far away from the Nazis as possible."

"How close can you get me to the Roumanian border?"

"Depends. The Polish officer's uniform still carries respect in some quarters. I've got an extra officer's uniform I hardly ever use which I can 'loan' to you. D'you have your major's insignia with you?"

"I do."

"Good. We're about the same size and build, so the uniform should fit. If it doesn't, our quartermaster can make adjustments. We'll sew the shoulder-boards on and you'll look official. I can get you to the Lublin station in our base staff car. I've got a friend who's a supervisor on the Polish Railway in Lublin. I'm sure he'd agree to put you in military command of a small local train that plies the route from Lublin to the southeast ..."

November 19, 1939 – Lublin Station

The platforms and waiting rooms were jammed with people babbling in different languages. The trains had stopped running. A reedy male voice issued through the public address system. "Ladies and gentlemen, I regret to announce there will be no more service ..." The voice was drowned out by the rumble of an approaching train. People surged to the edges of the platform. Railway guards tried to hold them back. As the sound became louder, the crowd fell silent and stopped struggling.

A war train. A Russian armored train, a peasant killer. It meant burnt villages and weeping women and everybody in Lublin station knew it. The train slowed to a crawl, so the crowd could see the soldiers' faces, cold and attentive. Then it passed. Silence once again.

A few minutes later, another train appeared, the very antithesis of the behemoth that had just passed. A relic from a different time, a time of peace. A little four-car train headed ... who knew where? There were no signs on the sides of the coaches. Sergei Rabinovitz, forty-five, a small runt of a man, pressed by the crowd against a marble column, felt his heart rise.

He needed desperately to get on that train. The Germans would make quick work of him and he knew it. But God had made him small, and as the crowd surged toward the empty little train, he found himself actually moving, pushed and shoved by an ocean of humanity. After a few moments, all he wanted to do was stay near enough to watch the train leave, to imagine that some part of his spirit would fly with it to safety. Out of the corner of his eye, he glimpsed the apparent commander of the train, a tall, handsome major wearing a Polish uniform.

Watching from the cab of the minuscule locomotive, Stefan Varga tried to show an impassive face, despite the churning inside his stomach. The crowd was now an unruly mob. Those who made it onto the train might live. Babies howled, men and women clawed and fought, station guards swung their clubs. A huge, brawny peasant shoved an old woman out of his way and started to climb onto the train. The fireman waited until the brute's weight hung on his hands, then kicked him full force in the face. The peasant's head flew up and he tumbled backward into the crowd.

But, in the end, the ones who pushed to the front were the ones who got on.

When the train was so full that people were hanging out the windows and seated on the couplings between the cars, Varga started to raise his hand. Then, suddenly, he stopped. His eye locked on a tiny man in a long black overcoat, with a black homburg hat. The little fellow barely managed to hold onto an old-fashioned valise in one hand, while pressing a handkerchief to his bloody nose with the other. "Get me that man," Varga said to the nearest guard, pointing.

With the help of the guard and two colleagues, the little man was carried through the crowd by the elbows and hoisted up to Varga. "Better get going," the guard said to the major.

Varga signaled to the conductor, who swung himself onto the train. The engineer blew a long blast on the whistle as the overloaded little train moved slowly out of Lublin station.

"Thank you, Major," the little man said. "I am Sergei Rabinovitz." He extended his hand and Varga shook it. Rabinovitz saw that the major was staring at his battered case. "I am — or until most recently I was — the principal second violinist of the Krakow Symphony Orchestra."

Varga inclined his head in acknowledgment.

"So," Rabinovitz said, evincing a tone of profound politeness, "we are going to Lvov?"

"South of there," Varga replied.

Just before the train left Lublin station, Varga approached the engineer.

"Is there any place you can hide this briefcase during the journey?" he asked quietly. "Someplace so secure it will not be found unless this train is totally destroyed?"

"Is it that important, major?"

"It is."

"There's a lock box under the coupling between the engine and the coal car that looks like an integral part of the connection. It cannot be identified as such by anyone not familiar with the workings of the unit itself and it's the most secure container available to us. I'm happy to provide you with one of the two keys to the box, but you should know that it cannot be unlocked unless a different key is used to open the container from its opposite end. With your permission, I will be the only one with access to the second key."

"That suits me, sir," Varga replied. "Let's be on our way."

The conductor was a man of old-fashioned manners and consummate dignity, with a droopy mustache, a conductor's cap a size too large, and a limp from wounds he'd received in the First World War. When he'd reported to Varga in the railyards, two miles from the entrance to Lublin station, he had stood at attention and produced from his belt a 9 mm Parabellum pistol,

1913 vintage. He informed Varga that he was prepared to send a significant number of Germans straight to hell if he got the opportunity.

As the train chugged through the Polish countryside, the conductor went from car to car, delivering the same speech. "Ladies and gentlemen, if I may have your attention, please. In less than two hours, we will be stopping at Zamosc. Those who wish to get off the train are invited to do so. However, this train will not be returning to Lublin. It is going all the way to Lvov with brief stops along the way. The military situation where we're going is unclear, but the railroad will take you as far as it can. Passage is without charge. Thank you."

Watching the crowd carefully from the last car, Varga discerned that the Polish passengers had already absorbed the first shock of war and dislocation. Now it was a question of survival and the will to live through catastrophe. When the train stopped at Zamosc, only a few people got off. *The farther from the war, the better.*

South and east of Zamosc there was no war, only the light snow of a November morning, a strip of pale sky on the horizon, harvested fields, tiny streams, and birch groves, the leaves of the trees brittle and starting to fall.

14

"Do you have a current map, Sublieutenant Nowicki?" he asked, as the locomotive, a small, ancient LNWR Samson class 2-4-0 towing four cars, pulled out of the station.

"Yes, sir," the young officer, who looked to be about eighteen, responded, snapping to attention.

Varga studied the map, tracing the route with his right index finger. "We're approaching Tomaszów Lubelski. I estimate that after we cross the River Tanew into the Ukraine, it's about sixty miles to Lvov. Does that sound about right to you, sublieutenant?"

"I don't really know, sir. I've never been as far as Lvov."

"Well, we'll find out together," Varga said. "With luck, this old locomotive will make a steady thirty-five miles an hour."

Each of them heard the airplanes at the same time.

A flight of Heinkel He-111 twin-engine bombers heading north, Varga thought. *That meant they've attacked the industrial cities in the south and are on their way home. Hopefully their bomb bays are empty.*

The Heinkels droned on. Below and behind them, a fighter escort of Messerschmitt Bf-109s. *Nursemaids for the big birds, nothing more.* One of them sideslipped away from the formation, swooped down in a long, steep dive, flattened out, and fired his 20 mm cannon into the train. Varga instinctively threw himself to the floor of the locomotive as several bullets raked the interior just above his head. Immediately afterward, the fighter slipped back into formation.

Varga called out to Nowicki, "Go through the cars, get the dead and wounded out. See if there's anybody who can help."

He ran along the track and climbed into the locomotive's cab. The engineer was kneeling at the fireman's side. Varga cursed to himself when he saw the fireman's face, which was ash-colored. The engineer went down on one knee and put a hand on the fireman's shoulder. "You did well. You'll be alright," he said, trying to comfort the injured man. As the crewman closed his eyes, the engineer pressed his lips together and shook his head. "My sister-in-law's husband," he said. "My wife told me not to let him go."

Varga nodded sympathetically.

The engineer said, "She —," but there was nothing more. It was quiet in the fields. The only sound was the slow beat of the locomotive's pistons running with the engine at rest.

The fireman raised his hands, palms up, then made a face. "Shit," he said. Then he died.

Nowicki had the casualties laid out in a beet field. Varga put him to work tearing shirts into strips for bandages for the wounded and sent him running up to the locomotive for hot water. Meanwhile, Varga organized a grave-digging crew. Its members took turns using the fireman's shovel. A priest said prayers, and the earth was piled on.

As a logistics expert, Varga had learned how to hide trains — at least in theory. Using Nowicki's map, he intuited where it was most likely he'd find branch lines or spurs. Sure enough, he directed the engineer to a branch line that wound into the hills above the Vistula. Within half an hour of turning off, the locomotive came to an old mine that had been closed for years. A railroad spur, wildly overgrown, but still usable, ran to the mine site. A roofed shed nearby was still standing. It would make the train very close to invisible.

Once inside the shed, the engineer patched the hole in the firebox. A hefty farm boy from a village they had passed volunteered to work as the fireman. Nowicki found four rifles and a few boxes of ammunition, which had been hidden behind a panel in the last coach. He chose four men to be armed in case of emergency.

The countryside was dark and deserted as the engine moved cautiously over the old track, heading east. The passengers were quiet, left with their own thoughts. *Maybe they would have been better off staying in Lublin.*

The train climbed into the uplands east of the Carpathians, the ragged edge of Europe. They ran dark, the lamps turned off in the coaches. Beyond the uplands, the steppe. Treeless, empty, sometimes a few thatched huts around a well and a tiny dirt road that ran off into the endless distance, to Russia, to the Urals. Now and then a village, a station house with a Ukrainian name. But it was mostly the track and the wind.

Varga stood beside the engineer and stared out into the darkness. The boy who'd volunteered to be the fireman fed coal to the firebox. His palms blistered after an hour of shoveling, so he'd taken his shirt off, torn it in half, and tied it around his hands. He might have been all of fifteen, but he was a man that night.

At some nameless settlement, the train stopped at a water tower. The engineer swung the spout into position, and he began to fill the tank. It was long after midnight, and deserted — only moths fluttering in the engine light and the splash of water.

Then, suddenly, a girl was standing by the locomotive. She was fifteen, perhaps sixteen, barefoot, wearing a soiled cotton shift, a head scarf, and a thin shawl around her shoulders. She was, quite simply, one of the most beautiful creatures Stefan Varga had ever seen. "Please, Your Excellency," she said in a soft voice that Varga barely understood, "may I be permitted to ride on the train?"

She raised her hand and opened her fingers to reveal a pair of tiny gold earrings resting in her palm.

Varga was speechless. The hem of her shift was spattered with mud, her ankles thin above dirty feet. She stood patiently, her eyes not quite meeting his, a sign of submission, her other hand clutching the shawl at her throat. But when Varga did not speak, she looked directly at him and just for an instant her eyes lit up as they caught the light, then she hid them away.

"Please, Excellency?"

The earrings must not be worth what she had thought. Her voice faded in defeat.

"You do not have to pay," Varga said.

Her face hid nothing. It was plain how she had struggled all her life to understand things. She had never been on a train before, but she knew one or two people who had, and they had told her one certainly had to pay. Atop the locomotive, the engineer swung the water spout away and shut it off.

Varga waited for her to ask where they were going, but she never did, "You may ride the train," he said.

Still hesitant, she closed the earrings in her fist and held them to her throat, then turned toward the passenger coaches. *Did he mean what he said? Or was he just making fun of her? No, he meant it.* Before he could change his mind, she ran like a deer, climbed cautiously onto the iron step of the first coach, peered inside, then vanished.

Past Lvov, the train started climbing a grade that ran through a pine forest, then deeper into the mountains that marked the southern boundary of Poland. Varga and the engineer saw a dim shape ahead at the same moment.

The engineer swore and hauled on the brake. The wheels locked and screeched and the train shuddered to a halt just short of tree trunks piled across the track.

The bandit leader was not to be hurried. He walked his horse to the locomotive's cab and stared at Varga. "Get out," he said softly in Ukrainian. Well into his fifties, he wore a peaked cap and a suit jacket. Varga and the engineer jumped to the ground, but the boy did not. All along the train, passengers were filing out of the coaches, hands high above their heads.

The leader kept staring at Varga. "Who are you?" he finally asked.

"No one of interest to you."

"I don't believe that. You ready to die up in a tree?"

Varga did not react.

"You people are so damned hardheaded," the bandit leader said. "Doesn't matter. You're finished, you know. Now it's just the Germans and us."

Varga remained silent.

"Carrying anything valuable on that train?"

"No. Just people headed for the border."

One of the man's colleagues rode up to the leader. "Any good?" the first bandit asked.

"Not bad."

"Gold?"

"Some. Polish money. Jewelry."

"Women?"

"Good. Five of them."

The bandit leader winked at Varga. "You won't be seeing them again. Give me your watch."

Varga undid the strap and handed up his watch. Helena had given it to him as a birthday present two years ago. The bandit, still sitting astride his pony, glanced at it, then dropped it in his pocket. "Not exactly a standard issue railroad watch, is it?"

"No."

With one hand, the leader raised his rifle until Varga was looking down the barrel. "What do you see in there?" Varga took a deep breath.

Suddenly one of the passengers screamed. The bandit leader's associate, riding a gray pony, dug his feet into the stirrups and the small horse trotted toward the sound. A rifle fired, then another. The bandit leader's horse shied and whinnied. Varga grabbed the harness and pulled himself close to the horse's body. The barrel of the leader's rifle probed frantically, looking for him. Somewhere above, the bandit was wailing and cursing, a muffled scream. Varga hung on to the reins with one hand and snatched the rifle barrel with the other. The weapon fired but he didn't let go. Then the boy came out from behind a locomotive wheel and smashed the bandit on the head with the shovel, which rang like a bell as the rifle came free in Varga's hand and the horse tore away from him.

The other bandit turned his pony around and shot the boy again and again. Varga could hear the bullets hit and the boy grunted each time. Varga flinched as something hissed by his ear. Then Nowicki called to him from the coal car and he ran up the ladder. Two horses thundered past, then a cluster of rapid rifle shots and a yell of triumph.

Nowicki was lying on the coal at one end of the car. Between the train and the forest dark shapes were sprawled amid clothing and suitcases. A yellow spark from the trees. Varga swung his weapon and pulled the trigger. There was a click as the hammer fell on an empty chamber. He threw it aside and worked the pistol free from beneath his sweater. "Who has the other rifles?" he asked Nowicki.

"Don't know, sir. It's chaos."

Varga couldn't allow chaos. He rolled over the lip of the car, slid down the ladder on the other side, stood between the cars for a moment, then ran along the length of the train. Passengers were climbing through the coach windows. Some of them had gotten a horse off its feet and it kicked and whinnied in terror as they tried to kill its rider, who howled for mercy. Varga tripped as he leaped for an open doorway, then went sprawling into the last coach.

A bullet from the forest went through the car and a triangle of glass fell on a seat without breaking. A silhouette rose suddenly in the middle of the car and began returning the fire. As Varga crawled along the aisle, the train moved. Barely. But he thought he could feel the logs being slowly forced off the track.

The engineer is alive, using the locomotive like a bulldozer, he thought.

Meanwhile, the unknown rifleman knelt quickly, moved on his knees to a neighboring window, straightened up, and fired again and again.

Good God, it's Rabinovitz, the violinist.

The homburg was jammed down on his head and he was muttering under his breath, "Stay still, you —," as he took aim.

Varga reached the far end of the last car on the train just as something started to give way and, with the sound of splintering wood, the train moved a little faster.

"Wait!"

A running shape burst from the forest — the peasant girl who'd begged to be let on the train at the water tower. "She got away!" Rabinovitz had appeared beside him. The girl ran in panic, tripped, went sprawling on her face, struggled back up again, limping now and much slower. She waved her hands and screamed as the train gradually picked up speed.

Varga felt himself abruptly shoved aside. A man in a dark suit leaped off the train and ran toward the girl, circled an arm around her waist, and tried to help her. No longer young, he could barely run fast enough to keep up with the injured girl. "For God's sake, don't leave us!" he yelled.

The bandits on horseback in the woods saw what was happening. Varga pinpointed the muzzle flashes in the half light. The range was absurd, but he aimed with both hands, changed the action to single shot, and squeezed off round after round. Rabinovitz muttered angrily and kept firing his rifle. A young woman in a sweater and skirt jumped from a window, stumbled, came up running, and took the girl around the waist from the other side. Nowicki, running down the roof of the car, fired into the trees.

Somebody shouted, "Save her! Save her! Save her!" and others took up the cry. Varga stood on the lowest step as the three people gained on the car. Rabinovitz was firing over his shoulder and Nowicki was shouting something from the roof. The three faces were beyond exhausted. With tears of effort, mouths gasping for breath, they clawed frantically at the railings beside the door. But as the last log rolled away, the locomotive accelerated. The three runners flailed and staggered as the platform moved away from them.

Then, a loud bang erupted from the locomotive. The shock slammed Varga against the wall, and suddenly the runners were close. He reached out and grabbed handfuls of shirt, coat, hair, whatever he could get, and hung on desperately. Someone caught the back of his coat, just as he started to fall onto the tracks. Other hands reached over his shoulders. People yelled, shoes scraped on the boards as somebody fought for traction, and the girl and her two rescuers were hauled aboard with a cry of triumph.

Varga ended up on his hands and knees as the train, something wrong with the way it now ran, slowly ground through a long, gentle curve. When Varga worked his way forward to the locomotive's cab, he found bullet marks everywhere, and a very pale engineer.

"My briefcase —?" he asked.

"Safe, major. I took the liberty hiding the second key in the engine's safe the moment I first saw what the bandits had done to block the track."

They were well up in the Carpathians. Some of the passes topped seven thousand feet. The train switched back over ridges and granite outcrops, through sparse grass and stunted pine forests. Barely moving now, the locomotive crawled along a trestle as the passengers prayed silently and not-so-silently, as oil trickled from beneath its engine.

They crossed the Tisza River. There'd been a fire on the bridge, but it still held. Varga walked in front of the train, his heart pounding, trying not to hear the sounds the wooden girders made. When the train had cleared the bridge, he reboarded. They traveled beside a deeply rutted dirt track, where some mileposts gave the distance to Roumania. A burned-out Polish army car had been shoved into a ditch in the middle of a mountain stream.

Slow as their progress was, there were no other trains. The Polish railway system didn't really exist any longer. A few miles before they reached the Roumanian frontier, Varga and Nowicki changed into officers' uniforms.

The train stopped at the Polish border station, but that station had been abandoned — an empty hut and a bare flagpole. As the train stopped just short of the frontier, a Roumanian major and two Polish diplomats — complete with steel-rimmed eyeglasses, Vandyke beards, and overcoats with velvet collars — appeared at the wooden barrier pole. Major Varga stepped off the train and onto Roumanian soil. He saluted, then shook hands with his opposite number.

A diplomatic solution had been reached. The Polish passengers could enter Roumania as temporary immigrants, the Polish train could not. Poland could no longer insist on anything. It was a *former* nation now, with questionable status under international law.

The sun dropped lower in the sky. The children cried because they were hungry. The truth could be seen in the eyes of the passengers: despair, boredom, fatigue. The refugee life had begun. Things started to happen. Roumanian soldiers delivered hampers of bread and onions and wormy pears. A train appeared at the Roumanian border post: a small but serviceable locomotive, a few freight cars, and Polish regular soldiers who would ride in this conveyance to an uncertain destination.

Varga watched as the Roumanian train departed to the south. He himself remained just on the Roumanian side of the border waiting for the arrival of the Polish staff car which he'd been told would take him to the Polish army's base station.

And yet … and yet … as he stood by the tiny, heroic Polish train, Varga felt his heart swell with pride. From the sad little train with its shattered window and bullet gashes, its locomotive reeking of singed bearings and burnt oil, the passengers emerged; blood had been shed, but Varga did not believe it had been shed in vain, as his little army struggled past: Sergei Rabinovitz, his battered violin case carried proudly in the same hand that had helped save them all, the peasant girl, the man and the woman who had run onto a battlefield to rescue her, a few country people, a few workers, women and children. Poland had lost a war and Poland had lost its land. But it had not lost its soul.

15

Colonel Rowecki reached into a nearby refrigerator, took out two bottles of Tyskie beer, opened them, and passed one to Varga. They reached up and clinked the bottles in a toast to one another.

"Your next assignment is more meaningful and, I might add, right up your alley."

"I'm listening, *Grot*," Varga responded, using his superior's familiar *nom de guerre*.

"This one hits closer to home. It seems a large number of your coreligionists don't exactly trust Mr. Hitler's motives as being helpful to their cause," Rowecki said sardonically.

"And…?"

"They've run off into the forests and formed partisan groups."

"They don't intend to use sticks and stones to break the *Wehrmacht*'s bones?"

"Correct. Our British allies have not poured any manpower into our war against the *Boches*, but they've thrown a little money into our pockets to help fight the battle."

"As in …?"

"£25,000 sterling."

Varga whistled. "$106,000 U.S. How many guns do the partisans want and what kind?"

"As many submachine guns and as much ammunition as they can get."

"What's available, *Grot?*"

"It's your job to find out, Stefan. How long would it take you to explore what's available and at what cost?"

"If we were the government producing them, a few days. But it will take me at least two weeks to find out if anything is even out there."

Two weeks later – end of December 1939 — Iaşi

"What did you find, Stefan?"

"I've narrowed it down to six types of submachine guns, assuming we're not interested in the STEN, which we can pick up new for $11 American apiece and which may last a week if we're lucky. Ideally, if we could buy 2,500 weapons and a thousand rounds of ammunition for each… We can't afford any of the new guns. The best we can hope for is some 25-year-old weapons that still work, assuming someone is willing to sell at less than outrageous prices.

"Have you established any kind of budget?"

"A very tight one. No more than thirty-dollars per weapon delivered to the closest port, Odessa or Constanţa. And that doesn't include a single round of ammunition. Do you think it's possible to get a little more from the Brits?"

"Anything's possible. Not likely, but possible."

January 8, 1940 – Molyvos, Lesvos, Greece

"Yannis Kakis." The man who extended his hand was in his mid-forties, short, with tousled black hair, bushy mustache, and the sharp, wind-chiseled face of the stereotypical Greek Islands fisherman. "Arms merchant if and when the mood overtakes me."

"Not your regular occupation?" Varga asked, his eyebrows raised.

"Would I have suggested we meet in Molyvos if it was, Major Varga? Let's just say I put sellers and buyers together. A broker. Might I ask how you came to learn about me?"

"Two months ago, I met a man named Sergei Rabinovitz on a train …"

"Sergei Rabinovitz, the violinist!" Kakis exclaimed, his face taking on a distinct glow. "My wife's cousin, a wonderful human being! I'd heard he got trapped when the *verkackte* Nazis destroyed Poland, and … but how can you know him? Your name is Varga." His glance turned suspicious. You're a Polish major. The Poles have been the biggest *anti-semites*."

"Originally Szymon Vaynshtok from Wilno. Are you, by any chance, Jewish, *Kýrios* Kakis?"

The smaller man embraced Varga, kissing him on both cheeks. "We can talk of such things when we're a little better fed and watered. I know the perfect place down by the port."

It took them less than five minutes to walk along Molyvos' harbor to the restaurant-bar. At 4:30 in the afternoon the pale winter sun sat low in a sky, casting a golden flame over the Aegean Sea. As the two men approached a small storefront with the hand-lettered sign, Καφένιο Μήθυμνα (*Kafenio Mithymna*), Kakis nudged his companion toward the front door. They entered a noisy twelve-by-twelve-foot room where they observed a dozen older men playing *tavli* — Greek backgammon — sipping ouzo, and nibbling on seemingly endless appetizers. Kakis found a small table toward the rear with just enough room for the two of them to be seated.

A tall buxom woman with thin, orange-colored hair, somewhere on the far side of forty, came to their table almost immediately. Varga nodded to his companion, assuming the Greek would order for them.

"*Barbayannis Evzone kai meh meze, parakalo.* Your best ouzo and a plate of appetizers, please," Yannis said. The waitress nodded, and headed back to the kitchen. Turning to Varga, he asked, "How hungry are you?"

"Quite," Varga replied. "You were about to explain how you're related to the Jews of the Pale."

"My ancestors migrated south to Salonika, which has had a strong Sephardic Jewish community ever since the Jews were expelled from Spain. Over the years, we Ashkenazi intermarried, and here I am."

"You're a part-time arms merchant?"

"By education and training, I'm a lawyer, Major Varga, but over the years I've associated with some less-than-savory people. Sometimes folks have needs that cannot be met through entirely legal means. Other times things just need to be made right. I render a service for such people. I suppose some of our smug, high-risen citizens would call me a whore," he continued.

"I've heard lawyers called that," Varga responded. "People generally don't like lawyers."

"Until they need one," Kakis replied, a ghost of a smile on his lips.

The waitress reappeared with a bottle of ouzo, a carafe of water, and two glasses. She walked back to the rear of the kafenio, then returned with a huge tray filled with platters of food.

"A *few* appetizers, Mister Kakis?"

"*Mezes,*" Kakis said. "Absolutely necessary if you're not going to fall into the sea when you stumble out the door. Ouzo's 45% alcohol. Three rules: you sip it *slowly*, you pour water into the cup to cut it, and you damned well better have some food to help wash it down. Clams, mussels, stuffed tomatoes, grape leaves, octopus, and anchovies marinated in olive oil and lemon." He pointed to three plates containing tiny fish about the size of his thumb. "Fried sardines, grilled sardines and *sardeles pastes*."

Varga stared uncertainly at what looked like *raw* sardines.

"They're not cooked. They come straight off the boat, they're packed in layers of salt for a day or two, then marinated in lemon, olive oil, and some garlic, the scales are rubbed off, and you eat them with your fingers."

"Would you mind if I pass on those, Kýrios Kakis?"

"Of course not. More for me."

For the next several minutes the two men gorged on the tasty assortment of food. Varga, heeding Kakis' advice, poured water into the glass of ouzo, which turned it a cloudy, milky-white color, and sipped the Greek firewater slowly and cautiously.

"What do you need and what've you got to spend?" his host asked at last.

"As close to 2,500 submachine guns and a thousand rounds of ammunition per gun as I can get. I've got access to a hundred thousand U.S. dollars, more or less."

"How close to new do you need them to be?"

"As long as they can kill Nazis, I'm not particular."

"Good. If you'd have said 'new,' I'd have said not a chance. As it is, it won't be the easiest order in the world to fill, Major Varga."

"If we're going to be short-term business associates, we may as well be on a first-name basis. Szymon or Stefan, whichever you prefer."

"Very well," Kakis replied. He extracted a small pad and a mason's pencil from a side pocket. During the next several minutes he scribbled notes in precise Greek script, occasionally mumbling in a language Varga did not understand. Finally, he looked up. "Would Beretta 1918s be acceptable?" Kakis asked, referring to a 21-year-earlier predecessor to the latest Italian-made submachine gun. "I know where there are 2,500 available. They cost about half as much as when they were new, they're two pounds lighter than the MAB 38, and they kill a man just as dead as the newer weapon."

"How much, Yannis?"

"Twenty-five dollars U.S. apiece, if your people pick them up at the dock in either Constanța or Odessa, twenty-seven if they're shipped to Klaipėda."

"Where would you get them?"

"Ethiopia, shipped out of Djibouti."

"And the ammunition?"

"Different story and quite a bit trickier. Nine millimeter Parabellum is pretty standard for submachine guns, but everybody wants 'em. You'd either have to hijack a shipment or buy stolen ammunition. You could end up doubling your outlay, maybe more, to get decent stuff, most likely from Odessa or one of the smaller Ukrainian ports."

"I don't know if we have that kind of money."

"Could you get more from your sponsor?"

"You're talking a minimum of thirty-five percent more than they've allotted me. How much is your commission?"

"Included."

"Any quantity discount?"

The Greek laughed mirthlessly. "The more you want the higher the premium. I like you, Szymon. On top of that, you're saving *Jewish* lives and hopefully kicking the shit out of the Nazi bastards."

Half an hour later, the two men continued their discussion as they ambled among Molyvos' small, picturesque waterfront. "First, there's the matter of end-user certificates," Yannis said. "Almost every firearms-producing country limits who they'll sell to by this treaty or that treaty, by an embargo, by a neutrality act, by any excuse they can manufacture to raise their prices to astronomical levels. Poland's now part of Germany — they're calling it the General Gouvernement — so you can't risk antagonizing the Reich by sending anything that would remotely threaten the government unless you're shipping to one of the Tripartite signatories, Germany, Italy, Japan or one of their client states."

"That leaves a great big wide world," Varga said.

"Not quite. America's isolated itself behind its Neutrality Act. France and England won't buck the Great Western Hope. It's got to be a state that's not involved with the players in our current war. And it's got to be a state that needs arms to protect its own interests. And that state has to issue an end-user certificate promising the selling country or company that they are the *final* user, the *end* user, and they have no desire to sell the weapons to anyone else."

"Don't various unsavory types buy arms every day? The street gangs of Odessa, the Sicilian Mafia …"

"Of course, once the end user certifies its *bona fides*, nobody gives a damn where the armaments go. Just as long as sufficient money changes hands and some of that money ends up in the hands of the 'right' people. That's just another service I provide for my clients."

They stopped at a wharfside candy shop where Kakis ordered two pieces of baklava for each of them and plunked down several *drachma* coins.

"You procure end-user certificates." It was a statement, not a question.

"Sometimes even legitimate ones," Kakis chortled. "In your case, the order's large enough to excite the interest of port police or other officials, who'll be more upset if they don't get their cut. That's why we'll need genuine certificates issued by a country that has a real reason for wanting them."

"Do you have such a country in mind?"

"The Republic of China. More than half of Europe has no idea China's even a country. At the moment it's got a nasty little war going on with Hitler's ally, Japan. When it's too far away to matter to you, someone else's war is always a *little* war."

"That means you have a connection."

"In this case, the ideal connection. The consul general of the Chinese Republic to Austria. One of the best friends we Jews have ever had in that part of the world. ..."

16

"Thank you so much for agreeing to meet with us, Mister Ho," Kakis said. "How are things between you and Ambassador Jie?"

"Never worse, I'm afraid. He's in Berlin trying to impress the Nazis while, I'm still in Vienna. Last month I was informed of a sharp rebuke on my diplomatic record and he was eager to deliver it to me in person. I imagine I'll be transferred out any day now." The dapper Chinese man, elegant in a modern, trim charcoal suit with narrow maroon-and-gold stiped tie, silk pocket handkerchief, and closely-cropped dark hair looked distinctly Eurasian. Kakis had arranged a suitable room for their guest at the Grande Bretagne Hotel.

"Permit me to introduce my associate, Major Stefan Varga, late of the Polish national defense forces. Stefan, this is my friend Ho Feng-Shan, China's consul-general to *Ostmark*."

"I'm pleased to meet you, Major. But don't the Poles —?"

"Not me, Mister Ho. I'm a Jew and a Litvak," Varga said, smiling and shaking hands with his new acquaintance. "Yannis told me your relations with the new management in Vienna are not good, since you've managed to get four thousand Jews out of the city."

Ho Feng-Shan nodded modestly. "It's gotten more difficult by the day," he replied. "Two months ago, our beloved ambassador ordered me to stop issuing visas and await new instructions from the Foreign Ministry. When I didn't receive any communiqués, I told my office to resume issuing visas. Last month, the illustrious, ass-kissing Mr. Chen sent one of his lackeys to learn whether I was selling exit visas from Austria and Shanghai entry visas to the Jews for profit. Of course, there was no evidence of that."

"Because …?" Stefan asked.

"I still have friends in Vienna, Major Varga. Even some who work in the Seyss-Inquart bureaucracy. Chen Jie would have done anything he could to curry favor with the Reich."

The three men rose, walked over to the buffet counter, and filled their plates with an assortment of crisp hot rolls, grilled fish, stuffed grape leaves, and shepherd's salad. When they returned to their table, they found their tuxedo-clad waiter had left a pot of strong black coffee, one of hot water, and an assortment of teas, lemons, and milk.

"I believe it's only a matter of time before Mussolini gets tired of being the Führer's junior partner and comes after General Metaxas." This from Varga.

"Could be," Kakis mused. "But we'll kick the shit out of the *guappos* if they think we're such an easy target. Enough of such talk. You know what we need, Ho?"

"A legitimate end-user certificate for a lot of weapons and ammunition to be delivered to Shanghai to help us in our war against the Japanese invaders. The prey banding together to survive the predator."

"I still can't understand what's in it for you Mister Ho," Varga said.

"A couple of months ago I met a pastor named André Trocmé, from a small town in the Haute-Loire. He's certain the Führer will attack France within six months and it'll be hell for the Jews when he does. He's making contingency plans if that happens. 'Love your neighbor as yourself,' he said. 'Sometimes you just have to do the right thing.'"

"Does he think he can protect France's Jews?"

"He hopes he can. There are a few of us like that. But we're very much in the minority and I fear the Nazis will make sure people like us will be long gone before we're able to make any kind of a dent in their plans. Speaking of which, assuming the toys you want won't be coming anywhere near Shanghai, would you mind telling me where they'll end up?"

Varga glanced at Kakis, who nodded.

"Somewhere southeast of Warsaw," Varga replied.

Two hours later, the three men arrived at Syntagma Square. Even though it was far from chilly, Ho Feng-Shan wore a lengthy trench coat with capacious pockets. He gestured to a row of buildings across the street and a block away. "The embassy," he said. "On a Sunday afternoon I doubt if there's more than one low-grade clerk on duty. You don't have to say much. Just follow my lead."

They crossed the esplanade, heading toward the tallest of the buildings. Ho Feng-Shan nodded at brass sign on the front: *Zhōnghuá mínguó dàshǐ guǎn*, Embassy of the Republic of China. Although it was Sunday, the gates and the doors were wide open.

Walking through the open doorway of the Chinese embassy, they passed racks of travel posters printed in Chinese, Greek, and English. Beyond them, a bespectacled young Chinese man sat behind a small desk. He greeted them politely, explaining in schoolbook English that he was the second deputy consul.

"Good afternoon, Honorable Consul," Ho said in Mandarin. "My name is Jacob Sheung-Lo." He reached into one of his coat pockets and extracted a thick business card printed on high-quality vellum. He pointed at Varga. "I am privileged to introduce you to my American client, Szymon Vaynshtok, who is visiting Athens from New York."

Varga glared at Kakis, who was innocently fingering a nearby brochure, seemingly oblivious to Ho Feng-Shan's use of his birth name.

"Doctor Vaynshtok is interested in making a substantial capital investment in the Republic," Ho continued. "Can you supply him with detailed information about the possibilities?"

The deputy consul, who was on his first diplomatic assignment and had drawn the lonely duty of being the only one at the embassy that day, stammered, "Honored Xiānshēng Lo, I'm afraid my English is very minimal."

"Do you speak any other languages, Consul?"

"Greek of course. And a little German."

"Fortunately," Ho continued in Mandarin, "Doctor Vaynshtok is fluent in German and the Hotel Grande Bretagne, where we are staying, has designated Kyrios Kakis as our guide since we arrived in Athens. Have you any promotional material? A film perhaps?"

The junior diplomat pulled out several glossy folders. Ho Feng-Shan picked up one of them, pretended to study it, and said to his confederates in Mandarin and English, "This man seems very knowledgeable."

"I will do my best," the underling said eagerly. "Would you gentleman please accompany me to our auditorium?"

"I'm quite familiar with our beloved country," Ho said. "If you don't mind, Consul, I've had a long journey. Is there a small room in the building where I could simply rest while you're engaged?" Under his breath, he murmured to Varga and Kakis in English, "Go with him and keep him busy as long as you can."

After the diplomat had shown Ho to a quiet place, Kakis assumed an air of companionable charm and walked with Varga and the young diplomat to a room down the hall.

When they were out of sight, Ho Feng-Shan rose and prowled through the hall in the opposite direction trying doorknobs until one of them turned. It revealed a large, imposing, and unoccupied office.

Feng-Shan slipped inside, closed the door, and began ransacking the adjacent supply room. He found a number of end-user certificates, grabbed several pieces of assorted stationery, matching envelopes, and two large metal seals — 'chops' — inscribed with Chinese characters, and stuffed all of them into his trench coat pockets. Then, noticing some official correspondence that bore imprints of the seals in red and purple, he pilfered stamp pads inked with both colors.

He had made it back to the room to which he'd been shown earlier with two minutes to spare, and was pretending to read a tourist guide to Peking on an adjacent table, when the deputy consul reappeared. Kakis and Varga followed him, armed with piles of commercial literature. Ho Feng-Shan thanked the young deputy profusely for his gracious assistance, asked him for the name of his superior so he could write a note about how well he'd been treated, and casually left the embassy with his friends in tow.

When they were several blocks away, the trio dumped the Chinese literature in a nearby wastebasket and returned to the Grand Bretagne. Once there, Ho asked the concierge to refer him to a Chinese translation service that provided typists, then told Yannis and Stefan that he'd meet them for dinner at the hotel later than evening.

Over dinner, Ho Feng-Shan presented them with perfectly typed and officially sealed end-user certificates for three thousand submachine guns as well as separate certificates for an unlimited number of 9 mm. parabellum ammunition.

The following morning, after thanking Consul General Ho and dropping him off at Ellinikon International Airport in nearby Glyfada, Kakis addressed Varga.

"Szymon, can you get me $120,000 U.S. *today*? I can get you the guns *and* the ammunition, but I need an answer and a deposit in an account at Union Bank of Switzerland, Zurich by no later than tomorrow."

"How certain are you that this will work?"

"Nothing's guaranteed in this life, Szymon."

"I'll see what I can do."

At the appointed time, Colonel Rowecki booked a call to the Grande Bretagne and was put through to his subordinate within minutes. "Let Mister Kakis know the money will be deposited in the numbered account he provided you in Zurich."

"Great news, Szymon," Kakis enthused. "Don't ask me how I intend to do this. All I can tell you is that I won't have to leave Athens to make the ammunition happen."

THREE DAYS LATER - WEDNESDAY, JANUARY 17, 1940 - ATHENS

"Yannis, it's been four years. To what do I owe this pleasure?"

The speaker was five-and-a-half feet tall, slender with unnaturally black, brilliantined hair, which he parted in the center. A thin black mustache traced his upper lip below his long, semitic nose. To Yannis, he looked closer to sixty than fifty. He'd aged poorly since Kakis had last seen him, and his sagging face portrayed a man under intense pressure.

"You're being fucked over by Göring and your Rheinmetall-Borsig partners who're under his control."

"Tell me something I don't know," the man seated across the desk from him replied. "I also know that when — not if — the Wehrmacht comes marching into little Greece and they throw Metaxas out, they'll use Pyrkal to screw my adopted homeland into the ground and I'll most likely be hanged as a traitor."

He offered Kakis a Havana cigar from a humidor on the credenza behind his desk.

"Don't undersell yourself, Prodromos," Kakis said, accepting the Montecristo tendered by his friend. "You've obviously done well for yourself."

In truth, Kakis' host — as well as his trusted old friend — Prodromos Athanasiadis, commanded an industrial empire that dwarfed that of anyone else in Greece.

"How long do you think it will be before the Axis invades Greece?"

"Ten, eleven months tops. Adolf will most likely goad Mussolini into starting the war. Then, after we've beaten the Fascisti but bled ourselves dry in the process, he'll finish the job. But enough of such happy talk. You're looking for something, yes?"

"Something that will help the Polish Resistance and, at the same time, give you a chance to kick the Nazis in the balls."

"I'm listening, Yannis."

"How much 9 mm. parabellum ammunition does Pyrkal's Greek Powder and Cartridge Division pack a month?"

"More than three million rounds. The shipping arm transports five times that."

"How much would it cost Pyrkal to purchase an insurance policy that would cover your oldest tramp steamer and 2½ million rounds for a single trip to a Black Sea port?"

"Less than ten thousand U.S. for a single use old tub."

"What if I were to offer you twenty-five thousand, cash up front, on condition you buy the policy from *Allianz A.G.?*"

"What kind of joke is that, Yannis? If you know so much about how Pyrkal is getting screwed over by the Germans, you'd know that Rhein Metall-Borsig forces us to buy at least forty percent of our marine coverage from Allianz."

"Not a joke, Prodromos," Kakis said. "How would you feel if Pyrkal sent a leaky old tub carrying ammunition to the Port of Sulina, insured the whole thing with Allianz for twice its value, and the ship went down for no apparent reason somewhere between Razim and Sulina."

"This is not a joke, my friend?"

"Could you somehow see that the tragically lost ammunition, which was probably sitting at the bottom of the Black Sea, found its way to Uzhhorod for another twenty-five thousand?"

"Ruthenia? That's tricky, Yannis. I could maybe get it to Iași for thirty and from there you'd have to move it on your own."

"Twenty-seven, five."

"American dollars?"

"Or Swiss francs if you prefer."

"In a different numbered Swiss account?"

"Deal." The two men shook hands and Kakis handed his friend a copy of the Union Bank account number with a letter directing the bank to release the agreed sum to Prodromos Athanasiadis personally.

17

Three in the afternoon. Kayla Meda, the Jewish quarter of Gondar. Inside one of the largest warehouses Varga had ever seen, two forklifts were lifting several wooden crates onto pallets.

Good afternoon, gentlemen. My name is Malachi Kahen. I trust you are Kýrios Kakis and Major Varga?"

Both men nodded affirmatively. Kahen continued, "As you can see, we're preparing your 2,500 Beretta M-1918 weapons for shipment. Since I anticipated you'd want to examine the merchandise, most of the cases are unsealed and you may inspect the guns at your leisure."

They thanked him and proceeded to do so.

"These look almost new," Varga commented. Indeed, from their random inspection, the submachine guns appeared to be in immaculate condition. each of them coated with cosmoline and packed tightly in wooden crates.

"Are they serviceable?" Kakis asked.

"Of course. Pick out any guns you want from anywhere in the shipment. I'll drive you over to the police firing range and you can test them at your leisure."

Less than half an hour later, the Polish officer and the Greek merchant returned and reported to Kahen that each of the weapons they had tested appeared to be perfectly in order.

Yannis Kakis had negotiated the purchase before he had left with Malachi Kahen, whose family had traded coffee, spices, oil seeds, and, when the opportunity arose, arms, for the past hundred years. Kahen, a leader of the *Beta Israel* Jewish community, had been among the first to welcome the Police of Italian Africa, when they'd arrived in Ethiopia four years ago.

"When that police force received its new MAB 38-A submachine guns six months ago, I purchased their 'retired' 1918s. If you need more, I've got another five hundred units available. I'm only too happy to sell them to my Jewish brothers, but of course I can't let Mussolini's people know where these weapons are really going, *farshteyn?*"

"I understand your concern Imebēti Kahen," Kakis said, winking and handing the end user certificate over to the supplier. "As I told you when we spoke last week, I represent the Chinese government and this shipment is destined for Shanghai to help China's glorious leader Chiang Kai-shek defeat the vicious General Matsui."

"How do you intend to get this shipment to Djibouti?" Kahen continued. "It's six hundred miles from here to the Port, and you can be sure you'll run into bandits and hijackers at least every fifty miles."

"Could you arrange for the shipment?" Varga asked.

"Of course, but it will cost you 75,000 lira, three thousand American dollars."

Kakis had already advised Varga they could expect to pay an extra five thousand dollars to insure the safe shipment of the guns to Djibouti. At least half of the *baksheesh* would go directly into the pocket of the Police Commandant.

Reaching into the pocket of his khaki-colored safari jacket, the Greek merchant extracted forty $100 bills and handed them to the brown-skinned Jewish man. "A little extra for your troubles."

Kahen rubbed has hands together and smiled, somewhat wolfishly Varga thought. "Most generous of you, Mister Kakis. You obviously understand how business is done in our country."

"When will this happen?"

"In order to justify the discounted price I quoted you, I'll have to secure at least two other shipments from here to Djibouti at the same time yours goes out. You understand that I can't guarantee you a specific time and date."

"Does that mean next week or next year?" Kakis asked.

In response, the Ethiopian shrugged his shoulders.

Kakis extracted two more hundred-dollar bills, which he handed to Kahen. "This week, Imebēti," he said. It was a statement, not a question.

"Of course, Kýrios Kakis," Kahen responded.

Two days later, Varga and Kakis received calls from Kahen at seven in the morning. His message to both of them was similar: "Please meet me at the warehouse by nine o'clock, prepared to ship off to Djibouti.

When they arrived, two forklifts were loading a huge Lancia Ro military diesel truck, its sides bearing the words *Polizia dell'Africa Italiana* and the emblem of the Italian police force. Kahen introduced Varga and Kakis to the commandant, a tall, stern-looking man in his mid-fifties, who wore a cavalry mustache of a style popular with army officers during the Great War twenty-five years before.

Impressed with the man's dignified demeanor, Varga addressed the officer quietly in Italian, "*Comandante, sono onorato di conoscerla. Anche se sembra che possiamo essere su fronti opposti in questo momento sfortunato, ti auguro ogni bene.* Commander, I am honored to meet you. Even though we seem to be on opposite sides in this unfortunate situation, I wish you only well."

The Commandant looked startled for a moment, then broke into a wide grin and responded, "For a Chinaman, your Italian is impeccable." He continued in Yiddish, *"Ken ikh fregn fun vos teyl fun Tsheyna ir zent? Vilne afshr?* — May I ask what part of China you're from? Wilno, perhaps?"

Nothing more needed to be said, except that the two men embraced, then saluted one another.

After the Commandant had departed, eight laborers loaded the truck and installed a sturdy canvas covering behind the cab so that the contents could not be seen. A sergeant dispatched one of his officers back to headquarters. Less than ten minutes later, two covered Sahariana reconnaissance cars, each carrying four armed troops and a driver, appeared. One of the cars positioned itself in front of the truck and other brought up the rear of the cavalcade.

Once in Djibouti, it took half a day to load the cargo, which was designated on the manifest and the end-user certificate as "Sardines," onto a small tramp steamer, the *Laodicea*, and another day to clear customs before the ship was allowed to depart for Istanbul.

Two weeks later - February 6, 1940— Istanbul, Turkey

As bitterly cold as any day Varga could remember. Despite the fact that he had walked the mile from Taksim Square to the Park Hotel wearing a thick woolen coat, a matching scarf, a karakul cap, and soft chamois gloves, he was shivering as he approached the lobby.

The Park was anything but imposing from the street, a low edifice of indeterminate age. Its elegance became evident only when one entered the portals held open by white-gloved doormen. Varga took the elevator two stories *down* to the most dramatic view in the city. The Park had been built into the side of a hill overlooking the Bosphorus. Years ago, an enterprising young architect had decided, with a stroke of genius, to position the lounge at the lowest point in the hotel. The result was a large, deep room that floated above the buildings on the street below.

As Major Varga entered the room, he marveled at the sweeping view. Immediately below him was *Kabataş*, the sea-bus pier. Less than a mile across the Bosphorus he could see the lights of Üsküdar on the Asiatic side of the city. To his left, Dolmabahçe Palace dominated the horizon.

Earlier that year, Turkey, neutral since the beginning of the European conflict, had been forced to allow the so-called 'commercial' ships of the warring nations to travel through the Turkish straits. Since then, the Park Hotel's lounge, with its unobstructed view of the passage between Europe and Asia, had become the most exciting place in Istanbul. Spies of every European nation gathered here each night and watched traffic pass through the Bosphorus. If a particularly large ship hove into view, there was a flurry of activity at the Park's bank of telephones.

A violin, piano, and string bass trio completed *The Blue Danube* for the hundredth —or was it the thousandth? — time that year. The audience applauded politely. The three white-haired musician s bowed stiffly and left the room. Varga ordered a shot of *rakı*, Turkey's potent anise-flavored version of *ouzo* — and poured a half-glass of water into the cup in which it had been served, watching it turn the whitish color of its popular name, "Tiger's milk."

As he was nursing his drink, the two men he had been expecting approached him. One was short and round-shouldered and spoke with an accent he recognized as Balkan. Bulgarian? Roumanian? The other was young, with steel-rimmed glasses and the severe haircut of a man who doesn't like to give money to barbers. Serious, square-jawed, wearing a suit meant to last a lifetime. Most likely an engineer.

"Good evening, gentlemen," Varga said, indicating the two empty chairs at the square table. "An aperitif before we eat?" Each inclined his head, somewhere between a nod and a bow. The older man ordered a shot of *Ţuică*, strong Roumanian brandy. The engineer, eschewing alcohol, asked the waiter for a bottle of Tekır sparkling mineral water.

Without preamble, Varga asked, "Well?"

"They're good," the engineer responded.

"I couldn't find any 38As for the amount we had available."

"Doesn't matter. The 1918s are perfect for our needs. When is the ship supposed to leave port?" the shorter man asked.

"Some time after midnight," Varga replied. "What made you decide on Odessa instead of Constanţa?"

"Better friends in Ukraine than in Roumania."

"You're Roumanian, yes?"

"True, but there are different sets of eyes in Bucharest nowadays. Antonescu's new friends would be far more interested than Besarionis in the cargo. Plus, it's easier to get to the forest by way of the steppes than over the Carpathians. Does that inconvenience you, Major Varga?"

"Not at all," Stefan replied. "I intended to take passage on the ship from here to its final port destination, where I'd assumed your people would take delivery. It should be a peaceful journey, so I'll simply have an extra day or two to relax and catch up on my reading."

Later that night – North of Istanbul

At midnight that same day, Leutnant Karl Havel and Feldwebel Sergeant Franz Weissbrot entered a two-story apartment building in Sariyer, fourteen miles north of central Istanbul and four miles south of the point where the Bosphorus meets the Black Sea. The Abwehr had purchased this particular building two years prior to use as an observation post to watch the traffic traversing the strait from the Black Sea to the Sea of Marmara.

The two men assumed their twice-a-week shift, sitting side-by-side in front of the window and tracking the area with their binoculars. Some time after two that morning, the sergeant said, "It's a pretty boring watch tonight if that's all there is."

"Where?"

"A mile to the south, single stack."

"I see her. She's the — *Laodicea,*" he said, adjusting his binoculars.

The sergeant thumbed through the shipping register on the desk to his right. "Out of Panama City, which means out of God-knows-where. An old tramp by the looks of her. Wonder where she's been?"

"South," the lieutenant replied. "Which could mean anywhere."

"The way she rides in the water she's hauling cargo," the sergeant said.

"Good for her. At least she's earning her keep."

"Is she worth an inquiry?"

"I doubt it. She's just an old freighter headed to Bulgaria, Roumania, maybe Odessa ..."

"Look at her stack. In a hurry for some reason," the sergeant continued, noting the gray smoke issuing from the *Laodicea's* single smokestack.

"Yeah? Doing what, nine, ten knots?"

"If that. What do you think, Leutnant? Should we just let her go?"

"Hmm," the lieutenant said, squinting through his binoculars. "Oh, what the hell, we may as well inquire." He filled out a form for the wireless operator: date, time, name of ship. "I'll take this down later. I wouldn't mind knowing the cargo and where she picked it up. Probably nothing we should worry about, but still ..."

18

On board the *Laodicea,* there were two seamen in the wheelhouse, a helmsman and a wireless operator. When the Morse code started up, the radioman wrote the message down in the logbook. "What is it? The helmsman asked.

"An operator at the port of Burgas. Wants to know what we're carrying and where we're going."

"Sounds official. What do we say?"

"I don't know," the wireless operator replied. "Better go ask Captain Mávros."

The helmsman descended to the captain's cabin on the deck below the wheelhouse. When he knocked at the door, the captain called out, "Come in." He was sitting at a high table reading a chart of southern Bulgaria.

"A message from the port at Burgas. They want to know our cargo and destination. What do I tell them?"

The captain thought a moment, then said, "Acknowledge reception, nothing else. If they try again, do the same thing. We're in international waters, we don't have to tell them anything."

The next evening, just after eight, it began to rain. A steady, windblown rain. The *Laodicea* began to rise and fall as she fought through the heavy swell. On the platform above the wheelhouse, the seaman keeping watch tried to use his binoculars, but it was hopeless. When the waves hit the ship's hull, a cloud of spray burst over the deck and was caught up in the wind, so he had to wipe saltwater from his burning eyes. The ship had now entered Roumanian waters and was twenty-five miles south of Constanța, its original intended port.

The watchman, who was standing on the *Laodicea's* flying bridge, squinted into the night, then turned aft and looked over the ship's stern. Where he thought he saw a light. Just for a second, then it was gone. Was he seeing things? With the spray blowing over him, he tried to find the light with his binoculars. A minute went by, then another. At last, he gave up, told himself there was nothing out there, and started to rise. Then he saw the light again. Off the aft beam, then gone, or hidden when, whatever it was out there, wplunged into the trough of the rolling waves.

Hanging onto the railing, the watchman went down to the wheelhouse, its interior lit by a faint green light of the compass on its post.

"Wet out there," the wireless man said. An enamel pot sat on the table by his transmitter. "Coffee's cold as hell, but you can have some if you want."

"There's a light out there, somewhere astern of us."

The radioman shrugged. "Another ship. Want me to see if I can raise her?"

"Try it."

The wireless operator tapped out some code, then listened to his headphones. "No answer." He tried again, using a few different frequencies, but there was only silence.

The watchman flipped his hood back on and said, "I'm going to have another look." He worked his way up the metal steps, and again flattened out on the watchman's platform. The wind was howling much louder and he could hear each wave as it slammed against the hull, then burst into spray.

He almost missed the light, because he hunted for where it had been earlier, but the positions of the two ships had changed. Now it was on other side of the *Laodicea's* stern. A tall wave towered to the level of the lower deck and the freighter shuddered as it hit her. But there it was again. Brighter. And now it didn't disappear.

The watchman returned once again to the wheelhouse, where the helmsman was struggling with the big, spoked wheel, trying to keep the *Laodicea* on course. The wheelhouse window streamed with water. The radioman asked, "Well? See anything?""

"There's a ship out there and it's catching up to us."

"In this shit? What the hell is he doing?"

"I'd better go find the bosun," the watchman said.

"What'll *he* do?"

"That's what I was told. He said to report anything at all. And whoever she is, she's keeping radio silence."

"I guess so. Or they're drunk or asleep."

"A few minutes later, the watchman returned with the boatswain, Lefkó, by his side. The bosun asked the wireless operator to keep trying the usual frequencies, then the two climbed up to the platform. The storm was growing worse. The wind was now howling through the freighter's deck cranes. Lefkó and the watchman focused their binoculars on the stern.

"There it is!" the watchman said. "Twenty degrees off the starboard beam."

When Lefkó saw the light he said, "It's getting closer. He should be changing course, moving away, but he isn't." A minute later he said, "Closer now and staying off our aft beam. The sonofabitch is *chasing* us!"

Down in the wheelhouse, the wireless came to life. A signal. Fast. Then repeated as the radioman translated the Morse code into words and wrote down the message. "Is that him?" the helmsman asked.

"Affirmative. On the emergency frequency."

"What did he say?"

"They're the Roumanian naval launch *Mărășești* and they're ordering us to make for the port of Mangalia."

"Go up and tell Lefkó," the helmsman said. "He'll get Captain Mávros."

By the time Mávros and Stefan Varga reached the wheelhouse, the motor launch *Mărășești* was running two hundred fifty yards off their starboard side and its powerful light held the *Laodicea* in its beam.

"Send this," the captain said. "'Cannot follow your order. Nikos Mávros, Captain, *Laodicea*.'"

The radioman tapped out the message and the *Mărășești* operator was back on immediately. "We repeat, this is naval launch *Mărășești* and we order you to make for the port of Mangalia *immediately*."

At Mávros' direction, the *Laodicea's* wireless operator sent the message, "We are *Laodicea* of Panama City, a Panamanian vessel in international waters."

There was no reply.

The men in the wheelhouse were holding onto whatever they could reach as the ship pitched and rolled. The wail of a siren from the *Mărășești* cut through the howling wind.

"Helmsman, put the light on her," Mávros commanded.

The helmsman worked the control by his wheel and the illuminated *Mărășești* turned from a gray ghost to a white motor launch. A machine gun set in a metal shield on its bow was aimed at the *Laodicea's* wheelhouse.

Then a naval officer in a white uniform covered by an oilskin coat appeared on the deck of the motor launch, a megaphone in his hand. He raised the megaphone to his mouth and enunciated in German, "*Laodicea*, we are ordering you to change course and make for the port of Mangalia right now. We will follow you in."

The freighter's loud-hailer was hung from a wire loop by the light control. Mávros grabbed it and stepped outside the wheelhouse. Raising it, he broadcast slowly and clearly, "*Mărășești,* you have no authority to order us to do anything."

The officer on the *Mărășești* rejoined, "We will fire on you if you do not obey our order."

Captain Mávros stepped back into the wheelhouse. Suddenly a stream of sparks flew across the *Laodicea's* bow.

"*Gios mias pórnis!* Son of a whore!" the boatswain swore.

"That's tracer," Varga said. "Bullets make an impact, tracer ammunition sets a target on fire."

"Lefkó," the captain said. "Go find the gangway watch pistol, then get the ship's rifle from my cabin."

The boatswain returned quickly with the weapons. The rifle was an old German Mauser from the Great War. As he handed the captain a box of bullets, another stream of sparks whizzed over the bow. An amplified voice came from the motor launch. "*Laodicea,* that was your final warning."

Lefkó took the big revolver from its holster. Mávros put a handful of bullets in his shirt pocket, worked the bolt of the rifle, and slid a round into the chamber. Together, crouched low, they ran out of the wheelhouse and lay flat on the deck. The captain wound the rifle's strap around his upper arm to steady his aim.

Then, the *Mărășești's* machine gun fired at the freighter. They could see the tracer as it hit the hull. The radioman mumbled a prayer and the helmsman crossed himself as they waited to die. The *Mărășești* fired again. A buzzing orange flash lit the wheelhouse as the round punched through the wall. The helmsman said, "Unh," and sank to one knee. There was blood on the wall by his side.

Varga, breathing hard, came running into the wheelhouse. The radioman was trying to stop the helmsman's bleeding and was tying a belt into a tourniquet above the wound in his thigh. Varga ran out onto the deck, where Lefkó and Mávros were firing their weapons.

"It's impossible to hit anything," the captain shouted. The target is moving and so are we." Turning to Varga, he said, "Maybe you're better at this than I am." He started to hand the rifle to the major.

Varga, struggling to keep calm under fire in accordance with his military training, recalled that when he'd spoken to the partisan representatives in Istanbul, they'd told him they had tested two of the Beretta 1918s and they'd worked perfectly. They'd obviously used rounds of ammunition to test the submachine guns and just before he'd boarded the *Laodicea* they'd handed him a large canvas bag to carry with him. When he'd opened the sack, he found two submachine guns and two unused belts of 9 mm parabellum ammo. He'd stored them in the closet of his cabin without giving them a second thought.

"Captain, you and Mister Lefkó keep firing. I may have the answer in my quarters."

When he returned moments later brandishing one of the weapons from his cabin, he said, "What do you want, Captain, the officer or the light?"

"The light. It's our only hope."

Varga squeezed off a shot at the light. The bullets hit the *Mărăşeşti's* wheelhouse. The officer, offended that someone had the nerve to shoot at him, shook his fist and ran for cover. Once again, the *Mărăşeşti's* gun raked the *Laodicea's* hull, but the tracer flew away into the night.

As Varga checked his submachine gun to see how much ammunition was left, Captain Mávros said, "The iron hull is too thick for a light machine gun."

"What about our wheelhouse??

"That's thin steel. I better get everybody out of there."

The captain rose slowly to his feet. The *Mărăşeşti's* gunner fired at him. One of the rounds hit the deck in front of Varga and sailed away over his shoulder. Concentrating hard, Varga exhaled, then held his breath and put slow pressure on the trigger. The light stayed on.

Captain Mávros took the helm. The boatswain and the radioman carried the helmsman out of the wheelhouse, headed for the stairway that led down to the second deck and the crew quarters. Meanwhile, the officers on the *Mărășești,* realizing that their machine gun would not penetrate the freighter's hull, sent out a sailor with a high-caliber rifle. The boatswain, having left the helmsman to be tended in the crew quarters, reached the deck by the wheelhouse. "We were on fire," he said to Varga,

"Where?"

"The storage room. A tracer came through the porthole and hit a pile of tarred rope. The crew took care of it."

Varga showed the Beretta to the captain. "No more rounds in the belt. There's one last thing we can try."

Mávros was at the helm, trying to keep the freighter on course. When the others arrived and stood next to him, he nodded at the motor launch. As the sailor on the *Mărășești* fired, they could see an orange muzzle-flash. "Captain Mávros," Varga said, "I think all we can do is run for it."

"He's a lot faster than we are."

"If you change course so that our stern is facing him, he can shoot all he wants."

The captain nodded and used the engine-room telegraph to call for full speed, then turned the wheel to bring the *Laodicea's* stern around.

It took time for the motor launch to react. Then, when it did, it also sped up, giving chase. Faster by several knots than the freighter, the *Mărășești* closed, in a few minutes to thirty-five yards off the aft beam.

"He'll hit us if he doesn't slow down," the captain shouted.

"I'm going down into my cabin for just a moment," Varga said. "We can only hope to God there's one more belt of ammunition in the sack."

There was.

Returning, Varga attached the belt to the Beretta, issued a brief prayer to whatever God he hoped was looking after them, and lay flat on the deck. The *Mărășești's* searchlight was a lot closer now. Varga made sure of his aim, then squeezed the trigger.

The light exploded.

In the wheelhouse, Captain Mávros turned off the *Laodicea's* searchlight and ordered that his second-in-command, bosun Lefkó, put out every light on the ship. The machine-gunner and the rifleman on the *Mărășești* took this as a challenge, now firing at a dark, bulky shape in the driving rain. But the upward angle made it difficult to aim and the tracer flew up over the wheelhouse. The *Mărășești's* captain kept his position for twenty minutes, then gave up and set course for Mangalia.

A week later - February 16, 1940 - Odessa, U.S.S.R.

Friday night. 10:00 p.m. The bar stood at the foot of a wharf in Odessa's port, where the lights of the quayside buildings were reflected in the still, black water. Inside, in clouds of cigarette smoke, the odor of coarse *makhorka* tobacco was overwhelming. Off-duty stevedores were drinking vodka, beer, or both until it was time to offload another freighter.

Varga and the two men with whom he'd met in Istanbul took an empty table, then were joined by Fyodor and Alexei, two young stevedores. Both of them wore brimmed caps down over their eyes and had unlit stubs of cigarettes pasted to their lower lips.

"Andriy said to tell you he's been held up," Alexei explained. "He'll be here as soon as he can." He took a sip of his vodka and said, "You got here right on time. Any trouble on the way?"

"Some," Varga said. "Our cargo is ready to be unloaded. Do you know when that will be?"

Fyodor shrugged. "What ship?"

"The *Laodicea*, out of Istanbul."

"Maybe after midnight. They'll let us know when they need us."

Varga was drinking beer. He would have preferred vodka, but in his present state of exhaustion that would have finished him off.

"You're Polish, right?" Fyodor continued.

"That or Lithuanian, depends on where you were born and when," Varga replied.

"*Yevrey?*"

"Or *Zhid*, or whatever."

"Sorry to hear about what the fucking Nazis did to you after our glorious Russian comrades entered into a treaty with them last year. That marriage sure as hell won't last long," Alexei said.

Something across the room caught Fyodor's attention and he said, "What's *he* doing here?" Then tapped Alexei on the shoulder and pointed out a man having a drink at the bar.

"Somebody you know?" Varga asked.

"Russian crane operator. Russians don't come in here. This is the Ukrainian bar."

"He seems to be just having a drink."

"For now. You know Andriy?"

"I don't," Varga replied. "He's my commander's friend."

"He's our union's boss. He'll make sure your shipment gets into the trucks. The Russkies don't like the Pollak partisans. Now, look at this," Alexei said. Two men had entered the bar and stood next to the Russian, "What do they think they're doing?"

Fyodor shook his head. "Making trouble, maybe."

"They better not," Alexei retorted.

A minute later, the man Varga had called 'the engineer' back in Istanbul went over to the bar and bought a bottle of vodka. As he turned to go back to the table, the crane operator bumped against him. The engineer stared at the man, who said, "You made me spill my drink," and poured some beer on the bar.

The bartender said, "Hey, take it easy."

The engineer returned to the table.

"He pushed you," Fyodor said.

"Forget it," the engineer replied. "He's drunk."

"He's looking for a fight is what he's doing," Alexei said.

"He'll find it," Fyodor remarked. "I haven't hit a Russian for days."

"Ignore him," Varga said placatingly.

Fyodor snickered. *As if I could.*

Two more men came into the bar. Some of the stevedores stopped talking. Outside, a ship's foghorn cut through the night.

The engineer unscrewed the cap of the vodka bottle and said, "Who's ready?" Alexei and Fyodor drank their vodka. "Major Varga?"

"I'd better stay with beer."

Fyodor stood up.

Varga said to Alexei, "Tell Fyodor not to start anything. We're going to need you to unload our freight and get it onto the trucks. We don't need to have you locked up."

Alexei said, "We won't start it, but if they do …"

Another man came into the bar. He wore a loden jacket and a green hat. "Uliakov," Fyodor said.

"Who's Uliakov?" Varga asked.

"Russian Fascist."

Uliakov spoke briefly to the man next to the crane operator, then left the bar. "I guess he's not staying for the fun," Alexei said.

A shout issued from the bar. "Hey! Watch the fuck what you're doing, asshole!"

"You watch!" the Russian said.

The man swung and connected. The Russian hit him back. The bartender vaulted over the bar. A table went over with a crash of broken glass. Another fight started. Alexei came on the run and said to Fyodor, "Get them out of here!" He grabbed Varga by the shoulder and started to shove him toward the door as Fyodor did the same thing with Varga's two companions.

Two big men came running through the door, and a group of stevedores went for them, hitting hard. Varga could hear the meaty thuds of body punches and snarled curses. One of the Russians had blood running from his nose, another one swung at the engineer, who blocked his hand with his forearm, then Fyodor grabbed him by the head. The two struggled for a few seconds, then another man broke a vodka bottle over the Russian's head. The Russian went to one knee. He started to rise and Fyodor kicked him in the stomach. He folded in half and something fell from his hand. Varga saw that it was a knife and tried to reach for it, but there was somebody in his way, so he kicked it across the floor.

Then Varga and the two partisans were pushed out into the street.

It was after one in the morning when Varga stood with Andriy and watched the crates being unloaded from the *Laodicea* and loaded onto two heavy trucks. An hour later, the trucks took off to the west and an exhausted Major Stefan Varga tumbled into bed in the elegant Citadel Hotel, where he slept peacefully for the next sixteen hours.

SUMMER
1940

19

June 2, 1940 – Barcelona, Spain

"A dreadful, dreadful time to arrive," he said. "You've been following the reports?"

"I have, Mister —?"

"West will do, Miss Gard. Denmark, gone Belgium, gone. Holland, gone. Luxembourg, such as it is, gone. I anticipate Paris will fall within a week, ten days at most. I give France two, maybe three weeks at most."

Lara looked *down* at the man addressing her. Not looked down *on* him, looked down *at* him. Five-foot-two at most. Not disagreeable, simply not *anything*, a *nonentity*. Somewhere in indeterminate middle age, bald with just the slightest fringe of colorless hair combed down in front. Dressed in a rumpled suit that looked like it hadn't been *un*rumpled in the past decade. A long, wide green and mauve-striped tie which attempted to cover, but did not conceal, a flabby paunch. She choked back a laughing thought: *if he was in a room with three people, he would somehow manage to disappear into the woodwork.*

Yet here he was, greeting her at the front desk of an equally nondescript hotel at an address she'd been given by the O.S.S. country representative when she'd boarded the plane from England at six, earlier this morning.

"I don't mean to be rude, Mister West, but what, exactly is your position vis-à-vis my assignment?"

"I have been designated your guardian angel, your *fixer* if you will," West responded. "Colonel Donovan apparently thinks quite highly of you and I've been designated to make sure your head stays firmly attached to your shoulders and that you continue to breathe. You might think of me as a babysitter. I've been called a lot of things in my time, mostly things you don't hear in polite society," West replied equably. "A goodly number of people think I have a remarkable talent for saying things they find abrasive, demeaning, and downright insulting. And, by the way, my dear young lady, you most likely picture me as a nonentity. You undoubtedly will continue to do so … up to the moment when your life depends on me. And then …"

What am I supposed to make of this man? Lara thought. *Here I believed he was a buffoon, but he's read my very thoughts, so he's clearly anything* but.

"I see you're somewhat underwhelmed by your surroundings, Miss Gard." He continued.

"Now that you mention it …"

"There's a good reason for that. The Office of Strategic Services is not only penurious, but downright stingy. More important, we do not look kindly on losing even one of our agents."

"Is 'West' your first name or your last name?" she asked.

"Yes."

"I notice this hotel doesn't have a name."

"Not on any sign you can see. It is registered with the city as Hotel Calidad, but the guest list is confined to agents and contract employees with the O.S.S. It's the same in many cities in quite a few countries, Miss Gard. The Agency leases older, inconspicuous hotels on an annual basis. But I can assure you that every one of these places has been renovated to the standard of modern comfort. There are good reasons for this."

"Security, I suppose?" Lara said. "And the ability to know where agents are — or where they're supposed to be — at bedtime each night. I assume you think because I'm a woman …"

"Miss Gard, I don't care if you piss standing up or squatting. Or if you're black, yellow, Jewish, Irish, or Chinese. There are good people and bad people all over the world. I try not to take sides."

"What about someone like Hitler?" Lara asked.

"Point taken. Back to your living conditions, Miss Gard …"

"Lara will do."

"Is that your first name or your last name?"

"Yes."

That broke the tension and they shared a genuine laugh.

"Now that we've broken the ice, there's no reason for you to stand out in the heat. *Rioja?* I believe you got used to that last time you were in Spain?"

"I'd appreciate that, West."

"One other thing. Your private life is your own. Whatever your needs are, your room is *your* room for whatever duration you're here. If Señor Caceres …"

She blushed nearly scarlet.

"Very few secrets within the Organization," he continued smoothly. "If there were, we'd be far less able to protect you."

"How long will I be in Barcelona?"

"Until you leave. I'm not trying to be facetious, but there'll be times when you'll be in Madrid one day, Geneva the next, with almost no notice. As I said, there'll always be a clean room waiting. The elevator's down the hall to your left. It's been here for forty years and it's not going anyplace but up and down."

Much as advertised, the wooden floors on the ground floor protested with every step Lara took and the elevator creaked and groaned and threatened to give up the ghost as it propelled her to the third floor, seemingly traveling inch by inch.

But when she opened the door to room 307 with a large old-fashioned key, she found herself in utterly charming fin-de-siècle surroundings: a generous, well-furnished living room, an intimate bedroom with one of the most comfortable beds she'd ever sat on, even a serviceable, well-stocked kitchen.

No sooner had she become comfortable in the suite of rooms, when Lara instinctively found a way to have a short message delivered to Ramón Caceres in Castellfollit de la Roca, 75 miles to the north.

"Ramón: It's been almost a year. I miss you, and I am in a small hotel at 32 Calle Ferran, Room 307. Can we see each other? Lara."

For the next two nights, she slept very little and remained in her rooms for the better part of each day, pretending to "study" the area neighborhood.

Sometime between five and seven in the evening of the fourth day, the magic hour which in Paris was known as *l'heure bleue* — the time when one met one's lover before returning home from work to one's spouse — there was a soft knock, more of a hesitant scratching on her door than anything else, on the door to her apartment. She had no idea who it might be, since she had not yet met anyone other than West in Barcelona.

She glanced quickly in the gilt-framed mirror in the entryway. The bulky, dark-green sweater she wore over her mid-length skirt, no makeup, and tangled hair certainly did not present her at her best. Nor had she bathed that day, but … what if it *was* Ramón?

The knock-scratch came again. *Oh, well …*

"*¿Quién es?*" — "Who is it?" she called out.

There was no immediate response, but, trained as she had been in Canada, she was not afraid. "*¿Quién es?*" she called out again.

"A friend."

My God, it's Ramón's voice.

Quickly finger-combing her dark hair to straighten out the knots, she opened the door to see … Ramón. She felt a momentary weakness in her knees. *What on earth was I thinking when we separated last summer?*

She reached out for him, but just before her fingers made contact, she saw a stern-looking older gentleman immediately behind her erstwhile lover.

"Señorita," he said, inclining his head, somewhere between a nod and a bow.

"Bienvenidos, Señor," she replied, smiling uncertainly. "Please forgive my appearance. You are —?"

"El Padre de Ramón."

"Ramón' father. I'm so sorry we didn't have a chance to meet during the war. Ramón spoke of his family often. Always with respect and love. I was so sorry to hear about the passing of your eldest son last year. Won't you come in? I'm afraid I don't have much in my flat. Some tea and crackers, perhaps?"

"Lara —" Ramón interjected, his voice unusually tense, almost choked.

"Dear, dear Ramón," she said, reaching out to him.

Surprisingly, he backed away. "We … we can only stay a few moments."

"Did you get my message?"

"Yes, Lara. That's … That's why I'm … that's why we're … here." He mumbled the last words. Suddenly, he reached out and crushed her to him, whispering so the other man couldn't hear. "I've missed you … I love you so much."

As her arms went around his waist, he said, "I'm so sorry … so sorry."

"What is it?" she asked, feeling a chill in the room.

"My son has come to tell you, Señorita …"

"Yes?"

"He is marrying Maria Cristina Gómez y Mayo next Sunday in Castellfollit." His voice, though not unkind, had a no-nonsense finality to it.

"Is it so, Ramón?" Her voice stumbled as she choked back the tears.

"Y… yes, Lara. I'm …" He started to sob uncontrollably.

"It has been arranged, Señorita," the father continued. "You must understand. Our two villages need one another to survive. Don José was affianced to Maria Cristina when he passed. The Gómez family and ours must somehow continue the line and …" He coughed uncomfortably. "That is not to say …"

"No, Señor Caceres. That *is* to say," Lara said, summoning up her last shred of dignity. "I will not interfere with a marriage, and once that marriage takes place, Ramón and I will share memories of a lifetime, but nothing more than that. Ramón," she continued. "I wish you and your family well."

"Lara …"

"I think it's time that you and your father leave."

And as they did so, and Ramón looked back, his face drenched in tears, Lara shut the door to her room and shut the door to a future with Ramón Caceres. Very, very gently.

20

Two days later, Lara had shed her last tears over Ramón. West had told her that her stay in the capital of Catalunya would be "Until you leave," and that could be on as little as a few hours' notice.

At breakfast that morning, she thumbed through the hotel's glossy black-and-white travel folders, which boasted the marvels of Barcelona. With her last emotional tie to Spain severed, she emerged into the bright Mediterranean sun at ten that morning and spent the next few hours strolling down Las Ramblas, Barcelona's main pedestrian road, from Plaça de Catalunya toward the harbor. Fruit and vegetable markets, swank shops, overpriced souvenir kiosks, cheap travel agencies, and merchants urging mamas with small children to purchase caged canaries or parakeets.

As Lara passed the Liceu Opera House, she felt a magnetic sense of familiarity as she approached the Jewish quarter. *Ramón once told me that Spain's largest Jewish community lives in Barcelona.* Here, less-touristed establishments proliferated: fish markets, tattoo parlors, tailor's shops, and seedy bars. The streets were so narrow there was hardly room for two people to walk abreast.

Shortly after noon, she entered a small shop in the *El Call* neighborhood — Jew town —with Hebrew lettering adorning the front, and asked the proprietor if there was any place nearby where *Shabbos* services were conducted.

"You are Jewish?" he asked.

"*Si.*"

"The *Sinagoga Mayor* has not been used for more than six hundred years, but a small group of us gather in a vacant storefont a few blocks from here, every Friday night. It's not the best area in town …"

"I am," Lara replied. "If you could write down the directions …?"

"I'll do better than that," the man said. He went into a back room of the store and returned with a boy of about fourteen. "Shmuel here witll show you where we hold services. You are not from here?"

"America."

"Ah, I'm told it is a wonderful country where the streets are paved with gold."

"For some," Lara answered. "Not necessarily for all."

It took Lara and her young guide less than ten minutes to arrive at the storefront in *El Raval.* Bright banners of different colors hung suspended from crumbling three- and four-story buildings.

"A celebration?" she asked the boy.

"No, Señorita," the lad responded. "There are all kinds of bad people in this part of town. Those apartments are owned by drug dealers. If a red flag is out, no drugs are for sale. A blue one warns that police are nearby; and a white banner means drugs are available. I wouldn't recommend you come here after the sun goes down."

He probably means it's not safe for tourists or goyim, non-Jews. But I lived in Spain during the worst of times, I'm a <u>landsman</u>. A Jew will always protect a Jew.

"But your congregation comes together every Friday night …"

"Yes, ma'am. We've known one another for years. We know what streets to avoid and *they* know what will happen if they disturb any of us."

And I've been trained for this kind of thing back in Canada …

"What time do services start, Shmuel?"

"Sundown. They only last an hour, but still …"

"Is there a Metro in the area?"

"The Line 3 stops at Carrer De Roig station, an eight-minute walk from here. But …"

By five o'clock, Lara had ridden the Metro back to Plaça de Catalunya, taken a brief nap at her hotel, and eaten an afternoon snack, knowing that dinner time did not start in Spain until long after services concluded. To be on the safe side, she took a taxi to the storefront, where she arrived at six forty-five. Alighting from the cab, she felt less nervous about her surroundings when she saw two Sabbath candles burning on a table and a small group of people inside.

Nine people attended the services. Women were separated from the men by a *m'chitsa*, an opaque linen curtain. While she recognized most of the prayers, she was unfamiliar with the melodies and what seemed the disorderliness of the service. *No rabbi.* Then she remembered that Spanish Jews were *Sephardim.* The Jews she'd grown up with in New York City had been *Ashkenazim*, a wholly different sect.

Ten minutes into the service, a striking man, taller than the rest, who appeared to be in his early forties, entered the room. Looking at her wristwatch, Lara saw it was a little after eight when services concluded. It was still twilight when she left the building. Adhering to the route she'd taken to get to the Metro that afternoon, she entered a short, narrow alley within two or three minutes. The street was empty, very quiet, with only a single streetlamp some fifty feet ahead,

As she moved down the alley, she felt, rather than heard, a presence behind her, and felt the hairs on her forearms prickle.

"Excuse me, Miss," a man's voice rasped, "but a bird dropped something on your shoulder. Here, let me clean it off for you."

She felt a light brush on the back of her shoulder, then involuntarily stiffened as a hand roughly grabbed her shoulder. She turned abruptly and found herself facng two men in their twenties. The man who'd touched her was thin, with long, greasy hair. His companion, heavier, reeked of sour sweat and whisky breath and looked menacing. As he pressed a button, the switchblade knife he was carrying sprang open.

"Hey, Gonzalo," he said, turning to his associate. "Look what we got here. A nice sassy *turista*. Lotsa' money and … other things."

"Why don't you two crawl back into the hole you came from?" Lara snarled. She was surprised at how calm she felt, notwithstanding she was alone."

"Listen, *putana*, one shout, one scream and they'll find your body in fifty separate pieces, *me entiendes?*" The heavier thug grabbed Lara's arm and spun her around.

In that instant, everything came together in her head, the separation and ultimate end of the relationship with Ramón, the impotent rage she felt at what the Nazis were doing to her coreligionists throughout Europe, and, the grisly images she'd seen at O.S.S. training camp. She felt no fear at what her assailants were threatening to do. In the midst of it all "Dandy" DiGirolamo's voice and image came to her. *It's all in using a stiff hand. You can kill a man by jamming it up under his breastbone and tearing his guts, or you can smash his Adam's apple so he strangles. Or you can hit him hard under the nose. That breaks the bone at the bridge of his nose and drives the splinters up into his brain. You must always be in control of your inner self to prevail against the savage onslaught.*

Lara started to feel almost sorry for the thugs who had assaulted her as she realized that unless they knew more than she did, something she sincerely doubted, neither of them stood a chance. She silently thanked God she had worn loose-fitting clothing and slacks rather than skirt.

Perfectly calm, she reared back, stiffened the index and middle fingers of her right hand, and jabbed them hard into the first tough's carotid artery. He hadn't even collapsed to the ground when she drop-kicked her attacker's companion in the groin. The second man fell to his knees, clutching desperately at his crotch.

The first man was conscious, but gasping for breath and crying. The second was in too much pain even to do that.

A tall figure emerged from the shadows. "Señorita," a male voice called out.

Lara turned, ready to face a third potential assailant. She saw to her surprise it was the man she'd seen in the storefront synagogue.

"Are you alright, Señorita?" he asked gently, in English. "I saw you leave the synagogue and walk toward this alley and I thought, 'This can't be safe. I'd better follow her and make sure …' And when I saw … If I had been the one walking down this street, I'd have wanted *you* with *me* as protection."

"Thank you, Señor," she said, smiling at him.

"Fucking bitch nearly killed us, Señor," one of the thugs moaned. "Better call the *policía* if you want to survive. Better still, get the fuck away from her while you can."

The man glared at them for a moment. "You expect me to believe this young woman set out to attack *you*? Is that what you're telling me? I think you're right. I *will* call the *policía*."

"Wait, Señor," the second man pleaded. "We didn't exactly mean call the *policía*."

"What exactly *did* you mean?" the man growled. He reached into his pocket, drew out a military-style whistle, and blew it several times, hard and long. It took less than two minutes for a police cruiser to arrive.

The two policemen listened to Lara's and the stranger's stories. Her assailants were unable to answer the officer' sharp, targeted questions. Next thing Lara knew, her attackers were handcuffed and shoved roughly into the back of the cruiser. As the police car drove away, Lara and her new companion heard diminishing howl of the law enforcement vehicle's siren blaring the sharp *ooh-EEE, ooh-EEE, ooh-EEE* of such European vehicles, and saw its blue lights flashing as the cruiser disappeared from view.

Turning to Lara, the stranger continued in English, "Señorita, would you feel offended if I asked where you are staying and offered to hire a cab and ride with you to make certain you arrive safely? Not that you'd need me, of course."

"Not at all," she responded. "I notice you didn't speak Spanish."

"Is that why you answered me in English? I heard you speaking fluent Spanish in the Catalonian dialect."

"A combination of training and … other things." She reached out to shake his hand. "Lara Gard."

"Stefan Varga, late of the Polish armed forces."

"With all the excitement that's gone on, you probably haven't had a chance to eat. I saw a decent-looking restaurant I saw on Plaça de Catalunya as I was being driven to the synagogue.

"I certainly wouldn't stand on ceremony, Colonel …"

"You know my name?"

"I don't, but I heard the police sergeant address you as *Coronel*. And I *am* starved. I'd appreciate *anything* you choose."

"Thank you so much for suggesting this restaurant. The is delicious, Colonel Varga."

"Stefan, or Szymon, take your choice, Lara. No need to stand on formality. I've given you the short version of how a Litvak-turned-officer in an army that no longer exists got here. I would think an American Jewish woman would want to stay as far away from Europe as possible."

"That's exactly what I thought when I left Paris last September." She sipped slowly from her glass of *Penedès cava*.

"So you left Paris to come to Barcelona?"

"Via a circuitous route. I went back to Manhattan and rediscovered the reason I had *left* New York."

"But *Spain?*"

"Trying to recapture a lost love affair I thought had burned out. We got together during the Civil War, escaped to Paris at the end, and found that hard work, long hours, and hardly any money is not the recipe for 'happily ever after.'" She reached over with her fork and pushed a generous helping of shrimp, mussels, sausage, and rice from the large serving platter onto her plate.

"And?"

"I found out two days ago that Papa had arranged for Ramón to marry a local princess and inherit two villages, one owned by each of the families. So much for 'happily ever after.'"

"You don't seem exactly heartbroken, Lara."

"Oh, I spent my first two days worrying what it would be like if — when — he showed up and the next two days crying because I felt it was the proper thing to do, but by then I realized that had it worked out, it probably would have been for the worst. Liberal university graduate Jewish girl and Catholic boy with not even a high school education, from the staunchest conservative upbringing you could imagine."

She reached over and poured him some *cava*.

"Thank you. So, you're on the next ship back to the States?"

"Well … not really. I've taken a job with an American firm based in Geneva." She thought it best not to say anything more. "What about you, Colonel … Stefan …?"

"Hard to say. For now, I'm the one they trot out to show at diplomatic parties. A uniform, a few medals … As long as my so-called 'diplomatic status' keeps me far enough away from the *Geheime Staatspolizei.*"

"The Gestapo."

He rose. "Would you mind of I excused myself for a moment. It's been a long evening and …"

"I saw the signs on the way in. It's right down the hall."

He returned several moments later, looking obviously relieved, then bent over and scooped a mound of paella onto his plate.

"What about you, Stefan? A wife? Children?"

"I had one of each. A wife and a son back in Warsaw. Both of them were killed when the Germans overran what was then my country."

The silence hung heavy between them, After several moments, she said, "I'm so sorry … and that must sound so empty."

"Life goes on. I suppose that sounds equally meaningless, Lara."

"What happens now?" she asked.

"I'm supposed to return to Paris within the week. Assuming there'll *be* a Paris. The word from my sources is that it'll fall to the Reich within the next fortnight."

"And then?"

"We hide from the war," Stefan replied. "In the mountains, in small towns to the south, inside ourselves. In the Metros, in the sewers if need be …"

"They'll try to get rid of us, won't they?"

"Us?"

"All the little bits and pieces that always seem to wind up in Paris: Russians, Jews —mostly Jews, of course — Republicans fleeing from the new Spain,

Poles, emigrés from the Balkans …the refuse of Europe. Artists, writers, publishers of certain periodicals."

"The *real* French will be safe if they mind their manners," he replied. "For the rest, it's best if we disappear."

After they finished their late-night dinner, a waiter approached them. "Coffee or tea?" he asked.

"Have you any real coffee?" Stefan asked.

"Nescafé, Señor."

"Better than chicory," he replied.

Since there were only a few customers left in the restaurant, an attendant turned up the radio. A silky male voice came clearly over the airwaves. "For our allies who are so valiantly defending the Free World, we salute you with the latest from Europe's most popular jazz guitarist, Django Reinhardt, with Stéphane Grappelli, and the *Quintette du Hot Club de France — Nuages.*"

"The B.B.C.," Stefan remarked.

The music faded and returned, disappeared into static, then came in strong. When the announcer could be clearly heard, they listened to the newscast.

"The French government has left Tours and moved to Bordeaux. In the United States, the chairman of the Senate Foreign Relations Committee suggested the British should consider surrendering to Germany, since the situation was growing more hopeless by the hour. The Maginot Line has been abandoned. German troops have crossed the Marne and secured their positions in Norway, Denmark, Belgium, and Holland. And now, to lighten our mood, we take you direct to the Savoy Hotel where we join Victor Silvester and his Ballroom Orchestra on the North Bank of the Thames … Maestro Silvester, if you please …"

Shortly after eleven that night, they left the bistro and walked the few blocks to Lara's hotel. They shook hands collegially, and he hailed a late-night cab that had stopped half a block from the hotel.

Now <u>that</u> is a real man she thought, as she saw him enter the waiting taxi and drive off.

21

MONDAY, JULY 1, 1940, 11:00 A.M. - PARIS

The man, who was slightly shorter than Varga, carried his fifty-nine years with the vigor and magnetic dignity of someone who'd lived to command and who'd survived numerous attempts on both his life and his career. Varga had seen him on two or three occasions before the war, but they'd never formally met.

General Władysław Sikorski, former prime minister of Poland and now the Prime Minister of the Government in Exile, met Varga just inside a café at the southwest corner of the Hôtel des Invalides. The café had been well and truly used. What had once been pale brown walls were tinted darker through years of tobacco smoke. Etched glass windows gave a clear view onto the street. An old woman with yappy white Bichon Frisé sat at the bar, nursing some sort of pink-colored drink.

Although the general wore corduroy slacks and a grey open-necked shirt, Varga recognized Sikorski from his photos and snapped his most militarily correct salute. The shorter man smiled and held out his hand. "At ease, Colonel," he said. "Thank you so much for coming. I've been looking forward to chatting with you."

As they sat in a booth facing one another, each man ordered a glass of Konenbourg 1664, France's most popular prewar beer. General Sikorski spoke first. "Hard to believe it's over. The French army collapsed after one month."

"It *is* over, then?"

"As you've no doubt seen, the Wehrmacht is everywhere in the city."

"But surely France will fight on, General —?"

"No, it won't. When Roosevelt declined Reynaud's request for American intervention, that was that."

"But France has army units in Morocco, Syria, Algeria. It could have fought on for five years!" Varga exclaimed. "In Warsaw —"

"This isn't Warsaw," Sikorski responded, shrugging his shoulders. He took a pack of *Gauloises* from his pocket, offered one to Varga, took one for himself, then lit both their cigarettes.

On the Rue de la Croix Nivert, a refugee family trudged by. The man pulled a cart with quilts tied over the top of a mound of furniture. Here and there a wooden table leg poked through. A woman walked next to him leading a goat on a rope. Three small children, a girl holding the hand of two smaller boys, followed the cart. The farm dog, large and of an indeterminate breed, panted hard in the noontime sun, and walked in the shadow of the cart. The family, which had obviously been on the road a long time, slogged on, their eyes glazed over with fatigue.

The café's proprietor put his newspaper down for just long enough to stare at the family as they labored past, then went back to his paper with an imperceptible shake of his head. The old woman's dog barked fiercely at the goat. The farm dog glanced up for a moment, then resumed his exhausted march, looking back with disdain. *Some little woolly thing in Paris that thinks it's a dog. The things you see when you travel.*

"I suppose we're going to London unless there's a miracle," Varga said.

"There will be no miracle," Sikorsky replied. "The Polish government will be based across the Channel."

"Am I to presume I'll accompany you?"

The general shook his head. "No, Colonel. You're going to stay on the Continent as my eyes and ears for the time being.

At that moment, the elderly lady with the dog glanced in their direction and dropped her head in a slight nod. "She's one of ours," Sikorski remarked. "Let's you and I continue our talk outside. One never knows who might be listening in a closed area."

"I'm sure you're wondering how you suddenly ended up in Paris, let alone as a Lieutenant-Colonel."

"I can't say I hadn't given it a thought, General," Varga remarked.

"Very well. Let me enlighten you, Colonel Varga, or Szymon Vaynshtok if you will."

They exited the Jasmin Metro station and headed toward one of the city's most beautiful walking venues, the Bois de Boulogne, at the western edge of the sixteenth arrondissement.

"If you know that about me, you must know I rose pretty high for a Jewish *Litvak*."

"Assistant professor of Logistics at Warsaw Higher War School, commissioned as a captain in the Polish army reserves in February 1939 when you turned forty — rather late in life to begin a military career, I'd say. Transferred to Section II Intelligence command a month later, escaped to Romania after the invasion…"

"Although there are a lot of us in Poland and Lithuania, we Jews have been as popular as lepers in those countries."

The general stopped, lit another cigarette, and they continued toward the Cascades. A pair of brown squirrels stopped at the edge of the pathway, five feet away from where they stood, glanced inquisitively at the two men as though expecting a handout, and scampered away when they realized none was to be forthcoming.

They passed a playground, where some two dozen youngsters were pumping their legs or cajoling their *au pairs* to push the swings on which they sat ever higher, screaming in delight as small merry-go-rounds whirled faster and faster. Others jumped up-and-down on seesaws ever more mock-viciously, totally ignorant of the terrors facing the world immediately beyond their vision.

"You're wondering how you ended up in Paris?" Sikorski said.

"Not really. I assumed I would not remain in Warsaw. Even under Occupation, I prefer Paris to Iași. And with the way the war is going, there aren't many safe havens left in Europe."

"There's always England, Canada, America ..."

Varga glanced sardonically at the prime minister-in-exile of a country to which he could not even return. "If you talked to the passengers on the *St. Louis* you might get a different story," he said. "England has closed its doors to Jews, even to that useless pile of sand in Palestine."

"Politically necessary to mollify the Arabs."

"Maybe from England's point of view, but I don't see a single Arab threatened with loss of his life, his legal status, or his ability to make a living."

Two days later, on July 3, 1940, Sikorski departed for London, while Varga remained in France. A week later, 120 German bombers and fighters struck a British shipping convoy in the English Channel, while 70 more attacked dockyard installations in South Wales. The Battle of Britain had begun.

August 5, 1940 – Haamstede, The Netherlands, 20 miles north of the Belgian frontier

Varga could hear his own footsteps as he slogged up the wet, hard-packed sandy beach toward the town, *shhh-sss, shhh-sss, shhh-sss*. Behind him, the crashing of waves, the sound receding as he moved farther inland, and the sucking sound as the surf rolled back toward the open sea. Once in the center of the small town where he'd been sent overnight, his attention focused on a sharp crackling, popping sound. The docks were burning. The harbor smelled of dead fish and rotting seaweed. Varga could identify the lone attendant, an old man, from the metallic *click-click* as he fastened the snaps of his 'Norwester.

"Damn!" the man grunted. The sloshing of water inside his soaked galoshes seemed louder than the splintering sound of cracking, old wood. The plop-plop of a heavy rain pelted the rubber sleeves of his raingear.

Suddenly, a growling roar drowned out everything else. Varga's eyes widened as he recognized the only surviving Polish bomber to have escaped capture by the Romanian government, a PZL.37 *Łoś*. The twin-engine medium bomber, "Moose," came tearing over the coast at fifty feet. Its high-pitched whine combined with a loud *whoosh* as a herring boat caught fire, and a splash as a sailor jumped into water abutting the harbor, to create a cacophony of disparate sound.

Rat-tat-tat-tat-tat-tat-tat-tat-tat-tat. Ten rounds from the *Łoś's* guns raked the side of the harbor's gasoline tank, following by an explosive ka-BOOOOM! The seaman shouted he couldn't swim. A taxi driver ran to the edge of the pier to try to rescue the flailing body, but when the *Łoś* screamed around the town, he threw himself on his belly. When he arose seconds later, the sailor had disappeared below the mild chop of seething waves.

German antiaircraft guns fired, *pfft-WHAM, pfft-WHAM, pfft-WHAM* from their position on a small hill atop the town and sent red fireballs over the port in a fruitless attempt to hit the *Łoś*. The Polish bomber screamed as it tore out over the sea and came skimming back into the town, its three machine guns raining further havoc on the German-occupied port town.

After he'd made it back to the top floor of the only lodgings available that night, the dingy, pretentiously named Hotel Amsterdam, where the seaport's whores regularly plied their trade, Varga watched the bomber through one of two windows in his shabby room, just as he heard the sharp *cll-r-aaack* as the adjacent window burst and the silvery tinkle of glass showered the pavement three stories below. As he recognized the insignia on the tail, Varga involuntarily burst into a round of applause and shouted, "*Yes!*" for the whole city to hear,

Moments after Varga heard the loud flush of a toilet down the hall, a half-drunk Greek sailor wearing only his underpants burst into Varga's room, belched loudly, and passed gas with a flatulent *bbrrrppp*. The seaman, who'd gone to the communal bathroom to relieve himself after his time with a woman in a different room, didn't realize his mistake and seemed surprised to find another man there. He mumbled his apologies and left the room, just as a blast shook the window glass, a high explosive bomb going off on the other side of town. Varga looked out the window and heard, rather than saw, a tall building collapse onto the street.

His attention momentarily diverted, the Polish colonel looked back toward the waterfront, where a man ran up to the herring boat, now fully ablaze, threw a completely useless bucket of water on the roof of the wheelhouse, then ran away as the loud sizzle and crack added its momentary solo to the symphony of destruction.

As Varga turned back to the window, the PZL.37 flashed by, its wingtip less than thirty feet from where he stood, its engines howling, rattling the window in its frame. The pilot circled low over the town and headed out to sea, toward his home base. The engines' noise sank to a lower pitch as the pilot put his plane into a steep climb, then a sharp bank at the top of the climb, and vanished into the cloud.

Moments later, Varga heard the anachronistic high tinkle of a tin bell as the town's sole fire truck, an ancient Volvo 71-S, slithered and skidded around the harbor to where the burning herring boat had set the pier on fire. A late-model Citroën Traction-Avant commandeered by the occupying force, its six-cylinder engine purring smoothly, pulled up behind the truck, its brakes protesting with a loud squeal, its tires skidding noisily on the wet cobblestones. Its driver, a *Wehrmacht* soldier, leaped from the car, his heavy boots pounding *clack, clack, clack* as he approached the truck driver's window. Banging on the hood of the truck with a glove-enclosed fist, the soldier shouted in guttural German through the pouring rain, and pointed back the other way. The fire truck, its gears clashing, its engine growling, and the *chuff-chuff-chuff* of greasy smoke pouring out of its exhaust pipe, its little tin bell still incongruously tinkling, slowly backed up, trying not to drop a wheel over the edge of the pier.

Good! Varga thought. *Something's really gone wrong and the Germans are pissed off about it.* Even so, it didn't seem to slow them down. They patched and fixed and improvised and did without. *Somehow, they find a way to get things done and move on to the next objective.*

Another plane came roaring past the hotel. *No, the same PZL.37. Take that for destroying our country, you fucking bastards!*

This time, the huge gasoline storage tank erupted in a great ball of orange flame and black smoke. Once again, the aircraft circled the town, its pilot waggling its wings, and sped out over the sea toward the English coast. "*Yes!*" Varga shouted for a second time, raising his right arm and shaking his fist in victory as the bomber disappeared from sight.

Afterward, the sounds abated until the only noise Varga could hear was the pitter-patter of a light rain as it moistened the town, falling with varying degrees of noise on the wharfside streets, cooling them. The water sizzled as it touched the still-hot metal and dying embers that abutted the alleyways. In the distance, the fire truck's bell never stopped tinkling as the small vehicle fought to be heard against the deafening silence which now enveloped the town. Haamstede smelled similar to the way he remembered Warsaw in September of 1939: charred plaster, burning oil, and cordite.

"The hell with everyone and everything," he muttered. By now, Varga had grown tired of the four-walled cage in which he had observed everything. He decided to go for a walk.

Once outside, he luxuriated in the quiet, punctuated by rain still hissing on a few small fires here and there. Some of the town's citizens poked through a burnt-out café, lifted a blackened timber, then dropped it quickly when they saw what was under it. Soot drifted down on him as he walked — carefully, because the sea fog hung over the town. Quiet water that night, lapping gently at the foot of the quay as the tide went out. Walking away from the center of Haamstede, he was stopped by a pair of *Wehrmacht* sentries. They desultorily waved him on. Varga moved off the beach and onto the dunes, where he sat quietly, listening as peace descended on the town.

As it turned out, the *Łoś's* attack was only the opening act.

The main British assault came half an hour later. Bristol Blenheims, at least a dozen of them, maybe more. Although these planes were individually smaller and lighter than the PZL.37, their combined number sounded like a hundred kettledrums pounding the town from above. The beach shuddered as the bombs hit. Once or twice, they came close, showering sand down on him. The antiaircraft defenders finally chalked up a small success; they hit a Blenheim with a full bomb load a little way out to sea. Varga swore he could see the night cloud for ten miles from the light and corrosive BLAMMM! of the explosion. But the rest of the English armada got through, hitting the town and the sea and God knew what else. Pretty soon, most of Haamstede was ablaze. As he turned back from whence he'd come, Varga saw that the Hotel Amsterdam was nothing more than a pile of smoking brick.

As the sun rose over the still-smoldering remains of the town, it was clear that the Germans had put on a dress rehearsal for their proposed landing on the beaches of Britain.

And it was equally clear that the British had put on a dress rehearsal of their own.

BOOK THREE

A NEST OF VIPERS

1939 - 1943

22

There is a vast plateau in East Central France, more than 150 miles from its northeast corner to its southwesternmost point. Lyon, France's third largest city, is almost exactly in the center of the plateau, where the Rhône and Saône Rivers meet. Le Chambon-sur-Lignon, a commune of some three thousand inhabitants, occupies the southwestern part of the plateau, sixty-five miles from Lyon. Diametrically opposed to Le Chambon, on the plateau's northeastern cusp, lies Cerdon, a much smaller village, perhaps one-quarter the size of Le Chambon.

During the four years the Germans occupied France, these two settlements were colloquially referred to by the Nazi overlords as a "nest of vipers."

Each fought the *Boches* in their own way. Le Chambon's impoverished residents saved the lives of more than five thousand refugees, most of them Jewish, most of them children. The moral brilliance of the villagers did not light up the moral darkness around the village so much as it made the vast darkness seem darker by contrast.

For centuries, France has been one of the most visited countries in the world. How could it be otherwise? Paris, *La Reine du Monde*, the City of

Light. The Eiffel Tower, Nôtre Dame, the Louvre and Versailles. The very center of the Western world's culture. Paris. Ground under the heel of German oppression during the Holocaust. But never changed. Not really. The *petits cafés* where one could still find *filet mignon* if one had the wherewithal, or, more likely, lentil soup, *filly* mignon and sour wine. *Brasseries* and *bistros* filled with the National Socialist elite and their French girlfriends. Shamed and humbled, yes. Beaten into submission. But still *Paris.*

Marseilles, where one trod carefully — *very* carefully — even under the Vichy government, even under the Nazis. Where one could be anything or buy anything, from sliced swordfish to the sliced-off head of a competitor, an erstwhile lover, or the leader of an abhorrent political movement. The Loire Valley Châteaux, the coasts of Normandy and Brittany, the wines of Bordeaux and Burgundy, the stunning Côte d'Azur meccas of Nice, Cannes, and Saint-Tropez.

But there is so much more to France. Thousands of tiny villages and townlets which are simply too poor, too remote, or too insignificant to be of interest to anyone.

France, has always been — and still is — sharply divided among the 96% who are Roman Catholics and 2% Protestants — Huguenots. Before 1598, the French state persecuted the Huguenots as *schismatics* and *heretics.* But in April of that year, King Henry IV signed the Edict of Nantes, which guaranteed religious freedom to the Protestants and granted them fifty areas of safety in France, effectively ending the French Wars of Religion.

Le Chambon-sur-Lignon is one of those thousands of villages in France, but with a difference: it is an almost wholly *Protestant* village.

Thick pine forests and vast mountains surround Le Chambon. One can see the great dead volcano of *Le Mézenc* from every structure in the village. It often seems as though Le Chambon is far from being hospitable. Perhaps that's because this mountain village has relied for over two hundred years on the tourist industry – mountain climbing, bicycling, golf, and communing with nature. Chambonnais, that's what its inhabitants are called, survive a nine-month-long winter, when they keep to their houses because the weather is bitter cold, the streets are too icy to be walked upon, and because there is nothing much do to in the village after the tourists have left.

Chambonnais have, for years, repeated the wisest of their maxims: "*Neuf mois d'hiver, trois mois de misere*" — "Nine months of winter, three months of trouble." During the three summer months of trouble, they throw themselves into making money from the tourist trade. In winter, they burn the bitter-smelling *genet*, a bush that brightens the land when it bursts into golden blossoms in June. Their typical reaction to some new misery is a shrugged, "*Que voulez-vous?* — Well, what did you expect? What can you do about it? Nothing, that's what."

The *presbytery*, a gray granite house with a stone roof that seems to weigh it down like a heavy tombstone, dominates the *Rue de la Grande Fontaine* at the center of town. Its closed shutters are a drab gray, from which it seems that all life has been washed out. Save and except for the inscription over the front door. *Aimez Vous Les Uns Les Autres — Love One Another.*

Le Chambon has been a sanctuary village, a place of refuge, since time out of mind. And so it was during the time of this tale. And so it remains, even today.

During the holocaust that consumed the second half of the Thousand-Year Reich, Le Chambon was largely ignored by the Nazis because, until the very end of the War, it was not a place of active resistance. What happened in Chambon-sur-Lignon was nothing more than a footnote to history. But it was not unimportant to the 3,000 people who lived in or near this mountain village during World War II. And it was a matter of life for some five thousand human beings who, for no other reason than an accident of birth, would have perished but for its existence.

Cerdon, on the other hand, conducted its resistance in an entirely different manner than LeChambon. Less than fifty miles west of Geneva, it was a French spearhead, albeit a small one, but that made it no less bloody, and no less vicious, much like a pit bull, or other terrier which, despite its relatively small size, is utterly fearless.

23

Roger Darcissac, thirty-six, glanced at his wristwatch as he heard the whistle and clanging bell of the one o'clock local from Saint-Etienne. One-oh-five, just about on time. As director of the public school and unofficial historian of the village, Darcissac made it a point to be at the tiny railway station that served Le Chambon and its sister village of Le Mazet each day to meet any new arrivals.

Most days, the minuscule train produced hardly any passengers. Once September arrived, the tourists left, and Le Chambon went into its nine-month hibernation. But today promised some excitement. The new Protestant pastor was scheduled to arrive. A change in spiritual leaders usually meant new ideas, which might, but never really did, shake up Le Chambon's Protestant majority.

The new fellow, André Trocmé, a few years Darcissac's junior, had most recently served at Sin-le-Noble, a stone's throw away from Belgium. *I wonder which higher-up he annoyed to get that assignment, not that Le Chambon's a great prize either.*

The small locomotive, hauling its three cars, hissed white steam from its wheels as it came to a stop at the far end of the platform. A graybeard

Darcissac recognized as a farmer from the high country above the village, clambered out of the first car.

Soon, the only other passengers emerged: a man close to six feet tall, wearing a clerical collar, followed by a robust-looking woman with short, dark hair plaited in ringlets. Behind them, a little girl of about seven held the hand of a toddler, followed by two boys, both younger than the girl but older than the little fellow whose hand she held.

The woman carried two suitcases. Each of the older boys carried a child-sized cardboard satchel. When he was certain his family stood firmly on the platform, the cleric, who walked with a slight limp, returned to the railroad car and retrieved two more large bags.

Although the family looked weary, the *paterfamilia* spread his arms as though to embrace the entire village and exclaimed, "Le Chambon sur-Lignon! How much lovelier than our last two postings! Magda, Nelly, boys, come stand beneath the sign while I take your photograph!" As he extracted a Brownie camera from his coat pocket, the woman arranged the children from the tallest to the toddler.

Darcissac approached the man. "Pastor Trocmé? It would look more complete if you were in the picture as well. Allow me to act as your photographer."

"How gracious of you!" the new pastor said, handing Darcissac the camera and arranging himself next to his wife. His smile was bright enough to light up the entire platform. "And you are …?"

"Roger Darcissac. I teach at the public school."

"Ah, a bit more than a 'teacher,'" Trocmé replied. "I believe you are the director of the school, and, I'm told, a man of excellence in the community."

"How could you …?"

"Monsieur Darcissac, I was not surprised when you addressed me by name. Would you not have expected me to do my homework as well?"

"Thank you, Father? Père?"

"André. And this is my wife Magda," Trocmé continued. "I must warn you, she's a Florentine who must have been a Medici in an earlier life. Lord help anyone who tries to stand in her way."

"Monsieur Darcissac," Magda said, reaching out and grasping Darcissac's hand in a firm, almost masculine handshake. "Would you know where I could find a cab to help us to our destination?"

"I could," Darcissac replied, "but it would be a waste of time, energy, and money, since your presbytery is directly across Avenue de la Grande Fontaine, just the other side of this station."

"In that case, would you care to join us for a late lunch, Monsieur Darcissac?"

"Roger."

"Roger, then. We haven't eaten since early this morning."

"Madame ... Magda, I'm afraid there are very few restaurants open at this time. And if there were, there'd be precious little to eat, since this is a rather poor village as soon as the summer visitors leave."

"A grocer, then? A vegetable market?"

"Close by. But ..."

"Then I insist you join us."

"The presbytery may need a bit of work to accommodate a large meal. You see, the previous pastor was a bachelor and, if you'll pardon my saying so, not the greatest housekeeper."

"Nonsense, Roger, we'll make do and you'll join us."

"I see what you mean, Roger," Trocmé said, as an afternoon storm raged outside the door. "A lot of work needs to be done, but if we look on the bright side, some poor craftsmen will survive the winter nicely on the largesse of the greater Protestant community."

"Meanwhile, while we're waiting for God's miracles, I'd say Magda wrought a miraculous meal from what she was able to buy at the market."

"Agreed. We're quite used to vegetables and my wife is an artist when it comes to creating tasty dinners from whatever comes to hand."

At that moment, the Trocmés' daughter, who'd been eating with them, asked, "Excuse me, Mama, Monsieur Darcissac. The trip has worn Daniel out. Is there a bedroom close by where he could take a short nap"

"What a lovely young lady," Darcissac remarked. "Lots of spirit, yet so well behaved."

"Thank you," Magda remarked. "Nelly is a little mother to Daniel, the baby. The two boys care for one another. André is right. This place is going to need a lot of work." *And my husband is being wildly optimistic if he thinks we can depend on the Central Protestant Authority to send us much of anything. It would be nice if they gave us some heat for starters.*

"What was your last posting like, André?" Darcissac asked.

"Most clerics I met remarked that Sin-le-Noble was a miserable stepchild of the church in one of the poorest backwaters in Europe. I found it to be six years of the most challenging and rewarding proofs that perseverance could turn a sow's ear into a silk purse."

"So why did you give that parish up?"

Trocmé chuckled. "One silk purse did not a paradise make. Coal-fired soot, inhospitable winters, and wondering how unhealthy it would be to raise four young children there wasn't quite the life I'd promised Magda when we met in Manhattan."

"It might have been nice if they'd sent my husband to Lyon or Marseilles. But his pacifist, nonviolent ideals didn't sit too well with the powers-that-be. And so … Le Chambon."

"Mama," seven-year-old Nelly piped up. "Didn't you tell me two other parishes wanted Papa to be their pastor?"

"Yes, darling, but more important people said he couldn't go to those places.

"So, you love a peasant's life of hand-to-mouth poverty?" Roger asked. "Well, you'll certainly find it here."

"I've not heard you complaining," Trocmé rejoined. "What keeps *you* here, Roger?"

The school director lit a pipe, then placed his chin between the thumb and forefinger of his left hand thoughtfully. "Le Chambon may seem like a dying little mountain town, and it probably is. But you probably didn't notice the inscription above the front entry to the presbytery."

"I did," Trocmé replied. "'*Aimez Vous Les Uns Les Autres — Love One Another.*'

"That's more than just a nice saying in these parts," Darcissac continued. "Although our *Chambonnais* may seem cold, even aloof, on the outside, I've never heard one of them refer to 'a Jew,' 'a Moor,' 'an Abyssinian.' We have 'men' and 'women' and 'children' here. As long as anyone can remember Le Chambon has welcomed and protected everyone who came here to live…"

24

NOVEMBER 1937

The Trocmé family's nearly four years in Le Chambon-sur-Lignon had wrought changes in their lives, not the least of which was the 'correction' of the deferred maintenance in the presbytery.

Entering the residence through what Magda called the poetic gate, a visitor came upon a small, square hallway facing a door which opened into the kitchen on the right and a vast dining room on the left. The large kitchen had a big, black iron stove with four round holes in its cooking surface. The dining room on the south side of the house had three windows, two of which faced onto the Lignon River. The room had a sycamore ceiling and paneling, with a coarse pine floor that made it painful for the children to run across it in their bare feet because of the splinters.

A large dining table covered with a colorful Basque design tablecloth dominated the middle of the dining room. Large, potted geraniums filled the three windows. A small parakeet lived in a cage adjacent to the third window, which let in the most light. From time to time, Nelly went to the piano in the corner where the east and south walls joined, and played her favorite piece, Mozart's *Rondo alla Turca*.

Next to a fireplace that didn't work, a wooden door opened into a dark passage that led to Pastor Trocmé's office. During those rare moments when the residence was comparatively quiet — usually late at night after everyone went to bed — one could hear the large grandfather clock next to the entrance to Pastor Trocmé's office ticking loudly and steadily.

Inside Trocmé's office, an orange, brown, black, and white Turkish carpet warmed the floor. The walls, covered with books and pictures, provided André with welcome companionship during the many evenings he sat in this, his favorite room, wearing large rabbit-fur-lined slippers to protect his feet from the cold.

On one such evening, Roger Darcissac, with whom he'd become very close, came to visit. As he and Roger were wont to do, they made short shrift of the niceties and got down to more meaningful conversation,

"I know we've talked about this before, André, but it's such a shame Le Chambon is slowly dying," the schoolmaster said. "Young people are simply bored here. Two-thirds of *Chambonnais* are peasants living on scattered farms in the area. It's no secret that our young people migrate to Lyon, Marseilles, even Saint-Etienne, from which they never return. If only there were something to keep them here."

"We've tried some ideas already …"

"Your toy factory idea wasn't a bad one. It just didn't take hold.'

The two men sat for awhile in companionable silence. After several moments, Trocmé brightened. "What about a secondary school?"

""We've got that already. My school's the largest within several miles,"

"Not enough," Trocmé responded. "I mean a private university preparatory school that would draw students and faculty from around the world. No bureaucratic red tape." Darcissac saw his friend rapidly warming to his latest idea. "A school that would prepare teenagers for their entry into a world-class university, one that taught students to *think* rather than simply follow traditional instructions … a place where students from many countries could come and exchange ideas."

"I hate to throw cold water on your idea, André, but why would anyone want to come to a small village like Le Chambon and pretend it would get them into a world-class university?"

"Every journey has its beginning." Trocmé's 'little engine that could' had now started to gather steam. "I've got just the person I need to help me start it…"

FEBRUARY 1938

André Trocmé and Roger Darcissac stood inside the marginally-heated railway station, wearing the heaviest coats they owned, fur-lined leather gloves, thick woolen scarves, and stiff rubber boots. 12:30. Half-an-hour to go. Trocmé kept removing his eyeglasses and rubbing them with a white handkerchief. The cold pinched Darcissac's face, emphasizing his thin-lipped saturnine smile and dark, watchful eyes.

At quarter-to-one they both heard the familiar whistle of the Le Chambon local.

"Fifteen minutes early," Darcissac noted. "You've known this fellow for …?"

"Almost two decades," Trocmé replied, rapidly rubbing his gloved hands together and watching the steam erupt from his mouth as he exhaled into the sharp, icy air. "I'll wager Edouard's the first one off the train."

As if to prove Le Chambon's pastor right, no sooner had the locomotive come to a stop amidst steam pouring from beneath its wheels than a huge man who looked half-a-decade younger than his forty years and had a smile as broad as his face, practically leapt from the first car onto the platform. He reached back to where a small, very attractive woman, had just stepped onto the top rung of three stairs leading from the railroad car to the platform, grabbed the woman by the waist with both hands, and swung her down to the platform. She seemed not the least disturbed by the man's action. Two teenage girls followed the couple at a sedate distance.

"Edouard, Mildred, over here!" Trocmé bellowed.

The giant turned. Although André was by no means a short man, the newcomer towered over him as the two embraced. Trocmé turned to the woman. "Mildred, I'm so glad you came. Someone has to keep control of the big fellow. And my, how Jeanne and Jacqueline have grown in just two years! Do I detect another one on the way?"

"You do, André. Maybe a boy this time."

Darcissac stood watching the four others silently as Trocmé continued, "Edouard and Mildred Theis, I'd like you to meet my closest Chambonnais friend, Roger Darcissac, superintendent of Le Chambon's public school."

Darcissac and Theis shook their gloved hands. "I hope you're hungry," Trocmé said. "We live just across the square and Magda has laid on a lunch for everyone that'll help all of us deal with this pre-spring 'thaw.' Let's wait inside the station while the porter brings your luggage inside and then we'll adjourn to the presbytery,"

Over steaming bowls of thick soup filled with lentils and root vegetables, and four loaves of warm, freshly-baked country bread, lubricated with pitchers of red and white *vin ordinaire* from the Haute-Loire, and the warmth of a roaring fire, conversation between the Theises, the Trocmés, and Roger Darcissac was spirited and convivial.

"What's this about you wanting to start some kind of private school in this village out in the hinterlands halfway between Lyon and Geneva, André? You wrote that you wanted me to become involved. Exactly how am I supposed to make a living?"

"The same way I do. God will provide. You won't starve, at least not that often, but don't expect to dine with the Rothschilds. My congregation's at the point where I can certainly use a half-time pastor, and if this proposed school shows any signs of life, you'd be the director and teach French, Latin, and Greek. Mildred and Magda could fill in where needed at first. I would hope that eventually we'd start to see some income. If you decide to accept my proposition, Edouard, you'll find things a bit different from your work in Cameroun and Madagascar. As you noticed when you got off the train, the weather is a bit cooler ..."

"A *bit?*" Theis exclaimed, his eyebrows raised.

"Yes, but as I recall, you always came back to Paris or the U.S. during the summer months to teach at the University Faculty of Theology. You could continue to do that during the summer break to supplement your income."

"All well and good, my friend," Theis said. But if – and it's a mighty big 'if,' — we'd need more faculty...? And you'll pardon me if I ask, but Le Chambon-sur-Lignon is not exactly Paris. Where would we find experienced, qualified teachers?"

André was quick to reply. "You've been following the news coming out of our neighbor to the Northeast?"

"Who hasn't?" Roger Darcissac interjected. "The anti-Jewish laws get tighter every day. The crème de la crème of every major university is steadily losing its most brilliant minds. The symphony orchestras ... the finest scientists and mathematicians ..." He cocked his head to one side, holding his chin between his thumb and forefinger. "The newspapers are speculating about what will happen next."

"That's easy to predict," André said thoughtfully. "Soon enough there'll be no work for Jews anywhere in the Reich, forcing them to move or starve."

"It could be much worse," their giant visitor remarked.

"Surely you don't mean ...?" Magda interjected.

"Surely I *do* mean," Edouard replied. "Once the hungry monster develops a taste for what he's eating or destroying, his appetite continues to grow, seeking out new ways ..."

"How beastly!" Mildred Theis said. "How inhumane!"

"True," Darcissac responded cautiously. "But think for a moment. Aside from the fact that Le Chambon-sur-Lignon is a small, dying pimple on the arse of an extinct volcano where the wind never stops blowing and people can't seem to wait to leave here for more interesting places, there is one thing that makes our village different. It may not be rich or powerful or even very interesting, but as long as anyone can remember, Le Chambon-sur-Lignon has always welcomed the stranger — any stranger, regardless of his or her background or belief. We may not be the world's friendliest place, and it sometimes takes an inordinately long time before we view any newcomer as 'one of us,' but I've never known anyone in Le Chambon to turn anyone away … or to deliberately destroy anyone …"

"A small university preparatory school in a poor, tiny village that no one has ever heard of, let alone cared about," André Trocmé mused. "Except that that small university prep school would welcome those who are being thrown out of what is becoming the nastiest bully in all of Europe. A faculty made up of political and religious cast-offs from the Universities of Vienna, Berlin, Heidelberg, places where Mozart, Beethoven, and Bach composed some of the greatest music ever written. Where Albert Einstein and Sigmund Freud moved the world's knowledge forward hundreds of years. A sanctuary for those of any faith, where someone simply needs to follow his or her beliefs, whatever they might be …"

December 1938

"Well, André, you can't say we haven't tried," Edouard remarked as they watched the last of the students and the only paid faculty member board the 2:30 train to Saint-Etienne. "D'you think any of our students will even return after winter vacation?"

"God knows," Trocmé replied somewhat sadly. "I expected far more than the eighteen we started with when we opened our doors last September."

"Doors?" Theis said. "As I seem to recall, the somewhat optimistically-named *Collège Cévenol* has a single door leading to the temple annex which consists of two rooms separated by walls so thin you can hear everything that's going on in both rooms at the same time. Of course, if you really think expansively, the temple annex is on one side of a busy road and Roger's public school is on the other side, so our students have to walk around the temple and cross the road in order to study the sciences."

"Perhaps the problem is that we're teaching nonviolence and conscientious objection?"

"I don't for a minute doubt that, André. France hates — but even more so it fears — the Nazis more and more every day. Let's face it, many of the pacifists who supported our proposals based their beliefs on Hitler's promises, but as Hitler and his gang broke more and more of those promises, those same conscientious objectors gave up their pledges of nonviolence."

As they turned back toward the presbytery, Trocmé thought *I continue to believe with all my heart that feeling, thinking, and acting as if life is precious beyond all price will, in the end, prevail over Nazism.* Out loud, he said, "Edouard, my friend, Collège Cévenol *will* go on, even if we have only eighteen students, even if we only have *one* student. And even if you and I have to nibble on thistles for awhile. ..."

August 1, 1939

As the early afternoon train from Saint-Etienne pulled into the station, a distinguished-looking man of medium height and early middle age, with a well-trimmed beard and goatee, wearing a thick, obviously careworn, greatcoat, carefully descended the three steps from the railway car to the platform and approached the Le Chambon – Le Mazet stationmaster.

"Excuse me, Monsieur," he said. "May I ask where I would find the Cévenol School?"

In response, the functionary swept his arms around and proclaimed, "The school is everywhere! You'll find students, faculty, and classrooms throughout the village!"

The newcomer extracted a small piece of paper on which something was handwritten. "Might I inquire where I would find Pastor Trocmé or Professeur Theis, please?"

"Most likely across *Rue de la Grande Fontaine*, just opposite the station." He looked at his railroad watch. "Of course, this time of day you'll probably find Madame Trocmé inside the presbytery, usually stirring a huge cauldron of soup or mixing an equally large bowl of salad, whatever comes to hand, for newcomers like you, sir. May I ask from where you've come?"

"Saint-Etienne," the man replied.

"I didn't mean that, Monsieur," the stationmaster replied. "I meant the place from which you embarked."

"Uhh … the East …"

"Germany, Austria?"

The man's face reddened.

"You needn't respond if it's uncomfortable. We get a lot of folks from Central and Eastern Europe nowadays. Not to worry, you're safe here. Le Chambon has seen a lot of refugees lately. Are you *Juif?*"

"*Oui.* From Pressburg."

"Bratislava?"

The man nodded uncomfortably.

"Then, for sure Magda Trocmé's home is the best place for you to go."

"Come in, come in! You must be Herr Professor Rozenmayer, yes?"

"Yes, *Frau … Madame* Trocmé."

"André told me you'd be coming today or tomorrow. You are, I believe, a professor of physics at Comenius University?"

"Was," he replied, removing his overcoat and a top hat of similar age, "The new administration calls it Slovak University, and they do not welcome my kind."

"I'm sorry to hear that, Professor. Not to worry, though. Bratislava's loss is our gain. The Cévenol School has grown to seventy-five full-time students, plus another hundred part-timers. But we can discuss all that later. First, you must warm yourself at our fireplace. You must be famished as well. Always a full cauldron of soup to be had here."

Over the bountiful and filling meal, the loquacious Magda Trocmé continued nonstop in a hodgepodge of French, her native Italian, and German. "One of the reasons our little school has grown so fast in the last year is the coming of refugees from the German and Slavic-speaking countries. Indeed, the educated and cultured Jews of those countries have not only found open doors in Le Chambon, but places as teachers and students in the Cévenol School.

"Have there been many refugees?" Rozenmayer asked.

"Not at first, but the numbers increase every day. Last year at this time, we had eighteen students. now more than four times that many. And God has blessed us with the ability to pay our faculty wages on which they can live; not generous, but since our Chambonnais provide free, safe housing and reasonable food, everyone seems to make do."

"Is it really safe?" Rozenmayer asked earnestly.

"So far, yes. Herr Professor. No one can predict what the future holds, since the German spider seems to be spreading its web everywhere. We cannot propose a neat blueprint for fighting Hitler's hatred with love. But my husband preaches, 'Work and look hard for ways to make little moves against destructiveness.' He doesn't tell his parishioners what those moves should be, only we must somehow make such moves when the occasion arises."

25

His back nagging painfully, in part because of his advancing age, and in larger part because of the *mistral*, the great wind that roars down the Rhône River Valley from the icy Alps, André Trocmé walked stiffly out of the Gare Saint-Charles, Marseilles' main railroad station. Just outside the terminal, he turned onto the Boulevard d'Athènes and walked a block-and-a-half to No. 29, a beige-and-black four-story building, headquarters of the American Friends Service Committee. He had received permission from the presbyterial council of his church to make this visit, having told his parishioners he felt the need to help the many refugees who were pouring into southern France from Central and Eastern Europe.

Pastor Trocmé had come to the Quakers, convinced he could best work with the Friends, who were already bringing desperately needed supplies to people in the horrendously overcrowded, understaffed internment camps at Gurs and Argèles, a stone's throw from the French-Spanish frontier.

Trocmé walked into the stark little offices where he saw a man of his own age, as tall as he but much thinner. The man stood and held out his hand.

"Pastor Trocmé?"

"Burns Chalmers?"

"That's me."

The two men struck up an instant affinity for one another.

"Is it true that the Friends consider themselves no nation's enemies and no nation's friends?"

"Correct, Pastor — may I call you André?"

"That goes without saying. I'm told your only enemies are human suffering and killing."

"Again correct. I understand you have great influence and prestige in southern France. You need not demur or pretend to insincere modesty."

"I don't, Burns. I'm here 'hat in hand' because I need your help. I trust you and I have exactly the same ethical commitment to treat human life as something beyond all price."

"What do you need, André?"

"I'd like to work in the internment camps, but I need help from the Friends as well."

"I appreciate what you say, but the eyes of each and every refugee reach out to me."

"Do I read what you say as a definitive refusal, Burns?"

"Not at all, but we can't continue to meet in Marseilles because our office is busier than Gare Saint Charles. Why don't we agree to meet once a month in Nimes and talk without interruption about how we can best help one another — and, more important, those who need our help so desperately?"

FRIDAY, MAY 23, 1941 – NIMES, FRANCE, A SMALL RESTAURANT NEAR THE MAISON CARRÉE

"The children should be our most important concern, Burns. That's a 'given.' We've got to show them there are human being outside their own families who care for them."

"Agreed. But you said you wanted to help by working in the internment camps. That's a great idea, but I don't believe that's the best use of your talents. We've already got various organizations doing this."

"Do you have any better suggestions for what you call my 'talents'?"

"I think I might. You come from a small mountain village surrounded by rugged mountains, a difficult place to reach, a place where one can still enjoy certain *security* ..."

"Yes, and ...?"

"The Friends are presently trying to deliver as many medical certificates as possible to the inmates of the camps stating that the persons named on those certificates are medically incapable of forced labor — *Zwangsarbeit* — in Germany. If we can't save the father of a family by delivering a medical exemption certificate, we try to save the mother. If the parents are still deported, we take charge of the children and arrange for them to be boarded outside the camps. Our problem has been, it's very difficult to find French communities that will agree to shelter such dangerous 'guests.' What we *really* need, more than anything else, is a sanctuary community, a place of refuge for these children."

"Are you saying what I think you're saying?"

"I am, but I'll put it bluntly, André. Would Le Chambon, be willing to be a place of refuge for these children?"

"I would hope so. But it will be necessary to board, feed, and educate them these children, and Le Chambon is woefully short of funds."

The thin man stood to his full six-foot height, stretched, and cracked his knuckles before responding. "Find some houses and some monitors. The Quakers will support you financially."

"Are you committing ...?"

"Pastor Trocmé, I don't have the authority on my own initiative to bind the Friends' leadership in Marseilles or Toulouse to a sum certain, but ..."

"What about this idea?" Trocmé suggested. "Your people fund the project and I'll obtain the houses, appoint the monitor, and distribute the supplies."

"What have we got to lose by trying?" Chalmers responded.

26

JULY 1942

"Can you imagine a tiny village like ours hosting such an event? What do you think of that, sir?" the 28-year-old head scout of Vichy France, Julien LeBlanc, addressed Aristide Bach, head prefect of the Haute-Loire Department.

"What a feather in our cap!" Bach responded. "The marshal is sending Georges Lamirand, the Vichy government's minister of youth, to Le Chambon for this occasion."

"Of course, we want to make certain everything goes perfectly. The program will be covered by the French state radio and every major newspaper in the country. Afterward, all the leaders will adjourn to the temple for a major conclave, and finally we'll hold religious services in the temple. It will be magnificent."

"You won't be disappointed, sir, that I can promise you."

"What do you think, André?" Theis asked his friend that evening,

Trocmé's face was sour as he replied. "For two years we've been able to

197

escape Vichy's attempts to indoctrinate our young people," as he observed the small parade coming down LeChambon's main thoroughfare. A group of young teens passed, wearing blue shirts with yellow lettering, 'Companions of France.' To the accompaniment of a drum and bugle corps, the young men stretched their right arms toward the sky in Fascist salutes.

"Thank God that garbage never touched Le Chambon 'til now," Trocmé nearly snarled to his assistant. "But now we've got a problem, Edouard. It's confrontation or compromise, and one alternative is as dangerous to Le Chambon as the other."

"What do you suggest, André?"

"This requires some careful planning. We can't be seen to throw a monkey wrench into the proceedings, not obviously at least. But …"

August 1942

Minister Lamirand, tall, ramrod straight, looking a good decade younger than his fifty-six years, and wearing a splendid marine-blue uniform, which looked vaguely like a German military uniform, marched into the town's main square. Pastor Trocmé, in his pastoral robes, was the very picture of dignified respect as he and Lamirand walked together to the refectory of the YMCA camp, where they took seats next to one another.

The first course was served. Minister Lamirand seemed mildly discomfited.

"The menu I was handed during the planning stages said we'd dine on Bresse chicken in wine, *choucroute garni*, potatoes Lyonnais, Burgundy wine, and fresh fruit. There must be some mistake. All I see is a thin greenish vegetable soup and water.

"Ah, yes, Monsieur Minister," Trocmé responded mildly. "It seems with the austerity surrounding our brethren throughout *la belle France,* we should appear to stand as one with them, don't you think?"

"Well, Pastor, you're probably right. It is better this wa — WHAT?" Lamirand gasped and gave a sharp cry of surprised pain.

"Oh, how dreadful, Monsiuer Le Ministere!" Trocmė purred sympathetically. "Hot soup poured accidentally on the back of your scout uniform." He hastened to start wiping the greasy liquid off the finely-tailored uniform which had been delivered to the minister's quarters in the next town that very morning. The grease spots could not be eradicated, and had now spread to the front of the jacket. Minister Lamirand, his dignity now irretrievably offended, grabbed another napkin from the table, dipped it in water, and started scrubbing his jacket. In so doing, he accidentally spilled the cup of water, which dripped onto his necktie and trousers.

He was now speechless.

"Naughty child," Trocmé roared in mock horror at the teenage serving girl, who happened to be his daughter Nelly.

Quickly regaining what was left of his composure, Minister Lamirand turned to his luncheon companion and remarked, "No need to berate the poor, sweet child, Pastor. No doubt she is unfamiliar with celebrations such as this."

Trocmé said nothing.

"I must say, Pastor Trocmé, I had expected Vichy flags, posters of the Marshal, flowers, perhaps some bunting, and military music to excite the crowd."

"I could not be more surprised, myself, Minister Lamirand," his host replied. "Scofflaws and malcontents must have destroyed what I'm sure the village elders installed this morning before you arrived. Had I known ..."

"Why, what flags there are look like they've been hanging on the flagpoles since the beginning of time. Where, by the way, are the crowds I was promised?" he asked rhetorically, looking at a street containing perhaps half a dozen people dressed in ordinary work outfits of drab gray, faded blue, or worn-out beige. "And your colleagues, the Protestant ministers?" he continued.

"Mister Minister, all I can say is I have no explanation. I am embarrassed, humiliated in front of my very flock. I'm sure the crowds will be eagerly awaiting your arrival at the sports field for the day's grand conclusion."

Shortly afterward, Minister Lamirand, Prefect Bach, and Head Scout LeBlanc arrived at the sports field. A dais had been set up, but the anticipated 'crowd' consisted of a couple dozen curious children, who pushed and shoved, trying to shake the hand of the dignified official.

"What are those stains on your uniform, Monsieur?" a voice issued from an anonymous child. "Did the laundry make a mistake or is that some kind of new decoration, sir?"

Lamirand, again maintaining his poise, turned to Prefect Bach and remarked, "So charming, all this spontaneity."

During a speech in the temple, a Charbonnais citizen gave a short talk on the thirteenth chapter of Saint Paul's epistle to the Romans. "As the sainted Paul himself said, 'You shall not kill, you shall not steal, you shall not covet. Any other commandments are summed up in two sentences, 'You shall love your neighbor as yourself' and 'Love does not do wrong to a neighbor.'"

Lamirand was obviously puzzled. He had prepared a long speech, but he replied with only a few words.

Then a visiting Swiss pastor gave a sermon on the theme of obedience to the state, emphasizing that, "*The state should be obeyed, but only when the state does not try to force the people to violate the laws of God and does not try to violate the one law that sums them all up: 'You shall love your neighbor as yourself.'*"

Afterward Lamirand and Pastor Trocmé walked out of the temple and into the front court that faced the road beyond.

And then it happened.

A dozen senior students of Cévenol School walked up to Minister Lamirand. The eldest student politely but firmly asked, "Honored Minister Lamirand, please acknowledge that you have received this document." He handed an inscribed piece of parchment to the Vichy minister. He continued, "To make sure you and our honored Marshal Pétain know precisely what we mean by what we say, I will read it out loud so you and those assembled here will know how we feel.

"Dear Monsieur Minister:

"We have learned of the frightening scenes which took place three weeks ago in Paris, where the French police, on orders of the occupying power, arrested in their homes all the Jewish families in Paris to hold them in the Vel d'Hiv. Fathers were torn from their families and sent to Germany. Children were torn from their mothers, who underwent the same fate as their husbands. Knowing by experience that the decrees of the occupying power are, with brief delay, imposed on Unoccupied France, where they are presented as 'spontaneous decisions of the head of the French government,' we are afraid that the measures of deportation of the Jews will soon be applied in the Southern Zone.

"We feel obliged to tell you that there are among us a certain number of Jews. But we make no distinction between Jews and non-Jews. It is contrary to Gospel teaching.

"If our comrades, whose only fault is to be born in another religion, received the order to let themselves be deported, or even examined, they would disobey the orders received and we would try to hide them as best we could."

At that moment, the maneuvering between the two obligations to be 'subject to the governing authorities' and to 'love your neighbor as yourself' was past. The moment had come for the people of Le Chambon to pass their ethical judgment publicly, and they had done so.

Minister Lamirand turned pale and mumbled, "These questions are not my affair. Speak to the prefect of your department." And he hurried into his automobile and away from Le Chambon-sur-Lignon.

Prefect Bach was furious. Instead of addressing the young scouts, he rounded on André and practically shouted, "Pastor Trocmé, this day should have been a day of national harmony. How *dare* you sow division?"

Trocmé shot back, "It cannot be a question of national harmony when our brothers are threatened with deportation."

"I have already received orders and I will put them into effect. Foreign Jews who live in the Haute-Loire are not your brothers. They do not belong to your nor to our country! Besides, it is not a question of deportation."

"Oh? What is it a question of, Prefect Bach?"

The prefect responded, "My information comes from the marshal himself. Just as the English have created a Zionist center in Palestine, the Führer has ordered the regrouping of all European Jews in Poland, where they will have land and houses. They will lead a life that is suitable for them and they will cease to corrupt the West. In a few days my people will come to examine the Jews living in Le Chambon."

Without batting an eyelash, Trocmé replied, "We do not know what a Jew is. We know only men and women."

"Monsieur Trocmé," the functionary warned, barely keeping his temper in check, "you would do well to take care. If you are not prudent, I shall be obliged to have *you* deported." The prefect turned on his heel and left.

27

AUGUST 29, 1942

Retribution struck two weeks later. Saturday night, to be precise. At first, a few automobiles entered the village marketplace. Later, four khaki-colored buses surrounded by police motorcyclists descended on Le Chambon. As soon as they arrived, the police chief summoned Pastor Trocmé to the town hall. He immediately addressed the Protestant cleric.

"Pastor, we know in detail your suspicious activities. You are hiding in this commune a certain number of Jews, whose names we know. I have an order to lead these people to the prefecture for a census. You are therefore going to give me a list of those persons and their addresses, and you will advise them to be on their good behavior, so they should not try to flee."

"I do not know the names of these people," Trocmé responded. *And I'm telling the truth,* he thought. *They have false identity cards. I don't know — and I don't <u>want</u> to know — their real names.* He continued aloud, "and I wouldn't tell them to you if I did. These people have come here seeking aid and protection from the Protestants of this region. I am their pastor, their shepherd. It is not the role of a shepherd to betray the sheep entrusted to his keeping."

The police chief was becoming angry. "What I said to you is not advice but an order. If you oppose authority, you're the one who will be arrested and deported. I hold you responsible for resisting the laws of your country."

"Monsieur *Polizeipräsident*," Trocmé responded with equal force, highlighting the German word for chief of police, "this conversation is over."

And he walked out of the town hall.

"Young men," he addressed the Boy Scouts of Le Chambon, who had gathered in his large office. "We have a little operation which we'll call the 'disappearance of the Jews.' I would like each of you to go to outlying farms in the area, to Crickets, to the House of the Rocks, and even to the Ardèche and warn the Jews to scatter and hide in the woods around Le Chambon. The police are crawling all over town like lice, so here's our plan …"

Saturday night in Le Chambon. Something went wrong with the lighting system. It was almost impossible to see anything but gray, ghostlike figures that might have been Boy Scouts or Bible class leaders crossing town to get to and from houses and farms around the village. The police slept on straw pallets, waiting for the chief's ultimatum to expire.

When Sunday morning came, Pastors Trocmé and Theis expected to see police coming into the presbytery to arrest them. But they did not appear. At three that afternoon, one of the Boy Scouts came into Magda's kitchen and asked to see the clergymen.

"Of course," Madame Trocmé replied. "They're in my husband's study having an afternoon cup of tea."

When the boy entered the office, the two men, who recognized him immediately, asked, "What news?"

"Oh, lots," he said, grinning broadly. "The police spent the entire morning searching the village houses and outlying farms. Nothing. Now they've all surrounded the four buses and they're standing around smoking and joking and looking at every girl that passes by. An hour ago, the village councillors, who were sitting between machine-gun-armed police, passed out an 'Appeal to the Jewish refugees,' which asked the Jews to present themselves at the town hall for a census."

"I'll just bet this will be a fine census," Theis intoned acidly. "With four large buses standing in the market square ready to take them away for deportation."

Not a single Jew presented himself or herself at town hall.

At five in the afternoon, the police started searching every house in the village. They demanded to see identity papers from everyone. They opened cupboards, went down into the cellars, climbed to the attics, knocked on walls to see whether they were hollow, and finally returned to their stations at nine o'clock that evening.

Without having found a single Jew.

On Monday morning, the police fanned out to the farms in the surrounding countryside. Nothing.

By late Monday afternoon, one Austrian Jew named Johannes Steckler had been arrested. He sat in one of the buses, surrounded by several policemen. The villagers smiled at him as they passed through the square.

"Would you look at that silliness?" a graybeard remarked. "Thirty policemen guarding one lone prisoner who's already sitting in a bus."

Another Chambonnaise, a fat older woman, waddled by and piped up, "Look! There's Pastor Trocmé's son Jean-Pierre handing the 'prisoner' a piece of imitation chocolate!"

An hour passed. Other townspeople brought more presents, which they laid at the foot of the bus until the stack of gifts reached up to its windows. Meanwhile, Herr Steckler, who had tired of all the excitement, had fallen asleep and was snoring softly when a police sergeant stepped to the front door of the bus and announced to the gathering crowd, "Ladies and gentlemen, *Madames et Messieurs*, there's been a slight mistake. Two of Herr Steckler's grandparents practiced the Jewish religion, but we've found no one else on his family tree who's Jewish. Thus, under French law, he is legally *non-Juif* and we've been ordered to release him."

The police remained in Le Chambon for three weeks, but they found no more Jews. The dogs on the farms of Le Chambon warned their masters, indeed the whole countryside, of new arrivals, barking at even the most distant sounds. And the inhabitants of the community knew everything that happened.

The day after the police departed, the Chambonnais regained their sense of humor. When asked about Jews, they stared back in astonishment and asked, "What would Jews be doing here? Have you seen any Jews yet? They say they have crooked noses."

One lazy afternoon in September, the mayor's son, Étienne Grand, was sitting with his back against a tree reading a book when a local gendarme stopped at some distance from him, and noisily whispered, "Psst!"

When Étienne looked up, the gendarme raised his voice and continued, "Go away! I haven't seen you."

"What do you mean you haven't seen me?" Étienne replied. "What are you trying to say?"

"I'm looking for Jews. If you don't leave, I'll be forced to arrest you."

"But I'm not Jewish, I'm the mayor's son!"

"Ah," the gendarme sighed, obviously relieved. "You aren't one of them? So much the better, I do not like the task they make us do."

As the Resistance in Le Chambon continued to develop, many of the Vichy police were 'converting.' Even as the official policy of Vichy France toward Le Chambon and the Jews was hardening, *individuals* among the police and Vichy bureaucrats more and more frequently resisted their orders to catch people who had done no harm to anyone. Caring became infectious.

Shortly after the Germans occupied southern France, the Vichy police were closely supervised by the Gestapo, and the danger of sheltering Jews became greater than ever. In the face of this new development, the Chambonnais concentrated on making Le Chambon a place of refuge.

28

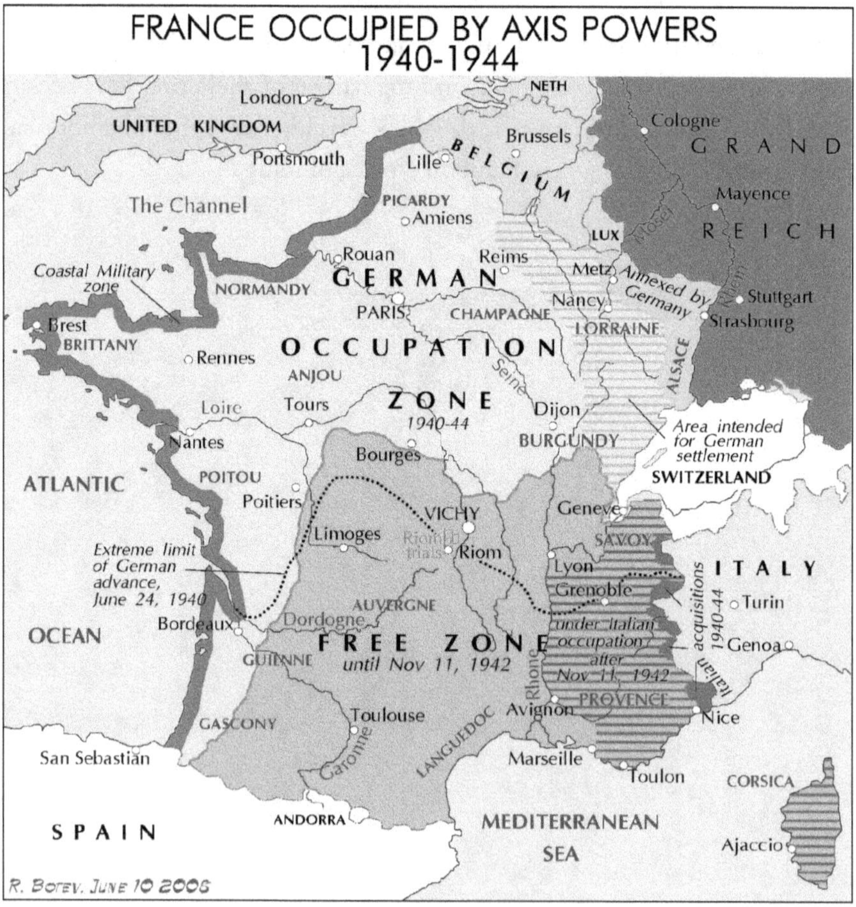

FRANCE OCCUPIED BY AXIS POWERS
1940-1944

UNITED KINGDOM

London

Portsmouth

The Channel

NETH

Cologne

Brussels

GRAND

BELGIUM

Mayence

PICARDY
Amiens

LUX

REICH

Coastal Military
zone

Rouan

NORMANDY

Reims

GERMAN

Metz Annexed by
Germany

Stuttgart

Nancy

Strasbourg

PARIS

CHAMPAGNE

LORRAINE

Brest
BRITTANY

Rennes

OCCUPATION

ANJOU

ZONE
1940-44

Loire

Tours

Dijon

Seine

Nantes

POITOU

BURGUNDY

Area intended
for German
settlement

Bourges

ATLANTIC

Poitiers

SWITZERLAND

Extreme limit
of German
advance,
June 24, 1940

Limoges

VICHY

Riom

Geneve

Riom
trials

SAVOY

ITALY

AUVERGNE

Lyon

Grenoble

Turin

OCEAN

Bordeaux

Dordogne

FREE ZONE
until Nov 11, 1942

under Italian
occupation
after
Nov 11, 1942

Genoa

Italian acquisitions 1940-44

GUIENNE

GASCONY

Toulouse

Garonne

LANGUEDOC

Avignon

PROVENCE

Nice

San Sebastián

ANDORRA

Marseille

Toulon

CORSICA

SPAIN

MEDITERRANEAN
SEA

Ajaccio

Rhone

R. Botev. June 10 2006

SEPTEMBER 12, 1942 - TRAVAIL, FAMILLE, PATRIE

On Thursday afternoon, Varga received a handwritten note under the door of his Paris flat. "SV: Proceed Ambassade Suisse, M. Dubigny. Hôtel Chanac de Pompadour, Ile-de-France. S."

After he arrived at the Swiss Embassy, an elegant eighteenth century building in the prestigious seventh arrondissement and presented the note to the duty officer, he was escorted to a suite on the second floor. A discreet sign on the door read *"Conseil d'Affairs des Nations."*

When the escort officer led him into the capacious office beyond the reception area, Varga was greeted by a shorter man his own age, wearing a full beard and mustache, dressed in a conservative charcoal-colored suit with white shirt and grey-and-red tie. The man radiated a warmth, which Varga had been told was atypical of Swiss diplomats.

"Colonel Varga," he said, reaching out to shake hands. "Won't you have a seat?

"Thank you, Monsieur Dubigny. I received this note less than two hours ago," Varga said, handing it to the man who'd sat down opposite him.

"Ah, yes. You're no doubt aware that our embassy serves as the good offices for a number of countries and regimes, even those whose duly constituted governments may not be able to act as such at the moment. Case in point, that of independent Poland and others that are presently aligned, willingly or not, with the Third Reich. You need not say anything, Colonel Varga. I've met General Sikorski recently in London. He asked me to speak to you at the earliest moment. You're Jewish, are you not?"

"I am."

"He told me he'd spoken with you at the beginning of July about an assignment that would be very close to your heart. One that would fit your talents."

"Briefly, Monsieur Dubigny."

The diplomat reached into a credenza behind his desk and brought out a round crystal bottle of amber liquid and two brandy snifters on a wooden tray.

"It's four-thirty, Colonel. Might I suggest we enjoy a libation while we talk?"

"I would be hard-pressed to say no. Particularly to Rémy Martin XO."

Dubigny poured a snifter for each of them and held his up in a silent toast. "How much do you know about the Jewish situation in France?"

"I'm aware that Premier Blum was Jewish, and more than fifty thousand refugees from Central Europe entered the country within the past five years."

"Bringing the current Jewish population in France to 330,000, on par with Britain as housing the largest number of Jews in Western Europe," Dubigny continued. "And most of them were as popular as a herd of locusts. More than half of them are not French citizens. A high percentage of those who are, acquired their citizenship after the First World War."

"About as well-liked as Polish Jews," Varga remarked.

"Precisely. And now that the world's leading anti-Semitic force has occupied France ..."

"The northern part, Monsieur Dubigny."

"*France*, Colonel Varga. Don't let titles fool you. The Marshal has a long history of right-wing conservatism. And he despises Bolshevik Communism, translation *Jew-motivated* godlessness, which he believes led to the recent humiliation of the French army."

Varga took a sip of his cognac. "And your point is?"

"Occupied France or Free France makes no difference. They've already started passing anti-Jewish laws, just as they did in Germany with the Nuremberg laws. First, Jews will be prohibited from engaging in certain professions. For example, the media. Then businesses will be 'Aryanized.' Then ..."

"But Mister Dubigny, France is …"

"Under the control of Hitler and his gang. And they won't hesitate to bargain with Jewish lives to bring about a 'negotiated' peace with England. That's one of the reasons General Sikorski wanted me to speak privately with you."

"He could have written me …"

"And you think the occupying forces wouldn't have intercepted any message he'd sent?"

"But I'm …"

"A Polish officer. A resident alien in a country where the conquerors of Poland — whom the Nazis despise as *ubermenschen* — subhumans — and a Jew to boot. Don't undersell the Germans, Herr Varga. They're not the beer-swilling buffoons the Brits like to think they are. Even the Swiss Embassy is not safe from their probing eyes. No, Colonel, General Sikorski believed a private conversation would be the safest alternative."

Dubigny lit a *Parisienne* cigarette and offered the pack to Varga, who declined.

"General Sikorski says the *Boches* will occupy the *Zone Libre* within the next month or two. He thinks it is urgent that you meet with a Protestant minister, Pastor André Trocmé, two weeks from today, September 26, at 1400 hours at the Aletti Palace Hotel in Vichy. After you speak with him, you'll receive further instructions."

"Vichy's in the Unoccupied Zone," Varga replied.

"For now," Dubigny said. "When the Nazis occupy the free zone, it'll become more and more difficult to cross the frontier. But for now … given Sikorski's confidence in your abilities, and …" He withdrew a manila envelope, which he handed to Varga.

The Polish officer opened the envelope and spread out its contents on Dubigny's desk.

The first item was a single page document printed in German with a red stamp, a black stamp, and the entries, "Stefan Varga, Militar" and "Vichy, *l'État français.*"

"An *Ausweis*," the Swiss continued. "An identification card issued by the German Occupation Authority authorizing you to leave the Occupied Zone."

The second piece of paper contained a printed name and address in a small town on the border of the two zones. The third item was a packet containing 25,000 *Reichsmarks*, the equivalent of one thousand U.S. dollars.

ONE WEEK LATER – SEPTEMBER 19, 1942

4:10 a.m. Varga lay on his stomach at the top of a low hill, wrapped in an overcoat and muffler, his dark hat worn at an angle, a small valise at his side. The damp wet earth above the river, where it shoaled over low islets, was so cold he could barely move, but there was nothing he could do about it.

Two border guards stood at the foot of the hill, near the edge of the river, rifles slung over their shoulders, sharing a cigarette and talking in low voices. Guttural German sounds drifted up the hillside.

The young man, Henri, perhaps sixteen, maybe a little older, lay next to him. It was his job to guide Varga across this branch of the river into the *Zone Libre*. Henri stared intensely at the *Boches* below him. *What the hell do you think you're doing invading _my_ hills, _my_ stream, _my_ ancestral land? Who the hell do you think you are? Just wait, you fucking schleuhs. Not tonight, maybe not even in a month or a year, but given enough time I'll settle accounts with you arrogant bastards.*

By his side, his dark-faced, chestnut Malinois shepherd, Fidèle, waited patiently, his breath steaming as he panted in the icy morning air.

Historically these *were* Henri's hills. His family, the DeCollines, still resided in the same rundown chateau they'd occupied since the fifteenth century, twenty kilometers southeast of Bourges just outside a village so small it didn't even have a name. He raised his hand a few inches, a signal to Varga to be patient. "I know these two. Lazy, gossipy old ladies, but eventually they'll resume their rounds."

Varga gritted his teeth as the wet grass crushed beneath him, slowly soaking his clothing.

Had we left the chateau at two as we'd planned, this would not have happened. But he said nothing. He knew it wasn't Henri's fault and he was grateful for the younger man's presence.

He'd been scheduled to go across with an older man and his wife, both Jewish, who wouldn't — or couldn't — get a permit to enter the *Vichy* zone. The man had arrived from whence he'd come forty minutes late and insisted on masking his nervousness with endless tales of his boyhood in the north, fortified by two jugs of country wine he'd brought with him, and which he eagerly shared with the DeCollines clan. Everyone had some wine and handfuls of cheese cut from a huge round. The fire burned low. Then, at 3:25, a telephone call from the man's wife: this was not a propitious night to travel, not for their kind at any rate, and he should come home to where they'd be safe for the time being.

That left Varga and Henri DeCollines to make the crossing later than they should have, almost dawn, and that invited discovery. The sentries shared a final laugh, then parted, heading east and west along the stream. The dog made a faint sound deep in his throat.

Typical, Varga thought. *These dogs' stock in trade is herding stock to safety.* He shivered as a small, cold breeze rustled the grass around him. He'd been offered an oilskin back in the gunroom of the chateau, but he'd declined. *Next time I'll know better.*

Henri, wearing nothing more than short pants and a sweater, seemed not to notice. "Don't worry, sir," he whispered. "We'll go down the hill now. Stay low to the ground and we'll run. Now I count one, and two, and three."

The youngster rose and scrambled down the rise in a soldier's crouch, the Belgian sheepdog in a fast trot just behind his left heel — dogs were always trained left so that the right side, the gun side, remained free and unhampered. Varga did the best he could, shocked at how stiff he'd gotten just lying on the damp earth for less than half an hour.

When they got to the foot of the hill, Henri took his shoes off, tied them at the laces, hung them around his neck, then stuffed his socks in his pockets. His charge did the same. When Varga stepped into the stream, the water was so close to ice that he gasped, "My God!"

Henri shushed him sharply. Varga couldn't move as the water washed over his shins. Henri grabbed his elbow and shoved him forward. The dog turned to make sure of the colonel, his eyes anxious. *Does this recalcitrant beast need a nip to get it moving? No, there it goes, swearing with every step.* Relieved, the Malinois followed, close by his master.

For Varga, the gravel of the midstream island provided comfort for a few seconds. Then, the water was even deeper and the dog had to swim. At last, the far bank. The Malinois shook off a great cloud of icy spray — just in case part of Varga's clothing had accidentally remained dry.

"Ah, Fidèle," Henri remarked, hugging the dog's neck. The Malinois almost appeared to smile at the compliment.

Henri sat in the grass putting his socks and shoes back on. Varga did the same. Together, they ran up the side of a low hill until they reached a grove of poplar trees. The young man stopped to catch his breath. "*Ça va, Coronel?*"

"*Ça va, Henri. Merci.*"

Varga stayed quiet for a moment, hands on his knees. Then the whipcrack sound of a pistol rent the air. Instinctively Henry and Varga flinched. Two more cracks, close together.

The dog — fear had been bred out of him many generations ago — looked at them inquiringly. *Is this something you'd like me to see about?*

Henri shook his head, raised the bottom of his sweater, and hauled out a huge, ancient revolver. This time, Varga grabbed the youngster's elbow. Before this particular battle could get under way, they were galloping down the reverse slope of the hillside. They took cover for a moment, then headed south toward a little road that would eventually take Varga to Vichy. Henri saluted Varga, wished him well, and as if it were an everyday occurrence, which it was, grabbed his dog by the scruff of the neck, hugged his four-legged companion, and the two of them departed for home. At the next hilltop, Varga looked back toward the river; a dull silver in the first light of dawn, and remarkably beautiful.

Without ever having met the large, robust man before, Varga felt the magnetic warmth emanating from him as soon as he entered the public area. The clerk at the front desk had pointed out the cleric when Varga had asked if '*le pasteur protestant*' had left a message for him.

Now, he faced a man roughly his own age, dressed in a Geneva gown, the standard outfit of Protestant ministers throughout Europe.

"André Trocmé," he said, a smile as wide as his face, as he shook hands and embraced the Polish officer simultaneously. "You are, I trust, the fellow sent by my friend Władysław Sikorski." A statement, not a question and no mention of military rank. "You had a refreshing swim?" Trocmé continued, his eyes glinting merrily behind a pair of cheap, steel-framed glasses.

"Thank God, it wasn't winter," Stefan replied. "It was much easier once I crossed into the Free Zone. The Swiss consul said I'd be interested in hearing what you have to say, Father …?"

"André's fine."

"Stefan."

"You've undoubtedly heard of Le Chambon-sur-Lignon, Stefan?"

"I can't say I have."

"To use your statement, thank God not too many people have. It's a small village, less than three thousand, a hundred and twenty-five miles southeast of here. It's where I've set up shop. I became parish pastor in thirty-four and I've lived there ever since. I helped open a school to prepare country boys for college four years ago. But I forget my manners. Monsieur," he said, summoning a nearby attendant, "a plate of petits-fours and two bottles of Perrier if you please?"

"*D'accord,*" the waiter said, returning a few moments later.

"If you don't mind my asking, André, how did an obviously likeable fellow like you end up in that village?'"

"I'm a pacifist, Colonel. I try to live in peace and help all kinds of people. I know that sounds very naïve and simplistic, but as old-fashioned as it may be, I truly believe Christ would have acted much the same way. That doesn't make me very popular among French Protestant clergy. Even less so among the eighty percent of Christians in this country who consider themselves Roman Catholic." He grinned. "Those who've even heard of Chambon refer to it as 'a nest of vipers, Jew-lovers in Protestant country' and that's the nicest thing I've heard about it."

Varga uncapped his bottle of sparkling water and held out the plate of pastries to his host.

"A sea of calm in a violent continent."

"Yes, but …"

"They say when someone puts the word 'but' in the middle of a sentence, you ignore everything that went before."

"A Polish statement, Stefan?"

"A universal statement, André."

They sat in companionable silence for a few moments, before the pastor took up the conversation. "We Huguenots represent a tiny percentage of the Christians in this country, maybe twice as many of us as there are Jews. And, we're about as popular as you Jews are in Poland. Władysław told me all about you, which is precisely why he thought you'd be perfect for what my project needs."

"Your project?"

"Yes."

"I'm listening."

"Chambon's a very different place from the rest of the world. The best example I can give you is my wife. Last winter Chambon's wind, *la burle*, was blowing a great deal of snow through town when two Vichy French policemen drove into town in a *Traction Avant* police car, searching for some Jewish refugees who'd supposedly hidden in someone's cellar. Seeing that it was dark and cold and that the police seemed tired and hungry, she invited them into our home for dinner. Later, some friends asked her, 'How could you bring yourself to sit down and eat with these men who were there to take poor refugees away, perhaps to their death? How could you be so forgiving, so decent to them?'

"Magda always gives the same answer. 'What are you talking about? It was dinnertime, they were standing in my way; we were all hungry. The food was ready. What do you mean by such foolish words as 'forgiving' and 'decent?'"

Trocmé nibbled at a petit-four, then guzzled half a bottle of Perrier water down at a single gulp before he continued. "When strangers come through Chambon, I often hear, 'Is everyone in your village so good and moral?' There was an old fellow who was still living in our town when I came. He died a few months later, when he was ninety-eight, but he came closer than just about anyone I ever met in describing Chambon.

"One day, he looked me straight in the eye and said, '*Mon garçon,* how can you call us 'good?' We do what has to be done. Who else can help them? And what does this have to do with goodness? Things have to be done, that's all, and we happen to be there to do them. There's nothing 'moral' or 'ethical' about it. It's just the way it is.'"

"Father, could you let me know what you and General Sikorski talked about?"

"Of course, Stefan," he began. "After the Germans defeated France, every Jew in France — indeed every Jew who'd not been able to escape to North America, South Africa, Palestine, or China — knew which way the wind was blowing and the smell was one of death. Of course, the Nazis had to keep up the pretense that there was such a thing as France, a *free* France. And so, they 'allowed' Marshal Pétain to have a state of his own, so long as it was a neutral ally of the Reich.

"Pétain truly believes France fell because it was morally bankrupt. And he finds it hard to resist that he's treated like a god. So, one by one, a small restrictive law against the Jews here, a little larger one there, the confiscation of a small Jew-owned shop, followed by the seizure of a larger one …

"Colonel Varga, mark my words, what took place in Germany after the Nuremberg laws, is being replicated in Vichy France. A year ago, German-occupied France *and* the so-called Free Zone started deporting Jews …"

"And your plan is?"

"Le Chambon-sur-Lignon is a village of three thousand people. There's no way we can save over three hundred thousand Jews. But if we can somehow save three hundred or, God willing, three thousand …"

"How?"

"By hiding them. By falsified passports and *Ausweis* documents. By what Negro Americans called 'the underground railroad' a hundred years ago. By planning …"

"And my part in all this, Pastor Trocmé?"

"General Sikorski said you were not only Jewish, but you were an expert in logistics…"

"If it gets this cold in mid-October, I shudder to think what it's like in winter," Varga remarked. He pulled his thick coat, which he was wearing over a Shetland sweater, tighter about him.

"Worse," Trocmé replied. "I'm glad you had a chance to meet my thirteen *responsables*. They've been the backbone of the parish as far as sheltering and hiding refugees. We meet every week to see where we've been and where we're going, and, as you saw, they not only have a deep understanding of what we're about, but I trust they were able to answer your every question."

"Monsieur Chazot referred to you as 'the great *responsable*.'"

Trocmé brushed off the flattery with a curt, "I feel more like the *governor* of a European circus. All is not always peace and harmony in Le Chambon. You hear all sorts of languages in the streets. You see all sorts of people: Christians, Jews, Westerners, Asiatics. The Cévenol School has converted this little village into a Babel of languages and cultures.

"One of the main problems is with the peasants on the outlying farms. They feel themselves to be economic outcasts with less influence than the refugees, while the refugees — students, and teachers, who consider themselves far more sophisticated than the 'natives,' get irritated by what they see as the slow pace of thinking and action. And the liberal attitudes of the Cévenol students and faculty clash with the three-hundred-year-old conservatism of those who've lived here all their lives."

"But it still works?" Varga asked.

"Yes, but only because Chambonnais, for whatever reason, manage to put aside their differences when it comes to rescuing innocent human beings. The presbytery and the temple could not have moved an inert mass of self-centered people into doing what's being done here. It's the houses, the homes in Le Chambon that make a village of refuge work.

"A family of refugees might come to town in winter," Trocmé continued. "The morning after their arrival they might find a wreath of holly leaning against their front door from an anonymous giver. Or a little boy might come to Miss Maber's door screaming in a high-pitched voice that the English teacher had better hide Henri because the police are after him. Miss Maber will calm the boy down, glance around to be sure no strangers have heard him, and then go straight to the house of someone known to have an empty room. Miraculous as it may seem, no one has ever turned a refugee away."

Varga and the pastor turned in to a well-heated small restaurant fronting on the Rue de la Grande Fontaine. Since coffee and chocolate were rare commodities in wartime Le Chambon, which was by no means wealthy in the best of times, Trocmé ordered tea and Colonel Varga signaled he would happily enjoy a cup of chicory.

"Are all of the refugees in private homes, André?" Stefan asked.

"No. Le Chambon is a community effort. There are different kinds of houses and different kinds of rescue activities. Some houses, like Crickets, are funded by the Quakers, and even by national governments like Sweden and Switzerland. We've already opened seven of them in and around the village. Flowery Hill is our most effective in starting the refuges on their journey to Switzerland. A large part of its funding comes from Cimade."

"The women's organization?"

"Uh-huh. They've actually formed teams to lead the Jews through the mountains to Geneva. Then we have *pensions*, small hotels and boarding houses. The one thing we need more than anything else at the moment, is the one thing we somehow haven't been able to attract, a qualified medical doctor."

At that moment, a young man of eighteen or so, with a thin scraggle of chinwhiskers approached the Pastor. "Pardon, Monsieur L'Pasteur," he said. "A note from the Cimade an hour ago. Their representative is waiting for a response at Flowery Hill. She said it was a matter of some urgency."

"Thank you, Matthieu," Trocmé said.

The pastor pored through the one-page missive, bade the young messenger to have a cup of tea in the kitchen, and said he would return with a message for the Cimade agent within ten minutes. He then turned to Varga. "I'm sorry for the interruption, Stefan," he said, "we were talking about whether you'd be willing to lend some assistance to our cause?"

"Andre, you don't have to ask whether I'm interested or not. Whatever time I have to devote to the cause — and as a soldier with no troops to command at the moment that's a lot of time. What do you need me to do?"

Trocmé smiled benignly. "As a matter of fact, something came into my hands this very moment which might interest you." He handed Varga the single sheet he'd just received:

"From Hagen2, Protectorate of Bohemia

To Cimade, Geneva

"Agent in place Berlin, American, masquerading as a Swedish foreign correspondent. Subject has acquired extremely sensitive information. She has been requested to remain in Berlin this weekend to attend a high-profile meeting of newspeople. Unknown to subject, extensive secret investigation by Sicherheitsdienst have been conducted over the past week. Believe subject's cover will not survive investigation as German intelligence intends to arrest her Monday noon. Urgent you get subject to safety before 0800 hours this coming Monday."

"Well?" he asked Varga. "I was told you were the expert in logistics."

"I trust Hagen2 means something to you?"

"Hagen2 means one of Cimade's agent in Olomouc, Moravia. My guess is that he or she would not communicate with Berlin, since the target would suspect she's being watched everywhere she goes. The Berlin agent has no idea of what is going on.

"Nor does Olomouc know who you are," Trocmé said. Is there any way you can exfiltrate her from Berlin?"

"Getting into the Reich is not the problem," Varga replied. "*Der liebe Gott steckt im Detail,*" he said, reverting to German.

"*Le bon Dieu est dans le detail,*" Trocmé riposted. "God – or the devil – is in the details."

29

Conseil d/Affairs des Nations
Confederation des Suisse
Hôtel Chanac de Pompadour
Ile-de-France. S.

14 October 1942

Honorable Ulrich Friedrich-Wilhelm Joachim von Ribbentrop
Minister of Foreign Affairs
Aussenpolitisches Amt der NSDAP
Hotel Adlon Annex
Unter den Linden, Berlin

Honored Herr von Ribbentrop:

My personal emissary, Stefan von Glarus und Varga, will be engaged in diplomatic business on my behalf in Berlin during the period 16-20 October. I ask that you and your associates kindly afford Herr Varga every diplomatic courtesy. *Vielen danke.*

> Yours,
> Mattias Dubigny
> Deputy Director of Foreign Affairs

14 October 1942

Fr. Hagen2
Prague, Protectorate of Bohemia

Dear Father Hagen,

My personal representative, Pastor Stefan von Glarus und Varga, will arrange to meet with you and Sister Gisella any time after 17 October, 1800 hours when he is expected to arrive at Anhalter Bahnhof. If you have not made contact by then, Pastor Varga will meet you outside the South Portico of the Berliner Dom, where he will serve as acolyte to the afternoon services. Pastor Varga is 1.8 m. tall, 40 years of age, and will be wearing appropriate clerical clothing. Thank you so much for your kind assistance. If he is not at either of these places, you may locate him outside the Hotel Fünf Mönche, Room 23.

Yours in Christ,
André Trocmé

"The Five Monks Hotel?"

"Yes, Stefan. Do you know Berlin at all?"

"Never been there."

"It's about as far down in class from the Adlon as you'll ever find, but it's entirely reputable and both Cimade and the American Friends have used it for at least five years. Here's a pocket map, which you should commit to memory."

"And the Berlin Operative?"

"Her real name is Lara. The note I sent to Hagen2 contains false information in the event it is discovered, which it most likely will be by the Sicherheitsdienst. Here is what you really need to know, and what Hagen2 will know through a Cimade intermediary ..."

"Lara?" Varga intoned softly. "I once met an American by that name. I wonder if ... no, I'm sure it's a mere coincidence ..."

October 15, 1942

"Varga checked his wristwatch. Eight a.m. Two hours to go before the *Koblenz* left the dock for its 23-hour voyage to Hamburg. Perfect timing. The ship would arrive at nine the next morning. Allowing for the four-hour bus ride to Berlin, he should arrive at *Sydsvenska Dagbladet's* Berlin offices between two and three hours before Lara got off work at 5:00 p.m. His papers were in order, and he felt reasonably safe. Last night, he had arrived at Memel, which, until it had been ceded to Germany had been Lithuania's chief port, Klaipėda.

His letter to the German authorities from Pastor Trocmé could not have been better timed, since the *Koblenz* had been commissioned by the German Foreign Office to transport more than a hundred Vojvodina Ethnic Germans, many of them men between twenty-five and forty, back to the Fatherland, even though most had never seen German soil during their lifetimes.

When the Axis powers had overrun Yugoslavia in 1941, many of these residents, who called themselves *Shwowe,* had joined the Nazis' hastily-established Seventh Waffen SS Volunteer Mountain Division, Prinz Eugen. But the tide of war had started to turn with the accession of Josip Broz Tito. The Ethnic Germans' property was confiscated and their Yugoslav citizenship revoked at precisely the time when the *Wehrmacht* needed additional troops to fight Stalin's forces in the Soviet Union. Thus, the propitious timing of the *Koblenz* and its sister transports.

Varga had allowed himself a three-day growth of beard, and a somewhat tattered clerical garb, which made him look a good ten years older than his true age, and walked with a stiff, bent gait to hide the fact that he was taller than most of his 'compatriots.'

At precisely 8:45 a.m., not a minute before and not a minute later, the dock in Memel was packed with Germans, their baggage, their cuckoo clocks, their dachshunds and German shepherds, and a band to play rousing Swabian patriotic anthems. At 8:55, the assemblage strutted up the gangplank, herded, like so many sheep, by *Wehrmacht* noncommissioned officers who had spent the last fortnight training new inductees at a camp outside Kaunas. German newsreel cameramen, their Zeiss and Leica instruments grinding away, were very much in evidence.

As he ascended the platform leading to the deck, Varga felt himself hailed by a sharp, commanding voice. "Excuse me, Father, your papers please?"

Momentarily unnerved, Varga recovered quickly and smiled broadly. "Of course, Herr Obersturmbannführer," he said, promoting the major to lieutenant colonel and giving an enthusiastic Nazi salute. He withdrew the letter from Prefect Savic, replete with its gold-embossed seal and purple franking stamps, and handed it to the officer.

Without giving the document, which had been printed in Bratislava's O.S.S. field office the week before, a second glance, the major snapped, "*Alles in Ordnung, Vater,*" and handed the letter back to the earnest-looking cleric. "Fine work you are doing for our long-forgotten brothers. Have a pleasant journey."

As he glanced at the myriad passengers crowding the deck, Varga felt, rather than saw, a deep and patient anger. They were glad to be 'going home,' for the newsreel cameras, but among themselves he heard barely concealed utterings of discontent as they promised one another that they would be 'going back soon enough.' At which time, certain scores would be settled, many of them with Jews who had 'appropriated' their homes.

Lieutenant Colonel Varga had no desire to be singled out or caught, because he knew that as a *Czechoslovakian* cleric, while he was a Slavic cousin, he was by no means a Serbian brother, thus not to be trusted. As a result, he kept to himself at a point farthest from the majority of the crowd, assiduously reading and mouthing the words from his book of Scriptures.

A hefty young fellow, a decade younger than "Pastor von Glarus und Varga," wanted to strike up a conversation and offered the religious leader a greeting. Varga stared at the man, as though her were intruding on a world of private anguish, and mumbled, "I watched as they came through our village. They took … everything."

As Stefan watched, the man's expression went from surprise to pained sympathy, to righteous anger. "I understand, Father," he said, laying a great paw of a hand on the cleric's shoulder. "But in God's great universe, things will even out. *Heil Hitler*. It was meant as a very warm human gesture. If only this sympathetic peasant with brain to match, knew what Stefan Varga was thinking. …

A calm sea. A comforting sea.

Life aboard the *Koblenz* was tightly organized. The numerous officials in attendance seemed benign, meaning to ease the transition of the passengers into German life. His processing — a matter of saying yes or no — given a temporary identity card and told to report to proper authorities wherever he settled, was perfunctory. Did he have any notion of where he wished to live? Family in Germany? Friends? A church to which he would be assigned? "Don't worry, old fellow," more than one of them tried to comfort him. "You're in good hands now."

The public address system was constantly at work. A dachshund had been discovered urinating in the crew's quarters. An uplifting message of welcome from Dr. Goebbels. The *Winterhilfe* charity was stationed at Table VII just before the bow. Those with last names beginning A through K should report to the dining room promptly at 1:00 p.m. N through Z at 2:30. To promote the appetite, a songfest would begin in precisely twenty minutes on the foredeck. The singing would be led by the well-known second soprano, Irmgard Von Schmiedkampf from the Augsburg State Opera Company and the well-respected baritone, SS Untersturmführer Heinz-Maria Holz of the Okenheim Soldiers' Chorus, two inspirational artists who had volunteered to accompany the voyage and join their fellow *Volk* in singing some of the grand old songs.

Varga stood for the rousing performance of *Deutschland Über Alles,* which signaled the beginning of the performance, then watched the breasts of the second soprano swell mightily with patriotism Almost all of the passengers were deeply affected by the singing. Both men and women shed unashamed tears. There was a kind of joyous agony on their faces as they raised their voices together. The performance closed with Germany's most famous of all prewar songs, which, Varga knew, had actually been written in Austria.

> *Stille Nacht, heilige Nacht*
> *Alles schläft; einsam wacht*
> *Nur das traute hochheilige Paar*
> *Holder Knabe im lockingen Haar*
> *Schlaf in himmlischer Ruh!*
> *Schlaf in himmlischer Ruh!*

The mass rendition of *Silent Night,* a Christmas carol familiar to all, was extraordinary, sung with great and tender feeling as the ship rumbled through flat Baltic waters.

Varga maintained his neutral appearance, nodding in time and mumbling the old words to himself, but his internal reaction to the performance was unutterable fear. It was the instinctive passionate unity of the singers that frightened him. You couldn't find three Jews in the world who would agree on what it meant to be Jewish. But there were fifty million of these people who knew exactly what it was to be German, even though the majority of human beings on this deck had never set foot in Germany.

Something was wrong. It took only moments for Varga to decipher what it was. Obviously, they had suffered injustice without end. That was plain to see on every face. They swayed and they sang, held hands, wept, and together formed a wall of common emotion: nostalgia, regret, self-pity, resentment, hatred … The words bounced around inside him. None of them right. None of them wrong. None of them mattered. What he did know was that these human beings were poisoned with themselves. And the rest of the world would suffer for it.

As the sun set, the voice on the public address system changed subtly from cheerleading camaraderie to reverence and awe. "There has been a remarkable change of plans. The ship will be met at Hamburg by a train comprised of only first-class coaches. All passengers will proceed to Berlin where the Führer himself will address each of you. Please do not be concerned for the friends and family who will come to the dock to meet you. There will be plenty of room for everybody. *Heil Hitler!*"

Next morning, a wall of cheering Germans stood to either side of the disembarking passengers, an aisle of welcome as effective as barbed wire, that lined the way to the railroad station. And thus it was that Pastor Stefan von Glarus und Varga came to Berlin.

30

Lieutenant Colonel Stefan Varga emerged from Tempelhof Airport looking totally different from the weary and decrepit passenger who'd endured the long journey on the *Koblenz*. When he'd arrived at the aerodrome, he'd immediately shaved, then removed the tickets from his briefcase, proving he'd taken a direct train from Lyon to Geneva, where he'd boarded an AB Aerotransport DC-3, which had a daily flight from Geneva to Berlin and thence to Stockholm, returning the following day.

From Tempelhof, he'd taken a taxi to the Fünf Mönche, which appeared from the outside to be the kind of hotel that rented rooms by the hour. However, once inside, the Five Monks seemed well-kept, and Herr von Glarus und Varga was directed to the second floor, where Room 23 awaited.

No sooner had Varga entered the room, he found a clean, freshly-pressed outfit which he would wear when he left the hotel, and an unsigned note on the bedstead: "Leave hotel by rear entrance. A gray BMW 321 will be waiting at the back of the building and will transport you to your destination. – Cimade."

Varga, who had learned to expect the unexpected, was not surprised by the message. The BMW, half a block away, fired up its engine and slowly approached. The driver, a slender, bullet-headed man about sixty, nodded once and stopped beside him. Varga walked around the rear end of the car and entered on the right front passenger side. Without a word, the driver pulled into the alley and drove to the nearest main street. Twenty minutes later, the car entered a distinctly upper-class neighborhood. The tree-lined streets here were clean and quiet, and from the looks of the elegant stone-and-brick three-story buildings set back some distance from the curbs, Varga concluded that the elite of the National Socialists resided in places like this.

"Charlottenburg," the anything but loquacious driver remarked. "*Alte reichturm,*" he continued in a neutral, but not particularly impressed, voice. "Old wealth."

As they approached an intersection, Varga read a discreetly-placed street sign. 1 Giesebrechtstrasse. The BMW cruised slowly past number 11, a faded yellow five-story office building.

"Here is where Fräulein Nygard works," the driver said. A small, discreet sign announced this was the Berlin headquarters of *Sydsvenska Dagbladet, Malmö.*

The car continued to the end of the street, then turned right, into a busier boulevard. A sign on the outside of a narrow building sandwiched between two much larger buildings read *Schlafenszeit Residenz Hotel.* The driver nodded as he pulled up to a curb adjacent to the lodging, but said nothing.

"Ah, Sturmbannführer von Glarus und Varga," the obsequious toady at the front desk said brightly, clicking his heels. He handed an old-fashioned key with the number 307 to Varga. "Enjoy your stay. *Heil Hitler!*"

The room was small, but not cramped. Varga hefted his overnight bag onto the double bed, then approached the dresser to hang his extra pair of corduroy slacks and tan open-necked shirt. As he opened it, he thought he must be in the wrong room. There were two outfits hanging from the closet bar. The first was a Geneva gown of the type universally worn by Protestant ministers. It was the second outfit that truly surprised him. Pinned to the second outfit was another unsigned note. "This may be more appropriate, considering ..."

October 16, 5:00 p.m.

Lara, who'd been using the name Nygard for the past eight months, watched the minute hand on the hall clock as it crept toward the 12. Almost 5:00 o'clock. While she was slightly annoyed that her weekly trip to Olomouc had been canceled, she was more than a little excited, and a bit nervous.

This morning, she'd received a memorandum from Colonel Walter Schellenberg: "Mademoiselle Nysrom: An important meeting among high-ranking senior SS officers will be held this evening at 1800 hours this evening. Request you cancel your plans for this weekend and appear as one of only three foreign correspondents invited to attend. You will be escorted by a member of my staff. This may well result in your elevation in the council of the Overseas Deutche Press Confederation. Regards. *Heil Hitler!* – Walter Schellenberg, *Sonderbevollmächtiger* von Heinrich Himmler."

5:05 p.m.

As Lara exited the front door of her employer's office, she did not see anyone else in the vicinity until she was grabbed from behind by her right arm. She turned sharply to accost whoever it was, and stifled a gasp as she beheld an SS major, wearing the current grey-green uniform of the *Allgemeine Schutzstaffel.*"

"Wha—?" she instinctively blurted out.

"Keep walking," the man, who was several inches taller than she, said brusquely. "You're supposed to be attending a private press conference, and as far as you know, I am escorting you there."

"But I know perfectly well how to get there without your assistance," she said peremptorily, recovering her composure. "How do I know you are who you say you are? For all I know, you could be a kidnapper." She reached into her purse and withdrew a police whistle.

As she looked around and lifted it to blow, the man next to her said, in quiet, controlled English, "Please don't do that, Fräulein Nygard. That could well be the last sound you'd make as a free woman."

Despite the chill that came over her as she heard his words, Lara felt a much stronger emotion as she looked more carefully at the man beside her. *I've seen him somewhere before. Not here, but …*

The SS major did not once raise his voice, nor did he tighten his grip on her arm, but said softly, as if speaking to a child, "Fräulein Nygard, please understand that I mean you no harm. I am not who or what you think I am. Now, you can trust me or not, but all I can say is that I have no intention of escorting you to the press conference, nor anywhere else near the *Sicherheitsdienst*, the foreign ministry, or the Adlon Hotel."

Suddenly, her face colored and her fear faded entirely as recognition dawned. "You're … you're …"

At that moment, a prewar Skoda, its color a mixture of dirt and rust, with dents on both front fenders, pulled up adjacent to where they were walking. A graybeard with a luxuriant moustache that looked twenty years out of date looked up and down the street. Noticing no traffic at that hour, he pulled up the handbrake, opened the driver's door, and walked around the car to where the woman and the Schutzstaffel officer stood, and opened the passenger door. Lara entered the car, noticing that her escort had unhanded her and gotten into the driver's seat.

The older man approached Varga, who said a few words to him in flawless German, and handed him a piece of paper. "That's the address where we're going. It's only a few blocks away.

AN HOUR LATER, THE SCHLAFENSZEIT RESIDENZ HOTEL

"And that's the 'elevation' they would have given you – East."

"But … but … how did you even find out?"

"There are those very few right-thinking people in Germany who aren't taken in by the big, bad wolf at the door. Cimade, for example, and … others, like the Polish military-in-exile."

Now, if you'd please sit in this not-so-comfortable chair… "

He approached Lara with a hairbrush and a pair of barber shears. "Time to say goodbye to your beautiful long hair for awhile. Also, your most attractive appearance."

Before she had a chance to answer, Stefan Varga showed that among his talents, being a beautician was not one of them. By a combination of snip-cut and electric razor, within twenty minutes, Lara's pate was now almost as short as a man's haircut. Shortly afterward, she felt some kind of liquid being massaged into what was left of her hair, and when she opened her eyes to look, she found what had been shimmering dark brown to be an outrageously brassy orange-red, the product of a very inept dye job.

As if this weren't enough, Lara's skin, both on her face and on her hands, was artificially aged and roughened by powdery pancake makeup and dark cream, which highlighted her veins. Finally ….

"You wouldn't dare! How *could* you?" she grinned, as she looked at her impossibly long blue-green polished nails.

"If you don't mind my saying so, my dear," Varga said, "to quote an Americanism, you look like the original twenty-five-cent piece."

Shortly thereafter, each of them glanced out the third-story window to the street below. Dusk had given way to twilight and then to nightfall. The pristine sidewalks of this section of town were lit by old-fashioned yellow sodium streetlamps, which did not seem out of place in this genteel neighborhood, despite the militaristic aura which had cast a pall over Hitler's *Germania*. At this hour, the streets were eerily deserted. As was becoming increasingly obvious as the war dragged on, the populace retreated early in the evening to their homes, to their clandestine assignations, or to the artificial gaiety of tightly-regulated cabarets and nightclubs, which would have seemed as risqué as a Sunday school a scant decade before.

"Stefan, while I can't tell you how much I appreciate what you've already done for me, I'm still in the middle of Berlin. Any idea how I can leave Doctor Goebbels' heaven on earth – and by that, I don't mean East?"

"I just took another look from our window," Stefan said, pointing to a Mercedes Benz W136, the Gestapo's favored vehicle, which was rolling very slowly down Giesebrechtstrasse. "One thing is for certain. They suspect something already. I suggest we decide what we're going to do very quickly, because they'll most likely investigate every building on this block within an hour."

7:20 P.M.

SS First Lieutenant Georg Gmeinde found it unnecessary to flash his credentials to the night clerk, whose face had turned ashen at the officer's peremptory tone. "We saw two of them enter the hotel a little over an hour ago."

He whipped out Lara's photograph.

"*Jawohl*, Obersturmführer," the clerk replied. "This one I can recognize for certain. A very attractive young woman. Can you describe the second person?"

"We have no positive identification. Our information is that he — or she — may have been a bit taller than the woman in the photo."

At that moment, an SS Sturmbannführer, two ranks above the lieutenant, entered the hotel, his arm holding that of an obviously hard-used *nachtvogel*, a woman of the night. He glanced briefly at the captain's name tag. "*Alles in ordnung*, Leutnant Gmeinde. I trust you are looking for Lara Nygard, the Swedish reporter?"

"Indeed we are, Major."

"Is this woman she?"

The lieutenant looked at the photograph, then at the disheveled woman, who wore a very short, tight skirt and a sweater two sizes too small which did nothing to hide her pronounced breasts.

"Does this look like the same woman?" the major asked again.

"You tell this 'gentleman' who I am," the woman snapped at the night clerk, who had been briefed barely five minutes before.

"She is not the same woman shown in the picture," the clerk replied.

"Do you know who she is?" the lieutenant pursued.

"I'd rather not say."

"Leutnant Gmeinde didn't ask *who* she is," the major snapped, impatiently. "He asked if you *know* who she is."

The night clerk hesitated for several moments, glanced at the obvious prostitute, then stammered quietly, "I ... I do."

"Well?" This from the lieutenant, who saw by the four squares on the tall man's collar insignia that he was two ranks above his own.

"Answer the question, Sachbearbeiter," the major said. "We're not interested in *what* she is. We're men of the world and that seems obvious to all of us. And we're not hunting some *nafke* who'll give us the clap," he continued dismissively.

"You won't arrest her if I tell you?"

"Not unless she is Fräulein Nygard or someone in league with her."

The woman glared balefully as each of the men in turn, but said nothing.

"Her name, or at least the name I know her by, is Malina Fenstermacher. She's been 'working' this area for at least five years, and I've seen her in this hotel more than two dozen times. I have no idea where she lives or anything else about her."

"Is this true?" the lieutenant asked the woman.

"Fuck off!" the tart lashed out at him. "I don't have to tell you a goddam thing. If you're looking for State secrets, you can arrest me and you'll get nothing more than I've already said. If you're looking for some action …"

In response, the major slapped her, not particularly hard. "Well, Leutnant Gmeinde?"

"Waste of time, *Sturmbannführer,*" Gmeinde replied. "In the time we've spent here, the real Fräulein Nygard could be halfway to Köln. What about the other one?"

Lara answered bitterly. "*He's* probably halfway to Köln by now with two hundred Reichsmarks that should have been mine, thank you very much. And *you* 'gentlemen' have probably screwed up my business for the next week. If there's nothing more to say, if you'll excuse me, I'd be happy to let you boys play with yourselves."

And with that, the tart performed a mock curtsy and left the hotel.

Embarrassed, Oberleutnant Gmeinde addressed his superior in a subdued tone. "Best we just let this thing go, Sturmbannführer. Shall we canvas the rest of the block?"

"Probably a good idea, Leutnant. *Heil Hitler.*"

That night, Stefan and Lara, who'd managed to escape Berlin by taking separate trains to the outlying town of Werder-am-Havel, met at a farmhouse run by Cimade volunteers, where they had additional time to plan their proposed escape from the Nazi state.

31

6:30 A.M. THE NEXT MORNING

Stefan Varga awakened to horrendous shrieks and screams, followed by intermittent piteous moans. Wide awake in an instant, he grabbed the sidearm next to his bed, and rushed into the adjoining bedroom, ready for confrontation.

The scene which confronted and concurrently horrified him was a writhing, screaming Lara. Perspiration was running down her forehead and the odor in the room was one of consummate fear. She alternately grabbed her midsection and twisted her body into grotesque positions. Attempts to quiet her screaming, mewling, and moaning only resulted in making things worse.

"A doctor, any doctor, the pain … the pain is excruciating. Help me! Please help me!

I'm dying and I don't care …" She doubled up and Varga froze in his spot.

Moments later, Varga ran out the door, banging on the door of the Cimade house until a woman in her fifties, devoid of makeup, her eyes filled with sleep, answered the door.

"I'm sorry, Frau … Fräulein … but my companion is in desperate agony and we've no one to turn to."

"I understand," she said. "Werder has very few medical practitioners in these times. All of them must be screened and approved by the National Socialist government and they donate a substantial portion of the time they have to war effort."

"Going to Berlin is out of the question," Varga replied. "You know of our mission …"

"Of course. The only exception I know who might be willing to risk his life in attending to Miss Nygard is an assistant clerk to the local veterinarian."

"The local —?"

"You heard me right, Colonel. It's an impossible choice, of course, but when you consider the alternative facing this poor young woman..."

"You're right, of course. How do I find this person? Every moment counts."

"I have the telephone number where he's staying. I'll have him on the phone within moments. The address of the veterinary clinic is …"

"Mr. Hale, I can't thank you enough," Varga said, and sincerely, as he entered the less-than-impressive surroundings."

"It is my privilege. The patient is …"

"Thank God you were able to see her. How did you get the morphine?"

In response, the clerk said nothing but signaled them, the woman from Cimade and Stefan, to follow him into a small, barren room on which there was a single bed. "You must understand, we have no staff here on a Saturday morning. The veterinary office is not open on the weekend. It would not have been a good idea to ask anyone associated with the clinic to be here.

On entering the room, they saw that Lara lay semiconscious on the bed, but her writhing has stopped and she was silent. Varga watched in undisguised amazement as the 'clerk' gently and expertly prodded the area in the lower right side of her abdomen. After a few moments, he spoke quietly to Varga and the woman from Cimade. "I'm fairly certain it's acute appendicitis."

"Is it fatal, Mister … Mister —?" Varga asked.

"Hopefully, the appendix has not burst," the other man said. "Appendicitis is a serious medical emergency. If the appendix has burst, it can cause a deadly infection. Since we have no medicine in this clinic to treat such an infection, we can only pray that the appendix is whole. But it is absolutely imperative that we perform surgery to remove the appendix immediately."

"Is there anyone in the vicinity who can perform such a surgery?" Varga asked.

"Almost no one I know of," the man replied. "That means you'll have to trust me."

"You?" Varga rejoined. "How can you —?"

"You'll simply have to trust me and trust God," the clerk replied.

"There's really no alternative," Varga said. "If we do nothing, it's handing Lara a painful death sentence." Turning to the clerk, he said, "We've never even met before and now you're asking us to trust you with a woman's life."

"And I added that you must trust God as well."

"Very well, then."

"You may assist me if you wish."

"How in the world can I do that?"

"Just hand me certain tools when I ask you to. We've already administered morphine, which is the strongest anaesthetic I know of. We may have to give her more if the current dose starts to weaken."

With that, the man reached into an ancient doctor's bag, which Varga had not previously noticed. He saw a number of instruments which he would never have expected a mere clerk to have: medical instruments that appeared pristine and remarkably well cared-for. The would-be surgeon asked his two guests to don white aprons, masks, and hair nets. Without a word, he glanced at the drip tube, administered a small additional dose of morphine, then scrubbed his hands thoroughly with antiseptic soap before sheathing his hands in latex gloves.

He addressed Varga and the Cimade woman matter-of-factly. "I will cut into the lower right-hand side of her belly, find the appendix, and remove it. If there are no complications, the operation should take less than an hour and she'll recover in a few days. If the appendix has ruptured …"

He stopped speaking, signaled Varga to hand him a #15 scalpel, and without further ado commenced making deft, sharp strokes that were so thin and bloodless that the latter hardly noticed Lara's abdominal cavity open. The clerk searched with sure hands until he found a finger-shaped tube, some four inches long. As he nodded, Varga reached into the doctor's bag, extracted a pair of surgical scissors, and handed them to the older man.

With a sharp, apparently painless snip, the clerk removed the appendix. He expelled a sign of relief, and breathed, "Thank God. Swollen, but had not ruptured." The remainder of the operation was anticlimactic.

"I think it best that she remains hidden in the Cimade house, would you not agree?" he asked the woman, who nodded gratefully. "It's best that I not be seen in your company. I'll come to the house in about an hour."

"Will you take tea with us?" she asked.

"I think that's a good idea," he said, smiling for the first time. With all the excitement that's gone on at this early hour, I seem to have forgotten I've not had breakfast."

"So, you're not a clerk?"

"Correct, Colonel Varga."

"If you'll excuse my saying so, you sound rather highly educated to be an assistant clerk in a veterinary office, Mister Hale."

"Thank you for your observation," the man said. "It's not frequently I hear kind words like that."

"I don't understand —" Varga started to say.

"Perhaps if I told you that Hale is not my real name. If you add a 'v' and an 'i' —"

"I still don't understand." Suddenly the shock hit him. "Your name … that is … you are …"

"The lowest of the low in the National Socialist pecking order. And, I daresay, fortunate to still be among the living. Chaim Halevi."

"So, if I may be so presumptuous, you are … were … a bit more than an assistant clerk?"

An hour later, the three of them were still seated in the alcove adjacent to Lara's bedroom-cum-recovery area.

"I was born fifty years ago in Pressburg. It was called Bratislava then, but our new overlords changed the name back. Just before the war started – the Great War – I moved to Germany, which, at that time, was one of the few places in Europe where a Jew had almost unlimited opportunities if one were so disposed. Just after the War started, I was admitted to Charité-Medical University of Berlin. Four years later, I'd taken a degree in neurosurgery."

"So your 'clerkship' is a sham?" Varga asked.

"My 'clerkship' is a way of preserving my life," Halevi rejoined, "although I would hardly have thought I'd end up where I am today. As I said, Germany was the land of opportunity for Jews during the Weimar Republic. Would you mind if we walked for awhile? The Havel is lovely at this time of year, and I try to exercise a bit each today to try to forget where I am and what I've become," he continued, sadly.

"So, you were the Dean of the Medical School until 1934?"

"Fourteen years. Until the Nazis came to power and practically every Jewish academic was peremptorily told his position had been filled by someone friendlier to German national aspirations. Translation, Jews need not apply."

"What happened then, Doctor Halevi?"

"Hannah and I had been married eight years. Hans was six, Leah five, and as more doors closed every day, we discussed the possibility of moving. Despite my religion, Jews, particularly educated Jews, particularly qualified surgeons, seemed to be welcome anywhere else in the world. We moved to Holland, where I taught at the University of Amsterdam Medical School for a year. It was a good year, but I missed the order and organization of the German mind, the cleanliness of its streets, and I believed, naively, that National Socialism would burn itself out and we would return to a rational life. After all, this was the land of Goethe, Schiller, and Beethoven. Where would the universities, the concert halls, and the art museums be without us?"

The two men walked in silence for several moments, allowing the quiet, slow drift of the Havel, a tributary of the Elbe, to infuse them with its quiet.

"Are your wife and children still in Germany?" Varga asked, not allowing for the possibility that they might not even be alive, or that they had been sent "East."

"They are," Halevi said. "But they are in hiding in a tiny, anonymous town just over the border in what used to be called Austria. I can't reveal their whereabouts, and, if you'll forgive me, not even to anyone, not even to you. We correspond through an intermediary and only once a month. It's been a year-and-a-half. And I need not tell you how difficult it's been…"

"And you are still twenty miles from the Reich's capital?"

"Yes. I believe the administration is quite aware of where I am and what I'm doing. I believe they are hoping I'll break, that I'll try to make contact with my family, and if I do, I have no doubt that the four of us will be on the next train to Poland. I don't have to tell you *where* in Poland."

"So, for the time being you are?"

"Hopefully too small a fish for them to merit attention. At least for now."

"Let me get this straight. The young woman was employed by the Haganah, a clandestine Jewish organization operating out of Palestine?"

"Not quite 'employed' by the Haganah, but for now that's close emough."

"And you?"

"I am a lieutenant colonel in the ZWZ, the *Związek Walki Zbrojnej*, attached to the Polish Government in Exile in London."

"I see," Dr. Halevi continued. "And you are in charge of spiriting Fräulein Nygard, who was about to be arrested as a spy, out of Germany to France?"

"Not to *France*, Doctor Halevi. Our information convinces me that Germany intends to invade the unoccupied zone and take over Vichy France, within the next month. The place I'm talking about is a particular community in the Haute-Loire, a Protestant community which has become a safe haven for Jews."

"In the middle of Nazi France? But how can that be?"

"In ways you can hardly imagine. Miss Nygard, not her real name, will be absolutely safe there. I tell you all this for a reason, Doctor."

Varga sketched a not particularly detailed map of France. In the south-central segment, he made a dot, around which he drew a circle. "This is its approximate location. Like you, it's been pretty well ignored by the Reich. You wouldn't believe the number and caliber of Jews currently living there. Among others, they've got professors from Europe's finest universities and more than a thousand of the most talented people I've ever met. What they do not have is a practicing physician of your rank."

The surgeon's eyes lit up as he sensed the immensity of what Varga was proposing. "Why me?" he asked."

"Because you saved Lara Nygard's life. The Talmud says, 'Whoever saves a single life is considered to have saved the whole world.' Could I do less than offer you and your family the same salvation you gave Ms. Nygard?"

"My and *my family?*" Halevi said. "How can I even consider that possible?"

"Haven't our people always believed that if you dare the impossible, you may well achieve it?"

"Wait a moment, Colonel. Might I dare suggest …?"

"I am. Szymon Vaynshtok. Wilno. And as fervent a *Yehudi* as you. Doctor Halevi, join us embracing a new life, courtesy of God, by reclaiming who you were — and what you, Hannah, Hans and Leah — can and will be again."

32

October 18, 1942 – Cimade House, Werder

"It was so good of you to see us on such short notice, Mevrouw Zimmermann, particularly since you came from Berlin on a Sunday morning when I'm sure you had better things to do."

"You're very gracious, Colonel Varga. It does not go unnoticed that you addressed me as I would have been called back home. I felt it was the least I could do. I was born and raised in South Africa. Whether we're subjects of King George or followers of Oom Paul Krüger, we learned early on that the prey animals have learned to protect themselves from the predators by working cooperatively together."

The leader of Sweden's Cimade contingent and a devout adherent of the anti-Nazi Church of Sweden, Hendrika Zimmermann had come to Germany as part of a trade delegation ten days before. Born more than sixty years before and barely five feet tall, her steel-gray hair styled in an unfashionable bun, she projected fearless, barely masked contempt for the current Nazi regime. However, Germany needed Swedish neutrality and, even more important, its iron ore, and so each co-existed uncomfortably with the other.

"As I understand it, Colonel Varga, you, yourself, have no need of stealth, since you are under Swiss diplomatic protection. Miss Nygard's situation is a bit different. Despite her claim as a Swedish citizen, she has recently been portrayed as a person living here under false pretenses and guilty of treason, to boot, while Doctor Halevi is a 'U-boat Jewish illegal,' who manages to survive in the National Socialist paradise, surfacing only occasionally, and then only at the sufferance of those looking to make Berlin *Judenfrei.*"

"That's not entirely true, Mevrouw Zimmermann," Varga said. She's actually a citizen of the one belligerent that Germany dare not mess with, masquerading as a Swedish reporter from Malmö."

"If you'll pardon my asking Mevrouw, how many organizations are presently assisting the 'prey?'" Lara asked.

"Many more than you might imagine, Miss Nygard.

"What about the American O.S.S.?" This from Varga.

"Officially, they don't exist. Unofficially, they'd probably be the best ones to spirit Doctor Halevi's family out of the Reich and into Switzerland."

Mrs. Zimmermann lit up an American Lucky Strike cigarette and passed the pack around to the others, each of whom declined. She inhaled deeply and emitted several short puffs, forming smoke rings. "Dreadful habit, that," she said, "but after enjoying an early morning and a late-night smoke for so many years, I can't — and don't particularly want to — break it."

"I trust you have an idea of how to get Lara and Dr. Halevi out of Germany?"

"I do, Colonel Varga. The next 'Operation Quiet Exit' will take place tomorrow night, under the command of my friend and colleague, Baroness Hilde von Nordin und Drakenberg."

"A baroness, Mevrouw?"

"Actually, yes and your friends couldn't ask for a better-placed guardian. She's a descendant of an old, noble Swedish family that migrated to Germany at least two centuries ago. She won two gold medals for the present regime in the 1936 Olympics, and she's been wildly popular with both the high-and-mighties as well as the ordinary *volk* since that time. She's Church of Sweden and views the *nouveau powerful* with undisguised contempt, but they dare not touch her, first, because her popularity parallels that of Generalfeldmarschall Rommel and Maestro Furtwängler, and second, because she knows everything there is to know — and many things they wish she *didn't* know — about some of the highest of the higher-ups."

"And how will this work?"

"We'll talk about it a little later. For now, here is where Dr. Halevi and Miss Nygard will be — where they had *better* be — tomorrow night ..."

October 19, 1942

Late that afternoon, a striking, blonde young woman took the train from Berlin. She got off at Frohnau and walked north through the attractive suburb. Its lush lawns were now faded and covered with dead leaves. The crisp, cold air hastened Baroness Hilde von Nordin und Drakenberg's steps. There was almost no movement on the streets. She'd been worried about encountering patrols, but she'd been assured there would be none, and there were none by 6:30, when twilight had descended.

A mile-and-a-half beyond the town, she entered the beginning of a forest. The baroness turned off and walked into the woods. Less than two hundred yards in, she found the people. Ten of them, including a woman of indeterminate years with outrageously reddish-orange, close-cropped hair and a remarkably pretty face, and a man as old as her father, who carried a well-worn leather satchel. The baroness had been told by Hendrika Zimmermann they would be arriving from Werder-am-Havel, several miles to the west.

Hilde felt a momentary chill, as she espied a man of forty in the uniform of an SS major, standing quietly at the rear of the group. While he appeared to have a strong, confident bearing, he did not appear to be menacing.

"Don't worry, Hilde," Frau Zimmermann had warned her offhandedly earlier in the day. "He'll look like everything he isn't. He's a Polish lieutenant colonel named Stefan Varga, who'll be an extra pair of eyes and ears, and perhaps a bit of insurance, just in case there are real bad fellows in the neighborhood."

It was dark now, but not so dark that Baroness von Nordin und Drakenberg couldn't see them. She motioned them to come close. As she approached them, she noticed that the six who were not of the Werder group were of all ages. They looked haggard and badly frightened, and pressed tightly together, as though taking comfort from their proximity.

"Try to walk very carefully," Hilde began. "Look down and take care not to stumble or step on anything that might emit a noise. Don't walk on the road. Stay in the woods. Don't crowd. Just follow the person in front of you." She paused, then continued. "This is the last short step to freedom. Be very careful."

None of them said a word. All of them nodded in unison.

They walked for a mile in the woods. The "SS major" trailed, some ten feet behind them. The column moved on, very quietly, but to Hilde their footfalls sounded like the pounding of tympani. At last, they came to a clearing. The baroness held up her hand and they stopped. Then, she beckoned and they came closer. Pointing across the clearing, she whispered, "Look."

In the broken light, they could see a tiny shack next to some railroad tracks at a point where a dirt road intersected the tracks.

"You're to hide in the woods on the other side, a hundred yards from that shack. When the train comes, stay hidden until someone fetches you. You'll be told what to do. Now move out, one at a time, and God be with you."

One by one they crossed the clearing and disappeared into the woods on the other side. At last, all was still, but Hilde von Nordin und Drakenberg felt uneasy. Even though the operation had been planned carefully, it did not seem logical that they should get away with it so easily. There were forced-labor camps in the area. The laborers were forever breaking out and their German overlords forever tracked them with dogs. If that happened tonight, the dogs could pick up the group's scent.

Hilde, herself, had been instructed to retrace her steps immediately after the operation, to be sure no one had followed them. *Thank God for the extra pair of eyes and ears. Certainly it would be difficult, if not impossible, to determine that he was not what he appeared to be.* If she encountered a patrol, she'd been told to sidetrack it somehow, so that she could divert the enemy from the people in the woods.

Momentarily, the leader of the expedition wondered who they were. Most of them were probably Jews, but a few of them may have been political dissidents. *How wildly terror and hope must be warring in their minds. They know nothing of what will happen — only that they're being smuggled out of Germany.*

It would happen any time now. A freight train, too old, too decrepit, and too slow to be of any use in the war effort, bound for the north of Germany, would make an unscheduled stop on the desolate stretch of track that cut through the woods. Hilde heard a soft, mournful toot as the tired engine slowed and wheezed as it came to a stop.

Suddenly, a group of men, whom the baroness and her charges had neither seen nor heard, rushed from the woods and opened one of the boxcars. As quietly as they could, which seemed to Hilde like the roar of ten thousand spectators at a Nazi rally, they broke the seals on a number of large crates and carefully pried them open. They removed the furniture in the crates, which they threw from the boxcar.

Moments later, the ten people, other than the 'SS major' and the baroness, ran from the woods toward the train. The men who had broken the seals and thrown out the furniture lifted the fugitives into the boxcar and gently whispered instructions to them to get inside the open crates. Concurrently, the 'railroad workers,' moved other things into the crates: chamber pots, lest the crates would 'leak' when the 'passengers' attended to their natural needs; sufficient food and water for the journey; extra ballast, since the attendants knew that the human cargo weighed far less than the furniture which had been offloaded and thrown to the ground. If the train were stopped and the 'light' crates were discovered, it would bring the entire operation to naught.

Once everything was in place and the 'new' cargo ensconced in the crates, the men who'd been responsible for what had happened so far, would nail the containers up once more. Counterfeit seals would replace those that had been broken. The men jumped from the boxcar and closed the door. Less than ten minutes after it had stopped, the superannuated engine hooted softly and moved down the track.

"What happens now?" Varga whispered to Hilde.

"The train is bound for Lübeck. Tomorrow morning, everything will be loaded aboard a freighter. Next day, they'll be unloaded in Sweden."

"And the missing furniture?"

"It was the property of Swedish diplomats and their families bound for home after a tour of duty in Berlin or wherever they'd been posted in the Reich. As expected, the Nazis gave the outlanders permission to ship their household goods back to Sweden. Of course, since it had been stolen or lost and presumably destroyed, those Swedes to whom it belonged would be compensated."

Varga looked down at the pile of furniture. "But certainly you'd need the cooperation of the train crew?"

"Easy enough," Hilde replied. "The crew has been told nothing of the plan. They'd simply been asked to stop the train in the woods outside Berlin for the amount of time it would take to make the switch. As far as they knew, this might be the work of black marketeers, thieves, smugglers, the kind of thing that had become quite common now that it appeared that the war would not be the short sprint to a quick victory the Germans had expected three years ago.

"Usually, the men crewing the train are too old or handicapped, or lucky enough to have missed being assigned to the Eastern front," she continued. "They're not such strong, pig-headed Nazis as the young trainmen who had gone off to war. We offer something to the engineer, the conductor, and the crew for their cooperation — food, coffee, sugar, chocolate, cigarettes, money, whatever entices them. These days, that's a lot ..."

Now, that part, at least, was over. Colonel Varga and the baroness walked back through the woods in a stillness so deep they could hear their own breathing. Just as they reached the edge of the woods, they heard the sound of barking dogs. And then — was it their imagination? —the thud of marching boots on pavement.

Suddenly, the darkness was pierced by a curtain of light thrown across the clearing a hundred yards ahead of them.

"It's not my imagination," she hissed. "You've got the protection of the uniform. Once you make it to Frohnau, you'll just assimilate and be one of *them*. Try and divert attention away from me. Since I know the area well and I've done this before, I may be able to escape."

"But ...?"

"I know what you're thinking and I thank you for your gallantry, but this way at least one of us will probably survive and tell the others. Now, get moving and godspeed!"

Seconds later, another curtain of light appeared behind Hilde. She knew, without seeing the other two light curtains, that she was caught in a quadrangle — and by the sound of their baying, the dogs had picked up her scent.

There was a narrow brook in front of her, and beyond it, if her nostrils told the truth, a pile of manure. She ran quickly to the brook, leaped across it, and raced to the manure pile. Without a conscious thought, she dove into the manure, making sure she immersed every part of her body and her clothing in the noxious stuff. When she was sure she was now nothing more than an odoriferous mass, she ran back to the brook, effectively having stopped her scent at the pile.

Once in the brook, she waded with the current until she reached a pond that was overhung with trees. She swam to the far side and waited under the trees until the sounds of the frustrated dogs receded. Only then did she lift herself onto the shore.

Hilde no longer knew where she was. Even if she did, she would have to wait out at least the night and then figure out how she could possibly make her way back to Berlin. Meanwhile, she prayed that the illegals had fared better than she had.

Dawn came. Baroness Hilde von Nordin und Drakenberg was frozen and hungry, but she was still afraid to move. Whoever had tracked her through the night would be waiting for her to leave the woods. With her wet and filthy clothes, she would give herself away.

She waited through the day, praying for an air raid, the only diversion she could imagine that would enable her to escape. As darkness fell, the four curtains of light came on again. She was still trapped, still hunted.

And then she heard the sweet, sweet sound of air raid sirens.

Moments later, the curtains of lights went out. She heard the bombers droning in and then the thudding explosions. *Now or never,* she thought. Crouching, weaving, she made her way through the trees until she reached the edge of the forest. Just then, there was a tremendous explosion as a bomb hit a factory. Soon, the factory was blazing, turning night to dawn. Hilde could see that the road was empty. The moment the all clear sounded, she made a dash for the factory. As she had hoped, everyone was suddenly too busy with the fire to pay attention to a lone figure running down the road.

She helped fight the fire for an hour. Soon, her clothes were no more wet or soiled than those of the others around her. As soon as the fire was under control, she approached an official. "I'm not from this area," she said. "I was busy visiting friends and got caught by the raid. I helped put out your fire. Can you give me some kind of paper saying what I've done?" She received the paper without so much as a single question.

By next afternoon, Hilde had hitched a ride on a truck going back to Wilmersdorf. When no one was looking, she scaled the wall of the Church of Sweden on the Kaiserallee. Hendrika Zimmermann opened to her knock. She took one look at the younger woman and asked, "Are you going to faint?"

"I don't think so," Hilde said.

Mevrou Zimmermann took immediate control, grabbed Hilde, and led her to a nearby couch. "How about the people?" the baroness asked.

"They made it," the older woman said. "They're now on their way to Sweden." She handed Hilde a glass of champagne. Hilde took a sip and fainted.

33

Almost no man except Dr. Chaim Halevi would have considered his wife, Hannah, to be a raving beauty, nor would any woman have considered her a threat to their sexual allure. By no means unattractive, she was, quite simply, someone who would disappear into the woodwork five minutes after you'd met her. Hannah Halevi gave stereotypical definition to the word "plain." Her eyes and her mouth were small and thin, her nose was a model of what the Nazis called a 'Jew nose,' and her mouse-colored hair was sparse. Although she was neither obese nor unusually thin, the unflattering attire she generally wore made her appear shapeless.

Still, her very ordinariness, when coupled with a sharp, incisive mind, had served as protective armor which had enabled her to survive more than nine years in National Socialist-dominated Europe. It was Hannah, who, despite her unflagging love and loyalty to her husband, had suggested a year ago that she and the children move from Berlin 450 miles south to the picturesque village of Seefeld, nestled in the northernmost section of the Alps. "At least until we can determine more clearly which way the wind is blowing."

Yesterday, Frau Kirstenbaum, her Catholic neighbor, a good friend, and a staunch anti-Nazi, who had been Hannah's factotum for the indirect, surreptitious mailings from Chaim, had delivered the cryptic message: "The doctor has left and is enroute to a new destination. Someone will contact you shortly."

Reading between the lines, Hannah Halevi gathered her two children, Hans, now fourteen, five-feet-ten-inches tall, and sturdily built, and Leah, a year younger and coltish, in Mrs. Kirstenbaum's apartment and imparted the news to them. "I've received word we'll be leaving Seefeld shortly."

To their questions, when, how, to where, and mostly why, Hannah responded, her voice betraying both her excitement and fear, the only response she could give was, "Very shortly, I don't know exactly how, where, or when, but I can answer the why. God willing, we'll be joining your father and we'll be free — and, assuming we make it, we'll be going to a safer place."

Tuesday, October 27, 1942

By next morning, the first snowfall had dusted the mighty Karwendelspitze, four thousand feet above the village of Mittenwald, just over the border in Germany, nine miles north of Seefeld, making Marketstrasse a wonderland of white, with old-fashioned golden streetlamps causing a fairytale glow. As Hannah Halevi walked purposefully down the main street, she was suddenly bumped by a short, nondescript man and nearly pushed to the ground. As she glared ahead and started to weigh whether to shout imprecations at the departing figure, she suddenly stopped in her tracks and dropped her gaze to the ground where three small, light brown booklets were clearly visible.

She stooped to pick them up, then gasped as she saw a recent likeness of herself, but with the name Annemarie Müller. With trembling hands, she opened the other two booklets. The second one had a recent photograph of Leah, which bore the name Hannelore Kreuz-Müller. When she opened the third booklet, she was not surprised to see the photo of her son and the name

Rolf Kreuz-Müller. Inside this booklet, Hannah found a small piece of cheap paper with a handwritten note, "Be prepared to leave in two days, each in different directions with a different escort. Now, return home immediately."

Closing the cover, the words "Passeport Suisse / Schweitzer Pass" and a cross enclosed in a shield, she had no doubt it was genuine, and, after five minutes of pretending to window shop and satisfying herself that there was no one following her, Hannah Halevi placed the passports in her purse, made sure it was tightly closed, and hurried home to tell her children and Frau Kirstenbaum what she had found.

The following morning, as Hans was riding his bicycle enroute to the neighborhood lake, the *Wildsee,* he narrowly averted colliding with a Grosser Mercedes which had suddenly pulled off the road and into his path. As he dismounted his conveyance, not knowing whether to be angry or embarrassed, a tall, stern-looking woman of middle years with a severely short haircut, exited the car and said, with no introduction, "Tomorrow will be a lovely day to go sailing on the Bodensee. It's a four-hour drive and a black BMW 321 will pick you up outside Frau Kirstenbaum's front door shortly before eight."

"But, I ...?"

She walked quickly back to the automobile, entered it, and drove off without another word, leaving Hans's face flushed with confusion as he considered what to do about this curt message.

That evening, when he told his mother what had happened, Hannah Halevi handed her son the Swiss passport in his new name, hugged him tight, and said, "You'll be the first to leave. God willing, we'll all be reunited in a short time." Concurrently, she handed Leah 'Hannelore Kreuz-Müller's' document and advised her daughter, "Keep this on your person at all times. I imagine the *Zollgrenzschutz* — the Border Patrol — will be alerted to what is happening any moment when they learn that your papa has escaped, and they'll be focusing on the three of us as hostages — or worse."

"Do you have any idea where or when someone will come for us, Mama?"

"No, darling, neither the Nazis nor those who are supposed to help us. We must, all of us, be prepared for something to happen, without notice, any time. That's why …"

"I understand."

THURSDAY, OCTOBER 29, 1942

"When" was the following morning, as Leah left her home to walk to the market, less than a half-mile from the Halevi home. "Where" was halfway to the market. "Who" were three ladies dressed in clerical outfits reminiscent of nuns she had seen over the years in and around the *Dom*, Seefeld's large Roman Catholic church, two of whom descended from an elderly black sedan bearing a foreign license plate, black with white writing.

The larger of the two, who seemed to be the leader, carried a similar habit draped over her arm. "Novitiate Hannelore," she called out to Leah, "I'm so sorry we were delayed. You must come with us right now, before Mother Superior starts to worry unduly."

"Uh…"

"Quickly, child," the second woman said. "We've got a long journey ahead of us."

"But the *Dom* …"

"We're going a bit farther than the village church," she continued. "Do you have your passport with you?"

"Yes," the girl answered.

"You'll need these as well," the woman said, handing Leah a sheaf of papers with official-looking stamps, identifying 'Hannelore Kreuz-Müller' of Seefeld-in-Tirol, Ostmark, as a registered novitiate of the Saint Florin Cathedral, Vaduz, Liechtenstein."

"What about clothing? Food? Money?" Leah asked.

"God will provide. We've got a long drive ahead."

"Haven't I seen you before?" Hannah asked.

"As a matter of fact, you bumped into me in Mittenwald."

"Excuse me. *I* bumped into *you*?

"Yes, and quite rude you were about it. Running ahead of me and trying to disappear into a crowd?

"Why, you presumptuous little man!" Hannah retorted, clearly irritated by this self-aggrandizing interloper.

"I have a name, Madame," he continued in fluent Bavarian dialect, not the least bit intimidated by the tongue-lashing she was prepared to give him. "If you want to take the train to Innsbruck and a two-hour flight to our final destination, you'll show me greater courtesy, and you may refer to me as 'West.'"

"Is that your first name or your last name?" she asked, in a tone only slightly warmer than she had used in her icy introduction."

"Yes," he replied.

Less than an hour later, they arrived at *Kranebitten* Airport. Hannah, who'd never flown before, was unnerved when she saw Alpine peaks surrounding the aerodrome on three sides, with the only apparent flatland directly to the east over Austria's fifth largest city. Nor was her nervousness alleviated when she and her companion were driven by an ancient DKW F-1 to the far end of the airport and to their conveyance, a tiny, single-engine, two-seat *Fieseler Storch* aircraft, which was devoid of any markings.

"Do you really intend to fly this ... this *thing*? It's smaller than the car."

"That it is, Madame, and this is the least likely vehicle that the Nazis will track and follow as we leave their precious Reich."

"And you think this will survive its journey through the Alps?" she inquired, nearly shouting with anxiety.

"So far, it's made in through more than twenty-eight such trips in this area. Of course, the mountains will flatten out significantly as we come closer to our destination."

"Which is ...?"

"To take my name in vain, west of here. More than that, you'd best not know."

"And exactly whom do you think I'll tell?"

"Most likely no one, because I intend to maintain radio silence until we're over the border. But I've no doubt the *Zollgrenzschutz* will be tracking us from the moment we take off until we leave Reich airspace."

11:00 A.M.

Oberzollrat Major Walter Gluckmann, forty-eight, sat at his desk in Innsbruck's Zollgrenzschutz regional headquarters, poring through the reports of traffic, including successful and unsuccessful attempts at leaving the Reich and entering the nearest neutral countries or those antagonistic toward the regime.

At first, Gluckmann had not been pleased when he'd been rejected by the Wehrmacht, invalided out due to a combination of age, nearsightedness, and a hearing defect, when he'd first been examined three years ago. After his discharge, his choices were to remain out of uniform and subject to the suspicious taunts of younger, more vigorous, and hence more virile German males, enlist in the *Heimwehr*, the home guard, with cast-off *old men*, or join the Border Patrol under Fritz Reinhardt's Finance Ministry. He elected the latter, and now, when it appeared that the Thousand Year Reich just might *not* win the War, he was gratified, both by his elevation to Major and this plum assignment in Austria's beautifully-situated city in the far west, well away from the battlefields.

Walter Gluckmann had no particular hatred, or even mild dislike, for the Jews, who were simply unfortunate *ubermenschen*, less than Aryan human beings. He was simply a loyal and quite diligent officer in the greatest armed force ever assembled. A week ago, the bulletin had advised him, not that it was worth any particular headline, that a formerly well-reputed Jewish physician and dean of Germany's most prestigious medical school, Chaim Halevi, whose wife and two children were being held in "protective custody" in Seefeld-in-Tirol, Ostmark, had somehow escaped from Germany, and that he might be attempting to communicate with them.

As a precautionary measure, Oberzollrat Gluckmann had detailed two junior officers to watch the Halevi residence in Seefeld. As of last night, it had been reported that there was no suspicious or unusual activity and that Frau Halevi and her children were at home. Since the daily report of all activity was not due on his desk until three o'clock this afternoon, and he had nothing to be concerned about, Major Gluckmann turned to the sports page of today's *Deutsche Volkszeitung*.

At 11:45 a.m., he glanced at his wristwatch, felt a pre-lunch groan in his stomach, and decided to treat himself — actually to allow the Reich to treat him — to lunch on Maria-Theresien Strasse. As he left his suite, he heard the ring of a telephone issuing from his inner office. "*Ah, well,*" he thought, "*my secretary's already left for an hour. There's no reason whoever is calling can't wait 'til I return.*"

"No answer, Heinz," *Zollwachtmeister* Horst Schwartz said to his partner. "Probably gone to lunch. D'you think he should know that the house is locked and there's no one home?"

"Naww. It's the middle of the day, kids are probably at school, and the woman's probably somewhere between here and Innsbruck. We'd most likely get our asses chewed out for disturbing the old man. Nothing will happen if we wait 'til this afternoon."

Major Gluckmann's attention was momentarily drawn to a small single-engine plane headed east over the city. Although the Deutsche Lufthansa flight to Vienna had passed over his head as he'd left his headquarters building and he knew there were no scheduled commercial flights before the 3:00 p.m. to Frankfurt, the sight of a Fieseler Storch at five hundred feet above his head did not unduly concern him.

1:00 P.M.

Alpine lakes are celebrated in story and song as among the most dramatic and beautiful in the world. However, few people, if any, have ever referred to the Bodensee, central Europe's third largest lake, and a source of the mighty Rhine River, as beautiful. Even fewer have considered it dramatic, with the exception of periodic upheavals which raised waves as large as one sees in the Atlantic Ocean. Konstanz, which lies near Germany's southwestern edge, is the largest and most populous city, as well as the premier tourist destination, on what is also called Lake Constance.

Because of its proximity to the Swiss border — only 3½ miles from Kreuzlingen in the Swiss Canton of Thurgau — Konstanz had escaped Allied bombing and had even kept its lights on fully bright at night to fool enemy pilots into believing it was actually in Switzerland.

Shortly after one that afternoon, the BMW in which Hans was riding, pulled into the parking lot of the Hotel Halm in Konstanz's old town. A blond man, a few years Hans' senior, stood a few feet away from the 321 sedan, holding two bicycles. He nodded at the car, which stopped and discharged Hans.

"*Guten Tag, du musst sein Hans Kreuz-Müller?*"

"Uhhh … *Ja*," Hans responded, using the name on his Swiss passport.

"*Zeit für eine Radtur in die Schweitz?* Time for us to go on a bike ride to Switzerland?"

"*Sicher.* Sure," Hans responded not knowing what else to say. The four-hour trip from Seefeld had been uneventful, and the woman who'd traveled with him had peeled off a hundred Swiss francs, given it to him, and told him that it would more than suffice 'til he made it to his destination.

As the two young men pedaled out of the parking lot and headed toward the road separating Germany and Switzerland, the BMW headed back in the direction from whence it had come.

The Swiss Border Guards knew Hans' companion well, and waved the two cyclists into Switzerland with a nod and without checking their papers. Hans' new companion spoke very little until they reached the Evangelical Reformed Church on Bärenstrasse, where he stopped and tolds Hans to dismount.

"There's a shared taxi that goes from here to St. Gallen twice a day. It's fast and cheap, and unless you want to pedal this bike for another twenty-six miles by yourself, since I have no desire to go there and back, you can catch it here in about forty minutes."

"But I know no one and nothing about Switzerland …" Hans started to say.

"I'll wait here with you for it to come. It'll drop you off at the Abbey Library. There'll be someone waiting for you at the front entrance. She'll be wearing a red blazer and will walk you to your destination for the night. Not to worry, Hans, someone will guide you right where you need to be.

"How safe will I be in Liechtenstein?" Leah asked, as the Church's car passed through Feldkirch, Austria's westernmost town."

"As safe as you'd be in Switzerland, child," the senior nun responded. "Liechtenstein's aligned with Switzerland as a neutral. Germany won't invade it for two reasons. First, of course, is that everyone seems to respect its neutral stance, much like the Reich won't invade Sweden or Spain. Second, and more important, Switzerland has something Germany needs: a safe place to store its money."

"Why would it need Switzerland for that, Sister? The National Socialists seem to have all the money the need safely tucked away in Germany."

"Yes, but some high-ranking Nazis think, although they'd never express it to their closest friends, and certainly not publicly, that Germany *might* not win this war, and if they don't, those Nazis will need an escape route, and they'll need money stored in a safe place where it won't be touched, to leave the Reich very quickly if they need to. Meanwhile, we've been traveling a long time. This care needs petrol, and I'm sure the four of us have other needs as well."

While they were stopped, a large sedan bearing Swiss diplomatic license plates, pulled up next to them. "Change of plans, Leah," the head nun said, using her real name. "We'll be going on to Vaduz, but you'll change cars here."

"Is this some kind of a trick?" the 13-year-old asked suspiciously.

"Not at all, dear," the nun replied. "We're still in Ostmark. One never can tell who'll be watching the border crossings. The only two foolproof ways to get to where you need to be are to walk over those mountains to the south or to ride in the one kind of vehicle that no one will inspect. That tall man driving that sedan is the one who arranged for us to pick you up in Seefeld. You need not be afraid of him because ..."

"That man with him in the car looks like ... it *is!*" she burst out. Opening the door, she ran to the sedan. "Papa! Papa!" she cried exultantly. "Oh, my God! Papa! You're safe! Thank God! How did ...?"

The two of them, father and daughter, rushed at one another, laughing, crying, *safe*! They'd been apart for more than a year, each writing and sending pictures to one another and they couldn't stop hugging one another. While they stood there, simply loving one another, the church's car pulled slowly away.

"Ahem," the sedan's driver interrupted their reunion. "Lest you forget, we're still in Austria, and no matter our 'protection,' we can't be certain we're safe until we're *out* of this country and *into* the Swiss confederation."

"You're absolutely right, Colonel Varga," Chaim Halevi said. "How far is it?"

"Thirteen miles to the border crossing at Hohenems, then we cross into Switzerland at St. Margrethen and take the A-1 another thirty minutes to St. Gallen."

Above Feldirch, the land flattened out as the foothills of the northern Alps gave way to the Bodensee basin. The animated conversation between the three of them continued nonstop for half of the journey into St. Gallen. Papa explained how they'd escaped from Germany. Once into Stockholm, papa and a Swedish news correspondent, Miss Nygard, had taken the AB Flight from Sweden's capital to Zurich. Meanwhile, Colonel Varga, traveling on a Swiss diplomatic passport, had taken a Deutsche Lufthansa flight from Berlin to Zurich. The three of them had landed within half an hour of one another. The woman continued on to Geneva, while Papa and Colonel Varga had walked over to the government parking lot, where they'd found the car in which they were now riding, and a set of keys, waiting for them, courtesy of the Swiss deputy director of foreign affairs, Varga's friend Mattias Dubginy.

"What about Mama and Hans?" Leah asked.

"Miss Nygard and some of her associates — she's American, not Swedish, by the way —helped get them to where they hopefully now are. Hans should be arriving in St. Gallen, just about now. He'll be in for a big surprise."

"And Mama?"

Doctor Halevi and Colonel Varga looked at one another.

"Truthfully, we don't know quite where she is at this moment …"

West of Innsbruck, they found themselves sandwiched in between Alpine peaks on the north and south. The plane's airspeed indicator showed a steady seventy-five miles per hour and, at 5,000 feet above sea level, it appeared from that elevation that they were crawling along and the ground scarcely seemed to move. For the most part, they remained at the same altitude, but there were times when the little aircraft experienced sudden updrafts and downdrafts which caused Hannah's face to turn pale as she grasped the stanchion above and to her right.

"Frightened?" West asked, not unkindly.

"If you must know, terrified," she replied. "I've never been in one of these before."

"And you're not likely to be during the remainder of this war. These sudden, unexpected climbs and descents are natural when you're flying through mountains. Think of the air as one big ocean and consider our plane as a small boat on that ocean. You'll have ups and downs as we travel through the 'ocean,' but we're not likely to sink. Air currents are like waves: they rise up and they come down. Fortunately, you'll get an updraft before you hit a mountain on the way down, or you'll get a downdraft before you hit the moon."

"Not very encouraging," Hannah said.

"Sorry, it's the best I can do."

As they continued west, thick cumulus clouds reared above the mountain tops, darkening the sky. Soon, there were brisk air currents, rocking the little plane from side to side, uncomfortably.

"I think I'm going to be seasick or airsick, or whatever you call it."

"There's a 'sicksack' under your seat. Grab it and use it if you need to vomit. I won't mind and you'll feel better if you empty out what's inside you."

"You seem so sure of yourself, West."

"I wasn't always that way," he replied. You get used to it … maybe."

At that moment two Messerschmitt Bf-109 fighters passed less than five hundred feet above them, causing their small aircraft to turn nearly on its side. Hannah could not stop herself from screaming with sudden fear.

"Thank God the radio's off," West said, gripped the stick tightly. "They're probably trying to signal us trying to learn what an unmarked aircraft is doing in German airspace. Hold on tight, Madame Halevi, we're going to descend fifteen hundred feet."

"But won't we crash?"

"No," West replied. "We'll still be at thirty-five hundred feet, about five hundred feet above the surrounding terrain. There are no airports of sufficient size nearby to allow the fighter aircraft to land, and no matter how great the pilots think they are, at the speed they're going, they won't risk smashing one of their expensive toys into a mountain.

Their descent was smooth and almost effortless as the *Storch* cut power only slightly. Thirty minutes later, the land had flattened out and Hannah Halevi pointed to a large body of water in some miles ahead of them.

"Lake Constance," West remarked. "See that patch of grass on the far horizon?"

His passenger nodded.

"Altenrhein Airport," the pilot responded. In what seemed like another hour, but was actually less than ten minutes, he said, "Welcome to Switzerland, Frau Halevi! You can relax now. We're beyond German airspace and we've left the Reich behind."

After almost unlimited tears and praise to the God who'd brought them safely together for the first time in over a year, the Halevi family spent their first night in a nearby *Gasthof* before Colonel Varga drove them to a Cimade Safe House, 4½ hours away in Geneva, halfway to their new home in Le Chambon-sur-Lignon, France.

34

LeChambon-sur-Lignon, November 5, 1942 – 7:00 p.m.

A six-year-old Citroën Traction Avant stopped not far from the Protestant presbytery. Two uniformed Vichy French policemen, Major Silvani, chief of police of the Haute-Loire and his lieutenant, Gaspar DeLamont emerged from the vehicle.

When they knocked at the door of the presbytery, Magda Trocmé hardly heard the slight noise, but when she did, she warned the two latest arrivals, the man from Berlin and the woman from Karlsruhe, to disperse to the attic and to the cellar respectively. She then opened the heavy old door and stood facing the two policemen.

"Madame Trocmé," Silvani asked, apologetically but with dignity, "where is your husband?"

"I don't know," Magda answered. "Would you like to come in and wait for him in his office?"

No sooner they went into the pastor's office and she'd closed the door behind them, she started trembling. *We've been expecting this since the LeMirand visit. Now the moment has come and there's no way I can warn him.*

Two hours passed. Shortly after nine that evening, André burst into the presbytery, across the dining room, and walked purposefully into his office to put some papers there. Less than five minutes later, he came back into the dining room and announced, "Magda, I am arrested."

The first thing his impulsive Italian wife cried was, "Oh, André! What about the suitcase with all those warm clothes in it, the clothes I packed for you months ago? We've been using them and now the suitcase is empty."

In less dangerous times, they would have burst out laughing about getting concerned over a valise. But the prison suitcase, which they kept in their bedroom closet upstairs had been packed in the very real expectation that any day the pastor would be arrested and most likely deported to a concentration camp in central Europe.

"What do we tell the Giberts, my love?" Magda asked. "We're supposed to go over to their house right after dinner." Almost simultaneously, Martine Gibert, their hosts' daughter, knocked on the door of the presbytery. Magda, thinking nothing about what was going on, invited Martine in.

When Martine entered the dining room, the first thing she saw was the police arresting her pastor. Without a word, she turned and rushed out of the house. Within minutes, half of the village knew that André Trocmé had been arrested.

After André and Magda rejoined the police in the dining room, Magda said, "Gentlemen, you may as well have dinner with us. It's late in the evening and you must be starved. By all means, eat."

Silvani's face hung down in misery. "I'm sorry, Madame Trocmé," he replied. "I don't have the heart to eat."

Meanhile, her husband, who was already eating heartily, asked Silvani, "Why am I being arrested?"

"I don't know, Pastor Trocmé," the chief replied shakily. "I really don't. I know nothing and I can say nothing."

While André, Magda, the children, and the two law enforcement officers were eating bowls of a thick soup made up of several kinds of vegetables, lentils, and scraps of lamb, there were continuous soft knocks at their front door. Before the meal was over, no less than fifty parishioners, most of them crying, had entered the presbytery to say their goodbyes to their spiritual leader. Some whispered criticisms to the police who were sitting at the table with their heads bowed.

As they embraced Trocmé, each congregant left a small gift at the table: candles, which were all but unobtainable at that time; sardines, chocolate biscuits, a large sausage, warm stockings. A roll of toilet paper. These were poverty-stricken days in the small village and any gift, no matter how small, was meaningful and extremely hard to come by.

At first, the two officers watched all this with amazed eyes. But as the crowd did not abate, Chief Silvani himself started weeping over his untouched food. "I have never seen such a farewell, never," he said, through his sobs.

Someone brought in a long, thin votive candle and handed it to Magda Trocmé. After the giver had left, she said, "But where will he get matches to light this?" Silvani walked up to her with a box of matches in his hand and said, "Please take these. I'll tell this story later. I'll keep it alive." The tears in his eyes expressed moral praise and moral dispraise more powerfully than any words could do.

As her husband was preparing to leave with the officers, Magda gave him three items: his freshly packed valise, a bulky package containing the gifts, and a pair of wooden shoes. In those days, the Chambonnais wore wooden shoes because they could not afford leather.

As the three men stepped out into the Rue de la Grande Fontaine, the narrow medieval street was dark and *la burle*, the icy wind which plagued the village every winter, blew thin snow around the broken, ice-covered stones in the road. Villagers lined both sides of the crooked street, silently staring at Trocmé as he walked between the two policemen.

As the guards and their prisoner continued down the street toward the high road that led to the village square, Silvani and his prisoner heard the soft strains of the old Lutheran hymn, *A Mighty Fortress Is Our God*, sung by a single female voice. As they continued walking, the woman was joined by another voice, then another, until it seemed that the entire village surrounded the three men with their spiritual sound, softly at first, then with greater force. As Chief Silvani, his deputy, and Pastor Trocmé passed, the villagers closed behind them and the *clop-clop* of their wooden shoes followed them up the street.

When they came to the main village square, the three men entered the Traction Avant. Major Silvani turned to Trocmé and announced, "We are going to find your colleagues, Edouard Theis and Roger Darcissac. They must come with us as well."

From *Le Chambon – Le Mazet* station, the sad little train bearing Pastor Trocmé, his associate Edouard Theis, and Superintendent Darcissac, accompanied by two deputies, traveled an hour on its daily run to Saint-Étienne-Châteaucreux station. When the three prisoners descended onto the main platform, they were met by three guards, none of whom looked particularly threatening. They were all in their mid-thirties, of medium height, and casually dressed.

During the exchange, Trocmé politely asked the man who appeared to be the senior of the three, "Might we ask where we're bound from here?"

The officer, who had no doubt learned who his charges were, responded with equal courtesy. "Pastor Trocmé, I have no idea of your final destination." He looked up at the large clock in the hallway. "It's now two thirty-five. We're scheduled to leave on the three o'clock express due west from here to Clermont-Ferrand and continuing on to *Gare de Limoges-Bénédictins*. It's a four-hour journey to Limoges, so you'll most likely spend the night there. You might want to get a bite to eat, since you've probably had nothing since breakfast and the buffet is open. We're supposed to turn you over to police chief at Limoges and return here tomorrow morning."

"You're aware that we face imprisonment?" the large man said.

"So I've been told, Curate Theis. I've not been told of the charges or anything else. You understand, of course, that I'm simply doing what I've been ordered to do. No reflection on anyone, but ..." he continued in a much quieter voice, "I just hope these abominable *boches* are gone sooner rather than later. Would it were *them* instead of you."

"Amen," Darcissac nodded.

Limoges, a city of 100,000, is situated on the northwest corner of the great Plateau de Velay. The three thousand inhabitants of Le Chambon-sur-Lignon lived diagonally opposite Limoges on the southeast corner of the same plateau, some two hundred sixty-five miles distant. The train bearing Trocmé, Theis, Darcissac, and the three men guarding them, arrived at seven-thirty that evening at Limoges' immense Benedictine Railway station.

"*Mon Dieu!*" Darcissac exclaimed, despite his exhaustion. "I've never seen a station this large! It must be more than three hundred feet long and nearly as wide!"

"Indeed," the senior guard who'd accompanied them said. "Most large railroad stations in Europe are built *next* to the tracks. There are ten separate lines into Limoges and the platform here is built *over* the ten railway lines, not next to them."

"There's more," the guard continued, a sour look on his face. He pointed to a yellow sign with black lettering adjacent to a stairway at the far corner of the platform.

"*Achtung! Nur für Wehrmacht!*"

"Fucking Nazis," the guard spoke *sotto voce*. "Leave it those bastards to build a roadway *under* the tracks as a defense shelter. And, of course, they mean business. They'll liquidate anyone who's not one of theirs, who tries to use it. Uh-oh. Here's comes the police chief. Time to turn you fellows over."

"You've been very kind Officer Jardin," Trocmé said. "May God protect you."

"Actually, you'll be the ones who'll need God's protection."

The man who approached them was smartly clad in a gray uniform bearing three stars on each lapel. Slender, in his early fifties, his face appeared to bear a permanent scowl, with thin lips and no hint of a smile. He addressed Jardin.

"So these are the three you've escorted from Saint-Étienne? I trust you have made arrangements for where you'll stay this evening?"

"Yes, sir, Préfet."

"Very well. You've done your job. You are dismissed."

With that the police chief, who was convinced that anyone who had been arrested was not only guilty of a crime, but beneath contempt, inclined his head sideways, signaling the two clerics and the third prisoner to move to a door several feet away. When Trocmé, Theis, and Darcissac entered the small office behind the door, they were four other officers waiting.

As the chief looked at their orders, he muttered, "Pastors! A teacher!" Then he whistled in mock wonder. "Where will evil hide itself nowadays? Come on, out with it. What have you done? Confess! The black market? Swindling, maybe?"

Theis answered. "We don't know the charge. Maybe they've arrested us because we have been trying to save Jews from being deported."

The chief's face turned an angry red, and he shouted, "What? Jews? Oh, that's lovely! Now, that doesn't surprise me. You're part of their conspiracy, eh? We all know they're the ones who've brought France down into the abyss. Well, you're going to pay for this! You're going to pay for all the harm you've done to the marshal!"

Trocme made no reply, but as he heard these words, his thoughts turned to something he'd never believed before. *People like this one may be patriotic, even sincere in their beliefs, but they are limited. They're capable of repeating hate-ridden clichés without any concern for evidence or for the pain of others. Before*

I arrived here, I thought the world was a place where two forces, God and the Devil, were struggling for power. But I've just learned from this man that there's a third force seeking to dominate the world: <u>stupidity</u>. God, the Devil, and halfwits of mind and heart are all struggling with each other for control of the world.

Le Chambon has been spared the cretins. In the south of France, people call my village "the republic of Le Chambon" because somehow it has managed to remain a world of its own, a fortress of civility in a murderous world, a place that cannot be made a party to the compromises and murders of the France around it. This moral isolation has kept out the cretins, or at least has quieted and assimilated them so that I have not seen them parading their cretinism.

From that point forward, and for the rest of his life, Pastor André Trocmé knew in his heart that there were some people — indeed many people — who did not realize what suspicion and hatred could do to their own minds — and to their victims.

"Excuse me, *Monsieur le Chef*," Trocmé asked, "but the hour is late and my colleagues and I have not eaten a solid meal since breakfast. Is there some place where we could, perhaps, purchase something small, simply to put us in condition to spend the night?"

"Oh, of course, *mon Vieux*," the captain replied feigning courtesy. He mumbled a few words to his deputies, who promptly brought in three glasses of water. "By all means, gentlemen."

As Darcissac, Theis, and André reached for the glasses, three of the deputies grasped the glasses and tossed the water in the faces of their prisoners.

"That'll cool you down from your uncomfortable journey," the chief said. "Now we'll escort you to headquarters where you can spend a restful night."

THE NEXT DAY.

"I trust you enjoyed your lodgings, *Pastor*," the police chief, already in a surly mood, greeted Trocmé the next morning.

"Thank you, yes, Your Excellency," Trocmé replied courteously. "I wonder if I might beg the indulgence of your department to allow the three of us to have breakfast with some of our colleagues in Limoges and attend services at the local Protestant church. We'll only be a few hours at most and we would certainly welcome any officers you would have accompany us to ensure our good behavior."

"Oh, you would like that, would you?" the captain snarled. "Well, *Father* or *Priest*, or whatever you call yourself in your religion, I would love to grant your request, but I'm afraid we have some other ideas in mind for you. Indeed, your transportation awaits you immediately outside, so might I request you pack your things and be ready in about ten minutes."

"Might we at least have a quick shower? We've not bathed since Friday, and …"

"Oh, my, you've not bathed for two whole days? How terrible. Of course, the three of you have the stench of *Jew* and the stench of *treason* about you, so I think if you must bear that odor for the next few days, that should not be too much for you to bear. And, indeed, your body should be able to cleanse itself without the need of extraneous food. So, gentlemen, ten minutes, and if you're not out in the parking lot, we'll help you hurry so you might be on your way."

35

Fifteen minutes later, André Trocmé, Edouard Theis, and Roger Darcissac were rudely shoved into a sealed bus with barred windows. Three armed guards accompanied them on the ten-mile journey from the Limoges police prefecture into a small valley and their "home" for however long it would be.

As the bus approached the camp, Pastor Trocmé felt fear grabbing at his innards. *This is not the ultimate destination, any more than last night's quarters was the final place. Refugees and Aryan resisters who had stopped in Le Chambon told me about these places in detail. There'll be lack of food, but we won't die here, not in France. This is only a collection camp, a gateway to the East. Starvation, torture, mass killing. We are on our way to our deaths.*

The three prisoners each held different thoughts as they observed the camp. Low, gray wooden barracks, built on a wetland surrounded by two ranks of high, barbed wire fences, dominated by watchtowers. Guards armed with machine guns, mobile reserve troops.

The Supervised Stay Center of Saint-Paul d'Eyjeaux was, in every way, a typical concentration camp. It housed French and foreign "undesirables," mainly Communists, Jews, anarchists, and anyone else deemed inimical to the Pétain government: men of all ages, factory workers, peasants, civil servants, craftsmen, merchants, mayors, or elected officials.

Several minutes after they'd first seen the camp, the bus pulled up to the administration building, a prefabricated two-story affair. Each of the Chambonnais stood by impassively, enduring their dehumanization as nameless, faceless bureaucrats registered them, took their fingerprints and photographs, and handed them numbers to replace their names.

Hustled to another waiting room, different functionaries catalogued and sequestered their personal possessions and, with a seriousness which only confirmed Trocmé's conclusion that they were "cretins," measured their noses to ascertain whether or not they were Jewish. All three men were aware that the French camp agents were as anti-Semitic as the Nazis could have wished them to be. In fact, Trocmé knew that the Vichy government had a definition of the word *Jew* that covered and condemned more people for the crime of being Jewish than the Nazi definition. With the help of the cretins, Vichy was going out of its way to please the current masters of France.

When they left the abject humiliation of the Saint-Paul d'Eyjeaux Administration Center, and passed into the no-man's-land between the two barbed wire fences on foot, the three former Chambonnais found themselves facing some thirty prisoners lined up to watch them. Those men were wearing ragged army coats. Their faces were jaundiced yellow and slack — walking corpses.

One of the internees asked, "Who are you?"

"Two preachers and a teacher," Darcissac answered.

To the extent the inhabitants were capable of any sustained noise, there was apparent guffawing as another inmate said, "Pastors! That's all we need! We've got a priest and a rabbi, and half the camp seems to be made up of teachers, and now we've got pastors, too!"

Yet, in the hellhole that was Saint-Paul d'Eyjeaux, Trocmé suddenly felt his spirits lift. *Even as ironic as this is, even as cadaverous and cynical as these men seem to be, they're trying in their own way to welcome us.*

That first evening was cold — not unexpectedly — and the surroundings made it more so. Dark puffs of smoke gushed out of stacks throughout the camp like billows of thick, black paint. The street adjacent to the Chambonnais' assigned dining hall was wet, although it had not rained, and a foul odor hung in the dampness, as if a large quantity of garbage had been scattered everywhere in the moisture.

Roger Darcissac had had nothing to eat that day and he felt his stomach gurgling and contracting. He'd worked up a ball of saliva and swallowed it. His hunger pangs had started coming that morning. His thoughts of food dulled the events of earlier in the day.

Potatoes. Garlic. Eggs. Greens. Onions. Salami.

He had thought he appreciated them properly when they had been in his possession only three days ago, but now he saw that it was not so. After the food in the south, potatoes and onions were nothing special. He'd considered them interim staples, so he had not conserved them. It took only a short while before his thoughts lingered jealously on each picture.

Dried, hard, brownish-red salami, speckled with white veins of fat, the round end casing tied in a knot, the sliced end smooth and oily, with a sharp, garlicky aroma. Potatoes, brown skinned, with dark, muddy eyes, sliced with onions and fried in oil. The eggs, lovely white enamel shells faintly tinged with pink, each oval pearly white and bright warm yellow inside, capable of reproducing the miracle of life. Salami. Potatoes. Eggs. Garlic. Greens. Onions.

Dinner that night, such as it was, did nothing to alleviate his hunger. Something that passed for soup.

Tasteless muck, Darcissac thought. *No fat, no bubbles, no film, no trace of skin or marrow, no carrots, no hint of salt, pepper, or paprika. A couple of rutabagas and a few lentils. How long can we survive on hot water with yellow food coloring?*

The inmates were invited to take seconds, even thirds. As much as they liked. The steaming yellow water filled bowl after bowl. Three-day old, moldy black bread provided just enough filler to take the sharpest edge off what would otherwise have been outright starvation.

After dinner, the thirty-odd men in the dining hall returned to their assigned barracks. Fifty cheaply-made metal cots with lumpy straw "mattresses" so thin that the three newest internees could feel and hear every loose spring beneath the fabric, gathered as close to the single heater as possible. The stench of dried urine permeated each bed, reminders of past inhabitants. If the mattresses provided little warmth or comfort, the "covers," consisting of single thin muslin sheets, were even worse. Each cot sported a few wisps of hay, which served as a "pillow."

Yet, despite the discomfort of their surroundings, Pastor Trocmé felt a camaraderie among his fellow prisoners. He and his two companions introduced themselves to their motley fellow inmates, who responded in kind. Most of the "old-timers" were eager to hear news from "the outside," even if the outside was less than twenty miles away.

"Fellows, I was able to bring something from Le Chambon that I'd like to share with you," Trocmé said, opening a small package he'd been allowed to carry with him from the administration building.

When his barracks-mates saw that it contained two rolls of toilet paper, an unheard-of, unimaginable luxury, they reached toward the Protestant pastor in apparent ecstasy. Even a single sheet would have caused commotion within the room. Trocmé was able to tear three sheets for each man before the roll was exhausted. Then, he pulled out the remaining roll.

"What in heaven's name?!" he exclaimed. "There's writing on the outer sheets!"

As Trocmé looked wide-eyed at the sheets, a graybeard asked, "What kind of writing?"

"I would swear ..." the pastor began and stopped almost immediately. "Yes ... each one of these sheets contains a different verse of consolation from the Bible." Suddenly, everyone in the room was silent as André Trocmé, who'd been a pillar of strength for such a long time, started weeping uncontrollably. "They remembered me," he whispered through his tears. "My congregation ... if Le Chambon couldn't join me here ... they made sure to remind me I'm still part of Le Chambon ... and their hearts and mine are still joined."

"Most of us are Communists," the older man, who'd noticed the writing on the toilet paper just after Trocmé's initial outburst, remarked the following day. "I'm Michel DeBre, Pastor."

"André Trocme," Le Chambon's spiritual leader responded, reaching out and shaking DeBre's hand. "I trust you're one of them?"

"Have been for thirty years. Spent two of them fighting with the International Brigade in Spain. When I returned in '39, the government had set up Gurs detention camp, and what a shithole that was. Makes this place look like a paradise," he said, reaching into the drawer of a small writing table and producing a small, faded picture.

"That's me, the guy all alone over on the right. Nice, huh?

"One of my Quaker colleagues told me about it," Trocmé replied. "It seems man's brutality to his fellow human beings knows no boundaries. How long were you there, Michel?"

"Two years. By that time, the Vichy government was in control and the last thing Marshal Pétain wanted running around 'his' little piece of rump France was a bunch of Communists. So, one day, little old Comrade Gourlay — my *nom de guerre* — was yanked out of Gurs and sent north to Saint-Paul d'Eyjeaux."

"So, you've been here ...?"

"A little more than a year-and-a-half, with no end in sight."

"Care for a cigarette?"

"I wouldn't say no," the older inmate said. "I trust you don't smoke, being a man of God and such?"

"A pipe smoker," André replied. "But some of my parishioners knew I'd be going to a place where there was nothing much to do *but* smoke and they thought if I had some small gifts for my fellow internees it might ease my entrée into the greater camp population." The pastor reached into his jacket pocket, extracted a pack of Gauloises, and handed it to DeBre/Gourlay.

"Appreciated," his new friend said, using a wooden matchstick to light up one of the cigarettes.

"You said 'most of the prisoners' are Communists. There are others …?"

"Catholics who opposed Vichy kissing the Nazis' asses and refused to play along with their anti-Semitic policies. A few Protestants. One nonbelieving Protestant in particular. I'll point him out to you. Be careful, he'll brown-nose anyone if thinks he can cadge a gift or gain some other advantage out of anyone. Between you and me, I think he's a *mouton*, a black sheep who's been passing all kinds of information to the Vichy guards. Be careful. He's given a bad name to Protestants and if you associate with him, some internees may paint you with the same brush as they paint 'Jean-Claude *Mouton*.'"

"Duly noted, Michel. Jews?"

"There are," Trocmé's companion said. "Poor souls. They're only here for a short time before they're sent to Drancy, and from there …"

"I understand."

It took a week before Trocmé and his two Chambonnais companions came under verbal attack from the Communists. When André sought out Michel DeBre to ask why, the older man replied, "They see you as collaborating with the enemy because you refuse to kill and you preach against violence. I can understand their feelings, André. We're in a state of war with Vichy and Germany. You're not actively participating, so they think you're peddling the same old opiate of the people that's kept the masses from moving forward to social justice."

"Perhaps if you could set up a meeting between four or five of their staunchest leaders. Just you, them, Edouard, Roger, and me? Hopefully, I could persuade them that we *are* on the same side, even though we might use different tactics than our Communist brothers."

"Thank you for allowing us to speak with you, gentlemen."

"Let me understand what you're trying to say, Pastor Trocmé. You acknowledge we're at war with the Nazis and with the Marshal's government."

"I do."

"Yet you refuse to engage them with violent acts."

"Also true."

"That makes no sense at all, Father," the Communist meeting leader said. "You're either a pacifist or you're not."

"Monsieur Rougette, that is, respectfully, where our thoughts part company. May I ask you, sir, how many Jews has your organization actively saved?"

"We've killed hundreds of men who've killed Jews …"

"Perhaps so, but from our viewpoint — and you may not agree and I respect your absolute right not to agree — in what you are doing, you are *indirectly* saving Jews, many of whom, by the way, have been the most vocal supporters of your ideology. Before the purges of 1936 and 1938, Jews were overrepresented in the Soviet leadership. Trotsky, Iurii Kamenev, Maksim Litvinov, Grigorii Zinoviev. For that matter, there's always Karl Marx's background … But while you are certainly *soldiers* in the war against the Nazis, you are *support staff* when it comes to our Jewish brethren. It is the people of Le Chambon who are on the front lines, *directly* putting their lives at risk to *hide* Jews, to *shelter* Jews, and, yes, to *save* Jews."

"But Pastor, you admit to being a pacifist?"

"Comrade Rougette, I concede no such thing. I must tell you in all honesty, I have always disdained the connotations of the term *pacifist*. That very word suggests passivity, even retreat, and that's *not* who I am or what I am. And for sure, it's an insult to the good people of Le Chambon-sur-Lignon. Trust me when I tell you that Edouard, Roger, and I — and the people of our village — are as vigorous and daring in our resistance to Vichy and Germany as the most aggressive inmates in this camp."

"Well ..." Rougette conceded, "you may have given us something to consider, Pastor Trocmé."

"This is London calling. You are listening to the World Service of the B.B.C. We interrupt our regularly scheduled news with the following announcement. The battle of Stalingrad is over. The Germans have suffered the most terrible defeat in the history of the Third Reich. ..."

All thirty men who were listening to the radio, which was concealed in a jar in the corner of the room nearest the heater, burst into cheers, pounding one another on the back, and breaking out hidden homemade brew that had been manufactured a week before.

Later that evening, Trocmé, Darcissac, and Theis had a much more subdued, quiet conversation of their own, in a tiny cloakroom off the main barracks hall.

"I'm afraid this great victory will reveal the basic differences among the various factions, each of whom wants their own piece of the pie," Trocmé began. "The Gaullists celebrate what they foresee as France's liberation after three years of deprivation, humiliation, and death at the hands of the Germans. It's the beginning of *France's* rebirth. On the other hand, our Communist friends see this, not as a *national* matter, but as a victory for all the downtrodden people of the world against the Fascists *and* the capitalists."

"But we're not into their politics."

"Correct, Edouard." The Pastor creaked the door open a couple of inches to ascertain that no one in the larger room was close enough to overhear their conversation. He continued, "Take it as a given that Hitler is a monster who invented and mobilized a great evil, and we're certainly pleased at his most significant defeat thus far. But the killing that's created this great victory over murder and humiliation is, itself, evil. DeGaulle's army is dedicated to military victory by means of killing. The Communists are eager to use any means, including killing, to eliminate what they perceive as institutionalized cruelty. But again, does the end justify the means? If we view all life as so precious, how can we justify the killing that has produced this great victory?"

"So, you're saying that unlike what we've heard from other groups in the camp during the short time we've been here, we're not dancing with joy at this latest development?"

Trocmé pondered this question for several moments before he gave his answer.

"Gentlemen, he finally replied. "I think I can safely say that we don't think in political terms. I, for one, view our dilemma as an ultimate ethical and religious judgment. God has shown how precious man is to Him by taking the form of a human being and coming down to help human beings find their deepest happiness. Jesus himself refused to do violence to mankind and refused to harm the enemies of his previous existence. He was always ready to forgive his enemies for their sins instead of torturing and killing them. Could we do any less if we wished to be close to Jesus than to emulate him?"

"What you're saying, my friend," Theis addressed his spiritual leader, "is that we should try, even if we fail, that our bravery lies not in killing or doing violence to others, even Germans, but in leading a whole village into stubborn, active resistance against the cruel ones of the earth."

"I believe that's correct, Edouard," said Roger Darcissac. "Bravery. And now, gentlemen, *myself* needs a good night's sleep."

Soon, gifts started coming to the camp from Le Chambon, brought mainly by Magda Trocmé and Roger Darcissac's son. The camp's shelves were loaded with packages, so that its storage area looked more like a grocery store than a prison barracks.

At first, the old inmates stared wide-eyed at each new bit of food or clothing, and they said, "We didn't know pastors were so rich."

To this, the Chambonnais would answer, "We aren't rich in the material sense by any means. These gifts are from the poor people of Le Chambon, who are used to giving and who love us."

An old inmate said, "I'll be damned! I used to be the chief of the Communist cell in Bézieres and I haven't received a thing from my comrades there. Those Christians in Le Chambon seem to resemble Communists, or at least what Communists *should* be."

36

Two weeks later

"Let me get this straight, Mister Trocmé, you're proposing that I let you use a spare room in the barracks, a blackboard and some chalk so you can conduct *Protestant* services?"

"Yes, Commandant, I am."

"You realize the three of you are the only three believing Protestants in the entire camp of over 600 prisoners?"

"I realize that, Sir. I also realize that every inmate in this camp, myself and my colleagues included, all expect to be deported, and none of us knows then the hammer will fall or the bell will toll. What harm can it possibly do? You and I are both aware that the morale in this camp is virtually nonexistent."

"But religious services …"

"And discussions which concern not only the Protestant religion but *all* religions. Matters that will prove that when it comes to religion, we are all children and there is only one Adult. Thoughts about why all of us are brothers and why the killing of anyone is an insult to the God who created us."

"How often would you wish to conduct these … meetings, Pastor Trocmé?"

"As often as inmates, or, for that matter, members of your staff, would care to attend. If only one person attends and his soul is comforted or moved, that will be one good person, one person who's come closer to God than there was before."

"Very well, Mister Trocmé, I've nothing to lose by granting what you ask."

At the first religious service twelve men trudged into the room, more out of curiosity than anything else. Theis wrote down the number of the hymns on the blackboard and gave a Bible reading. Then Pastor Trocmé gave a sermon. After this, Darcissac taught them a hymn that went, "Faith makes the strongest ramparts fall before our eyes; faith lifts the bolts and wins the battles." The three Chambonnais were surprised — and delighted — to hear the previously sullen attendees singing at the tops of their voices out of the sheer joy of being able to sing aloud together after so long a period of mutterings and fearful solitude.

After the benediction, the group sat around to talk. One of the Communists asked, "Are your hopes for the next world or for this one? If they're for the next world, they're too vague and too far away."

Trocmé replied, "Faith works on earth. I do not know about heaven. For me, the test of faith lays not in patience or rehearsed imagery, but in what that faith can do to make our own lives and lives of others precious *now*, in our homes and in our villages."

After the first meeting, the group insisted they meet not only on Sundays, but every evening. They finally agreed to meet three times a week.

On the first evening, there were twelve present, and the small room given them by the authorities was full. The next evening meeting attracted forty, and twenty inmates had to hear and sing while standing outside the open windows of the barracks.

The camp director began to worry: what could they possibly be saying to attract and keep the interest of all these long-term atheists. He detailed a policeman to become a regular member of the congregation and the discussion meetings that followed services. The police officer would sit in the front row in a seat reserved for him and he would take constant notes, although he said nothing.

The main topic of discussions was the relationship between Christianity and Communism. The three Chambonnais, cognizant of the dangerous waters they were treading because of the political implications, particularly the bitterly anti-Communist Pétain government, directed the discussions toward spiritual uplift, regardless of whether it was done in the name of religion or an economic system, and fostered the idea that trying to understand one another and to love one another and work together regardless of earthly differences, was the most efficient way of trying to bring the most promising life to all mankind.

The police officer was plainly impressed by the spiritual awakening the Protestants were bringing to this camp full of atheistic resisters.

In fact, the camp was becoming an organized group of resisters against Vichy right under the eyes of the government. After the first week of meetings, many of the formerly downcast, lethargic inmates could be seen walking across the area to and from meals or to and from the latrine singing and whistling the melodies of Protestant hymns. The camp had gotten completely out of hand, albeit *peacefully*, and the representatives of Pétain's national government never knew it.

The three leaders were creating another Le Chambon.

37

One morning, little more than a month after their incarceration, a strong male voice came over the camp loudspeaker and repeated a message three times in the space of five minutes.

"Your attention, your attention please! Camp Inmates 00681, 57592, and 71971 report to the Camp Director's office immediately!" Pastors Trocmé and Theis, and former School Superintendent Darcissac gathered nervously in their barracks when they heard the announcement.

"Oh, God, we could be in deep trouble," Darcissac said. "Maybe we were too aggressive in our discussion groups. We could even be sent to Drancy ..."

"Roger, anything *could* happen. Just remember, we've been teaching our congregants what faith is all about, and how would it look if we quivered on our boots and told them we'd been wrong all along?"

"Don't tell me you're not nervous," Darcissac persisted.

"Of course I am," Trocmé said. "If I said I wasn't scared shitless ..."

Trocmé's two closest friends, who knew of his temper, which often enough competed with his spiritual nature, were not surprised to hear him speak in this manner, and they said nothing.

"Gentlemen," Edouard Theis said, "what's that old saying, 'the coward dies a thousand dimes, the brave man dies but once ...?' We might as well march into the administration office together, just as we came here together, and face whatever music we have to hear."

When they arrived at the director's office five minutes later, the man was actually smiling. Even more surprising, he addressed them by their names and titles. "Pastor Trocmé, Pastor Theis, and Superintendent Darcissac, you are being released to return to your homes."

The three Chambonnais went back to their barracks, packed their things, and distributed the gifts they had left, mainly food which was much needed in that harsh camp, to the others. When they returned to the camp's administrative office, the commandant was waiting.

"You'll be boarding the 10:00 a.m. train for Limoges. There's only one slight formality you must observe before separation from the camp. You need to sign a certain document.

The paper had two parts. The first said, "I promise to respect the person of our leader." The other read, "I shall obey without question orders given me by the governmental authorities for the safety of France, and for the good of the National Revolution."

Darcissac, who was already working for the government as head of the boys' public school, had signed such documents in the past. He shrugged his shoulders and signed the oath.

Not so, André Trocmé. He was already about to sign the paper when Theis nudged him and pointed to the second part of the oath. "I have no problem with the first part. We respect the person of every human being. But obeying the orders of the Marshal *without question*? Are you sure you want to sign this?"

Trocmé lifted his pen from the paper. "We cannot sign this oath," he said. "It is contrary our conscience."

When he heard this, the camp director, who'd been standing behind them, became visibly agitated and shouted, "What's this? This oath has nothing in it contrary to your conscience! The marshal wishes only what is for the good of France!"

"I must ask you, Monsieur Directeur, exactly how much power does the Marechal have left? As I am certain you are aware, the fabrication that was Vichy collapsed in November, when the *Boches* turned what had been so 'bravely' called the 'Free Zone' into the Southern Zone. Other than Grenoble, there is nothing left of 'Vichy France,' *not even Vichy.*"

"You dare say such a thing, Prisoner Trocmé?"

"Indeed, I do," the pastor replied not even raising his voice. "Whether you say such things at home when no one can hear is a matter between you and your conscience. I sleep very calmly at night, by the way."

"How dare you defame the National Revolution!" the commandant growled, slamming his fist on his desk.

"I dare. Please listen so that you may hear that very clearly. We disagree with the *marechal* and his so-called National Revolution. He delivers the Jews to the Germans and thus to death. We are opposed to such an action. When we get home, we will certainly continue to oppose this policy and we will certainly continue to disobey orders from the government. How could we sign this now?"

"You refuse to sign?" the camp commandant sputtered. "This is insane. You know as well as I the vicious activities of the Jews. They're the rot that's polluting France and we must rid ourselves of them!" Suddenly he lowered his voice and confided to Trocmé, "Look, be reasonable. I appreciate your courage but you have wives and children. Sign. It's just a formality. Later, no one will notice what you did here."

"I'm sorry," the pastor replied. "If we sign, we must keep our word. We must surrender our consciences to the marshal. No, Commandant, we will not bind ourselves to immoral orders."

"So be it," the director said. "You can rot here indefinitely if the Germans don't deport you first." Turning to his deputy, he said, "Take these men back to their barracks."

Roger Darcissac had signed because he had already endorsed such an oath as head of the public school and also because he did not want to lose his job. But when he heard that his colleagues were not leaving because they had refused to sign the oath, he begged to be kept in camp with them. But the director would not let hm remain, so he said goodbye to his friends, who said they understood his position.

The next morning, Trocmé and Theis were called back to the administration building and were greeted by the director himself. "I have good news for you, Pastor Trocmé, Pastor Theis. I've just had a telephone call from the office of Pierre Laval, the marshal's second-in-command. I have been told to free you immediately."

"But we will not — we cannot — sign the oath of loyalty," Trocmé repeated, just as he had the day before.

"Never mind," said the commandant. "I have orders from the top to free you two without your signatures. You must have some good friends way up there. Anyhow, get ready. The train leaves at ten o'clock this morning, and I don't want any more trouble in this camp. Pack your bags."

To this day, no one knows with certainty why the ministers were set free. Some say that Marc Boegner, head of the Reformed Church of France at the time, spoke to Marshal Pétain on the pastors' behalf. From other sources, it was learned that the BBC had been broadcasting propaganda about how harshly Pétain was treating Protestant clerics, comparing the marshal's persecution of the Protestants and Hitler's attacks against the German Protestant churches. The Allies had won the Battle of Stalingrad, and it is possible that Pétain and Laval wanted to please the Allies in the event that the Axis might lose the war, just as they had been trying to please the Nazis when they believed that the Germans would conquer Europe and the world. For that matter, the camp director might have told the Vichy government of his fear that the Protestants were beginning to organize the camp in possibly mysterious and dangerous ways. It might have been a combination of some or all of these causes, or it might have been none of them, but as Trocmé and Theis approached the barracks for the last time, they were not concerned with this problem. They were at peace with themselves and with the world.

Just before they left, the two pastors gathered their closest friends together, formed a circle holding hands, and sang a song Roger Darcissac had taught them. The melody was the same as *Auld Lang Syne*, and its words meant, "It's only *au revoir*, my brothers, it's only *au revoir*."

The paper pledging allegiance to Marshal Pétain and the National Revolution was never used again. There had been a small breakthrough at Saint-Paul d'Eyjeaux.

But none of the prisoners except Trocmé, Theis, and Darcissac lived to go home. A few days after the Charbonnais left, all of the remaining inmates were deported to concentration camps in Poland and salt mines in Silesia. Almost all of them died at hard labor or in the gas chambers of a death camp.

38

December 14, 1942 – Pau, France - Hôtel de Gramont

"I trust you find these accommodations more to your liking than your residence during the past week?" West said upon entering her hotel room.

"Thank God for my credentials as a delegate of the American Friends Service Committee," Lara responded. "Do you mind …?"

He pushed his hand down sharply, frowning as if to emphasize *the walls have ears*. In a matter-of-fact tone, he continued, "I'm sure you're eager to see the Aviation Museum. Are you aware that after the Wright brothers transferred their operations from America to Pau thirty years ago, this fair city became the world capital of the aviation industry?"

"I am not. That sounds like a perfect afternoon's activity. I've nothing to do until tomorrow morning, when our group returns to Barcelona."

Half an hour letter, wearing a beige woolen coat, cap, and warm gloves to protect her from the icy wind descending from the nearby mountains, Lara and her "guardian angel" walked purposefully down the Boulevard des Pyrénées.

"Was it really that bad?"

"Worse," she replied. Her mind flashed back to less than a fortnight ago.

A shadowy street, strangely silent at midday. Suddenly it hit her like a punch to her gut. The unmistakable stench of human waste, sour, sickly body odor. She gagged and heaved, stumbling, and barely caught herself before she went down. Her eyes were watering as she reached the end of the block and turned the corner. "My God, what is that?" she thought, as the huge internment camp came into view. Flies buzzed in and out of barbed wire. Cheaply-built shacks strewn in rows abutting a single wide street which stretched to the far horizon. Narrow mud alleys separated the rows of at least five hundred shacks. She'd heard that Gurs internment camp had been designed to provide housing for a few hundred refugees from Republican Spain. How easily she could have been one of them. How easily Ramón could have been one of them.

As she approached the enormous courtyard in the middle of the camp, well over a thousand people, crammed in like cattle on a train — some of them crying, others screaming, still more with faces etched in wide-eyed defeat. Soiled children, silent babies, haggard elderly women, sobbing old men. Guard towers loomed over the crowd. French policemen patrolled the perimeter, their expressions blank.

One of the delegates from the A.F.S. Committee murmured as they approached the main gate, "This can't be right." He lit a Gitane *cigarette, cupping his hand to shield it from the wind.*

"Of course it's not," Lara replied.

"I mean, this can't be where they're keeping prisoners. It's not even fit for animals."

Lara felt like gagging again, but it was not the smell that was bothering her. It was the sense of suddenly being torn from anything that felt familiar. When she'd arrived in what was still Vichy France — the French State, the Unoccupied Zone — four months ago, the representatives of the Pétain government had carried out their duties with some small level of decorum. But this, this penning of humans awash in their own excrement, was barbaric beyond imagining. Worse by far than anything she'd experienced during the Civil War.

"Get your papers," the leader of their delegation had said under his breath. "Act calm, not outraged. The success of our mission, perhaps even our lives, may depend on it."

Lara couldn't imagine how she could pretend to the French police that all of this was fine. But then again, how were the guards here pretending to themselves that everything was fine? Dozens of officers walked around the area. None of them appeared bothered by the atrocity. Could they all be that evil? Did they go home to their families at night and simply flip a switch back on and become human once more?

The delegation leader exchanged words with an officer at the gate, who shuffled through their papers and ushered them inside, pointing them toward an office. As they walked, several of the prisoners penned inside another layer of barbed wire, called out to them.

"Please, you must call my brother Jean-Luc in Tarbes!"

"Please, will you find my daughter. Marie-Claire? Marie-Claire de Santos? We were separated in the recent ingathering …"

"My baby is dead! Is my baby dead? My baby, my baby …"

Lara drew a shaky breath.

A lean, dark-haired French officer, perhaps forty-five, his hair dyed a youthful light brown, stepped out of his office, his smile thin, as he ushered the delegation inside without a word. "So?" he asked, closing the door behind them. The plaintive wails outside were now muffled. The air in the room was hot, oppressive. "What brings you to our delightful establishment?"

That he could make a joke about the conditions infuriated Lara. Calm! *she commanded silently.* Let the leader do the talking.

"We are from the American Friends Service Committee," *the man announced, his tone determinedly neutral.* "Marechal Pétain …"

"I'm sorry," *the officer replied, his voice anything but,* "You are aware that the Reich has announced it will momentarily assume the duties that until recently the Marechal has had to carry on his shoulders?"

"Ah, a formality. But of course, our inspection visit was sanctioned by the duly constituted government of the French state. We only intend to be here for three weeks to give what assistance we can."

"Four days," *the functionary said peremptorily.* "During which time, you will be escorted by our stewards and you will be housed in accommodations commensurate with your station."

"But ...?"

"Let me see what I can do." *The man left, slamming the door behind him and leaving the delegation alone in the stifling mustiness of the office.*

"Not a pleasant visit?

"That, West, is an understatement, even by your measure," Lara replied. "Fifteen thousand Jews and counting. Dammit, there's got to be someone willing to help the Jews. If only America wouldn't turn a blind eye ..."

"What makes you think we aren't doing anything?"

"The newspapers, Congress ..."

"Lara, there's a lot going on that's *unofficial*, things you don't hear about. Such as *our* activities and ... others. Things which you're about to find out."

"Meaning?"

"Have you ever heard of LeChambon-sur-Lignon?"

"No."

"It's a village of about three thousand in the mountains of eastern France. Word has come down to the O.S.S. that Le Chambon has become a place of sanctuary for Jews, has managed to save at least that many Jews or get them over the border into Switzerland."

"Out of *millions* …"

"Your Talmud says, 'Whoever saves a life, it is considered as if he saved an entire world.' And just how many lives have *you* saved lately?"

Lara reddened. "I'm sorry," she said. "It's just that it's so damned frustrating …"

"Doesn't have to be."

"Meaning?"

"Save one Jew, save a universe of Jews. So far, the Nazis, and, for that matter, the Vichy government, such as it was, have left LeChambon alone. In order to make sure that continues, we have to create diversions to draw their attention elsewhere. Have you heard of the *Maquis*?"

"No."

"Even less people have heard of them than know about LeChambon. It's a throw-together organization, if you can even call it that, that's started two months ago, just about the time Vichy France issued orders to provide forced labor for Germany. Men — and women — escaped into the mountains to avoid conscription, and started a resistance movement. They've got the backing of the British Special Operations Executive, and the O.S.S. has jumped in as well. Ah, here's the Aviation Museum. I'll tell you where you come in when we're through."

"Come on, West, you can't throw bait like that into the water and expect me not to bite. I can see old biplanes in a museum any time I want. This sounds like serious business."

"Le Chambon either hides the Jews — mostly kids — for the duration, or they get them over the mountains to Annemasse, less than a mile-and-a-half to the Swiss border," West said. "Your boss man suggested he'd like to have you —under a code name of course — serve as the O.S.S.'s eyes, ears, and brains in a small mountain town called Cerdon, one hundred twenty miles northeast of Le Chambon and a little more than fifty miles west of the Swiss frontier, which seems to have become an important *maquis* center."

39

Two weeks later, December 28, 1942

On a chill winter afternoon in late 1942, "*La Lapine*" — the Rabbit — walked three blocks and crossed the border from Geneva into France. Since she'd gone back and forth every day for the past two weeks, her passage elicited not even mild interest from the border guards, who flirted with her halfheartedly before she boarded the Annemasse-Lyon express. Her mission: to contact a loosely organized group of French resistance fighters in the Auvergne-Rhône-Alpes region of eastern France between Nantua and Cerdon, direct their sabotage efforts, and turn them into a headquarters for underground operations in the area abutting Le Chambon sur Lignon. If she could establish a *courier*, a secret mail system, through that part of the Jura Mountains, so much the better.

Lara was not alone in the area. While there were several British communication and sabotage nets nearby, she had been briefed to stay well away from them. Both her American and British contacts had been adamant on that point. Three hours after she'd boarded the train, her conveyance arrived at Culoz Junction at the eastern foot of 5,023-foot-high Mount Colombier, one of the most treacherous mountain passes in France.

"Twenty-five minutes' stop!" the conductor called out as he strode through the four cars.

"Excuse me, Monsieur," Lara asked a man two seats in front of her and across the aisle, who'd been alternately napping, reading, and glancing out the window at the mountainous countryside. "Could you kindly direct me to the train to Cerdon?" Suddenly, she sat bolt upright as she recognized the man. "My God, Stefan! Is it really you?"

"It is, indeed, my friend. It's been …?

"Two months. Did the Halevis make it to Le Chambon sur Lignon?"

"They did, indeed, Lara. You can't believe what a blessing it's been, both to the four of them and to the village itself." He continued, "There's a local train to Cerdon, continuing to Nantua, due half an hour after this one leaves for Lyon. According to the timetable," he said, "it takes a little over an hour to get to Cerdon. How long since you've eaten?"

"Quite a few hours," she replied. "I had a late breakfast."

"Since this is the last major express of the day, if the buffet here is anything like those at smaller stations along the route, it'll most likely close just after this train departs. It'll be well after nightfall by the time you arrive and there probably won't be anything open in Cerdon. I hope someone will be coming to retrieve you?"

"Someone will be picking me up at the station," she replied. "West has made arrangements for me to stay overnight at *Maison de Vacances à Cerdon*."

"Ah, yes, that hero-in-disguise always manages to show up when least expected and most needed," Varga said. "Meanwhile, I trust you won't mind if I treat you to a meal while you're waiting?"

"Of course not," she smiled. "Once again the tall, handsome stranger saves the maiden in distress."

"As I seem to remember, Lara, we're one each in that department. And yes, I'd very much appreciate your companionship for the next half hour."

Descending the stairs of the train, Lara was momentarily stunned by the biting cold of the station's wind-whipped platform. Fortunately, the buffet was in its own closed-in space and heated to an almost-uncomfortable degree.

As Varga had predicted, the onion soup was excellent and the roasted chicken even better, leaving her in a much-improved mood when, half-an-hour after Varga had reboarded the express and it had departed to Lyon, a small, ancient steam engine hauling two cars arrived half an hour after the train to Lyon had departed.

True to West's promise, a man perhaps five years younger than Lara, was waiting at Cerdon station when the local arrived. "Do you have luggage?" he asked.

"Just my briefcase and a small suitcase," she answered. Lara had made sure her skirts, blouses, two sweaters, underwear and socks, as well as the woolen coat and sturdy shoes she was wearing were all well-worn, and of French manufacture. Her toilet articles were also French, and the pistol in her briefcase was Belgian, a Fabrique Nationale GP35 automatic with a thirteen-round magazine.

She'd been told her documents were quite good, and they'd proved to be when they'd been examined by the Vichy police or German street patrolmen in Annemasse. Should *la Lapine* fall into the hands of an intelligence section — Gestapo or SD — however, it might certainly be a different story. Her instructors back in Canada had told her in no uncertain terms that if she were captured, the sooner she tried to escape afterward, the better her chances.

Lara did not intend to be captured. She did not intend to mingle with Germans. She did not intend to be "brave." She'd been specifically cautioned against it. She would move cautiously in daylight, at most another face in the French countryside, and play the game at night.

The young man who'd met her at the station led her to an ancient, battered Renault truck, and within moments she was lulled into a sense of relaxation as she felt and heard the soft crunch of tires rolling over a thin covering of newly-fallen snow. As they traversed the country road, barely two lanes wide with no center line, Lara heard a distant engine. The driver pulled over to the side of the road and stopped on a narrow shoulder. As Lara listened to the two-stroke sputter of the engine, she determined it must be a motorcycle. She watched the German dispatch rider go by, sighting on him with her right index finger and silently mouthing *bam* just at the proper moment. The sound of the cycle faded into the distance as its rider shifted gears up and down quite frequently. *No need to shift that much* she thought. The German, alone on the road, was playing with his machine, lying low over the handlebars like a race car driver. But she, too, leading the rider for a perfect shot, had been playing.

What caught her attention in that first nebulous contact with the enemy was the intimacy of the moment. It now became clear what she had been tasked to do and how she would feel doing it. When her driver turned the key in the truck's ignition, its engine coughed a few times before it caught and, gears grinding noisily, the vehicle crossed over the tall weeds abutting the road and resumed its journey. The snowfall had now increased in intensity. By the time they arrived at her lodging great drifts covered the roadway.

That night, with a full stomach and no one to disturb her, "the Rabbit" slept deeply and dreamlessly in a firm single bed, shielded from bitter cold outside by a softly guttering fire and the warmth of a soft, thick featherbed.

Maquis, roughly translated, means "brush," and that was pretty much the story in the hills overlooking the lower village. The driver had picked her up promptly at 7:00 a.m., and in the weak, early-morning winter sun, she'd glimpsed the chipped stone *borne kilométrique* — the milestone marker — on the inner curve of the road. A few minutes later, they passed the first of Cerdon's vineyards, its vines now bereft of the grapes which, in the warmer months, gave birth to the region's famed Cerdon-Bugey rosé wines.

Upper Cerdon, backlit by a cold mountain sky, was a mud square surrounded by a handful of stone cottages and a rust-stained fountain with a tattered iron hen standing motionless atop the spigot.

As Lara and her driver alighted, several small, brownish dogs glared at them unpleasantly from a safe distance, but there were no people. The village, beautifully situated, climbed from a narrow, winding valley through three hills, but Lara's first sensation was the smell of damp earth and pig manure.

The *maquis,* alerted to *La Lapine's* coming, trickled from the doors of nearby cottages and formed up, more or less, in the square. After a period of awkward silence, they began to introduce themselves to the new arrival. There were the Cadieux brothers, Jean-Marc and Jean-Luc, short, dark-skinned, and vaguely menacing, each in their late teens or early twenties, dressed in tight pants and pullover shirts of the type that had been popular a decade ago. Aristide Monet, twenty-three, tall, blond, and classically handsome — watchful and silent — a shotgun slung, barrel down, diagonally across his back. *Le Taureau*, the bull, he was called. No one ever referred to him by any other name. No one would ever want to run across him in a dark, narrow space at night unless he was there to protect you. Eighteen and built like his cognomen.

Emile Serres, *"Homme de Garde,"* — the watchman — sixteen, the youngest of the group, who had picked Lara up at the train station and was her initial contact. His deceptive appearance, that of an innocent choirboy, masked his true character. Marie Vallade, *La Tasse* —"the purse," — a stocky young farm girl with the courage of ten men. Altogether six young people. The beginning of an army.

"*La Lapine?*" It was Jean-Marc Cadieux, the older brother, who spoke.

"*Oui,*" she replied.

The "army" looked uncertain, perhaps disappointed. They had probably anticipated a ten-foot-tall amazon with a machine gun, breathing fire. *Well,* she thought, *too bad.* They were dealing instead with a reasonably attractive woman close to their own age, who did not appear particularly menacing. *Probably we deserve each other.*

Shortly after the introductions, the half-dozen young people, lacking the appearance of a real army by a few thousand souls, took her into one of the nearby houses, where they ate a breakfast of cabbage fried with fat bacon and hunks of heavy bread, washed down with cups of chicory, since there was no coffee to be found in the villages of the *Haute-Rhone*. An older man of forty-five, Roland DesJardins, and his much younger wife, Jeanne, served *l'Americaine* and the Cerdon *maquis*.

After the meal, a grandmother appeared, five feet tall and almost equally round, swathed in black. She examined Lara, pinched her waist and her bottom, and clucked her tongue against the roof of her mouth. She muttered to Roland, in what he later explained was the ancient Occitan tongue of the mountains of the Haute-Rhone, "A good wind would blow her right off the mountain. We must fatten this one up."

And it was thus that the war against the *schleuhs* — the Germans — got started in earnest.

It was a war of mischief,

That became apparent in the week that followed Lara's arrival. Roland, in whose house she lived, said one evening that the people of Cerdon had always hated those bastards down there. It was the contempt of mountain people for flatlanders. *Down there* meant Bourg-en-Bresse, twenty miles to the northwest. *Down there* meant tax collectors and municipal authorities and Gendarmerie and all those blood-sucking leeches who made a poor mountain man's life a misery.

Between Cerdon and *down there* was a kind of truce, worked out over decades. The flatlanders bothered the *Cerdonais* only a little, and the mountain people accepted just about that much botherment. They lived with each other — just.

When, however, you added the heavy-handed *boche* authority to this chemistry, as had occurred in the two years since the Vichy "government" had become the Nazis' catspaw, a certain amount of hell was bound to break loose. The people of Cerdon took it as a divine mission to bother the German overlords, while avoiding too much interest from those they called *La Geste* — the Gestapo. It soon became apparent to everyone that these Gestapo people were best left alone. They had made that evident early on, had taken to strutting about in leather coats and tearing around the roads in Grossser Mercedes sedans. *Here we are,* they said. *Try your luck.*

So, in Cerdon, until *La Lapine* showed up, they'd had to content themselves with mischief. When *Homme de Garde* had contrived to obtain a concussion grenade, Jean-Marc Cadieux and the others had snuck inside the perimeter of a Panzer division encampment near Bourg-en-Bresse and dropped it into a septic tank which served as the officers' latrine, just about the time it was in full use, the noise inside the barracks had been spectacular. Better yet, there'd been no response from the Germans.

But when *Le Taureau* had become obsessed by an obnoxious poodle — the adored pet of a *Feldwebel,* a sergeant, who spoke German babytalk to it on the street — and had blown the thing's fluffy head off with an old army pistol he'd stolen, the local Notary and his wife had been stood against a wall in reprisal. The townspeople took the orphans in, but they had a good notion who had done it, and *Le Taureau* had to visit relatives in another village for six months. The *maquis* had learned that any people, *frightened* angry people, are dangerous, that they couldn't be sure what they'd do, especially when the means to a hard lesson were so near at hand.

In the same week, Lara began to have a feel for the currents that ran beneath the surface of village life. Her briefers had been crystal clear: "Village sexual life is quite complex. Don't be drawn in."

It soon became obvious that they'd been right, A servant girl of perhaps fifteen was visited on successive nights by Jean-Luc Cadieux and Aristide Monet. In addition, Jean-Marc looked at Roland's young wife in a quite explicit way. Lara hadn't any idea how Roland reacted to it. He seemed not to notice.

Meanwhile, she familiarized herself with her surroundings. She spent a good deal of time walking the vineyards and the forests around Cerdon, learning the trails from *La Tasse* and Emile, and listening each night to the BBC's *messages personnels* on the radio, which held an honored position on a table in the center of Roland's living room. The sheer volume of traffic surprised her.

A week after she'd arrived in the village, her activation signal crackled from the wireless. Lara told Roland she'd be away for a time. The older man offered to accompany her. "Nothing against the young ones, they are the patriots of Cerdon, but I am a patriot of *France*, a veteran of the last war. The *boches* gassed me at Verdun."

La Lapine thought about the offer for a moment. By the rules, she was supposed to go alone, but there was something of a test in Roland's manner, and she decided to trust the man. The briefers had told her, "Unless you are monumentally stupid or terribly unlucky, the Germans won't catch you. On the other hand, the chances of being betrayed are better than one would like."

But she had to trust somebody, so she trusted Roland.

40

A FEW DAYS LATER, JANUARY 3, 1943

The train ride from Cerdon to Mâcon was nasty, cold and sweaty at the same time. A great press of bodies occupied the aisle, including German soldiers. It made for two hours of sour breath, wet wool, a baby that wouldn't shut up, vacant faces, tired eyes, and icy drafts that blew through the spaces between the boards of the World War I vintage rolling stock. Most of the better French trains has been commandeered and had traveled east to Germany to be refitted for the different width of the tracks, then sent on to Wehrmacht units near Moscow.

It took them more than two hours to travel forty-eight miles over often-damaged and repaired track, shunted aside for flatcars carrying artillery pieces to the Atlantic coast, unable to attain much speed because of coal adulterated by sand and gravel. Roland turned out to be a traveling companion of great comfort, prattling away the whole time about the health of his pigs, the price of cheese, and his older sister. For her part, Lara grunted and nodded, pretending to listen to her "boring uncle."

At the Mâcon station, which was only 90 miles from Switzerland and thus a magnet for just about anything in occupied Europe, *La Geste* was very much in evidence, pointedly in the business of *watching*. To Lara, they had the feel of provincial police inspectors, stocky and middle-aged, clumsy looking in their high-belted leather coats, and stolid, their eyes forever searching. Clearly a game but, just as clearly, a game they were good at. When they saw something — anything — one of them would snap his fingers and beckon the individual over for a document check, holding the paper up to the white sky above the station platform. Roland, bless his heart, faltered not at all, blabbering Lara past *La Geste* and the usual police checkpoints with the story of "her *maman,*" insisting that the roof be retiled, just at planting time, not a seed in the ground, and rains coming. But, Roland shrugged, one must obey the *maman*. What else could one do?

It was not the usual Roland who went to Mâcon. The everyday Roland sported a permanent gray stubble of whiskers beneath a beat-up old beret, layers of shapeless sweaters, baggy wool pants, and rubber boots with dried pigshit from the farmyard. The Mâcon Roland, knowing he was to be no part of the business there, had shaved and produced a Sunday suit that wore its age with grace and dignity. In the street outside the station, he bade Lara farewell and went off whistling, with a light step. Clearly, his mission in Mâcon was a romantic one.

Contact procedures for Lara included a visit to the Post Office near the railroad station. *La Lapine* stood in line, and at last approached the counter attended by a man in his sixties with well-pomaded and recently poorly-dyed black hair. Lara pushed a letter across the counter and requested six stamps. The postal clerk barely glanced at her, tore six stamps off a sheet with bureaucratic efficiency, and handed them to her. She looked at the stamps, an occupation issue prominently featuring the new national motto — *travail, famille, patrie*. In the corner of one stamp was a lightly penned address.

This turned out to be an abattoir, a slaughterhouse, in a working-class neighborhood, twenty minutes from the railway station. Using every bit of her self-control to avoid gagging at the overpowering stench when she opened the door, Lara asked the young attendant, "Do you have any rabbit *paté?*" knowing that such a product was never sold in a place like this.

"You must be joking," the young man, clothed in a blood-stained apron and chef's cap replied, "to think we'd sell something like *that* in a place like *this.*"

"Ah, please pardon me," Lara continued, having memorized the drill. "The Dominican priest must have misguided me."

"You must return in twenty minutes," the young man said. "We might have some, then."

Lara returned to the slaughterhouse shop exactly twenty minutes later,

"So," the attendant said. "Perhaps we have some in the back."

As *La Lapine* went through the door the young attendant had indicated, she found herself in a room just above freezing, amid rows of bloody beef and horse quarters on ceiling hooks. An older woman appeared at the other end of the central aisle, her breath steaming in the cold. She appeared to be in her mid-fifties, silver-haired, clearly an aristocrat, in a finely cut gray suit with an overcoat worn around her shoulders like cape.

"Who are you?" she asked in Parisian French, each word shaped as if it meant something.

"*La Lapine.*"

"And who am I?"

"Dominique."

"Where do I live?"

"Château De Chambord."

"Would that I did," she sighed. "Papers?"

Lara handed them over. Dominique spent at least two minutes thumbing through the pages. "Excellent," she said. She handed back the papers and called out, "Very well, Alois."

Lara never saw Alois. There was some motion to one side of her that caused the red haunches to sway on their hooks, then the sound of a shutting door. She assumed there had been a gun aimed at her.

"What do you need?" the older woman asked.

"Stens, ammunition, enough for training as well as normal use. *Plastiques*, cyclonite, time pencils. A few hand grenades perhaps?"

"How many *maquis* are there?"

"Six. Probably eight."

"Not enough, *Lapine*. You must recruit."

"Is that safe?"

"Hardly. You'll take losses — everyone does. You should have twelve new recruits to start. Ask your people. They'll know whose heart beats for France. What do they have now?"

"Rabbit guns. An old pistol. A few cans of gasoline."

"That won't win the war. You shall have what you need, but wait for your *message personnel* before you move. There will be a courier for the date. You won't see him."

"Will I be in radio communication?"

"In time, *Lapine*, but not now. The German radio interception is very good. They have mobile receivers that move about the countryside and they'll find you quicker than you think. I'd suggest you enjoy your independence while you have it." Dominique glanced at her watch, a top-of-the-line Patek Philippe. "Well, goodbye then. I'll see you another time." They shook hands. Lara opened a door that fronted directly onto an alley behind the shop.

On the way back, as she waited with Roland on the Mâcon station platform, the two Gestapo officers made an arrest. How the man had gotten that far Lara could only imagine, His clothing was torn and blackened with railroad soot. His face was drained, white as death, and his eyes were pink from sleepless nights, He was obviously a fugitive on the run. They manacled his hands and he wept silently as they marched him away.

Two weeks after Lara's visit to Mâcon, the Cerdon *maquis* drove to the drop zone, then carried dry wood on their backs for half a mile after hiding the old truck well off the road. They triangulated the field with wood piles and covered them with canvas tarps. Immediately thereafter, it started to rain, the drops cold, icy, and as heavy as pebbles. They tried sheltering under the trees but this particular mountain meadow was surrounded by deciduous forest, so that they were splattered by raindrops hitting the bare branches. *La Lapine* was soaked through in minutes.

At 2:30 a.m. they lit the woodpiles, then stood back and watched them blaze and smoke in the rain. But there was no sign of an airplane, and by a quarter of three their bonfires were no more than smoldering piles of wet, charred wood. They couldn't return to Cerdon, so they groped their way into the forest in search of dead branches, falling and bruising themselves in the darkness. The wet branches were piled up on what remained of the bonfires and they tried to light them, using up most of their matches and swearing every curse they could summon.

To no avail. At last, Aristide produced an old piece of rubber tubing from a coat pocket and started siphoning off the gas from the truck. A bottle at a time, they soaked down the woodpiles while Aristide, who'd ingested a certain amount of gasoline in getting the siphon action underway, went off into the woods to be sick.

At that moment, they heard the sound of airplane engines above them in the darkness. coming from the east. The equation for nighttime air supply operations involved fuel weight, load weight, airspeed, distance, weather, hours of darkness, the phase of the moon, evasive flight paths, and fuel allowance for escape tactics in the event of pursuit. Lara figured the British pilot must have used his last margin of safety looking for them, and should he encounter Luftwaffe night fighters on the return trip, he'd be doomed unless he ditched over the Channel. They never saw the plane, but they could hear the engines quite distinctly. He'd come down low to look for their signal. The gas-soaked wood sprang to life and roared against the downpour for only a few moments before the flame turned blue and danced pointlessly along the tree boughs, burning up the last of the fuel.

But that was enough. The Halifax pilot must have seen the orange smudges beneath the clouds and signaled his dropmaster. Thus, the crates with parachutes attached were manhandled out the cargo doors and floated down through the darkness, one of them hanging up in the branches of a tree until Emile scampered up and cut the shrouds. They loaded the crates into the truck and silently celebrated their miraculous achievement — until Roland attempted to start the engine and learned that their precious gasoline had been burned up. The Cadieux brothers hiked back to Cerdon.

By midmorning, German patrols occupied the road. Someone else had heard the bomber, but it was raining too hard for the Germans to come up into the forest. Nevertheless, the *maquis* waited most of the morning in ambush by the trail, having voted to defend their arms, no matter what the cost.

Just before noon, as the rain turned to snow, six of the Cerdon women appeared at the edge of the field, pushing bicycles. They had traveled all morning, carrying the heavy metal petrol cans back and forth.

The entry into Cerdon was triumphant. The entire population of the village turned out in the wet snow and applauded the American woman, the English pilot, and themselves.

Four days later, Lara's *Limelight* message was broadcast, setting the first attack for the night of January 20, 1943. Ten days. That was no time at all, but she did what she could. Which meant preparing for the operation — doing the necessary intelligence background and simultaneously training her *maquis* in the new equipment. Back in Canada, her instructors had shown her that the pathway to minimize danger — and to maximize the opportunity for escape should the worst befall them — consisted of knowledge of the situation, objectivity, caution, secrecy, planning, and, above all, scrupulous attention to detail. But suddenly she was at war, so she found herself improvising, doing half a dozen things at once, making decisions quickly in the heat of the moment. Perhaps all the wrong things, perhaps not, but she could feel *something* in the air, and she was carried along by its rhythm. Lancasters and Halifaxes overhead every night. Searchlights criss-crossing the sky. Her *maquis* could see them from miles away. *Boche* patrols everywhere on the road, from Nantua all the way to Mâcon, and, she'd heard, perhaps as far away as Lyon. Increased interrogation in Gestapo centers.

The Germans felt it, too. And they were clearly unsettled. They knew *something* was going to come. They just didn't know *where* or *when*, and, as unwelcome invaders and rulers of a surly and sullen defeated population, that made them understandably and meaningfully nervous.

The new guns were a matter of great excitement to the Cerdon *maquis*. The Mark II Sten, properly a machine carbine, was *the* special operations weapon of their clandestine war. So simple. A few tubular components that screwed together quickly once you filed the burrs off the threads. Six pounds, essentially a skeletal steel frame carrying the most primitive bolt-and-spring firing mechanism. And it was fast, putting out rounds in a staccato spray.

For *La Lapine*, the Sten was the least alluring of their available tools. She realized that the reality of this war called for hundreds of thousands of these simple death machines to be placed in willing hands. It was a perfect assassination weapon, meant for the man or woman whose anger had pushed caution out of the way, to the point where he or she would kill up close.

The Sten was cheaply made, costing less than $12.00 to produce. The basic firing mechanism tended to jam. Thus, the thirty-two round magazine was better loaded with thirty rounds of 9 mm parabellum ammunition to reduce pressure on the magazine spring. And it was short. The fixed sight was set for a hundred yards. You operated at the length of a football field and could see the enemy quite clearly. It was, quite simply, a streetfighting weapon. If, as a guerilla, you had the misfortune to engage the enemy on his own terms, the best you could do was to get close enough to burn him badly before he killed you — which he could easily do by drawing back out of your range to give himself total advantage.

Lara had no intention to engage. Their target, identified in code by the courier, was the railroad yards at Oyonnax, just under twenty miles to the northeast. *La Tasse* had a cousin who worked in the storage yards, and, on the Thursday before the attack, it was *La Tasse*, and not the cousin's wife who, at noontime, brought him his lunch of soup and bread. Lara found a vantage point on a hill overlooking the yards and watched *La Tasse* ride in on her bicycle, napkin-covered bowl in the crook of her right arm, half a *baguette* balanced across the top of the bowl. The German sentry waved her through. Later, Lara was ecstatic to learn there were fifteen locomotives in the roundhouse in different stages of repair and readiness. She would, she knew, get them all.

On the following Sunday night, just before midnight, if one were close enough, he or she could hear a series of muffled *whumps* in the roadhouse and might see some dirty smoke dribbling from three or four broken windows. That was all. But fifteen tools critical to the Wehrmacht's war effort would now be permanently removed from the Nazi arsenal. *La Lapine* and Emile watched it happen from their vantage point, then retreated casually, by bicycle, back to the center of Oyonnax.

Lara had gone in accompanied by Roland and *Le Taureau*, almost casually surrounded by a dozen laborers on the graveyard shift. These laborers would suffer German suspicion after the sabotage, but the German interrogations would not be all that severe. No occupying force, particularly one as hated as the *schleuh*, could easily afford to sacrifice skilled railroad workers.

The men gathered around the American and her two male cohorts as they trudged into the railyard. To them, the three strangers constituted a weapon, plain and simple. A weapon against those they loathed beyond words, and they protected *Lapine, Taureau,* and Roland accordingly. The three invaders wasted no time in the roundhouse. They simply formed thirty pieces of malleable *plastique* explosive into a collar around the wheels under each locomotive and wedged a time pencil into each claylike mass. Then *Taureau* tied up two quite willing roundhouse workers with heavy cord and moved them behind a protective wall. The three interlopers snuck back out the back of the roundhouse through a well-used dog tunnel in the wire fence. The whole operation took less than forty-five minutes.

For the mere thud of an explosion and a little smoke.

The yard sirens went off, the firemen appeared, the French police followed, a few German officers ran about, but there was little to be done. One fireman, reducing the water pressure to little more than the volume of a garden hose, soaked down the area for ten minutes while a yard supervisor nailed boards across the broken windows. A dog patrol showed up shortly afterwards. The German shepherds went right for the dog tunnel in the fence, picked up a scent that led to the edge of an empty hill above the yards, accepted their dog biscuits and pats, peed, and went home.

A Gestapo *Sturmbannführer* took the rope that had bound the workers as evidence and put it in a leather pouch with a tag stating the time, place, and date. Then they all stood around for an hour smoking and talking. Bored. It was so insignificant.

The true rage was reserved for the German transport officer who had chosen that night to occupy a French featherbed rather than a German army cot and had thus arrived late. He was quick to assess what the loss of fifteen locomotives, half of which were not even in operable condition a few hours before, meant: fifteen locomotives weren't going anywhere ever again.

The officer stared at the mess and muttered *scheiss* through clenched teeth. His transportation mathematics were quite efficient. Each locomotive pulled sixty freight cars. In the three-month period it would take to replace these locomotives, assuming the German army, which was starting to run short of rolling stock *could* pull them off the increasingly urgent need to reinforce the forces on the eastern front, and replace them in that time, each engine could be expected to make nine round trips to the Atlantic coastal defense lines in the west and north. He multiplied that by fifteen out-of-service locomotives and came up with eighty-one hundred lost carloads which would never reach the German forces.

The transport officer wasn't really a bad fellow. In all likelihood he would have appreciated, once restored to his more reflective self, the words of *la Lapine's* British briefing officer as he'd reviewed Lara's operation: "For want of a nail, my dear young lady, and all that sort of thing."

41

JANUARY – MARCH 1943

They operated quietly in the first months of 1943. With the destruction of oil fields, railroads, factories, shipping, and lines of communications, coupled with an increasingly bleak outlook on the eastern front and in North Africa, the colossus that had earlier seemed perilously close to ruling its desired sphere of influence was starting to totter. And despite Goebbels protestations to the contrary, increasingly restive civilian populations in Hamburg, Frankfurt, and even Berlin were starting think something that was *never* to be voiced publicly: perhaps victory was *not* just around the corner. Likewise, as pins went up on maps in the Abwehr and Sicherheitsdienst analysis centers, a similar but opposing set of pins appeared in London, Arlington County, Virginia, and in the Kremlin.

La Lapine's operation had been only one of an increasingly broad range of allied actions concentrated of a period of several weeks against communications and transportation facilities, including railroads, factories, and shipping ports. The Germans surmised that a major attack was coming somewhere in Occupied Europe, but the *where* and *when* factors were critical. The chief intelligence mission, of which MI-6 and the O.S..S played a tiny but critical role, was to create a structure in which deceptions could succeed.

The techniques were not new: the practices of disinformation and special operations behind enemy lines had been well-known and used by Hannibal in his wars against the ancient Romans. It drove the Axis forces slightly mad, which was exactly what it was intended to do.

Locomotives had not been the principal objective in *La Lapine's* attack on the railroad yards at Oyonnax. This was not strategic sabotage on a grand scale; it was sabotage specific, a tactical maneuver. The actual target was a heavily-armed ammunition train which was, at the moment of the attack, over a hundred miles away, bound for a much-needed overhaul in the Oyonnax facilities prior to shepherding a series of smaller, unprotected trains to the defense lines of Picardy. There would be no major landing in winter — the Germans knew that — but they also knew about dress rehearsals. Two-and-a-half years earlier, the nearly moribund British had launched such a rehearsal at Haamstede. The Oyonnax operation was clearly seen by the Nazis as a feint, but toward what end?

German intelligence in the *Haut-Bugey* region was not able to find out precisely who had attacked the Oyonnax yards, but gossip did reach them, and was intended to reach them, that it was no more than a bunch of village toughs led by a low-level Special Operations technician. They sent a platoon up to Nantua, one of several villages that interested them, but the *maquis* lookouts on the road passed the word, and the group took to the hills with time to spare, crammed themselves into a woodcutter's hut high up on a nearby mountain, and waited it out.

Cerdon, covered by a thin layer of snow, was even less impressive than Cerdon in its normal condition. The German officer who looked in the houses, smelled the smells, and saw the frightened eyes peering from doorways and the rust-stained fountain with the iron hen standing motionless atop the spigot, wrote off the scene as insignificant.

So, ultimately, in Berlin, they stuck a white pin in Cerdon, not a red one. The information was wired back from Berlin to counterespionage filed units in the Ain sector and, because a Polish factory worker had stolen a

German cipher machine at the very start of the war and Polish and British cryptanalysts at Bletchley Park had broken the codes, the Allies knew they'd succeeded. And put a pin of a different color in their own map.

Lara's mission called for ongoing operations at a low level. Harassing the *boches* had to continue, of course, but gently, gently. A telephone pole cut down. Children's jacks with sharpened points strewn about to blow the tires of the telephone repair vehicle. A tree felled across the road, which halted supply columns. No ambush, just a tree. But it kept the *schleuh* nervous, busy, frustrated. Pranks, simple, innocent pranks at such a low level they did not warrant reprisals against civilians. The Cerdon *maquis* blew up metal casings that enabled the switching of locomotives from track to track. Rails pried apart so that a locomotive plowed up hundreds of ties as it derailed, then left a charge behind for the railroad crane that would arrive to repair the damage. But only a small charge, which would keep the crane out of commission for a week.

Under *La Lapine's* direction, the *maquis* slowly recruited five, eight, ten, then twenty-one new *maquis*. The creation of a courier service was put on hold. Lara had all she could do to operate her own small group and, concurrently, to find, enlist, and train new *maquisards*.

She got all sorts.

Soldiers of fortune — former criminals who hoped to make their new fortunes in wartime targets of opportunity. Everyday citizens, who had held themselves out of the fighting until they saw which way the wind was going to blow, and now started rushing to get in on things before it was too late. They now surmised that service in the underground resistance would yield important benefits after the war. The original *maquis* looked down on these citizen-soldier "volunteers" with contempt. "Mothballs," they called them.

Meanwhile, the original group of Cerdon male *maquis* strutted about grandly with cigarettes stuck in one corner of their mouths, eyes slitted, and Sten guns slung diagonally across their backs, mountain style.

Mountain style, which left the hands fee, enabling one to move swiftly and safely on the treacherous paths, better because that was the way it had always been done, since the time their village ancestors had slung muskets across their backs and gone off to fight as mountain troops in Napoleon's Grande Armée against the ancestors of the very same Germans they were fighting in 1943.

One day in late January, Jean-Marc Cadieux and Marie Vallade took two of the new recruits, "Charles," who claimed he was the nephew of the old loon who'd built a house up on a neighboring mountain, but whose accent sounded as though he'd originally hailed from someplace southeast of Zagreb, and Battistu, a dark-skinned Corsican from Ajaccio, out on practice maneuvers. The objective was to teach them some mountain lore and to familiarize them with the network of deer trails running through the forest between the road and the village.

Jean-Marc and Marie traveled down the path at great speed, testing the stamina of their pupils, leaving them far behind. *A good lesson, let them struggle.* It could well save their lives. The two veteran *maquisards* would race down a section of the path, then wait for the other two, who would arrive panting and red-faced. Just as they came into view, Jean-Marc would bark out, "Rest period over. Time to go," and set out again. The novices were left to get along as best they could, leg muscles twanging and rubbery from the shock of the downhill slope.

No one saw the German officer, who was bird-watching on his day off, until they almost ran smack into him. Jean-Marc and *La Tasse* came around a corner of the path and there he was, attended by a bored *feldwebel,* a sergeant, probably his driver, who leaned against a tree and picked his nails while his superior alternately peered into the sky through binoculars and consulted a field guide to birds in the *Ain.* The two Germans and the two *maquisards* saw each other at about the same moment. For a long second, they froze and nothing happened. It took each of them some time to realize they were in the presence of enemies because they were engaged in innocent pastimes, simply not at war that day. It was less than strange to meet a French boy and girl on a mountain path and all would have been well but for the Stens. The officer, a little to one side of the path for a better view through the pines, got a good look at the weapons and it wasn't long before he came to understand exactly what they meant.

There followed a moment when the officer scrabbled at the flap of his holster, and his *Feldwebel* attempted to grab his rifle which was resting butt down against a tree, only to knock it over. Jean-Marc and Marie had the most difficult time of all as they tried to struggle free of their slung weapons. It took them a hopelessly long time to do so, and they never quite managed it. The officer drew his pistol, thumbed the safety off, shot each of them once, then ran away down the trail, the sergeant galloping behind, dragging his rifle along the ground by its strap.

Charles, the new recruit, who really had come from the Balkans and was more experienced in guerilla tactics than any of them knew, had heard the shots and dove off the path, landing on his stomach with his machine pistol pointed in the direction of the gunfire. Battistu could not see. Charles heard the sounds of flight and a series of moans below him. Within a minute, he deduced that someone had fired and someone else had run away. Since those who fled were headed downhill toward the road, he assumed they were the enemy and that the moaning was coming from Jean-Marc and *La Tasse*, one or both of whom had been hit.

Charles circled wide of the trail and came in from the flank. Battistu arrived from the opposite direction about the same time. Charles gestured down the trail and Battistu took off in that direction, crouched, moving swiftly and gracefully. It was clear to Charles that the Corsican was not new at this.

When he reached Jean-Marc he saw the veteran *maquisard's* Sten gun on the ground. Jean-Marc lay flat on his back, a plea in his eyes: *please help me.* *La Tasse* seemed worse off. She lay on her back across Jean-Marc's lower legs. Her head hung backward. She had covered her face with her hands and was moaning softly every few seconds.

"Are you badly hurt?" Charles asked Jean-Marc.

The latter shook his head that he didn't know. "She has my legs pinned," he said. "It's somewhere down there,"

He circled Jean-Marc, knelt by Marie, and gently pulled her hands away. It was very bad. She'd been shot in the face. Just below and to the outside of her left nostril, a red bead of flesh extended from a puffy circle shaded blue at the exterior edge. Suddenly, she grabbed hold of his wrists and gagged. He realized she was swallowing blood, shook one of his hands loose, and raised her head, "Thank you," she mouthed.

"Can you spit it out?"

She tried, but couldn't manage. He cleaned out her mouth as best he could, then wiped away the water that ran from her eyes. "It's the wound," she said. "I am not crying."

"I know," he said. He probed gently in the hair at the base of her skull, looking for an exit wound, but couldn't find anything. God only knew where the bullet was. Somewhere inside her face,

Charles realized that Battistu was standing above him, breathing hard, "They're gone," he said, "I heard the car take off."

Charles nodded. That meant they would be back in force in less than an hour, He said to Jean-Marc, "I don't want to move her. Is she crushing your legs?"

"I don't feel anything."

"Can you move your feet? Your toes?"

"No."

Charles' heart sank. Battistu swore softly.

Suddenly, he heard running footsteps from the trail above him. *La Lapine,* the American leader, and Roland DesJardins came into sight moments later. Lara appeared pale and shaken. Roland carried a Sten and a tattered old book with its covers missing.

"What happened?" Lara asked, breathless.

Jean-Marc Cadieux told him.

Marie laid her head back in Charles' arms. One side of her face had swollen so that her left eye was a slit. She was beginning to struggle for breath as the damaged passages swelled shut.

Charles addressed Roland, who was hunting through his book, a medical manual which had belonged to the village for many years and was used primarily to set broken bones and treat burns. "Is there a doctor in the village?" he asked.

"The closest one is in Bourg-en-Bresse, twenty miles away."

"You'd better get him," Charles said. "Marie is dying."

Lara spoke. "We must bring them both down there," she said.

"No," Roland said. "*C'est impossible.* The *schleuhs* will be all over the place. They've seen the Stens."

"Where is the truck?" Lara demanded.

"By the logging camp on the other side of the road."

"Is there gasoline?"

"A little."

"Let's go," Lara said.

"Did you not hear me, *Lapine*?" Roland asked.

"It doesn't matter. We're going."

"*Lapine*," Roland said, grim. "They'll get us all."

"No, they won't."

"I'm sorry, *Lapine*," Jean-Marc said. "We didn't …"

They waited while Lara ran back up the path and warned the villagers. The remainder of the *maquis* and the new recruits took the arms and ammunition and moved up the mountain. When *La Lapine* returned, she, Charles, Battistu, and Roland carried the wounded down the path and across the road, and loaded them carefully into the back of the truck. They covered themselves with a canvas tarp while Roland drove alone in the cab.

The ride down the mountain road seemed to go on forever. The old truck's brakes were virtually useless on the steep curves. Every time Roland downshifted, the flywheel screamed and threatened to blow the transmission all over the road. Charles lay on his side in the darkness and tried to keep Marie's head from moving with the truck's motion. In vain. At first, she cried out, but as they went farther down the mountain, she fell silent. Charles felt her skin growing cold.

His training told him to sacrifice one in order to save another. To stop might put all their lives in jeopardy, but this was the leader's decision. Finally, he shifted over next to Lara and raising his voice above the truck's roaring motor, said, "*Lapine, La Tasse* is asphyxiating. She won't make it."

Lara answered a moment later, "Are you sure? It could be shock."

"It could be, but I think her windpipe is closing up. We can still save Jean-Marc if we continue."

"No," Lara answered firmly in a tone that brooked no objection. She reached out from beneath the tarp and pounded on the rear window of the cab. Roland slowed — they could feel him pumping the brakes gingerly — then pulled off the road onto the grassy shoulder. He raced the engine so that it would not stall.

On the other side of the road, a German staff car and a truckload of soldiers raced past, going the other way, but they ignored the truck by the side of the road.

"Hold her head," Lara commanded.

Charles cradled Marie's head in his lap and pressed his hands against the side of her face. Lara reached into her pocket and brought out a cheap fountain pen. She unscrewed the two halves, then broke off the nib and end cleaned up the shattered edge as best she could. She pulled her shirttail out and wiped ink from the open tube she'd fashioned. Charles could see that her hands were shaking.

"Ready?" Lara asked.

Charles nodded.

"Open her mouth."

Charles pulled her teeth apart. He could see Lara was sweating in the cold air as she pressed Marie's tongue down with her left index finger. When she forced the tube down the back of *La Tasse's* throat, the pain brought the French girl back from stupor and she screamed, a hoarse, choking sound that made Charles shudder. When Lara withdrew her hand, there was blood on it,

Lara wasted no time. She pounded on the cab window again and Roland moved back onto the road. Marie — *La Tasse* — tried to move her hand to her mouth, but Charles held tightly to her wrist. "Just breathe," he whispered by her ear, "Can you?" After a moment, she moved her head up and down to tell him that she could.

In Bourg-en-Bresse, the truck slowed, bumping along the cobbled streets. Suddenly, he took off quickly with all the acceleration the old engine could muster. They drove for several minutes, then rolled to a stop.

Charles peeked beneath the tarp and saw the Bourg-en-Bresse railway station. At Lara's direction, Battistu checked out the other side and reported that Roland was entering the Hôtel de la Gare, which, Charles knew, was to be found across the street from virtually every railroad station in France,

Some minutes later, Roland appeared at the back of the truck and spoke in an undertone. "There was a Gestapo car parked in front of the doctor's office. They know there's been a gunshot wound. I'm going to drive around to the back of the hotel. Once we get there, move quickly and get them inside."

The truck inched down a narrow alley, cornered, and stopped. They threw the tarp off and saw two men in dark suits with pistols in their hands. Charles immediately armed his weapon and covered them.

"What's this?" Lara asked.

"Pimps," Roland answered, climbing up on the truck bed to help with the wounded. "We're at the Bourg-en-Bresse whorehouse, the only place in town where the doctor comes and no questions are asked. They've already sent one of the girls to get him."

They carried Marie and Jean-Marc through the small bar adjacent to the lobby, then upstairs to a dingy room with faded wallpaper. A mustachioed man in long underwear jumped out of the bed when they entered the room. "See, here!" he demanded.

"Take a walk," one of the pimps answered, showing the man his pistol. "This is for France."

A heavy-set woman in her late forties, wearing a dressing gown, appeared as they lowered the wounded to the rumpled bed. Without a word, she handed the customer a sheaf of ten-franc notes.

He, in turn, drew himself up to his full dignity —all five feet, four inches tall — baggy underdrawers and all. "Never!" he exclaimed with great solemnity. "*Vive la France! Vive la Republique! Liberté, egalité, fraternité!*" He slapped the money back into the woman's hand, saluted crisply, and marched from the room.

In the highlands above Cerdon, Charles Bonheur, whose real name was Ekrem Beganović and who'd been born and had lived in Sarajevo until he'd moved to Paris a decade ago, kept to himself in his mountain aerie, cut off from time, lifeless and inert. A place where snow showered from the pine boughs, a place where the wind died and the water froze to perfect crystalline ice. He lived, like the rest of the village below him, on turnips and rutabagas. Sometimes there was bread and, in his case, some canned Polish hams, which he'd stored from the day he first came to the Juras and which he'd eaten judiciously during the winter while he waited for the warm days to return.

Most of the recruits had been sent home, told to return if they wished after the March thaw, because the village foodstocks could not support them.

But Ekrem — Charles, as he was known in Cerdon — and Battistu had been asked to stay.

The shooting of Marie *La Tasse* Vallade and Jean-Marc Cadieux continued to reverberate uncomfortably in Cerdon. They had both survived, for which everyone was thankful, but Jean-Marc had been wounded in the spine and would never walk again. Roland's young wife Jeanne, had taken this very badly. She had been, as everyone supposed, Jean-Marc's lover, and her broken heart showed for all to see. Roland was rumored to have shifted his sleeping quarters to the bed of the servant girl who lived in the house.

The doctor had arrived within minutes that day at the Hôtel de la Gare, a dignified, elderly white-haired gentleman who wore an old-fashioned silk vest beneath his suit. He had patched up *La Tasse* as best he could, then ordered both wounded removed to a convent near Crêches-sur-Saône, where he operated on Jean-Marc Cadieux. Both had remained and were said to be recovering as well as could be expected.

Within a day after he operated, the doctor's dismembered body was found in his office with a swastika carved into his forehead.

The Vallade clan, after continually muttering for revenge for the near-fatal wounding of the youngest daughter, managed one day to ambush the officer and the sergeant, whose misadventures had led to the tragedy in the hills above Cerdon, and slaughtered them in the same hills.

Four days later, the Germans repaid this outrage by publicly murdering over a hundred civilians, including no less than twenty of *La Tasse's* extended family.

It was a high price to pay for the Vallade honor.

42

"I must say, André, Grenoble is a lot closer to Le Chambon than Nantes."

"It's one of the last holdouts of 'Unoccupied France,' after the Nazis abandoned the pretense of a free and independent state," Trocmé replied, wiping his mouth with a napkin embroidered with the words *Café de la Table Ronde* before sipping the rosé wine and spearing a pair of large, breaded shrimp and half a dozen scallops from the platter directly in front of him. "And since this restaurant has been doing business here for more than two hundred years, it'll probably survive until after the Nazis have left."

"Speaking of that, how has the German takeover of the Hôtel Du Lignon affected your 'business'?" Chalmers asked his friend.

"Surprisingly, not at all, Burns. The Nazis are in the center of town, but the rescuers have spread so far, they're operating throughout the entire Vivarais Plateau. I wouldn't be surprised if there are rescue houses all over the Massif Central. In fact, there's a family named Gervoson in Biars-sur-Cère, 150 miles west of here, that's not only provided a safe haven for Jews like LeChambon, but has even given all of them jobs in a little company they've started, *Bonne Maman*, which produces jams and preserves. By the way, and needless to say, the Friends' contributions have been immense and much appreciated."

"How's the doctor working out?"

"Couldn't ask for a better man. And you've met Stefan Varga and the American woman, so you know how valuable they've been. Of course, being a pacifist and a Christian in the true sense of the word, I can't say I totally agree with some of their, shall we say, more vigorous activities."

"Agreed, but let's be frank. After the surrender at Stalingrad last month and the more prevalent rumors of 'resettlement centers" in the East, 'Charlie Chaplin' may be crazier than ever and DeGaulle's *maquisards* are starting to spring up like weeds all over France. Even down here, you're starting to hear a lot more *liberte, egalite, fraternite* than Pétain's *travail, famille, patrie.*

Le Chambon – Early April 1943

"I'm certainly in favor of nonviolent resistance," Trocmé said. "But there are others who have a somewhat different view of things, and while I cannot and do not openly condone what they're doing ..."

"*Maquis?*"

"Yes," the pastor said, clearing his throat. "They have all the fighting spirit in the world, but less than no experience in military maneuvers, tactics, or organization. If they had an experienced military officer, an adviser who might keep *me* advised..." He handed Varga a piece of paper on which a few words were written. "They're *not* meeting at this address in about thirty minutes. If you're curious, it's straight down the road about half a mile and it's inside a big red barn on the right side of the thruway."

Eight young men between seventeen and twenty, an older fellow of thirty, and two women in their early twenties sat on hay bales more or less in a circle. When Varga entered, each of them nodded. They had obviously been told he would be joining them. Each attendee introduced himself or herself as Monsieur Blanc, Monsieur Rouge, Mademoiselle Jaune, or some other obviously false name. Catching on quickly, Varga introduced himself as Colonel Polonais, "Colonel Polish."

The oldest among them *Grand-père Vieux* — "Old Grandpa" — who appeared to be the leader stood up and spoke briefly. "*Amis résistants,* fellow *combattants de la liberté*, it seems that our group, small as it is at the moment, has been recognized by brothers and sisters outside our small area. It's now been some months since the Pétain 'government' came crashing down beneath the jackboots of the *forces d'occupation*. The *Schutzstaffel*, the *Geheime Staatspolizei*, and whatever else these bullyboys call themselves, are demonstrating what a farce the last two years have been. Our 'unknown' benefactor, the very model of nonviolent resistance, has arranged for the presence of Colonel Polonais, an experienced field officer, to guide us in how to do what we do more effectively."

There was a smattering of polite applause and Varga, who was a head taller than 30-year-old "Grandpa," rose to speak.

"Ladies and gentlemen," he began, "'Grandpa' — although he's a decade younger than me — told you my job is to help you, to help *us*, reach *achievable* goals and *not* to interfere with your leadership or the way you choose to conduct yourselves. Please consider me as your coach rather than an authority figure."

A few of the men lit up *Gitanes* and *Gauloises*, France's most popular cigarettes.

"Let's you and I hash out some ideas of goals. Yes, Mademoiselle Violette?" he asked, pointing to an attractive blonde who wore her long hair over one eye like the American *femme fatale* Veronica Lake.

"Colonel, our first goal has always been to win the war as quickly as possible and drive every German out of our country."

"You're absolutely right, of course, and that's a fine *strategic* goal. But there are well over 100,000 German troops in the *Zone Occupée* and half-again that number down here in what used to be called the *Zone Libre*. How many *maquis* would you say there are in southern France at this moment?"

There was confused muttering among the group, and by the time they quieted down there seemed to be no consensus.

"There's no real way of knowing," Varga continued, "because each *maquis* unit has been operating separate from most of the others. Let's say there are eight soldiers on average in a given unit. Let's further estimate that those units are presently active in 2,500 villages in the southern zone. At a maximum, the *maquisards* have 20,000 freedom fighters operating in France. That means there are about seven well-armed, well-trained *Wehrmacht* soldiers to every one of our forces. What kinds of weapons and in what numbers do the eleven of you have?"

More confused muttering before a pugnacious-looking twenty-year-old replied, "Four Sten guns, one Welrod pistol, a Mauser 98k rifle, and four old farm rifles from our homes."

"And ammunition?"

"Less than a hundred rounds altogether."

"Against a minimum of one hundred thousand 98ks, MP40 submachine guns, antitank artillery, tanks, motorcycles …" Varga said.

"So, you think we're hopeless?" another young man sighed.

"Hopeless if you're fighting a conventional war, one side shooting at another across a flat field. But certainly not *helpless*. If you're fighting a guerilla war, you don't have the *fire*power the other side has, so you have to use the *brain*power *you* have."

"Can you give us some examples, Colonel?" the *maquisard* leader asked.

"Sure," Varga responded. "I'll start with a few ideas off the top of my head. First, there's not much you can do in LeChambon or LeMazet. They're 'off the beaten path.' Meaning, they're small. But more important, neither the Pétain 'government,' such as it is, nor the Germans have much interest in this area. No railroad connections of any importance, no major roads, no industrial facilities meaningful to the war effort. So, the best you can hope to do is to kill off one or two low-level government functionaries, which would result in the occupying powers killing a hundred times that many civilians. Or maybe you could spread nails or rocks on the road, which might slow down or delay a motorcyclist or even a police car for half an hour or so. Again, not much profit in that,"

"So, you're saying we can't do much of anything up here in Le Chambon?" another young voice asked.

"Exactly, but I don't say this to discourage you. Only to try to convince you to expand your horizons. How many of you have access to a motor vehicle?"

Four men raised their hands. A fifth fellow, not more than seventeen, piped up, "Does that include cars we can 'borrow?' Even if the owner doesn't know?"

"Depends, but I don't see why not," Varga replied.

Two more hands raised.

"Ladies and gentlemen," Varga continued, "Where is the closest large railway junction?"

"That's easy," *Grand-père Vieux* said. "Saint-Étienne."

"Does it have any important industries?" Varga persisted.

"Uh-huh," Grandpa said. "It's been an arms manufacturing center for four hundred years and produces more coal than any other city of its size in France."

"It's forty miles from Le Chambon to Saint-Étienne," Varga said encouragingly. "By borrowing three cars, or by boarding the Le Chambon-Saint Étienne local, our *maquis* can hook up with Saint-Étienne's *maquisard* units in about an hour. If there are a hundred resistance fighters in the larger city, you've added ten percent to their fighting force. If another nine small villages each send a similar number, you've doubled Saint-Étienne's freedom fighters.

"Larger numbers attract more attention: from the newspapers, from the British Special Operations Executive, and from those French citizens who are sitting 'on the fence.' Like a snowball rolling down a hill in winter, things grow large quickly. Before you know it, you have a *real* army, and ordinary townspeople begin to think, '*Maybe … Why not?*' Then, Nimes starts to look at what Saint-Étienne is doing and wonders '*Maybe … Why not?*' And then, Marseilles starts to wonder the same thing …"

"Great idea!" exclaimed the man who'd introduced himself as Monsieur Blanc.

"Maybe," Varga answered. "Then these community armies attract experienced veterans of *national* armies, who've developed tactics and strategies that know how to deal with opposing forces. You'll want to share ideas of your own. Maybe some of them will be accepted. Maybe the 'small steps' that you take will lead to larger steps, maybe even to '*liberte, egalité, fraternité*' instead of '*travaile, famille, patrie,*' maybe even to a united, independent *Republique Français!*"

Now a storm of genuine applause greeted "Colonel Polonais."

"Do you know if any of this is really happening, Colonel?" the second woman, "Demetria," asked.

"It is, Mademoiselle," Varga responded. "I can tell you that at least twice a month, between 1:00 a.m. and 3:30 a.m., Wellington, Hampden, and Whitley bombers flying out of High Wycombe, thirty miles northwest of London, drop crates of firearms, ammunition, pencil detonators, plastique explosives, and other gifts in various landing areas, both in the *Zone Occupée* and in the southern zone. And Saint-Étienne certainly qualifies as a drop zone."

"What you propose is certainly as good an idea as we've heard," *Grand-père* spoke up. "But other than the daily train, do any of us know anyone in the Saint-Étienne *maquisards* with whom we could connect?"

No one raised their hand or responded affirmatively.

"Not an insurmountable problem," Varga responded. "I can, and will, find a senior officer in Lyon. I propose that we all meet next Thursday at 4:00 in the afternoon, at Gare de Saint-Étienne-Châteaucreux. I'll arrange overnight lodgings for whoever wants to go — my budget allows for it — and I may even be able to fix things so that two or three of the main officers in the Saint-Étienne *maquisards* will join us for dinner."

The meeting turned out to be highly productive for both sides.

"We are delighted to welcome your cadré to our group. You'll maintain your independence, of course, but we'll share whatever bounty S.O.E. delivers to us with you, and we'll count on your participation when we have joint operations. Does that work for you?" the senior Saint-Étienne officer, Lieutenant Jacques Duval asked.

Varga noticed that the man used a *nom de guerre*, since the name he used was the French equivalent of "John Smith."

"Absolutely," *Grand-père* replied. "Do you have any other concerns, Lieutenant?"

"I do," Duval answered. "Security is always a concern with us. I cannot tell you the number of German sympathizers — even German agents — who have infiltrated the Saint-Étienne *maquis*. These are by no means fools, and they have clever ways of masking their duplicity. Do you have any such problems?"

"Not to my knowledge," the Le Chambon leader replied. "Of course, no one can be certain of everyone in every organization, but our village is a very small, tightly-knit community. I'm absolutely sure that anyone of consequence in the mountains knows exactly who the LeChambon *maquis* are, and they keep that knowledge very much to themselves. Still ..."

"May I ask you this, *mon Vieux*, and please don't feel insulted or offended. If we advised you that one of your own was acting as a double agent, would you have any hesitation — any hesitation at all — to *dispatch* such a person, even if it were a *her*?"

In response, the Le Chambon leader asked each of the other ten *maquis* around the table the same question. Each, including the two women, answered in the negative without demur.

"And to make it unanimous, Lieutenant Duval, I would have no such hesitation."

"Very well *Sergeant* Vieux. I accept your declaration and I welcome each of you into our brotherhood-sisterhood." He raised wine glass solemnly. "*Liberté, egalité, fraternité pour toujours et à jamais!*"

"Forever and ever," the assembly responded.

43

Le Chambon – End of April 1943

"One hundred seventy-eight students signed up for the next semester!" Theis crowed. "And that's not even counting the anticipated influx of new arrivals."

"But the flow from the East has slowed to a trickle," Trocmé replied nervously. "We all know why, of course," he added.

"So you believe there really are those 'camps?'"

"*Believe?*" the pastor responded. "From the reports of two or three who made it here after escaping, I *know*. Two months ago, the Gallup organization in the United States conducted a poll of Americans, asking, 'It is said that two million Jews have been killed in Europe since the war began. Do you think this is true or just a rumor?' How do you think those people answered?"

"I have no idea, André," Theis responded. "I say close to one-hundred percent thought it was true."

"Guess again, my friend. Although the Allied leadership had already confirmed a month earlier that at least two million had already been murdered by that time, only 47% of Americans believed that was true. 29% thought it was just an overstated rumor, and the remaining respondents – almost a quarter of what we view as our strongest ally, had *no opinion!* More than half the population either didn't believe it or had no opinion – and it's now sixteen months after the United States entered the War!"

"I don't believe it," his co-pastor said, shocked. "I there no one standing up to combat the Nazi lies?"

In response, Trocmé reached into the bottom drawer of his desk and drew out a single page of a newspaper. It was a full-page ad in the New York Times of February 15, 1943. Pastor Theis read only the huge boldface type at the top, which read, "FOR SALE TO HUMANITY, 70,000 Jews, GUARANTEED HUMAN BEINGS at $50 A PIECE!" The ad went on to state that Romania would be overrun by the Nazi juggernaut 'any day,' but as long as they were still independent, the government would ensure that for every $50 it would get one Jew to the Turkish frontier and safety.

Meanwhile, Roger Darsissac had entered Trocmé's office and, after listening a few moments, waxed sarcastic. "While Ben Hecht, Peter Bergson, and a few others have mounted a public pageant which, according to their promoters, will be playing in seven major cities across the United States to call public attention to the plight of the Jews, all of the mainstream Jewish organizations and so-called 'Americanized,' or assimilated Jews wanted nothing to do with what they called 'irresponsible rabble rousers.'"

The two of them turned to their leader. "What do you think of that?" Darcissac asked.

"It seems a shame that a country as big and powerful as America, which could comfortably fit every Jew in the world into a state the size of Montana, is, like so many other nations, dancing around the issue without ever addressing the underlying problem. At least in Le Chambon, we're not *talking* about it, we're *doing something* to combat it."

"All well and good," Theis said. "We've got what, two hundred Jews in and around Le Chambon at any time. Hardly a thimbleful of water in a great big ocean."

"Yes, my friends," Trocmé replied somberly. "But the U.S.A. is a great big country with a hundred and thirty-five million people. Le Chambon has three thousand. Two hundred Jews here is about the same as if the United States took in eight-and-three-quarter *million* Jews. So unless someone decides to give us some small recognition, which will never happen in our lifetimes, I suggest we simply go on sheltering those Jews we can and hope maybe there are several thousand other Le Chambons in the world who might follow our example. And the best way we can do that is by betting on peace instead of violence, and hoping we can spread our doctrine to an unhappy world."

BOOK FOUR

SONG OF SONGS

1944

44

Eight of them sat around a table in a conference room, in an anonymous building on the outskirts of London, which had been used as a field office by Britain's MI-6. Along with President-in-exile Sikorski, Brigadier General "Wild Bill" Donovan, American Friends Field Service Representative Burns Chalmers, representatives from the offices of Generals Charles DeGaulle and George C. Marshall, Colonel Stefan Varga, O.S.S. Representative Lara Rosensohn Gard, and a man known only as "West," attended the meeting.

President Sikorski chaired the meeting. "Miss Gard, Gentlemen," he began. "I trust each of you has seen the report prepared by my office on what we can now confirm has been going on in Poland, most notably the area around Krakow. It has become increasingly difficult for the enemy to deny the existence of these horrors, and what they portend for what will happen after the Allies emerge victorious from this dreadful nightmare."

"Beyond belief," rasped Chambers. "Not since ... indeed, not since the beginning of the world as we know it, has such a monstrosity been perpetrated on the human race. How could we possibly have ignored what should have been so obvious?"

"If I might interject," West said. "Mankind simply refuses to believe what it does not *want* to believe, and, as you pointed out, Mister Chalmers, it sanctions what seems too monstrous to conceive."

"What if we issued a joint communiqué from this group?" This from Donovan.

"I have the latest Gallup Poll here," André Trocmé spoke out. "Dated ten days ago. Not much changed from the one I had in my hands last April. Even in the face of what we've found, only 49% of Americans — barely 2% more than eight months ago, believe that the Germans are engaged in the wholesale slaughter of Jews. Worse, one-third of Americans, more than forty-five-and-a-half million people, believe that this statement grossly exaggerated, the result of Soviet propaganda. That means that *more than one-half of the strongest bastion of democracy in the world, remains unconvinced.*"

"Worst of all," Lara exclaimed, "notwithstanding that Goebbels told the German people, 'If you tell a lie big enough, often enough, it becomes the truth,' it's entirely different in America. If you tell *anything* to the American people often enough, they eventually react by claiming you are just a bully, trying to silence the 'underdog,' or, worse, it simply becomes *boring* and they stop listening altogether."

Stefan supported Lara's statement in a way that no one, even at this table, had dared to express, but which electrified them nonetheless. "Let's face it, gentlemen, they're only a bunch of Jews. And, if I may be frank, how many of you have ever, *ever* felt that way, even unconsciously, even if you've never said something like that out loud?"

Hushed, embarrassed silence followed the Polish colonel's statement.

Varga continued, "Can any of you think of anything worse than the ovens, which the National Socialists have foisted on their fellow human beings?" When there was no response, he stated, "I can. And if you are willing to support, and, if necessary, protect me, I am willing to go to such a place and expose it for what it is. For I've learned one thing that I believe with all my heart: what the Talmud said two thousand years go is true: 'He who saves one life, it is as if he has saved an entire universe,' And I am willing to prove it."

45

There was nothing secret about Theresienstadt. The German government made every effort to publicize the "Paradise Ghetto" in the Czech fortress town of Terezin, less than forty miles northwest of Prague.

Theresienstadt Fortress was built on the order of the Austrian Emperor Joseph II between 1780 and 1790 and named for his mother, Archduchess Maria Theresa, who reigned from 1740 until 1780. By the end of the 19th Century, the facility was obsolete as a fort. Early in the 20th Century, Terezin accommodated military and civilian prisoners. From 1914 until 1918, Gavrilo Princip, who'd been convicted of assassinating Archduke Franz Ferdinand, which had served as the catalyst for World War I, was imprisoned there. He died in Cell No. 1 from tuberculosis on April 28, 1918.

After Germany invaded and occupied Czechoslovakia on June 10, 1940, the Gestapo took control of Terezin and set up a prison in the "Small Fortress," the town citadel, on the eastern bank of the Ohre River. The first inmates, who arrived on June 14, were predominantly Czech. Later, political prisoners of other nationalities, citizens of the Soviet Union, Poland, Germany, and Yugoslavia were housed here.

By November 24, 1941, the Nazis had adopted the "Main Fortress," on the west side of the river, as a ghetto. From 1942 forward, the Nazis interned the Jews of Bohemia and Moravia, elderly Jews, and persons of "special merit" in the Reich, as well as several thousand Jews from the Netherlands and Denmark.

Theresienstadt, also called Terezin Spa, was reputed to be an island of peace, a safe haven for Jews, in the middle of the maelstrom. Wealthy or influential Jews tried to get sent there. The Gestapo collected enormous fees for selling them large, luxurious apartments with guaranteed lifetime medical care, hotel service, and generous allotments of the best food available in the Reich. Leaders from numerous centers of Jewish population found themselves shipped here, once disease, hunger, and transportation "to the east," had decimated their communities. Half-Jews, deserving old people, those who had achieved international renown, decorated Jewish war veterans, and privileged Jews from the Netherlands, Denmark, and even a few from the United States, dwelt in this town with their families.

News pictures showed these fortunate Jews, often recognizable by name or face, all wearing yellow stars, sitting at their ease in small cafés, attending lectures and concerts, happily at work in factories or shops, strolling in a flowery park, rehearsing for orchestra performances or plays, or wrapped in prayer shawls and worshiping in a bright, new, immaculately maintained synagogue.

Outside Nazi Europe, information about Theresienstadt was sparse, but the German Red Cross had given such favorable reports about the place that even Dr. Goebbels had remarked, "While the Jews in Terezin are sitting in the café drinking coffee, eating cake, and dancing, our soldiers bear all the miseries and deprivations to defend their homeland."

In neutral and Allied countries, there were veiled hints that Theresienstadt was just a cynical show staged by the Nazis, so German Red Cross representatives had been invited to come and see for themselves. They had publicly confirmed the existence of this curious sanctuary. The Germans assured any reporters who would listen, that Jewish camps "in the east" were all like Theresienstadt, just not quite so luxurious. The Red Cross and the world must take their word.

In November 1943, Liliana Traube, 32, who, ten years ago had been the loveliest, most sought-after comedy actress on the Viennese stage, and her daughter Sarah, twelve and promising the beauty of her famed mother, had somehow landed in the Paradise Ghetto.

Theresienstadt was a complete, utter hoax, but Lili's chances of survival depended on her remaining here.

The Paradise Ghetto, grotesquely named after the countless spas of Bohemia, was, in actuality, nothing more or less than a transit camp, a way station to "the east," a floodgate. But it was a transit station with a difference. Those Jews privileged enough to be sent to Theresienstadt were received cordially and courteously, served an abundant and delicious meal, and encouraged to fill out forms detailing what sort of hotel accommodations or apartments they preferred. For security and insurance purposes, they were asked to list what possessions, jewelry, and currency they'd brought with them. Shortly afterward, the new arrivals were ushered into a room where they were stripped naked and robbed of all their goods. Their bodies were thoroughly searched for valuables. Thereafter, they were treated like ordinary Jews, crushed into the cramped spaces of the ghetto.

Sometimes, when large shipments arrived at the welcoming center, the pretense of even minimal respect for their dignity was omitted. The newcomers were herded into a hall, their belongings were plundered *en masse*, they were issued cast-off clothing, and were then marched into the crowded, disease-ridden town to find shelter in four-tier bunks, in drafty attics already overwhelmed with sick, starving people; rooms built for three, which housed fifty filthy, lice-ridden bodies; or a hallway jammed to the rafters with suffering humanity. But at least the inmates were not asphyxiated immediately upon arrival. Welcome to the Paradise Ghetto.

At the beginning, the well-organized Jews of Prague prevailed upon the SS to let them set up a Jewish municipality in Terezin. Of course, the so-called Jewish "government" had to do whatever the Germans ordered, including the grisly job of drawing up lists for shipment "to the east." Yet, the leaders of the community did manage health, labor, food distribution, housing, and culture. While the Germans insisted on tight security, their own comfort and pleasure, the production quotas of the factories, and the delivery of live bodies to fill the trains, they allowed the Jews to look after themselves in other matters of seemingly less importance

The inhabitants of Theresienstadt even had a bank that printed special decorative currency, with astonishingly artistic engraving on all the bills, showing Moses holding the tablets of the Torah, which God gave to the Jews at Mount Sinai more than three thousand years before. The money was a macabre joke. One could buy nothing with it, but the Nazis required the bankers and the Jewish workers to keep elaborate records of salaries, savings accounts, and disbursements, which looked genuine to the casual eyes of the German Red Cross observers. This rictus grin of a joke never extended to raising the food ration above starvation level; it never provided medicines or sanitary facilities; and it never kept down the torrent of incoming Jews.

And yet, Terezin was a pretty town. Stone houses and nineteenth century barracks set along well laid-out streets, were pleasing to the eye, if one did not look inside at the crowds of sick, filthy, and hungry inhabitants, who were chased out of sight whenever visitors came.

In normal times, Terezin housed four or five thousand people. But in these times, the Theresienstadt ghetto averaged fifty or sixty thousand disaster survivors, where the disasters kept mounting, relieved only by the high mortality rate and by the sluice gate "to the east."

Still, lectures, concerts, plays, and operas went on. The German overlords allowed the Jews to forget the hunger, the illness, the crowding, and the fear by means of these "paradisical" activities. The cafés and the nightclubs did exist. There was nothing to eat or drink, but actors, dancers, and musicians were in long supply, and the Jews went through the ghastly motions of peacetime pleasure, until their time came to be shipped off.

The library was surprisingly fine and well-stocked. Why should it not be? The books had all been looted from arriving Jews. There were shop façades with windows full of goods stolen from half-dead throngs who drifted by. Naturally, none of these goods were for sale.

For a while, only German Red Cross commissioners had been allowed into Theresienstadt. No great effort was needed by the SS to obtain favorable reports from *them*. However, the very success of the hoax presented the Germans with an unanticipated problem: *Neutral* Red Cross observers demanded to visit the Paradise Ghetto. This led to the most bizarre episode in Theresienstadt's "unorthodox" history, the *Verschönerungsaktion* — the Great Beautification. Liliana's fate turned on this.

46

Lili was unrecognizable at work because a handkerchief masked her face below the eyes. The mica dust from trimming and grinding machines drifted over the rows of long tables, where women sat all day, splitting the laminated material into sheets. Lili's was simply another bent back in this grimy factory. While the work took dexterity, it was boring, but it was not hard.

Liliana Traube had not the faintest idea what the Germans used this stuff for. She knew only that it must be very rare, for scraps and table sweepings went to the grinder, and the powder was crated and shipped to Germany like the trimmed sheets. Her job was to take a block and split the laminations into thinner, more transparent sheets until the tool could not wedge off another layer, yet avoid tearing a sheet and getting clubbed by the arm-banded Jewish bitch who patrolled this section. That seemed simple enough, although in practice it seemed that each patrolwoman was given a quota of beatings she must administer during each work period or risk a beating from the next higher-up factory "supervisor."

Lili spent eleven hours a day in this crowded shed. During a four-minute break, which was allowed every hour, she surveyed her surroundings. Low-wattage lightbulbs hanging on long black wires. The unheated premises was almost as cold as the outdoors, damper because of the breath of close-packed women. It was hard to escape the stink from the single loathsome, overflowing latrine, which was cleaned out only once a week by the pitiful squad of former professors, writers, composers, and scientists, whom the Nazis had delighted to put to work hauling human shit. She'd gotten so used to the body smells of crowded, ragged, unwashed females that she'd become immune to the odor. To a visitor from the outside, the shed would have seemed like a living hell. Lili was used to it.

Most of the women, like Lili, were from a refined background. Terezin was a true melting pot: Czechs, Austrians, Germans, Dutch, Polish, French, Danish, even one or two English or Americans. Many had once been wealthy. The vast majority were highly-educated. The mica factory was a favored spot for women of privilege. The ever-present menace of "transport to the east" was a daily source of terror for all the inmates. The specter of death haunted normal life. But so far, mica workers and their families seemed to have escaped the worst.

Most of the women doing this easy work were elderly. Lili's assignment to the mica factory hinted at some sort of veiled "protection." Her ending up in Theresienstadt had not been a random act. Something was behind it. Meantime, she and Sarah endured from one day to the next.

The six o'clock bell buzzed sharply. The end of the workday.

The machines stopped. The women rose stiffly, stored their tools, and shuffled outside, clutching shawls, sweaters, and rags around them. They proceeded as quickly as their arthritic joints would let them, to get to the food lines while the slops were still warm. Outside, Lili pulled the handkerchief off. Her once-beautiful face was sharper, paler, and there was a harder set to her jaw; yet it was hard to hide that she was still an attractive woman. The pervading stench of Theresienstadt's clogged sewers, random excretions, rotting garbage, and sick, filthy people was momentarily lessened by a brisk, icy wind. Still, she could not escape the sight of hand-pulled hearses that rolled by day and night, where the crematorium beyond the wall would dispose of those Jews who had died of "natural causes," never murder. The mortality rate in the Paradise Ghetto was only slightly lower than the number whose lives had ended at the extermination camps.

Liliana hastened across town to the children's home. She detoured around the high wooden walls that shut Jews out of the main square, where she could hear musicians playing at the SS café. The streets were quiet, less crowded now, but some feeble old people, who poked in the garbage heaps, were still creeping around. Long food lines curled from some courtyards into the street. People stood scooping messes from tin dishes into their mouths, their eyes popping with eagerness. Even reduced to her present state, Lili was saddened as she watched these cultured Europeans gulping slops like dogs.

A tall figure in a long, ragged coat approached her. "*Nu, wie gehts?*" he asked softly.

"How should it go?" she replied automatically in Yiddish. "The lessons?"

"They're going as well as can be expected," he murmured. "She's bright. You know that. The trouble is, she's becoming a very attractive young woman. The boys — even some of the men — are starting to look."

"If they so much as dare, I'll kill them, one by one if I have to, and cut their ..."

"Ssshh. Sssshh," he cautioned in a low voice, which carried not nearly as far as a whisper. "There are those in this *shtetl* who will protect her at the cost of their own lives. You must know that you, yourself are an object of attention, even by our beloved SS."

Lili bent her head into her hands as the hot, bitter tears started to come. She could not control them and did not want to. *What kind of a cruel God would allow this sort of punishment to happen? And to what purpose?*

"Oh, Szymon, Szymon," she wailed. "If only she can somehow become a *Bat Mitzvah*. Two months, three months, no more. Then, at least, she'll be in God's hands."

"And you would entrust your only child, an innocent, beautiful girl to such uncaring hands?"

"You must not say that," Lili reprimanded him sharply, keeping her voice low. "He can bring greater calamity on us."

"Exactly what greater cruelty can He inflict, Lili? My wife, my four-year-old son. Your husband. Tell me that if you will," he said, his voice muted, his eyes blazing as he remembered that morning nearly a half-decade ago, when he had received the terse message:

```
"Regret inform you your wife and son killed when building
bombed STOP. Return HQ Warszawa soonest STOP. Rowecki."
```

"I thank Him if only because you arrived here two months ago and started teaching Sarah the law and what she needs to know to meet her Maker as an adult within the community."

Hearing the determination in her voice, Stefan Varga, who'd reverted to using his birth name, Szymon Vaynshtok, was starting to realized that this clandestine assignment, these moments in hell for as long as they lasted, were the most meaningful in his entire life, no matter what had transpired before.

His anger not abating by a decibel, he replied, "Such as that community is. Today's comrade is tomorrow's corpse. Today's community leader becomes tomorrow's latest passenger on the transport to …" The dreaded words "the east" did not escape his lips.

"Enough," she said. "I must go see my baby girl. Here," she said, thrusting a half-spoiled but still edible orange into his hand.

"Where …?"

"I found it just outside the factory. Someone must have dropped it in the rush to get to the evening meal."

Szymon gripped Liliana's cold hand in his. A silent gesture of thanks, a gesture that proclaimed louder than any words that in this hell on earth, humanity — *humane* humanity — had somehow survived.

Sarah was waiting in the doorway of her dormitory room. When she saw her mother, she leapt into her embrace. Feeling Sarah's body in her arms,

Lile forgot mica, boredom, misery, fear, and, yes, her ever-present hunger. Sarah's high spirits flooded and cheered her. Whatever hell the winds of Theresienstadt blew, Sarah's flame was not destined to be snuffed out.

Since she'd been born, Sarah had been the most precious thing in Lili's life, but never so much as here. Separated from her daughter, who spent her days in the children's home among several hundred children, seeing her for only a few minutes most evenings, regimented by strange women — with one exception — in this damp, dark old stone house, fed coarse, dark, indistinguishable mush, though the childrens' rations were the best in Theresienstadt — Sarah was thriving. Other children sickened, fell into a listless stupor, and died. The mortality rate in this home was terrible. But Sarah's ordeal seemed somehow to have toughened her, particularly during the last month, particularly when a new woman had been assigned to the home as housemother.

Sarah's a super-survivor, blazing with vitality. Lili thought back to her own childhood. Was Sarah the reflection of Liliana's earlier self? *She excels, without seeming to try. Even the new housemother openly loves Sarah, despite the child's indomitable spirit, which is in such desperately short supply in the Paradise Ghetto.*

This was where Lili ate and slept, since she took turns on the night duty staff. Tonight, the soup was thick with potatoes, spoiled by last winter's frost and rotten-tasting, but substantial. Mother and daughter spoke in low tones at a small table in a corner of the dining room. By some unwritten rule, the children and the house women allowed the Traubes to claim possession of one of the few private places within the large hall.

"I read the story you wrote," Lili began. "I can't tell you how proud I am of you, darling I would swear it was written by a seventeen-year-old. I know I could never have written such a thing when I was that age."

"Twelve or seventeen, Mama?"

"Take your pick. It really is *that* good."

"You think so?" The child glowed from within.

"I honestly do, *Shayna*," Lili said, using the Yiddish for "beauty," a nickname she'd given her daughter at birth.

"Do you think it might be published some day?"

"I don't see why not, darling. This war can't go on forever."

"But can *we*, Mama?" Sarah asked seriously.

Lili was stricken by the profound, thoroughly adult thoughts expressed by her only child. Sarah was by no means stupid or coltishly childish, but nevertheless it shocked her mother that such a child, such a miracle, could have come from her body.

Sarah continued, "Mama, if by some chance we *do* survive this terrible time, do you think you'll marry Szymon?"

"I ..." Liliana could say no more. She'd never dared utter such words or even harbor such thoughts since David had been sent "east" two years ago.

"You don't have to feel embarrassed about it, Mama. Things ... happen. And don't look so shocked."

My God, Liliana thought. *How much does this child know? Can she possibly be thinking ... "* She shuddered.

At the teenage boys' house, lessons proceeded day and night. Officially, the Germans forbade the education of Jewish children. But there was nothing else for them to do. The Nazis did not really check. They knew what lay in store for most of these boys, so they really didn't care how these teenagers spent their days in the precursor to the slaughter pen. These big-eyed, scrawny boys published a small newspaper, learned languages and how to play musical instruments, worked up theatrical performances, debated Zionism, and learned Hebrew songs. But they were also cynical, accomplished scroungers, thieves, and liars. What frightened Lili most was that they were sexually precocious. They knew their way around the ghetto like rats. They believed in nothing and harbored no illusions about their too-short-term destinations.

Their frankly unsubtle stares and greetings when she walked by made her feel naked and uncomfortable, even though in her baggy brown, yellow-starred prison uniform she considered herself a sexless, even revolting, female object.

It mattered not if they were bigger, possibly stronger, more aggressive. Let just one of them lay so much as a hand on her Sarah. Just let them try. And Szymon told her he had friends.

Despite all this, once the boys got down to lessons, they were all sharp, all focused and attentive. They were bright, all eight of them. Each had become a *Bar Mitzvah*, a Son of the Covenant, and regardless of their fundamental urges and desires, there was an indefinable sense of honor and duty among them. Much as they might want to sleep with a young girl, Lili had no doubt they'd fight to the death — most likely their own — to protect the honor of a *Jewish* girl attacked, or even touched, by a *Boche* swine.

All eight wanted to learn English, so they could go to America after the war. Two of the eight were missing tonight, rehearsing for the scheduled performance a week from now of Mozart's *Abduction from the Seraglio*. The two were replacements. The cast had just been decimated by a transport. But now her nightly hour of teaching them and her daughter English was over. She and Sarah returned to the childrens' home, just across the road from the teenagers' dormitory.

After joining her daughter in their recitation of the *Shema*, the most important prayer in the Jewish liturgy except, perhaps, the *Kaddish*, listening to Sarah recite her *parshah*, her Torah portion for her upcoming *Bat Mitzvah*, and tucking her amazing pre-teen into bed, Liliana hurried through the starry night to the loft where she would spend an hour before returning to the children's home where she and Sarah dwelt together.

The quartet was already playing at the far end of the low, slope-roofed room. Once used for large gatherings, it was now filling up with bunks, as more and more Jews arrived at the ghetto even faster than others were being sent "to the east." The hope of the entire ghetto was that the Americans and the Soviets would smash the rapidly deteriorating thousand-year Reich in time to save those piling up at the Theresienstadt floodgate. The sole object of life was to avoid being transported, and, while the ever-decreasing number of Jews was still living, to make the nights bearable with culture.

The Vishnovics Quartet, three gray-headed men and a plain, skeleton of a middle-aged woman, playing instruments smuggled into the ghetto, would, in normal times, have been welcomed in the first section of any major orchestra on the Continent. The quartet itself did justice to every selection. Again, in normal times, it could have commanded an eager, well-paying audience, whose attention and appreciation would be at least equal to the enthusiasm of the ghetto audience.

The loft was packed, People hunched or lay on the bunks, squatted on the floor, even lined the walls on their feet, standing beside the hundreds sitting jammed together on long wooden benches. Liliana Traube could almost — *almost* — have forgotten where she was and the ceaseless monotony of what she would face for as long as she possibly could. Maybe long enough, maybe not, but she vowed with her entire soul that she would somehow — *somehow* — make sure that even if she did not survive, her darling Sarah would.

47

"What in the world is *that?*"

A charcoal woolen suit of fine cut and quality lay across her cot. The yellow star in the upper left-hand portion of the suit was subdued. Beside it were silk stockings and new shoes.

The *protectsia* hovering over Lili and her daughter had been apparent since they came here: mother and daughter allowed to sleep in the same room, in the childrens' home. Though they occupied only a tiny space with one window, it was partitioned off with wallboard from a larger chamber, formerly the dining room of a prosperous Czech family's private house. Beyond the partition, hundreds of children were crowded into box-like bunks. But the Traubes' space contained two cots, a dim little lamp, a table, and a cardboard wardrobe, the height of ghetto luxury. Even council officials did not aspire to greater privileges.

Liliana held the suit up against her thin body. Excellent material, a bit loose, but certainly close enough to her measurements when she first came to the Paradise Ghetto. The suit exuded a faint scent of roses. Whatever had happened to its owner, she wondered. Alive? Dead? Transported?

As she was standing there wondering, she heard a light knock on her partition. No one confined in these surroundings expected such a courtesy.

"Yes?"

"Frau Traube, may I enter?"

"Of course."

The middle-aged man who entered was stooped, bearing the weight of the world on his 42-year-old shoulders. Lili was suspicious, not knowing what to think.

"To what do I owe the privilege of this visit, Herr *Ältester*? Isn't it a bit unusual for the head of our municipality to meet privately with a constituent? Am I to trust that the presence of these fancy clothes are your doing, Mayor?"

The man coughed uncomfortably. Paul Eppstein, a sociologist originally from Mannheim, Germany, was the present head of the Theresienstadt Jewish community. Earlier, Eppstein had been the speaker of the central organization of Jews in Nazi Germany. He'd been deported to Terezin with his wife and Rabbi Leo Baeck, in January 1943. Shortly afterward, he'd replaced the first head of the Terezin Community, Jakob Edelstein, former head of the Prague Jewish community, who'd served until he had been deported to Auschwitz and shot to death after being forced to watch the execution of his wife and son.

Eppstein was Theresienstadt's present head of the municipality, a mayor of sorts. Meek, beaten-down, the survivor of Gestapo imprisonment, he knew he was trapped in subservience to the SS. He tried, in his own way, to do some good, but the other Jews saw him as a German puppet, with little choice and little strength left to exercise what minimal choices he had.

"Well?"

"We're to go to SS Headqarters tomorrow. Don't worry. You're not in danger. It will be pleasant. You're due for more special privileges."

Lili felt a sudden void in the pit of her stomach. "Why are we going?"

"For an audience with Lieutenant Colonel Eichmann."

"*Eichmann?*" She felt a deep, horrifying chill. The interview would not be with some familiar local officers. Eichmann was a remote, evil name. Despite his modest rank, the Jews viewed him as just below Himmler and Hitler.

Eppstein's expression was kindly and sympathetic. "Yes. Quite an honor," he said with calm irony. "But those clothes bode well, don't they? Someone at least wants you to look good."

Eppstein himself came by the next morning to accompany Liliana to SS headquarters. He tried to be agreeable, complimenting Lili on how attractive she looked. Eppstein was in a pitiful position, a Jewish tool, a figurehead who carried out SS orders, a shabby Jew like the rest, with his yellow star.

Lili had never been in the SS headquarters before. It was separated from the Jews by a high wooden fence. The sentry passed them through the fence. They walked along a street bordering a park, past a church, and into the government building with offices, bulletin boards, and corridors echoing with typewriter noise. It felt very strange to come out of the grotesque, squalid ghetto into a place that, except for the large picture of Hitler in the lobby, could have been an office complex anywhere in the world. Its ordinariness was the last thing Lili had expected of SS headquarters. Even so, she felt an overwhelming sense of fear as she entered the building to which she and the mayor had been directed.

Lieutenant Colonel Eichmann looked surprisingly young, a man in his late thirties, at most half a dozen years her senior. He portrayed the alert air of an ambitious mid-level officer on the way to higher aspirations. When the two Jews came into his office, he sat behind a wide desk. Lili's sense of foreboding increased as *Obersturmführer* — First Lieutenant — Anton Burger, a man her own age, the brutal head of Theresienstadt, and, like Liliana, an Austrian, entered the room and sat next to Eichmann.

Although, like every other Jew in Terezin, Lili had done her utmost to avoid him, it had been impossible to do so altogether. She was aware that on those occasions when he had come across her path, she could not escape that he'd undressed her with his eyes a hundred times or more. The looks he gave her were those of a savage predator. Lili knew, as a woman invariably does, that he'd have liked nothing better than to have his way with her in front of Sarah, in front of the entire camp for that matter, for no other reason than to shame her beyond imagining.

Without getting up, Lieutenant Colonel Eichmann nodded at Ältester Eppstein and Lili to take their seats in two office chairs in front of him. So far, except for Burger's cold, nasty look and the black uniforms worn by both men, they might have been calling on a bank manager for a loan. Eichmann looked first at Liliana.

"Your accommodations are comfortable, Frau Traube?" he asked congenially.

"Yes, thank you," she choked out cautiously.

"Your daughter Sarah is a beautiful child. She is, I believe, approaching the age of her *Bat Mitzvah*,"

"That is true, *Obersturmbannführer.*"

"Five months from now," Eichmann said. He opened a booklet containing a desk calendar and marked it. She heard him murmur to Lieutenant Burger, "Two delegates from the Danish Red Cross are due to arrive on June 23. Interesting."

Burger nodded his assent obediently.

Eichmann turned back to Lili. "I recently inspected the entire camp, Frau Traube. I must tell you the conditions in Theresienstadt do not satisfy me at all. In the next months, you will see remarkable improvements, *gewaltige Verschönerungen.*" He smiled benignly, but the smile seemed cold, bereft of any human emotion. "I have directed Obersturmführer Burger to ensure that very special *prominenti* like you and your lovely young Sarah will be among the first to benefit from these changes."

He turned to Eppstein. "I believe you have a few words to say, Mayor."

The Ältester proceeded to reel off in a monotone, occasionally looking at Lili and Eichmann, but throwing worried glances at Burger, who alternately glared at Eppstein and gazed wolfishly at Liliana.

"The Council of Elders has recently voted to split off the Culture Section from the Education Department. Although cultural activities are the pride of Theresienstadt, our childrens' education, which is equally important, has not been properly supervised or coordinated. The average age of the Council of Elders is above sixty. We need an influx of vigorous, young, presentable members, including attractive female members, to balance out the Council. The Members have unanimously voted to bestow on you the great honor of requesting that you join the Council as teacher representative."

Abruptly, Eppstein stopped talking and looked straight at Lili with a mechanical smile. Lili was dumbstruck, confused. Her mind was working feverishly, weighing her limited options. If she accepted the offer, she might beat the odds of a transport. She was not unaware that the war had started to turn against Germany. By playing for time, she might survive until the world discovered what was really happening.

On the other hand, once she "sided" with the Germans by accepting their "honor," and the Allies prevailed, sooner rather than later, she'd be branded a collaborator, and her life after the war ended — God willing it ended soon — would be changed. At the end, her only possible motive for accepting Eppstein's offer would have been pity for the man. Clearly, he was doing what he had been ordered to do. It was Eichmann who, for some reason, wanted Lili to sit on the Council of Elders.

Lili, unable to make a decision, and hoping against hope that she could somehow avoid doing so, finally spoke, choosing her words carefully. She looked directly at Eichmann, searching his eyes for any signal of what he was feeling.

"*Herr Obersturmbannführer*, while I feel privileged I would even be considered for such a position, may I permit myself to point out that I have no educational or administrative background. I am — was — a musical comedy actress in Vienna, which hardly qualifies me to be a part of the governing Council. I am by no means refusing this offer, but I am ill-suited for it. Do I have a choice in this matter?"

"If you did not have a choice *Frau Traube*," Eichmann answered briskly, but cordially, his eyes betraying nothing, "this conversation would be pointless. I am a rather busy man. Obersturmführer Burger could simply have given you an order. However, I think this job would be a fine one for you."

Liliana was now appalled at the prospect of becoming one of the wretched Elders, who, for a few miserable privileges, most of which she already enjoyed, bore the awful burden of the ghetto on their consciences. It would mean giving up her endurable, but largely anonymous, existence for the limelight of the council, for dealing daily with the SS over terrible problems which had no decent solution. Lili gathered her nerve for one more try.

"If I may, Sir, and only if I may, I should like to decline the honor."

"Of course, you may. We'll say no more about it. We're keeping you from your work in the mica factory. How do you like it, by the way?"

Lili's voice came out hoarse and hollow. "I am very glad to be working there."

"I'm glad to hear that, Frau Traube, very glad indeed." He stood up graciously to bid her take her leave, then, as if reconsidering, he said, "Would you mind staying for just a few more minutes? I forgot there are a couple more things I wanted to chat with you about. Ältester Eppstein, would you permit us a few minutes alone?"

Eppstein knew this was not a request. He looked at Lili. In that moment, she became fully cognizant of what the "Mayor" faced each day. He took his leave silently.

Eichmann walked over to the door, shut it gently, and returned to his desk. His appearance had changed entirely. He looked positively ugly and very, very threatening. That look frightened her beyond anything she'd previously experienced in the ghetto. His mouth twitched to one side. Suddenly, he roared, ***"WHO DO YOU THINK YOU ARE? WHERE DO YOU THINK YOU ARE?"***

Lieutenant Burger jumped up, charged at Liliana, and slapped her hard. She felt the blood rush to her head. Her ears were ringing. As Burger raised his hand again, Lili winced. The blow knocked her off her chair, and she fell hard on her knees. Burger shoved her with his right boot that rolled her over on her side. He kicked her in the stomach, not with all his might, but in utter contempt, as though kicking a dog.

"*I'll* tell you what you are!" Burger shouted. "You're nothing but a filthy, sagging *bag of Jewish shit! You hear? You stinking cunt, did you think you were still Lotte Lenya on the Viennese stage performing* Die Drei Groschen Opera*?"* As he walked around her, Lili barely saw the moving black boots. Burger kicked her in the backside. "*You're in Theresienstadt! Understand? Your life isn't worth a pig's fart if you don't get that through that shithead of yours!"* With that, he kicked her harder with the point of his boot. Red-hot pain shot through every part of her body. She lay there stunned, shocked, in total agony. Through a fog, she heard him say, "*Get up on your knees.*"

Liliana obeyed dumbly, shaking all over.

"*Now, tell me what you are.*"

She clamped her mouth shut. She would not give that beast the satisfaction of seeing her crack.

"*Do you want more? Say what you are!*"

Lili turned her head away from him.

He gripped her left breast and twisted it. Hard.

Lili nearly screamed out in pain, but through some miracle, she held it in.

"*Next comes your cunt!*" He reared back with his right boot and moved it just to the edge of ... "*You have five seconds, shit-bitch.*" She could actually feel the tip of his boot digging around her private parts. Looking up through eyes blurred by tears of pain, she could see this animal was *enjoying* what he was about to do.

The kick was not hard, but it was the straw that broke her.

Almost insensate, she barely mumbled, "I'm a bag of filthy Jewish shit."

"Louder, cunt, I can't hear you,"

She repeated it.

"Scream it, shit pile! Scream it at the top of your lungs or I'll kick your greasy, filthy cunt, you stinking Jew pig, until you do scream it!"

"I'M A BAG OF FILTHY JEWISH SHIT!"

"You're a fucking Jewish whore!"

"I'M A FUCKING JEWISH WHORE!"

"You're not fit to suck my cock, Jew-girl!"

"I'M NOT FIT TO SUCK YOUR COCK!"

"That's enough," Eichmann said in a matter-of-fact tone. "All right, get up."

As Lili staggered to her feet, a hand caught her elbow to steady her. She had no consciousness of who it was.

"Sit down, Frau Traube," said Eichmann. He sat at his desk, smoking a cigarette, looking quite composed, like nothing so much as a bank manager. "Now, let's talk sensibly as adults, you and I."

Burger sat down beside him, grinning, obviously enjoying himself immensely.

Eichmann's tone was all business. "The SS knows you've been teaching the Talmud and the Torah. Since education in Jewish subjects is forbidden, we could simply send you to prison in the Little Fortress. We know of your friendship with Szymon Vaynshtok. Whether you're fucking him or not does not concern me, for even if he somehow knocks you up with that shriveled little Jew-prick of his, it's most likely neither of you will survive long enough to have the bastard."

Obviously, Eichmann used this ice-cold message to drive home the lesson of Burger's brutal assault: No vestige remained of Liliana's rights as an Austrian citizen or as a human being in Western civilization. As a Jew, she had crossed the line. The sword hung over her head every minute, every hour, every mortifying day.

I'M A BAG OF FILTHY JEWISH SHIT!

I'M A FUCKING JEWISH WHORE!

I'M NOT FIT TO SUCK THE COCK OF A GODLIKE GERMAN!

Eichmann continued, his voice surprisingly mild. "Not that we really give a damn how you Jews amuse yourselves. Teach away. If you stop seeing Vaynshtok, it will go harder for both of you. You will not tell anyone — *anyone* — what just happened in this room, do you understand?"

Lili mumbled something incomprehensible.

"To emphasize, Frau Traube, may I remind you that we are watching your precious, lovely little Jew-girl child every moment. From here on, we will attend to her even more carefully. After all, *one has to protect her innocence for as long as we can, Nicht War?*"

Lili nodded dumbly.

"If you breathe so much as a word of this to anyone, I will be sure to find out, and that will be too bad. You are looking forward to your daughter's *Bat Mitzvah*, are you not? As are we all. Representatives of the International and the Danish Red Cross will be arriving on June 23, a Friday, just in time for *Shabbos*. You are surprised that I know all about your traditions? You need not be, my dear. I am schooled in all things Jewish. Friday night, we will show the Red Cross how the Third Reich honors the Jewish Sabbath in Theresienstadt. That evening, Sarah will celebrate her *Bat Mitzvah* in the sight and hearing of the entire community and our Red Cross observer guests. *She will do the best job ever, and she will be the proudest, happiest child ever to celebrate her coming of age. You understand?*"

Lili choked back a sob and simply nodded. By now, she could see nothing except tears. She felt only that her humanity had been sucked out of her soul.

"Now, I will ask Mayor Eppstein to return and show you the ropes of your new Elder status."

The Jewish Ältester, who looked thirty years older than when he'd left the room, returned to the office as Obersturmbannführer Eichmann stood and dismissed Lili with a curt, offhand wave. She could hardly rise from her chair. Eppstein helped her hobble out. Behind her, she could hear the two Germans joking and laughing.

As they left SS headquarters together, Eppstein did not utter a single word. As they passed the sentry at the fence, Liliana forced herself to walk more normally. She found the pain was less if she stood straight and took firm strides. Eppstein brought her to the hairdresser's, where she got a haircut and shampoo and had her nails trimmed and painted. A cosmetician applied light makeup to her face. Lili was hardly aware of what was going on, since she was still in a state of shock.

Eppstein then led her to the council chamber, where a photographer was setting up for news pictures of the Council of Elders. A moderately attractive German woman in a fur coat, a reporter, asked questions and scribbled notes. Liliana Traube posed with the elders. She had her own picture taken. The reporter chatted with her and with the others. Lili was sure the woman was a genuine reporter and that she left with a highly plausible story, which she might even have believed, about the Jewish Council which governed the Paradise Ghetto, a serene, well-dressed group of distinguished gentlemen and one strikingly attractive young woman, who had formerly been a first magnitude star on Vienna's stage not so long ago.

Until the incident with Obersturmbannführer Eichmann and Hauptsturmführer Burger, Liliana Traube had refused to believe the stories of Nazi atrocities against the Jews, and even the evidence of her own eyes. Yet now, she was certain that the most alarming reports were the true ones. Why this turnabout? What was so very convincing about her encounter?

After all, she had already seen much atrocious conduct in Theresienstadt. She had observed an SS man clubbing an old woman in the snow because he'd caught her peddling cigarette butts. She had heard of children being hanged in the Little Fortress for stealing food. Three weeks ago, the SS had marched the entire male ghetto population out into a field and made the inmates simply stand there for twelve hours. Those who succumbed to the need to urinate or defecate were forced to lick up their waste, lest they pollute precious Reich soil.

Yet, none of this had brought home the truth. Her meeting with Eichmann had. One could not truly feel another's misery. Worse, Liliana now realized that the misery of others could make one feel glad and relieved that she or he had been spared.

Eichmann was not a low police brute, nor was he a banal bureaucrat. Much more than the flamboyant, fanatic Hitler, this businesslike official was a reasonable, intelligent, even affable fellow. He was one of the civilized men of the West. Yet, in a twinkling, he could order horrible savagery perpetrated on a harmless woman, and look on calmly; and in another moment, he would return to polite European manners, without the slightest sense of inconsistency. Like Hitler and like Liliana, he was an Austrian. Like himself in this dreaded time, he was *the German.*

Nevertheless, Lili swore she would go to her death refusing to condemn an entire people. There were *good* Germans, who must exist in large numbers. There *must* be, to have created the beauty, the art, the philosophy, and the science of Germany, what had been known as *Kultur* long before Germany became a name of horror.

Perhaps, what Lili needed to appreciate *who* she was and *what* she was, perhaps to proceed with what she must now do, was the *kick in the arse* given to her that day in the SS headquarters of the Theresienstadt ghetto. For despite uttering the words she had been forced to utter, she now understood more fully the words of the *Kol Nidre*, the prayer recited and sung by all Jews, even those who were not "observant," at the beginning of *Yom Kippur*, the Day of Atonement:

"Let all our vows and oaths, all the promises we make, and obligations we incur to You, Oh God, between this Yom Kippur *and the next, be null and void should we, after honest effort, find ourselves unable to fulfill them. Then may we be absolved of them."*

48

On February 8, 1944, Burger was quite suddenly transferred to Greece. Almost simultaneously, Szymon Vaynshtok quietly informed Liliana he'd be "gone" for about a week. Lili did not question her friend, although she feared the loss of someone she had come to believe was not only her friend but, by some mysterious circumstance which she never understood, her protector. She assumed he had told her truthfully who he was, but never *what* he was, or how he seemed able to enter and leave Theresienstadt at will, without a word ever being said about his unexplained absences.

Three days later, word circulated through the inmate community that Hauptsturmführer Burger's nearly unidentifiable, horribly mutilated body, had washed up on the shore just north of the town of Molyvos on the Greek island of Lesvos. Less than a week after that, Szymon returned to Theresienstadt and resumed teaching, much to Liliana Traube's relief.

Several days later, the members of the Council of Elders sat nervously around a long table in the Magdeburg barracks, awaiting their first meeting with the new Kommandant of Theresienstadt, SS Sturmbannführer Karl Rahm, a major.

He was reputed to be a run-of-the-mill Nazi, an Austrian, with a dangerous way of exploding on the slightest provocation, but his manners were said to be less coarse than Burger's. Still, the Theresienstadt Elders were worried about the change of command. Burger was the devil they knew. Even though the ghetto was functioning on a wretched basis, it was stable. There had been no transport for many weeks. What changes would the unknown devil bring?

"Ladies, gentleman," he began. "I am privileged to assume command of Theresienstadt. I intend to make this town the Paradise Ghetto in fact as well as in name. You, the esteemed Elders, know the town. I would deeply appreciate if you could give me ideas. I'm sure you'll agree that the present conditions are disgraceful. Theresienstadt is a run-down slum. I will not tolerate this. Starting today, I am initiating *die grosse Verschönerungsaktion*, the great beautification program."

Lili was struck by the very phrase Eichmann had used a month ago. Under Burger, there had been talk of beautification, but the idea had been so preposterous, and Burger himself had seemed so disinterested, that the Elders had taken it as just one more German façade of words. The Council had paid scant lip service to cleaning up a few streets and painting half a dozen huts and barracks.

But Rahm was talking a different language altogether. The Great Beatification was going to be his primary concern. He had laid down specifically what was going to be done. The old social hall would be rebuilt at once as a community center, with studios, lecture halls, an opera house, and a theater with fully-equipped stages. The cabarets would be enlarged. More orchestras would be created. Hospitals would be of the highest order, to the degree one would normally experience in the best of Berlin's *krankenhauses*. A children's playground, beautiful parks for the elderly. Every effort would be directed toward making Theresienstadt a model community for the whole of the Reich.

As she listened to these grandiose pronouncements, wondering whether Kommandant Rahm could be serious, Liliana suddenly seized upon the catch in this whole scheme: Rahm had not addressed anything that really mattered to the Jews interned here: the starvation diet, the hideous overcrowding, the lack of warm clothes, the lack of heat, the want of toilets, the absence of basic healthcare for the old and crippled, in short, everything that contributed to the terrible death rate. Rahm had not mentioned a single word about these things. He had proposed putting makeup on a corpse.

Rahm's approach seemed so simpleminded. No matter how hard he drove the legions of malnourished, drastically weakened inmates, no matter how thoroughly he renovated the buildings and grounds, how could he hope to conceal the overwhelming squalor, the crowding, the sickly faces, the mortality rate? A little more food and some attention to health would quickly have created happiness in the ghetto that would have fooled anybody. But the concept of treating the Jews themselves even a smidgen better, even to create a brief, useful illusion, seemed beyond the Germans' comprehension.

Rahm finished his talk and asked for suggestions. No one spoke. None would risk opening his or her mouth first.

Finally, Eppstein raised his hand. Rahm nodded. Eppstein stood up and saluted smartly. "Herr Kommandant, I am the stinking Jew, Eppstein —"

Rahm interrupted. "Now, then, this kind of shit will cease at once! New regulations! No more idiotic saluting and removing of caps. No more 'stinking Jew' talk. Theresienstadt is not a concentration camp. It is a comfortable, happy residential town. Mayor Eppstein, please go on and be assured of my respect."

Liliana looked about her. Surprise registered on every face. Before today, failure to pull off one's head covering and salute a German — any German — had been a major ghetto offense, punishable by anything from instant clubbing to time in the Little Fortress. These reflexes would take time to unlearn.

"I beg leave to mention, Herr Kommandant, that several departments are in need of paper. Any kind of paper, *mein Kommandant*, but music paper is in extremely short supply. The musicians will rule it themselves, although, of course, ruled paper would be best."

"How much paper?" Rahm asked, not unkindly.

"For the kind of expansion you are planning, perhaps five hundred sheets."

"It certainly will be done, Ältester Eppstein, and I thank you, sir. That is exactly the kind of idea I want. What else, ladies, gentlemen?"

One by one, other Elders now timidly rose with innocuous requests. Rahm received all of them warmly. Not one Elder mentioned food, medicine, or living space. Lili said nothing. What good would it do? She would destroy the sunny moment, bring trouble on herself, and would, at the end, accomplish nothing.

Kommandant Rahm bowed congenially. "Ladies, gentlemen," he concluded, "this has been an auspicious beginning. I am convinced it is the beginning of a new day for Theresienstadt. Now, I must beg your leave. I believe Mayor Eppstein has one or two more items of business to conduct and my presence is not necessary. I wish you all a very good day." He departed.

Moments later, Eppstein rose. His previously fixed smile faded. "There is one more thing," he announced. "The new commander has found the overcrowding of the town most unhealthy and unsightly. Five thousand Jews must be transported at once."

In a town of fifty thousand, the loss of ten percent of the entire population is a tragedy of unimaginable proportions. In Theresienstadt, there was no getting used to this periodic decimation. Each time it occurred, the fabric of the ghetto was torn apart. The sense of doom, which had been *almost* forgotten, rose again. Though no one was sure what "the east" really meant, it was a name that rang universal terror. The unlucky ones moved around in shock, making their farewells, giving away what meager belongings they could not pack into one suitcase. The General Secretariat was besieged with frantic petitioners pulling every string and trying every loophole to get exemptions. *Five thousand Jews must get on the train.* If one was exempted, another must take his place. If a hundred were excused, a hundred who thought themselves safe must be struck as by lightning with gray summons cards.

The Jews who ran the Transport Section were their brothers' keepers and executioners. Everybody smiled at them, but they knew they were cursed and despised. They had life-and-death powers they had never wanted. They were *Sonderkommando* clerks, disposing of Jews' living bodies with pens and rubber stamps.

Liliana wondered whether they were to blame, or whether they were simply motivated by the instinct for self-preservation? An astonishing number of desperate Jews stood ready to seize their places, much like the number of French had stood in line to collaborate with their historic enemy, the *boche*. Many never thought of anything but their own skins. A few tried to correct the worst hardships. More of the wretched showed favoritism, took bribes, held grudges. In this spectrum of human nature, what man could say where he would have fit? What man who was not there could judge the Central Secretariat and the Transport Sections?

The real power in Theresienstadt was not Eppstein, nor was it the Council of Elders. It was the Central Secretariat. Yet no one could talk to the Central Secretariat. It was friends, neighbors, relatives, or just ordinary Jews. It was a bureau carrying out the Germans' orders. The Complaint Section of the Secretariat, a row of faceless Jewish faces behind desks, was an impotent mockery, but it provided a lot of jobs. The Bureau was overstaffed because it had been a refuge. But this time, the gray cards struck, even inside the Secretariat. The monster was starting to eat itself.

Oddly, impossibly, a few people actually applied to go in each transport. In a previous shipment, their spouses, parents, or children had gone. They were lonesome. Theresienstadt was not such a paradise that they had wanted to stay at all costs. So, they would brave the unknown, hoping to find their beloved ones in the east. Some had received letters and postcards, so they believed those they still sought were still alive. This was one request about which the Germans were always gracious.

Szymon's face was grim, although the words he spoke around the small table were optimistic. "Maybe those tales about the east are exaggerated," he said. He was aware that half of the group had received the dreaded gray cards. He pulled out a plain piece of cardboard, at the top of which was the letterhead "Birkenau, Camp II-B."

"Where is Birkenau?" Lili asked.

"Poland. Outside Oswiecim. It's just a village. The Jews supposedly work in big German factories near there. They are said to get plenty of food."

Lili was skeptical. She had passed through Oswiecim once, on the way from Warsaw to Budapest, before stardom, when she was touring with a road company. She barely remembered it: a flat, dull railroad town, forty miles west of Krakow. A place to be *from*.

There was little talk in the ghetto about "the east," the camps, and what happened there. It was akin to talking about cancer, not the stuff of polite conversation. The word "Oswiecim" resonated with horror.

Afterward, as they walked back toward the children's home in the dark twilight, they spoke in a quiet monotone.

"Would you forgive me if I told you I passed what you wrote along to a friend on the outside?"

The back of Lili's hand involuntarily flew to her mouth, as conflicting emotions coursed through her. On the one hand, her written recollection of that day carried a certain death sentence. On the other, Szymon was her most trusted friend, indeed her only real friend in the Paradise Ghetto.

"How well do you know this friend?"

"I trust that friend the same as you trust me."

"Jewish?"

"Yes. More than that I cannot say, except that you know this person."

"Would you mind if I ask you why you did this?"

"Of course not. You've been told by the establishment that you're 'protected.' A '*prominenti.*'"

"Often."

"How safe do you think you really are? More important, how safe do you think Sarah is?"

Liliana's face reddened, "Are you saying we're not?" Despite her "high" position as an Elder, she was vaguely aware that Szymon had many more connections, both on the inside and on the outside, than she, and that he knew things he implied, but never revealed.

As if to underscore his words, a shadowy figure, small and of indeterminate sex, passed within a foot of them and handed something to Szymon. He said nothing and Lili knew better than to ask.

As they came within two blocks of the childrens' quarter, Lili gasped, startled, as an SS Lieutenant approached.

"You're out late tonight, *yid.*"

"I'm sorry, *Leutnant,*" Szymon responded. "I must have lost track of the time."

"May I see your papers?" he asked, raising his truncheon.

"Of course, Sir," Szymon responded respectfully. He reached into his jacket pocket, the one where he'd put whatever the shadow-figure had given him, and handed something to the officer.

"Do you have any papers, ma'am?" the officer asked Lili.

Without a word, Lili handed the man documents showing she was a member of the Council of Elders. The lieutenant looked at them cursorily and handed them back. "You're the new member of the council? The woman who used to be an actress in Vienna?"

"I am."

"Very good. It might be wise to be careful with whom you associate. And you'd best be home at this hour to protect your security. You should know better than to be out on the streets at night. *Heil Hitler!*" He raised his arm in the Nazi salute and departed.

Lili noticed that the SS officer had not handed Szymon's papers back. She looked questioningly at her companion, but said nothing until they'd walked another block.

"One of ours," Szymon said quietly. "Uniforms are not hard to come by if you work in the SS laundry room.

"The papers you handed him?"

"Czechoslovakia — and places much farther afield than you might imagine — are thick with our friends. For example, there's a small island in the Eastern Aegean, Lesbos, and a small town, Molyvos, on a remote corner of that island …"

"What —?"

"Best not ask at the moment, my friend. All in good time …"

49

The Beautification was a painstaking pretense that the Germans were Europeans, just like the others, conforming to the mores of Western civilization. The rumors and reports about the Jews were too silly for words, or else they were cruel Allied atrocity propaganda. The Germans were play-acting an elaborate denial of their central effort in this war, the eradication of a people.

The new Kommandant, Rahm, was thorough. His planning of the Beautification carried hypocrisy into a new realm. Because Liliana was involved as an Elder in the Education Department, and because Sarah's *Bat Mitzvah* was intended to be a showpiece of the visit by the International Red Cross, she was very much involved.

The Elders spent hours in Major Rahm's office poring over a detailed map of the town. The visitors' route was marked in red, with every stopping place numbered. A wall chart showed the progress of the renovation and new construction at each numbered halt. Lili's role on "the day" would be to show the visitors the education facilities. The height of her performance would be as the proud, gushing mother of the *Bat Mitzvah*.

The visit was planned to the last detail. It would be a spectacle involving an entire town. The action, however, would be limited to the route traced in red on the map. A hundred yards on either side of that route, filth, overcrowding, and starvation would prevail. A narrow pretense of an idyllic spa town was being created with intense labor. No expense was spared. Liliana wondered if the Germans really expected to get away with this grotesque fake. It seemed so.

She was aware that previous inspections by the German Red Cross officials had proved to be no problem, of course. The visitors had come and gone, and had spread glowing reports about the Paradise Ghetto. But this time, the visitors would be neutral outsiders. How could the Germans be sure of controlling them? A determined Swede or Swiss Red Cross representative had only to say, "Let us go down that street," or "Let's have a look at that barracks" a hundred yards away, and the bubble would pop. Beyond the film of fakery would lie horror of such unbelievable dimensions as to make one's hair stand on end. But the inmates were used to it.

Did Rahm have some cagey plan to deflect such embarrassing requests? Did he count on suave bullying to keep the visitors from seeing what he did not want them to see? Or was the whole Beautification just a master example of the thoroughness which had characterized what the Germans had done since Hitler came to power?

Lili, as an Austrian, knew the Germans were capable of the greatest charm, intelligence, and taste. With whole hearts and absolutely no reservations, they could throw themselves into the execution of plans and orders that seemed crazy or monstrous beyond human comprehension. The Beautification was a perfect example: the German face turned innocently to the outside world, asking — and totally believing it when they asked — "Why do you accuse us of doing bad things? Look for yourselves. See with your own eyes."

The thoroughness of this epic masquerade was awesome. Very little was finished yet, but the scenario had all been laid out. The bustling disorder of today's Paradise Ghetto was that of a stage halfway ready for dress rehearsal. Two or three thousand able-bodied Jews toiled from dawn to dusk in the Technical Department to build this fantastic, narrow path of illusion.

The visitors' itinerary had been fixed for months. Rahm carried around a thick document bond in black-and-red-striped cloth, "the Beautification Bible." Its final minuteness of detail could only be German. It included the selections the municipal orchestra would play in the town square: two Rossini overtures, the Radetzky March, several Strauss waltzes, Habañera from Carmen, and, of course, *Vltava — Die Moldau —* which, as the symbol of Czech patriotism, could not be played anywhere in Germany.

Copying paper was available in profusion. Excellent new instruments had flooded in. Theresienstadt had become a place where music filled the air.

Looking into the opera house, the visitors would see a full symphony orchestra and a large choir rehearsing Verd's *Requiem Mass.* More than 150 talented Jews in neat, clean clothing, yellow stars and all, were producing music worthy of performances in Paris, Vienna, London, or Berlin. Downstairs, in a smaller theater, the visitors would experience a run-through of *Brundibar,* the delightful children's opera composed by Hans Krása, a Jewish Czech composer, with libretto by Adolf Hoffmeister, also a Jew, who had somehow managed to escape the Nazi machine. Walking in the flower-lined streets, the Red Cross representatives would hear a string quartet in one private house playing Beethoven, a superb contralto singing Schubert *lieder* in another, a clarinetist practicing Weber in a third. They would refresh themselves at a café, where customers would pay, depart, and arrive in a thoroughly drilled, natural fashion.

Visitors would see shops stocked with all manner of fine goods, including luxury foods; shoppers would casually come and go, buying what they pleased, paying with Theresienstadt paper currency, engraved with a picture of Moses. Rahm's "Bible" contained a stern warning that as soon as the visitors departed, these "customers" must return all "purchases." Any shortage would be punished. For a missing food item, the offender would go to the Little Fortress.

The plan resounded through every phase of ghetto life: a mock, super-clean hospital, a mock children's playground, a mock sports field were all in the works. The bank was being completely renovated. A mock boys' school had already been finished, complete with chalkboards, chalk, and textbooks. It had never been, and would never be, used. A "main mess hall" was being erected for the sole purpose of serving exactly one meal, the visitors' lunch, where Jews all around them would dine heartily. Unfortunately, the SS had not yet figured a way to avoid feeding some Jews, just this once. It was the only lapse in Rahm's "Bible." The café customers were to indulge in coffee and cakes only while the visitors were in sight. Otherwise, they would go through the motions over brown slop and plates of cakes which they dared not touch.

Liliana had to get up at six in the morning. Before she went to work at the mica factory, she rehearsed for the visit at the children's playground and the kindergarten. She and several other young, attractive women, had just received their assignment. They would have their work cut out for them, training the kids to speak their scripted lines and simulate happiness. At lunch, the children were to cry out, "What? Sardines again?" It had all been written out. The SS had actually increased the childrens' rations because they wanted the visitors to see roly-poly tots at play. They were stuffing them, much like the witch in *Hansel and Gretl* had done.

How could so blatant a comedy hoodwink anybody? Even if it did succeed, what did the Germans have to gain? The Jews were disappearing. Millions were already gone. There was no sense to it. But no one pretended that today's world was a sensible place. The unbelievable, the monstrous, had become "business as usual" in a Europe dominated by the Third Reich.

For that matter, what sense was there to Oswiecim, which the Germans called Auschwitz? Calling the Germans sadists, butchers, beasts, and savages explained nothing. The root of the matter could not be Hitler. Such a thing must have been brewing for centuries to have encountered so little resistance among the Germans when it happened.

Liliana Traube, Szymon Vaynshtok, and Lili's daughter Sarah, propelled by her situation to be wise well beyond her years, talked in hushed monosyllables, in a back alleyway just off the childrens' residence. If anyone had heard them, they would have been on the next transport to the east. It had been Szymon's idea to bring Sarah into the picture. She had a right to know what was being planned for her.

Even if the chances of succeeding, of cheating the Angel of Death, were a million to one.

50

May 5, 1944. 7,500 persons must go. Nearly one-seventh of the entire ghetto. The Transport Section frantically shuffled and reshuffled index cards for the first shipment of 2,500. There would be three shipments, one train a day, for three successive days.

The transport would badly disrupt the Beautification, but the SS was unconcerned. Rahm had warned that the work would be done and the performances would shape up, or those in charge would be sorry. The Beautification was the cause of the transport. As the Red Cross visit approached, the Kommandant was becoming nervous about his ability to steer the visitors along a restricted route. The whole ghetto was being cleaned up. To relieve the overcrowding, the gate to "the east" had once more been opened.

Lili departed for the mica factory in the morning, unaware of the waiting train. The day faded into late afternoon. Nothing had happened. She began to hope that all would be well. But they came: two shabby Jews from the Trasport Commission, a big fellow with darkish hair, carrying the bundle of gray summons cards, and a smaller, weasel-faced man with the roster to be signed. Their expressions were bitter. They plodded through the rooms, hunting down each transport recruit, serving that person with a card and getting his or her signature.

Half an hour later, Lili approached Szymon, her expression grim. She held a single gray card. She had been assigned to the third train, departing on May 17, *"for resettlement in the direction of Dresden."* Her transport number was on the card. She must report to the Hamburg barracks on the sixteenth, bringing light luggage, one change of linen, and food for twenty-four hours.

"This is a mistake," Szymon said to her. "I'll go to Eppstein."

Lili's face was as gray as the card. "At least my Sarah is spared. For now. How will she ever perform her *Bat Mitzvah?*" She started weeping uncontrollably.

"Lili, listen," he said, grabbing her shoulders. "You're a *prominenti*, a mica factory worker, the head of the childrens' program for the great Fake."

"Szymon, don't try to palliate me. Half of the performers in the orchestra, half of the technical staff, people much more important than me have been …"

"I'm not trying to downplay this, Lili. This is a mistake. I'll go all the way to Rahm if need be."

"A lot of good that will do you." Her eyes were dry, hard.

They heard a roar erupting from the Magdeburg barracks. They saw a riotous crush. Cursing ghetto guards were trying to shove people into a line, using fists, shoulders, even rubber clubs. From the far end of the hallway came the angry, anxious tumult of petitioners jamming the transport office. A line had also formed outside Eppstein's suite.

Directing Lili to remain in the background, since being part of the mob would only make things worse, Szymon elbowed his way to the front of the line. At least Lili's position as an Elder gave him access to the big shots. Eppstein's pretty Munich secretary, looking cross and worn, managed to smile and passed Szymon into the Mayor's refurbished office.

Eppstein sat at a handsome new mahogany desk, the picture of a Prague advocate. The SS had scheduled a long briefing for the Red Cross visitors in this office. When Szymon Vaynshtok entered, Eppstein looked surprised to see him. Despite his appearance, Eppstein had heard about Vaynshtok.

Never any details, only veiled references, that the Polish Jew, who had been in Theresienstadt and survived for an indeterminate period of time without being "sent east," seemed to have had some bizarre, magical influence "in high places." Those who claimed to know him didn't really know him at all, an impression Szymon Vaynshtok, né Stefan Varga, had worked hard to foster.

Eppstein was cordial and sympathetic about Liliana Traube. Yet, his right hand shook with an unmistakable tremor. His answers to Szymon's questions were ambiguous, obscure. "A mistake is not necessarily unlikely. I will certainly look into it."

Vaynshtok tried to give Eppstein the gray card. The Ältester shrank from it. "No, no, no, let her keep it. Don't confuse things. When the error is corrected, she'll be notified to turn the card in."

For the next two days, no further word came from Eppstein. When Szymon tried over and over to see him, the Munich secretary turned surly, cold, mean. Pestering her was useless. The High Elder would send word when he had news.

The first two trains left. A third long string of cattle cars squealed into the *Bahnhofstrasse*. All over the ghetto, transportees trudged toward the Hamburg barracks in bright afternoon sunshine, carrying luggage, food, and small children.

Lili was scheduled to leave at midnight. It was now five o'clock. She had not mentioned a single word to Sarah. Liliana had somehow managed to keep up the pretense of normalcy for the past two nights, although she had slept less than an hour each night and dark circles had formed under her eyes. If Sarah knew or suspected anything, she had not revealed this. Nor had she asked any questions.

Liliana finished her packing, closed the suitcase, and tied the bundles. Now, there was nothing left for her to do. She had not forgotten what she'd learned about what happened "in the east," but she had suppressed that knowledge. The summons had not mentioned Oswiecim. All it had said was *"for resettlement in the direction of Dresden."* And Dresden was *north and a little west of here.* She had poured out her heart to Szymon until she felt like nothing so much as an empty shell, devoid of all emotion. No, that was not quite true. Fear gnawed at her entrails. Her heart was a locked stone inside her chest.

Vienna's former star of the stage, someone whom men once adored and would have paid a king's ransom to squire to Sacher's, could no longer wait for Szymon. Almost all hope was gone. She set out for the Hamburg barracks, a bundle of food and toilet things on her back, a small cardboard suitcase in her hand. She fell in with a stooped, shabby procession of Jews with their packs, all headed that way. It was a beautiful, balmy afternoon. Flowers bloomed everywhere, bordering fresh, green lawns that had been laid down in the last two weeks. Theresienstadt's streets were clean. The town smelled like springtime. Buildings gleamed with bright, new paint.

Lili got into the long line outside the Hamburg barracks. A black locomotive stood across the street in the terminal shed. Under the watchful eyes of SS thugs, Trasport Commission Jews officiously checked the transportees, asking questions, calling out names and numbers, irritably banging rubber stamps onto pieces of paper.

Liliana's turn came. A small man wearing a maroon cap shouted at her in German, stamped papers and scrawled notes. He collected her cards, bawled a number over his shoulder, and handed her a cardboard sign looped with string. The number of Lili's gray card was painted on the sign in huge black digits. She hung the number around her neck.

A large, pink-faced Austrian, who could not have been more than twenty-five, opened the office door. "All right, you. Get in here."

Szymon strode through an anteroom, and through the open door to Rahm's office, where the scowling Kommandant sat, writing at his desk. Behind Szymon, the adjutant shut the door. Rahm did not look up. Szymon had never been in this office before. The large pictures of Hitler and Himmler, the swastika flag, the double lightning-flash of the SS, blown up on the wall in a large silver-and-black medallion, bespoke the aura of raw power the Kommandant wanted to convey, the fear he wanted to engender in anyone unfortunate enough to be summoned to his sanctum.

Intending to intimidate his visitor further, Major Rahm shouted, "What the hell do you want, Jew?"

Completely unruffled, Szymon calmly replied, "I thought you said that kind of 'Jew' shit was to stop, Herr Major."

Startled, Rahm continued in the same tone, "Why should I even dignify your presence by lowering myself to your level, Jew?"

"Because you might be raising yourself in my esteem if you conducted yourself as your rank demands."

"Not a good way to start a conversation, J—" Suddenly, unexpectedly, even to himself, Rahm stopped in mid-sentence. "I know exactly who you are. You're that scum who's been fucking the Jew-whore actress. Say one word on behalf of that slut and you'll do time in the Little Fortress within a minute my snapping my finger."

"Or I may not," Szymon responded imperturbably.

Since his arrival at Theresienstadt, indeed, since he had become an SS officer, Karl Rahm had never faced someone like this, and a Jew to boot. But his authority must not be challenged. If word ever leaked out about this interview …

The Kommandant had a dangerous temper and he had been painted into a corner within the first moments of this meeting. Pounding the desk, rising to his feet, Sturmbannführer Rahm screamed at the interloper. "Well, Jew? You asked to see the commander, *ja*? I'll give you exactly two minutes, and if you so much as mention that Viennese cunt even once, I'll knock your teeth down your swinish throat! Understand?"

"Herr Kommandant, I suggest you may wish to comport yourself in a more civilized manner. Would you have me use such words when talking about Frau Rahm?"

"That's it, Jew." Rahm lifted the telephone and made to punch the intercom button. Just before he summoned his adjutant, the Kommandant glared menacingly at his visitor.

Szymon Vaynshtok sat quietly, his hands folded in his lap, looking directly at Major Rahm, not giving an inch. The two men sat that way for fifteen seconds. It was Rahm who quietly replaced the receiver. His temper tantrum abated as quickly as it had started.

"Who *are* you?"

"No one of any consequence," Szymon answered levelly. "Very few are." He reached casually into his pocket and withdrew two shoulder boards. One bore the letters "U.S." and at the sight of the other board, on which he recognized the silver eagle of a full colonel, the Sturmbannführer's eyes widened perceptibly and his face paled.

"As I'm certain you are aware, Major," Szymon continued, "my boss, General Donovan, has been meeting secretly from time to time with someone whose name is undoubtedly familiar to you, Reichsführer Himmler ..."

"Your name is Szymon Vaynshtok. Yet, I have no record of a Szymon Vaynshtok interned at Theresienstadt."

"For our purposes, Szymon Vaynshtok will do, Herr Rahm."

"That's not your real name?"

"As I said, Herr Kommandant, that name will do."

Rahm stood, walked over to a sideboard, and poured himself a shot of Johnnie Walker Blue Label. Neat. He swallowed it in one gulp, but did not offer any to his guest.

"So, this visit *is* about that Jewish c—, about Frau Traube?"

"It is, and for your information, not that it matters, I have not been engaged in any relationship, sexual or otherwise, with her, except as a friend. And, yes, I will accept your apology, not that it's of any consequence. She's been selected for the transport. Her daughter has not."

"I had nothing to do with that, Herr … Vaynshtok. The Transport Section, Jews, make those decisions."

"Perhaps, perhaps not. But you have the power to reverse the harsh decree."

"What could possibly move me to rescind any orders made in my name?"

"Eight thousand people have been handed gray cards. Five thousand have departed in the last two days. The final transport leaves at midnight, only a few hours from now."

"I'm aware of that."

"Three thousand are scheduled to leave. But you only have room for 2,500 on the train."

"That's impossible!" Rahm stormed.

"Not impossible at all, Kommandant. Over eight thousand summonses were served, but the SS contracted with the *Reichsbahn* for exactly seven thousand, five hundred transportees. The *Reichsbahn* charged the SS reduced third-class group fares for the *Sonderzüge*, the 'special trains.' There are cars for exactly seven thousand, five hundred passengers, not one more. So, at least five hundred summonses will need to be canceled."

"How can you possibly know that, Herr … Vaynshtok?"

"You ask a lot of questions, Kommandant."

"And *you* are taking an unwarranted risk in speaking to me in that impertinent tone."

"Major Rahm, I've been coming into — going out of — the Paradise Ghetto since before you arrived. Indeed, when your predecessor departed, I decided to take a brief holiday on the Greek island of Lesvos …"

There was an inordinately long, strained silence between them.

"I promise you absolutely nothing."

"I understand."

"Why should I?"

"Major, while your manners are not always the best, I don't doubt that you are a very perceptive man, or you would not have gotten where you are."

"And if I simply let you walk out of here and your lady friend leaves our Paradise Ghetto as scheduled?"

"You are very good at making threats, Kommandant. I'm willing to wait and see if you are as good as carrying them out."

The unexpressed, but pregnant, implication hung in the air. Karl Rahm SS major, commander of Theresienstadt, presently reigning lord of all he surveyed, was, at bedrock, a man, nothing more and nothing less. Put a hole in him just large enough to drain him of his blood and organs, and his life would end exactly as quickly as those who went to the "delousing" showers of Oswiecim or Birkenau.

On February 8, 1944, Burger was quite suddenly transferred to Greece. Three days later, word circulated through the community that Hauptsturmführer Burger's nearly unidentifiable, horribly mutilated body, had washed up on the shore just north of the town of Molyvos on the Greek island of Lesvos.

At that moment, Rahm felt the cold, jagged icycle of fear. Fear of his own mortality.

"Herr Rahm, I come bearing not only the stick, but a carrot as well. Regardless of what you may think, the Reich grows smaller every day, and as loyal a patriot as you believe yourself to be, there may be other considerations a year from now."

Vaynshtok reached into his other pocket and extracted a small, velvet purple pouch. He walked over to the Kommandant's expansive desk and lay the pouch halfway between himself and Rahm.

The Kommandant picked the pouch up and emptied five sparkling stones onto the mahogany desktop. He looked questioningly at Szymon.

"They're from Rome. They cost twenty-five thousand U.S. dollars in 1940. They appraise at double that today. You have less than four hours to decide, Kommandant. Surely, you can find an expert appraiser, probably a Jew, within a few hundred yards, to convince yourself." Vaynshtok's tone continued to be neutral, completely unafraid.

"Where did you get them?"

"Bulgari. You can check the trademark on the pouch."

"How did you keep them hidden?"

"I didn't. As I told you, I am by no means a permanent resident of Theresienstadt."

"That's it?"

"That's it."

One by one, Major Rahm picked up the diamonds and held them to the light. "Your woman knows about them?"

"She is not my woman, and no, she does not. Nobody in the world knows about them except you and me. And my associates."

Rahm stared at Szymon for long seconds. He dropped the stones into the pouch and placed the pouch in his pocket.

"I cannot promise she will not be gone by midnight." In a sudden, last attempt to salvage what was left of his dignity, Rahm said "Get your filthy Jewish arse out of here now, before I change my mind." The harsh words came out in an oddly unemotional way.

Szymon rose, said nothing, and made his way out the door and into the street.

51

Searchlights blazed down on the lawn from the roof of the Hamburg barracks. Blinded, frightened, Lili heard a deafening, harsh, loud voice over a series of loudspeakers.

"On your feet! Form a line by threes! Ghetto guards stalked the lawn, shouting *"Everybody out of the barracks! Into the courtyard! Hurry up! Line up by threes!"*

Transportees swarmed into the courtyard, hastily pulling on clothes. The SS had cleared the barracks for use as an assembly center. More than two thousand Jews who lived there were gone, staying wherever they could.

Everybody knew by now about the excessive summonses. The Elders, led by Eppstein himself, trooped into the courtyard as guards set up two tables on the cleared grass. Transport officials sat down with their stacks of cards and papers, their wire baskets, and their rubber stamps. Commander Rahm arrived, swinging a swagger stick.

The line of three thousand Jews commenced a shuffling march around the yard before Rahm. He pointed his stick to exempt one, then another. The freed ones went to a corner of the yard. Sometimes, Rahm consulted the Elders. Otherwise, he simply picked handsome young men and pretty women. The entire line passed in review, then started around again. It took a long time. As Lili came around a second time, the Kommandant looked brutal, menacing. The march went on and on under the floodlights.

The guards shouted, "Halt!"

Kommandant Rahm bellowed obscenities and swung his swagger stick at squirming, dodging transport officials. There had been a miscount. Another long delay. Whether Rahm was drunk or the Jews at the tables were incompetent or terrorized, this vicious game with peoples' lives had now gone on past midnight. At last, the line started moving again. Liliana trudged in a hopeless daze, following the back of a limping old man in a ragged coat with a black fur collar, the same back she had been trailing for hours. A rough tug on her elbow suddenly yanked her out of line.

"What's the matter with you, you stupid bitch?" muttered a whiskered guard. Commander Rahm was pointing his stick at her, sneering.

The floodlights went out. The commander, the Elders, and the transport officials left. The exempted Jews were trooped off into a separate bunk room. A transport official told them they were now "the reserve." The commander was furious about the bungled count. There would be another tally tomorrow when the train loaded up. Until then, they would be confined to this room. Liliana spent a hideous, sleepless night.

Next day, the official returned with a typewritten list and called out fifty names to proceed to the train. The list was not alphabetical, so until the last name was read off, the tension on the listening faces deepened. Lili was not called. The fifty unfortunates picked up their suitcases and went out. Another long wait. Then Lili heard the wail of the train whistle, the chuffing of the locomotive, and the clank of moving cars.

A man from the Transport Section looked into the room and shouted, "Pile your numbers on the table and get out of here! Go back to your barracks!"

As sick at heart as she was about the people on the train, especially those with whom she'd spent the last night, taking the number off her neck gave Liliana the greatest joy of her life.

Szymon Vaynshtok waited outside the barracks entrance, someone who could go unnoticed in the midst of any crowd. The reunions all about them were subdued. He only nodded to her. "I'll take the suitcase."

Lili lowered her voice. "For God's sake, we've *got* to put the plan into action.

52

A few days later, while she was at work in the mica factory, a ghetto guard came to Lili at noon and told her to report to SS headquarters at eight the next morning.

Liliana did not close her eyes that night. When the windows turned gray, she got up, feeling very ill, and did her best with her hair, trying to look as presentable as she could.

As the church clock struck eight, she entered SS headquarters. The bored-looking SS man at the desk nodded when she gave her name. "Follow me." They went down the hall, descended a long staircase, and walked through another, gloomier hall. The SS man halted at a wooden door. "In here. Wait." He shut the door on Lili. It was a windowless, whitewashed room, with a cellar smell, lit by a bulb in wire mesh. The walls were stone, the floor cement. There were three wooden chairs against a wall, and in a corner a mop and a pail full of water.

Lili sat on a chair. A long time went by. She could not tell how long.

The door opened. Liliana got to her feet. Commander Rahm came in, followed by his inspector, Horst Lendl, known throughout Theresienstadt as the most brutal of animals. Lendl closed the door. Rahm, who was in black dress uniform, walked up to her and roared in her face, **"So, you're the Jewish whore who plotted against the German government, yes?"**

Lili's throat clamped shut. She opened her mouth, tried to talk, but no sound came.

"Are you or aren't you?" Rahm bellowed.

"I ... I ..." Low, hoarse gasps.

"I think there's a brief movie you should see," Rahm continued.

Lendl prepared a projector and turned it on. Lili's eyes were drawn, not of their own volition, to a flickering screen. A group of young girls, Sarah's age, danced in a circle around the courtyard. Cut to another shot. Four of those same girls being brutally stripped and raped by vicious, fat old men. Then cut up, their prepubescent breasts sliced off, as they writhed in terminal agony just before they were shot through their skulls.

"I was insane. I was misled. I will cooperate. Please don't hurt my baby —"

"Don't hurt her? She's GONE, you dirty cunt. Don't you realize that?" Rahm gestured at the movie screen. "That's what will happen to your darling girl, your *Bat Mitzvah*, in ten minutes! She will be DEAD, but not before our fine young men have their fun with her. Maybe she'll even get pregnant before they do her in? Of course, you've heard of the medical experiments. Pig fetuses and such. Maybe we'll do that instead."

Liliana shrieked and rushed toward Lendl, but she tripped and fell to the cement. She rose up on her hands and knees. "Don't hurt my baby! I'll do anything. *Just don't hurt her!*"

Rahm, with a laugh, pointed the stick at Lendl. "You'll do anything? Fine. Let's see you suck the inspector's cock."

It did not shock her. Liliana was nothing but a crazed animal now, trying to protect her baby animal. "Yes, yes, all right, I will."

Unbuttoning his pants, Lendl pulled out a small penis, surrounded by a sparse mound of hair. On her hands and knees, Lili crawled to him. The exposed penis was limp and shrunken. Odious and unspeakable as all this would be if she were sane and conscious, Lili only knew that if she took that object in her mouth her child might not be hurt. Lendl backed away from her as she crawled. Both men were laughing. "Look, she really wants it, Herr Kommandant," Lendl said.

Rahm guffawed. "All these Jewesses are cocksuckers at heart. Go ahead, let her have her fun. German cocks are what they want most."

Lendl stopped. Lili crawled to his feet and raised her mouth to do the terrible thing.

Lendl lifted a boot, put it in her face, and pushed her, tumbling backward, onto the floor. Her head hit the cement, hard. She saw zigzag lights. "Get away from me! Think I'd let your Jewish shit-mouth dirty my cock?" He stood over Lili, spat down on her face. "Go suck off one of your own kind."

"Get to your feet," Rahm said calmly.

Liliana obeyed.

"Now LISTEN and LISTEN WELL, Jew-sow. When the Red Cross comes, YOU will be the guide for the childrens' department. You will be the happiest, proudest mother who ever lived when your daughter becomes a *Bat Mitzvah*. You will make an impression on them. They will write you up in their report, you will be such a happy Viennese Jewess. The children will be your pride and joy, *Ja?*"

"Of course. Of course. Yes."

"After the Red Cross goes, if you've misbehaved in any way, you'll come straight here with your darling little girl. The two of you will go to the hut of the POW road gang. Two hundred stinking Ukrainians will fuck the two of you by turn for a week. If your whores' carcasses survive, you'll go to the Little Fortress to be shot. Understand, cunt?"

"I will do everything you say. I'll make a wonderful impression."

"All right. And one word about any of this to your 'friend' or anybody else, and you're *kaput*." He shoved his face directly into her spittle-wet face, and howled with corpse-smelling breath so loud that her ears rang. "DO YOU BELIEVE ME?"

"I do! I do!"

"Get her out of here."

The inspector pulled her by the arm out of the room, up the stairs, along the hall, and shoved her out into the square, glorious with spring blossoms. The band had just started playing the morning concert, initiating it with the overture to Johann Strauss' *Die Fledermaus.*

Two nights later, while making his regular rounds of the refrigerated meat locker in the SS commissary, one of the butchers came upon a grisly discovery. Inspector Lendl's body was hanging from a meat hook. His ears and tongue had been cut off and stuffed into his mouth. His testicles, also removed, had been placed in a small, velvet, purple pouch displaying the Bulgari insignia and, so there would be no mistaking his identity, Lendl's SS number. The pouch hung around his neck, next to a cardboard sign looped with string.

The number of Liliana Traube's gray card was painted on the sign in huge black digits.

53

Lili was more frightened than ever of the retribution she was certain Major Rahm would exact, first on Sarah to ensure that Liliana would see every moment of the infinite brutality the Kommandant would visit on her daughter, then on her.

For all the abject humiliation she had suffered, while Lili was terrified of the unknown, she knew she could — and would — do anything to protect her child. She was the ultimate mother. Somehow, her resolve relieved her of fear of what would happen to *her*. She might well be tortured, as Rahm had threatened so graphically to do. She might be killed slowly, mercilessly, but she knew she was capable of killing before she died.

Although she had not mentioned a single word of this to Szymon or to anyone else, who but Szymon could have learned of what had happened so quickly?

It was now June 18, five days before the Red Cross representatives were due to arrive. She had learned, through Szymon, who the visitors would be.

Frants Hvass, the Danish diplomat who had been pressing Berlin about Theresienstadt.

Dr. Juel Henningsen of the Danish Red Cross.

Dr. Rossel of the German office of the International Red Cross in Berlin.

Eberhard von Thadden, a German career diplomat, Thadden handled Jewish affairs in the Foreign Ministry. Eichmann transported Jews to their deaths. Thadden had pried them out of countries where they held citizenship and delivered them to Eichmann.

In the mica factory, each second seemed like a day, each day seemed like an eternity. Lili must concentrate on her work. Each breath, each step, each word. It was still light when she got off work. She hurried to the childrens' home. Please, God in Heaven, let Sarah still be there.

Lili was within two blocks of the home when she felt someone suddenly yank her arm so hard it felt like it would be pulled out of its socket.

"Come with me, Jew bitch," the voice snarled menacingly. "Not a word, not a scream, or it will be your last, *understand?*"

She nodded, a defeated dumb animal. There was no one to see her suffering. Or, if there was, whoever saw her had turned his or her back away, lest they become involved and risk a trip to the Little Fortress.

Through her shock, she saw to her dismay, it was SS Leutnant Rolf Hauser, whom she knew to be one of Rahm's deputies. He said nothing more as he pulled her forward into one of the very few barracks that had not been spruced up for the visit. When they arrived at the barracks, he led her down a corridor very similar to the one she'd experienced less than a month before. Was this to be where she saw the sight promised by Kommandant Rahm?"

Leutnant Hauser opened a door halfway down the corridor. He shoved her into a room the same size and configuration as the one in the cellar of the SS headquarters. He pushed the door shut behind her and she heard the click of a lock.

Lili raised her head, not knowing what to expect.

Suddenly, she felt faint, a balloon from which all the air had been extracted.

There were four chairs in the room. Still in shock, she recognized all three people in the room. The first was a tall, distinguished-looking man in his mid-forties. Szymon Vaynshtok. But she gasped as she realized it was *not* the Szymon Vaynshtock she had known and to whom she had entrusted her life. This man was somehow taller, straighter. And he was wearing a military uniform, not an SS uniform, nor a Wehrmacht uniform, but one she recognized. On one side of his collar, he wore a silver eagle, which she recognized as the insignia of a full Colonel. On the other side of the collar were two silver letters, "U.S."

The man took her hand in his and nodded deferentially.

"Szymon?"

"Actually, that really is my birth name, but I've been Stefan Varga for so many years I can hardly remember when I haven't used that name."

"You're —?"

"Polish army in exile, temporarily breveted to the United States government."

Glancing around in confusion, she recognized the housemother from the childrens' home, the one who had always been so protective of her baby. "Fräulein … Frau …?"

"Laurie will do just fine, Frau Traube. Like my friend, the colonel, I've gone by another name for a long time. But at heart I've always been Laurie Rosensohn, a cultured Jewish girl from New York City, who found profound meaning to my life when I joined an American outfit called the O.S.S. — the Office of Special Services — and accepted this assignment."

"Lara, that's the only name by which I've known her, has been here the whole time, protecting Sarah when she didn't even know it, and liaising with me to ensure you survived as well," Varga said.

Her eyes now blinded by tears, all she could see was her baby girl, a strong, confident young woman.

"Sarah knows about the situation," Vaynshtok/Varga said matter-of-factly. "Young people grow up very quickly in this environment. You, yourself, saw a sample of her writing. It was not the scribbling of a child."

"You *know*? And you never said a word about it to me, *Shayna?*"

"I did not, Mama. You think I don't know about the transport? And some … other things?"

"But, why?"

"Why make you suffer more than you were already suffering? Why add guilt to the mix?"

"How long have you known?"

"Since Lieutenant Burger …"

"And yet, you said nothing. You're going ahead with this charade?"

"A *Bat Mitzvah* is *not* a charade, Mama. It's an affirmation of who I am and what I am. Even in hell, even if God abandons *us*, we can never abandon *Him.*"

"How can those be your words, Sarah, my angel?"

"They're not, Mama. I've been studying with Rabbi Baeck."

Lili stared at her daughter. Rabbi Leo Baeck was head and shoulders above Eppstein. Unlike the Ältester, Rabbi Baeck did not participate in the governance of Theresienstadt. He was wise, respected in the truest sense of the word, patiently trying to survive and comfort Jews wherever he found them, even if he had been forced by circumstances to hide the cruelest facts about Auschwitz, Birkenau, Treblinka, Maidanek …"

"Rabbi Baeck will supervise Sarah's *Bat Mitzvah*," Szymon said. "That will give us the added cover we'll need for the very few minutes we take putting our plan into action. "

"What you and I talked about in private?"

"Yes. I've told Sarah that as well."

"May I ask one thing, Szymon?"

"The answer to your question is yes, Leutnant Hauser is one of ours. A righteous gentile and an even greater rarity, a righteous *Schutzstaffel* officer."

"Does he know?"

"Not the details. There are certain things he does not know *and does not want to know*, for his own safety. We don't have much time here, five or ten minutes at the most. Let's go over the details quickly. Lili, you're an actress, a true professional. But in this instance," he said, squeezing Sarah's hand warmly, "your daughter will have to surpass you."

"Do you … do we … have others in place?"

"Yes, Lili, we do."

"Thank God!"

"Let us hope we'll be alive to thank God when this is over."

They reviewed the details of the plan in short order. Opening the door to the small room, they found it had been quietly unlocked. And Leutnant Hauser was nowhere to be found. Szymon, Sarah, and Laurie Rosensohn / Lara Gard exited from one side of the building. Lili waited a quarter of an hour, as Szymon had directed. The she emerged from another area, far away from whence her daughter, the housemother, and her closest friend and confidant had departed.

54

Friday, June 23, 1944. Sunrise. Squads of women were out on the street already, on their hands and knees, scrubbing the pavement in the orange-yellow light. The stench of those scarecrows from the overcrowded lofts fouled the morning breeze. Their work done, they vanished, and the perfumed, pretty ones in fancy clothes came out. Although dolled up and singularly attractive, Liliana felt nothing but fear of retribution if she didn't behave precisely as instructed.

Focus, focus, focus, she told herself. *This is a play and you are the star. Act One, get through the charade with the children. Kids are natural performers. They'll be fine. Just hope they stick to their lines.*

Act Two, be the proud, happy mother. Clap and shout "Mazel Tov!" *Throw the traditional candy at the smiling, beautiful* Bat Mitzvah. *Prepare for Act Three. And hope and pray with all your soul that we can bring it off.*

Lili and her three "assistants" spent the morning feeding the children a splendid meal: sausages, eggs, milk, all foods that the adults had been denied during their entire sojourn in Theresienstadt. Then they marched their charges to the hairdresser and the barber, where they were coiffed in the most flattering current styles. The childrens' clothing was uniformly bright, spotless, and stylish.

The charade was to begin at noon, when the four visitors were scheduled to arrive. At eleven, the thirty-five children began to warm up by singing. The most athletic of them started doing cartwheels on the soft, fragrant new grass of the childrens' playground. A few moved to the sparkling jungle gym, the oiled, noiseless swings, and the challenging bush-mazes. A child's fondest wish come true.

At five minutes past noon, Hvass, Doctors Hennnigsen and Rossel, and Herr von Thadden, in the company of high Nazi officials from Berlin and Prague, started Rahm's planned route by the timetable, without a hitch. They experienced one charming sight after another: pretty farm girls singing as they marched with shouldered rakes to the truck gardens, loads of fresh vegetables being unloaded at the grocery store, Jews in comfortable, casual clothing with yellow Stars of David on their chests, happily lining up to buy produce. A soccer goal, shot to the cheers of a joyous crowd, just as the visitors reached the sports field.

The hospital looked and smelled remarkably clean. Its aroma was natural, rather than carbolic. The linen was snow white, the patients were cheerful and comfortable, replying to all questions by praising the superb treatment and meals. Wherever the visitors went — the laundry, the bank, the Jewish administrative offices, the post office, the ground-floor apartments, the Danish barracks — they saw order, brightness, cleanliness, charm, and contentment. The Danish Jews outdid each other in assuring the visitors that they were well-off and treated with respect and courtesy wherever they went in this lovely spa town.

The outdoor scenes made it difficult for the Red Cross representatives to believe that less than fifty miles away, a bitter war was being waged that was tearing the very innards of the Continent apart. Here, the quaintly decorated street signs were a treat to the eye. Well-dressed Jews strolled at leisure in the sunshine. The café entertainment was first class. The cream pastries were still warm, freshly baked, and delicious. Von Thadden remarked, "The coffee here is better than you can find anywhere in Berlin."

Finally, they reached the children's pavilion, where they were joined by the handsome, urbane Commander of the camp, Major Karl Rahm himself. In response to his waving at the children, they outdid themselves in shouting, "Uncle Karl! Uncle Karl!"

"*Meine kinder*, my children! He called out jovially. "Did you enjoy your lunch?"

"Of, yes," a blonde-haired, pig-tailed urchin responded. "But is it necessary that we have chicken or sardines every day?"

"*Liebchen*, that's a diet you need to grow up big and strong. Did you eat your vegetables?"

"Oh, yes, Uncle Karl. Otherwise, we wouldn't have gotten ice cream for dessert."

Rahm turned and faced a smiling Liliana. "Frau Traube, have you a moment to speak candidly with our honored guests?"

"Of course, Major Karl," she replied. "I'm thrilled to be in this wonderful place. How glorious it would be if everyone in Europe would live as we do — no wars, no worries …" In her years on the Viennese stage, Lili had never acted so credibly. She was momentarily relieved to see the Commandant buying into her act.

As the tour group left the immediate area, she heard snatches of their conversation.

"She seems to be happy in her work …"

"Charming …"

"Such quick, positive responses to any questions we asked!"

"Clearly, she and Commander Rahm are on the friendliest of terms…"

They turned a corner and continued on their preplanned stroll. Lili called out, "All right, children, time for your afternoon rest period."

By the time the children were packed into their bunks, Liliana was teetering on the brink of nervous exhaustion, but she had survived Act One.

Of course, she could not tell for a moment how Kommandant Rahm *really* felt.

Defying every conceivable rational thought, the monster Rahm seemed to have brought the impossible off. From the minuscule snatches of conversation she'd heard, these intelligent, sophisticated Danes *were buying into whatever Rahm, the demonic salesman, was selling!* Of course, tomorrow, as soon as they left ...

Her day's performance completed, Lili rushed over to the childrens' house with its sparkling, fresh paint job, its newly enlarged rooms, its farcical refurbishments. As she walked through the door, she gasped as she beheld her darling little girl. But Sarah looked like anything *but* a little girl. She was radiant, stunning, and Lili was both proud and horrified to see that Sarah had matured into a fetching, beautiful, and *curvaceous* young woman, *If Act Three doesn't work out ...* She feared what might happen when *anyone*, Ukrainian, SS, Jew, *anyone* came near her daughter.

"*Shayna*, you look ... you look ..." Suddenly, Lili broke down in tears. "You look so lovely ... so unbelievably ..."

"Pretty good for a dead woman, Mama?"

"Ssshh! Don't you *dare* say that! God punishes those who blaspheme."

"Mama, you know it's only between us. And Szymon and Laurie, of course."

"The Rabbi?"

"Uh-uh."

"What about your *Parsha,* your weekly Torah portion?"

"I'm fine with it. Mama, you know tonight is *Rosh Chodesh?*"

"The beginning of the new month?"

"More than that. God willing, the beginning of the new month will be the beginning of a new life. I won't stay another day in this place."

"Are you afraid, Darling?"

"Terrified. Aren't you, Mama?"

"Beyond terrified. If it doesn't work …?"

"Don't say that, Mama. It *will* work. It *has* to work."

They were approached by the housemother. "Do you think you might need to rest for an hour or so?

"Thank you *Frau Direktor* … Laurie. I'm so excited I'll probably not even be able to close my eyes, but I'll try."

Shortly after eight, the guests of honor, including the Red Cross representatives, the high and mighties of the Nazis, the SS, and the Jewish Elders were seated in the first three rows of the extraordinary synagogue, which appeared to date back to the eighteenth century, but which, in fact, had been constructed two months ago by forced labor. It had been built to hold two hundred people, but twice that many pushed and shoved their way in that evening. A *Bar Mitzvah* or a *Bat Mitzvah* was a symbol of the continuation of Jewish existence, even in these extraordinary times, and it was an obligation to God to attend such an event.

Still, it had posed a major tactical problem for the SS to control the community at large. Once word had gotten out that a *Bat Mitzvah* was to take place, it had spread like wildfire. The authorities had selected only the best-looking, most prominent, malleable, and presentable of the inmates. They had provided the selected "guests" with clothing appropriate to the occasion and insured that they were clean and would act in a manner conducive to Rahm's orders.

But there were hundreds, perhaps thousands, of "others," and their sense of excitement had motivated those unfortunates to take grave risks they would otherwise not have taken. Malnourished, weakened, they still outnumbered the guards available to control and cow them. Even Kommandant Rahm knew that this imbalance could cause unforeseen and unexpected difficulties: how many SS were there to cordon off the four visitors versus how many guards were dispersed to ensure that "the others" were kept *away* from the *prominenti*? Rahm realized his manpower was stretched very thin, which only heightened his concerns.

The hospital was the focal point. It stood almost at the border between the Potemkin Village that had been created to mask the grand deception, and the rest of the camp. Sturmbannführer Rahm ultimately made a conscious decision to remain inside the synagogue to demonstrate his "solidarity" with the visitors and the most "respectable" of the Theresienstadt Jews.

After Rabbi Baeck's opening remarks, the service began in earnest: the lighting of the *Shabbos* candles by the proud and happy young mother of the *Bat Mitzvah,* the *L'cho Dodi,* the traditional welcoming of the Sabbath "Bride," the Queen of Days. At the *Shema Yisroel,* Sarah ascended the *bima,* the dais, amid the gasps of the audience, for she truly was, a Lili had told her, stunning. This was her moment, and she knew it.

After the *T'filah,* the Elders came forward for the opening of the Ark of the Covenant. Rabbi Baeck lifted the sacred Torah scroll from the Ark, and held it high for the Congregation to see. He passed the scroll to Mayor Eppstein, who led the Elders in a line around the perimeter of the worship hall. As the Torah passed the congregants, the men respectfully held the fringes of their prayer shawls, in their right hands, as they touched the velvet covering of the sacred object, then brought the *tzitzis,* the fringes, back to their lips and kissed them to the accompaniment of singing by the enraptured congregation.

When the Torah scroll had been brought back to the *bima* and the velvet covering removed, Sarah Traube, her voice strong and clear, recited the blessing over the Torah and seamlessly proceeded to chant her portion as she read from the now-opened scroll. Her performance was smooth, error-free, and effortless. After the Elders joined her in reciting the blessing concluding her Torah reading, Sarah chanted the *Haftorah*, a commentary on the Torah portion she had just recited.

When she concluded her masterful performance, the hall erupted with heartfelt cries of *Mazel Tov!* The audience threw traditional wrapped hard candies toward the *bima* as Liliana blushed and breathed an immense sigh of relief.

End of Act Two.

Now came the critical, crucial moments which would change their lives – or end them.

55

It was now ten minutes after ten in the evening. Since it was *Rosh Chodesh,* the first day of the month in the Hebrew calendar, there was only the tiniest sliver of a crescent moon in the nighttime sky. Commander Rahm, his entourage, and most of the Elders were quaffing prodigious quantities of the finest imported French wine and munching on sweet pastries at the *Oneg Shabbos,* the celebratory post-Sabbath-service party.

While Major Rahm was cognizant of everything going on in the *Oneg Shabbos* area, he concentrated mainly on drinking convivially with the Danish Red Cross visitors, celebrating the consummate success of the day, which had ended on this supremely high note. He had not the slightest doubt that the International Red Cross write-up of the affair would be highly laudatory. Thus, it somehow escaped his notice that the *Bat Mitzvah* and her mother had momentarily slipped away into a room off the hall, to speak quietly alone.

Nor did he notice when, a few minutes later, having removed their high-heeled shoes and donned flat shoes, black cloth coats, and dark wool caps, they left the building and walked in separate directions, each by herself. SS guards were so busy protecting the area from outsiders and ensuring that the *prominenti* inside were secure — and *secured* — that they paid no attention to two solitary, shadowy figures, who made sure to walk carefully outside the focus of the streetlamps abutting the avenue.

Shortly, they arrived almost simultaneously at the intersection of the main street and a narrow, unlit alley. As they turned into the alleyway, they found themselves surrounded by four SS men. The gravelly voice of their leader was familiar, and Liliana was immediately comforted.

"So, we meet again, Gnädige Frau."

"I never had the chance to thank you for the other day, Leutnant Hauser. I bless you with every fiber of my being."

He smiled, and she noticed, even in the dark, what a fine-looking young man he was.

"Shortly, you may not think I am so kind." The other two men, Waffen-SS enlisted troops, listened as Hauser explained. "We've only got a very few moments, so we must make haste. *Scharführer* Hahn, who's a qualified medical orderly, will inject each of you with a sedative. In less than fifteen seconds, you will feel nothing. Herr Vaynshtok said you will not feel any pain and you must not make any noise. We will then bruise the two of you up pretty badly. You'll show welts and you'll be far less attractive than you are now, but the marks will fade away quite quickly."

"How long will we be unconscious, Leutnant?" This from Sarah,

"Between four and eight hours, Fräulein Traube," Hauser responded. "Hopefully, long enough."

"And when we wake up?"

"Best you don't know or suspect that. When you awaken, let's just say you'll be in 'different' surroundings."

"Can you tell us what will happen in the meantime?"

"Let's move a bit farther down the alley," Hauser said quietly. At a nod, his associates moved to a different section of the narrow passage, guarding the entrance from others who might gather here. A few moments later, he continued. "If all goes right, shortly after you've been rendered unconscious and we've 'beaten you up a little bit,' we'll take you to the hospital, where we'll report we've found two bodies that have been trampled by the unruly crowd or knocked in the head by SS bludgeons while trying to get to the synagogue. You'll be photographed by professional hospital staff, who will take your fingerprints and compare them with those on file at Theresienstadt. A registrar will then certify your demise, cause of death brain injuries from a blunt instrument. This information will simultaneously be transmitted to your official records. A notation will be made that you have been discharged from the hospital and transported to the crematorium."

"How certain are you this will work, Leutnant Hauser?"

"Nothing is ever one hundred percent guaranteed, Fraud Traube, but we can tell you that all of the personnel involved are 'ours,' and we have taken precautions to keep everyone else away until the operation is completed."

"How long do you estimate that will take?"

"Ideally, between one-half and one hour from the time we get you into the hospital until your transport leaves."

"And if things don't work?"

"You'll never know, Fraud Traube. If it doesn't succeed, you and your daughter won't have to worry about transport to the east or anything else."

Lili shivered.

"Mama, you must trust *someone*. You and I know who enlisted these men. Have faith in God and have faith in Szymon's friends, who are *our* friends as well."

"All right, gentlemen," Lili said resignedly. "It's in God's hands."

"You'll feel a tiny pinch," Hauser said, "Count to ten immediately after you feel the pinch."

Mother and daughter held out their arms and did as instructed.

Neither one got past counting to eight before they felt nothing else.

It was 10:45 before Kommandant Rahm noticed that the Traubes had gone missing. He immediately convened a meeting of his guards and asked when anyone had last seen mother and daughter. To a man, the guards reported that they had left the worship hall and entered the room where the post-*Bat Mitzvah* celebration was taking place, but that had been more than half an hour ago, and no one had seen them since then.

Rahm did not want to upset the visitors or signal that anything was amiss. He ordered the guards to quietly, but thoroughly, search every nook and cranny, every room or space in the synagogue. Within fifteen minutes, one of the guards returned with two pairs of high-heeled shoes.

By this time, the attendees, both the dignitaries and the Elders, were exhausted. Commander Rahm maintained his calm demeanor, wishing them all a pleasant rest. He apologized that he would not be able to escort them to their comfortable and commodious quarters, but mentioned that he had a few post-closing matters to attend to. "No rest for the wicked," he remarked, smiling ruefully.

No sooner had the others left, than Major Rahm gathered the twenty-five synagogue guards and peremptorily commanded, "There will be an immediate perimeter-to-perimeter search of the entire camp. Every barracks will be thoroughly examined, millimeter by millimeter. Every possible hiding place or sanctuary, the church, the hospital, even the Little Fortress and SS headquarters. We will impress not only every SS guard and civilian employee, but the *capos*, the Elders, every inmate if necessary, into service. We will not tell any of them anything except that two criminals tried to sabotage the Great Beautification earlier this evening, and that there will be extra rations for a month for anyone who finds them, or immediate death to anyone found to have aided or abetted them."

Rahm turned to his aide-de-camp and remarked, very quietly. "Do we have a photograph of anyone called Szymon Vaynshtok?"

"I think so, Kommandant."

"Circulate it as well. There will be an instant monetary reward of ten thousand Reichsmarks for information leading to the apprehension of that person."

An hour after midnight. Rahm's men secured information from the central registry that Liliana Traube and her daughter, Sarah Traube, had been found bludgeoned or trampled to death in a small alley adjacent to the main red-lined street of the Paradise Ghetto. Their identity had been confirmed by grisly photographs, x-rays of their skulls, fingerprints taken by the night orderly at the hospital, and cross-referenced entries in their official records at the registry.

The hospital had dispatched the bodies to the crematorium at 11:15 the night before. In accordance with standard operating procedures, the crematorium night crew immediately immersed the bodies in lye and sulfuric acid. Twenty minutes after this "bath," the bodies had been charred beyond recognition.

Rahm's elite guard awakened the director of the crematorium, who groggily told them that the only way to guarantee positive identification of the bodies in their present state would be to ship them to the laboratory in Prague for analysis. Since that lab was closed over the weekend, if Kommandant Rahm desired, the director would be happy to shut down the entire crematorium until the following Monday morning, at which time he would exhume every female body from the holding areas and send them to Prague.

Furious and frustrated, Karl Rahm damned the entire population of Theresienstadt, vowing to punish every single inmate in the camp by torture and deprivation. He drank himself into a stupor before collapsing on his narrow bunk in his headquarters bedroom.

56

News of the Allied invasion of France on June 6, 1944, spread to every corner of France within a few days of the landing at Omaha Beach. The Reich moved every conceivable soldier from the small, remote areas of the country to the bastions which Germany had vowed to defend at all costs — Marseilles, Grenoble, Lyon, Dijon, and especially Paris. One of the first places to be evacuated by the *Boches* was the plateau which, in a remote corner, was home to the tiny village of Le-Chambon-Sur-Lignon, a notorious sanctuary for Jews, which the Nazis had long ago denounced as a "nest of vipers." Rumor had it that every Nazi in the area wanted to be the first to leave that hideous place.

Within two weeks of the Red Cross visit to Theresienstadt, word spread through Le Chambon, and most especially amongst the students at Cevenol School, that Pastor Trocmé had welcomed his close friends, Colonel Stefan Varga and O.S.S. representative Lara Gard to his home accompanied by two new arrivals, a striking woman in her early thirties and an absolutely stunning young teenage girl, who soon thereafter had taken up residence in a home situated in the hills surrounding the village.

Although the representatives of the International Red Cross and the Danish Red Cross initially praised the Paradise Ghetto of Theresienstadt in the Protectorate of Bohemia in lavish reports, it was only a matter of time before a totally different picture emerged from a very credible source, causing these otherwise respected gentlemen to admit, shamefacedly, that they had been "duped."

Sturmbannführer Karl Rahm was suddenly summoned to Berlin for "consultations."

Although the camp remained more-or-less "open" until the fall of the Reich in May 1945, no more transports "to the east" took place after October 1944.

EPILOGUE

Following the Red Cross visit, the Nazis decided to make a propaganda film directed by Jewish prisoner Kurt Gerron, an experienced director, who had appeared with Marlene Dietrich in *The Blue Angel*. After the shooting was completed, the director and most of the cast were deported to Auschwitz, where they were murdered. The film, *The Führer Gives a Town to the Jews*, was never distributed as intended.

In all, 144,000 Jews, most of them Czech, were sent to Theresienstadt. At the end of the war, 17,000 had survived.

Liliana Traube eventually moved to the State of Israel, where she married another Holocaust survivor. For years, they operated a successful restaurant-café in Haifa. Lili followed her husband into eternity ten years after his death at the age of 81, after a brief illness and a full life. Her daughter was at her side when she passed.

Karl Rahm, who actually stayed on as Commandant of Theresienstadt until May 5, 1945, was captured shortly thereafter by American forces in Austria. Turned over to Czechoslovakia in 1947, he was tried and convicted of crimes against humanity and executed on April 30, 1947, four hours after the Czech court had handed down its verdict.

Stefan Varga, born Szymon Vaynshtok, and Laurie Rosensohn Gard married in 1946. Ultimately, they both became advisors to the newly-formed

Central Intelligence Agency, took up residence in upstate New York, bore three children, and truly lived "happily ever after" for the next fifty years.

Finally, a word about Le Chambon-sur-Lignon, the sanctuary for so many Jews. That village was one of two in the world which was honored by the State of Israel as "Righteous among the Nations." It still bears that title proudly to this day.

THE END